THEN A
HERO
COMES ALONG

THEN A HERO COMES ALONG

ORDER OF OLYMPUS

✹ BOOK 2 ✹

MARIA SHIELD

*For my sister, who grew up to
be one of my best friends.*

Content Warning: Greek literature is unfortunately littered with nonconsensual situations and tragedy. This novel features character death, discussion/symptoms of PTSD, and traumatic experiences from war.
Please know that even with these moments in the novel, I will always promise you a Happily Ever After (HEA) for the characters.

And now I must care for incurable Ajax,
His mind infected by divine madness.
He was the one you sent overseas to win
The war with overwhelming force.
Now he is alone.

—Sophocles, *Ajax*

I T WAS A dangerous thing to keep a harpy waiting.

This was a rule as old as time, and most people knew not to break it. At least, they used to. At one time, she hadn't had to wait for anything. She had been a hound of Zeus, a creature who exacted righteous punishment on the mortals who dared to defy the gods above, while the furies exacted justice in the underworld. It was a good gig. She could do as she pleased, steal what she pleased, fly when she pleased.

But that wasn't the case anymore. Zeus had retreated to gods knew where, and now there were *rules about interacting with mortals.*

So the once-great terror of the sky was grounded.

She shifted in the plush restaurant seat, trying her best not to look put out. Her finger tapped against the screen of her phone for the hundredth time.

No messages.

"Ma'am?"

Allie snapped to attention, but it was only the waiter.

The young man gave her a sheepish smile. "Would you like a refill of your drink?"

He was being polite, but she could see the pity that lingered in his eyes. Great. Now a baby mortal felt bad for her.

She knew how this looked. Dressed in a sleek black sweater and skintight pants, sitting at a table, alone, for an hour. With only a glass of wine and an empty breadbasket in front of her.

"Sure." She picked up the menu, trying to save what little self-respect she still had. "And I'll order while we're at it."

"Do you want to order for your date?" he asked.

She didn't miss the unspoken question in the request. "No, I don't think she's coming."

The wine nearly sloshed out of the glass. Allie smiled at the reaction. "I was supposed to be meeting my sister."

"Oh?" Renewed interest filled his eyes.

Allie met it head-on. She was bored, after all, and it had been so long since she'd slept with a mortal.

The restaurant was one of the District of Columbia's nicer cocktail bars; men in business suits and women dressed to impress sat around having quiet discussions. None of them were really her type, but something was different about this guy. The sloppy knot of his tie and his pale-blond locks skewed from the biting winter wind, despite any attempts at taming them. He was probably the least put-together waiter in the place, but that was exactly what she liked about him.

"I'll have the salmon."

"Coming right up."

As soon as he was out of sight, she plucked a soft black feather off her sweater and brushed it to the side. And to think, she'd rushed to the restaurant for the meetup. Luckily, the winter eve had given her enough darkness for cover, allowing her to unfurl her wings. It had felt good, if not a little cold. It helped that her black hair, accompanied by dark clothes, made her melt into the backdrop of the night sky. With her bright-blonde hair and dove-colored wings, Celia wasn't able to fly very often. The last time her sister had taken flight, a local priest had run to the news, claiming to have seen an angel.

Oh, Celia. Her finger jabbed at the screen, unlocking it and bringing up her sister's contact. The phone rang once, twice, and went to voice mail. Allie sighed as her sister's bubbly voice filled her ears. *"This is Celia. I'm away from the phone right now, so please leave a message. Pecks and kisses."*

Beep.

"Celaeno"—Allie drew out her sister's ancient name in a long whine—"you suggested this posh-ass place and don't even bother to show up. What's with that? The babies are judging me." She paused for effect, hoping it would punch with an extra dose of guilt. "Look, I really need to talk to you, so call me when you get this. I hope you know that you owe me."

She hung up and fidgeted with her phone nervously. Celia wasn't usually the type to leave her high and dry.

She took a sip of wine and tried not to fret. Celia was becoming more and more preoccupied with her small graphic design company. It was becoming a habit now for her sister to stay late at work, passing on their usual Netflix-and-wine nights. If Celia wasn't at work, that meant she'd found herself a nice mortal customer to get wrapped up in. It wouldn't be the first time.

It drove Ocypete insane, but Allie didn't mind. This

century, their baby sister had grown into her own woman, and that meant spending more time away from the nest. She'd embraced technology and the power of being her own boss. Allie only cared enough about tech to buy the next new phone and binge-watch the latest on Netflix. But Ocypete was worse; their older sister barely knew what century it was. She would still have a flip phone if they let her.

Speaking of phones, hers buzzed to life, making the entire table vibrate against the force. Allie snatched it up quickly. Any excitement she felt quickly died when she saw it wasn't Celia, but Ocypete. She closed the screen and grabbed the wineglass again.

Sisters required wine. Lots of wine.

Her phone lit up again. Allie glanced down and saw an unsurprising text message. *"Can you bring home some chips?"*

Despite her annoyance, she laughed and typed up a reply.

"Here's your food." A delicious pink salmon appeared in front of her. The glaze on the fish made Allie's mouth water. Then a sleek, tall cocktail was placed next to it. "And something on the house."

She gave the waiter a thankful smile with the barest hint of flirtation. Why the heck not?

Her sisters had varying opinions on mortals. Ocypete would like to interact with them as little as possible, while Celia looked at them with fascination. Allie could admit they were beneficial at certain times. Like now. "What's the occasion?"

He shook his head, sending a crown of cherub curls bouncing. "Please, think of it as karma for your sister not coming to meet you."

"Maybe it was a good thing," Allie purred. "What's your name?"

"Leo," he replied with a delightful lilt of his tongue, which spoke the name in a perfect southern Italian accent.

Her smile grew at that. *Thank Mother Echidna for Leo.* "Well, I was going to spend the evening with her, but since she's not here, maybe I can spend my night with you, Leo."

He hesitated, and Allie could have kicked herself for the mistake. Too forward. She forgot mortal men didn't always like their women to be blunt. The rules seemed to change every decade. Luckily, this guy was willing to see the benefit of change. "I just need to find someone to cover for me. Do you mind waiting?"

"Not at all." Allie shrugged. "I need to pick up some things for my sister, anyway." He opened his mouth and she added, "Other sister."

"Oh, okay. Cool." He gave her another flirtatious grin, then sped off to take care of the other customers.

Satisfaction seeped into Allie's body as she took a sip of the sweet cocktail. Sending men scurrying gave her a sense of pleasure that few things did anymore. She checked her phone one last time. Nothing.

With a final sigh, she opened Instagram, picked up her fork, and began to do the exact same thing she would have done if she'd been at home: drink and scroll through her blog feed. *Oh, how the mighty have fallen.*

Barcus was in over his head.

He scowled, looking out the window and taking in the blistering cold city streets and the people who passed by. The outside offered no answers to his current predicament, but at least he could think without the winter wind cutting him to the bone. He took a gulp of dark coffee, closing his eyes as the bitter warmth washed down his throat. The coffee shop offered a quiet reprieve after nearly three hours of fruitless searching. It was the perfect place to warm up while he gathered his thoughts.

His eyes dipped down to his laptop, and his scowl deepened. Two things he absolutely hated were cities and technology. And both were making his night incredibly difficult.

After living through various centuries and hundreds of hunting expeditions, Barcus had once thought himself an expert when it came to hunting people down. There was a thrill in the chase, yes, but more importantly, there was a puzzle just waiting to be solved.

In the old days, it was much simpler. You got a clue—a broken branch, a print in the mud—then you used that clue to find what you were looking for.

Simple.

At least, it used to be.

But then forests turned into towns, towns turned into cities, and those cities turned into metropolises. And metropolises didn't leave room for footprints or tree branches. They had people, lots of people. And he hated people. The world was different now, and he hadn't had a proper hunt in centuries. He was out of practice and out of his league.

Artemis would strike him down if she saw the state he was in.

Outside, the city crowds were finally thinning out as they always did once the sun went down. Winter nights along the Potomac River proved to be miserable for the residents; the chill was enough to make bones tremble. People darted into the nearest restaurant or store, bundled in their coats and shivering. Fewer people made things a little easier, but the streets of the nation's capital became a labyrinth at night.

Fuck, he hated cities.

Hated the smell of them, the grime that lingered everywhere, the constant presence of people crowding against you. But it was nothing compared to what he had found inside of the city's apartments.

Blood and carnage. The remnants of a battle fought and lost and the remains of a fellow hero. His stomach tightened at the memory.

For five months, he had followed scraps of clues that Xanthus had left behind. Tracking the other hero was like finding a shade in the underworld. Nearly impossible, even for a hero blessed by the goddess of the hunt.

Look at the clues, he reminded himself, eyes scanning the bright screen. In this case, the clues took the form of a gruesome crime scene. Eosphorus had been a loner for a long time and had fallen out of touch with the Order. After the death of his second wife, he had changed his name to Erik Hearthright and moved to Virginia to live out the rest of eternity. It wasn't uncommon these days; watching the people around them die was exhausting.

Immortality wasn't meant to be spent alone. Barcus knew that better than anyone.

Erik had kept to himself, never once checking in with the Order or asking for their assistance.

And now he was dead.

Slaughtered. The word snagged in Barcus's mind. There was nothing left of the former hero but chunks and blood. It was enough to make his stomach roll.

As members of the Order, they had been blessed by

the gods with immortality, but they weren't invincible. In the wars before the Covenant, ancient creatures had killed heroes. Until a hero had created a blade forged in unmortal blood that could end any life it touched. *Former* hero, Barcus cursed.

Xanthus.

They had been brothers for a millennium—until Barcus saw Xanthus for what he was, a bloodthirsty killer, and the last shreds of their friendship had ended with a new scar along Barcus's collarbone.

They were supposed to be searching for Argos, fighting the monsters that had taken him, but Xanthus had a darker purpose. He was creating a blade that would kill any life it touched. Even those blessed with immortality.

Barcus had grappled with his role in Xanthus's bloodlust for three hundred years.

For years, he seemed to have disappeared from the face of the earth, but a couple decades ago he'd resurfaced with a group of heroes and taken to decimating the lives of Mythos, mortals who still worshipped the gods.

It was Argos who had struck a deal with the victim to find Xanthus and kill him. He had made the vow as a hero, but he was no longer one of them. It had only been a year since his friend had fought Circe and accepted life as a mortal with the woman he loved.

Barcus had taken up his vow, and finding Xanthus had nearly consumed his life ever since. The only thing he knew for certain was that Xanthus no longer had the *Theres* Blade, but that wasn't much to go on.

And then Erik had contacted him with information on Xanthus's whereabouts. His first real lead in months had turned up dead not even twenty-four hours later. It couldn't be a coincidence. Xanthus wasn't strong enough to tear a man apart, though. Barcus could think of only a few creatures who could. Giants, maybe. A cyclops, most likely. But why would those creatures do a hero's bidding?

If he had to worry about monsters attacking heroes as well, his job had just gotten a whole lot harder.

He quickly moved on to look at the more cryptic of the pictures, ones that showed the details of Erik's room, decorated in scattered notes and drawings of buildings in the neoclassical style, a style that hearkened back to a time Barcus was intimately familiar with. Corinthian and Doric columns elegantly decorated every piece of paper, next to fantastical buildings that would have once made awe-inspiring temples. It was the work of a true artist. There were designs for an elaborate entranceway, and marble statues of both gods and heroes.

Erik had been a talented architect back in the day. His designs and influence could be seen in every inch of the surrounding city. Maybe that had been his way of making the New World feel like home.

Among the drawings, there were other plans Barcus recognized. The unmistakable layout of the Lincoln Memorial, where the president sat like a godly figure. Another showed the Corinthian columns of the National Arboretum, laid out like abandoned ruins. A few of the drawings were more recent, showing that Erik had never really given up his passion for design. There were sketches of a pantheon of influential women, all dressed in the garb of powerful Olympian goddesses. More than a few drawings featured a beautiful woman from different angles. His wife, maybe?

But why kill a man who did nothing but draw?

When the recluse had contacted him, the other hero

had sounded haggard on the phone, his voice speckled with grit. *"I know where he's going next. Head to DC. We need to talk."*

Gods, why hadn't he asked more questions on the phone? Regret was a constant demon on his shoulder, and this was just one more thing to use against him. Erik's blood was on his hands as much as it was on Xanthus's.

The beginning of a headache beat behind his eyes. Barcus pawed at them and closed the pictures with a sigh.

Ever since he'd taken on the task of finding Xanthus, the headaches had been coming nonstop. *Just stress,* he told himself, taking a large gulp of black coffee. He'd been on the move for months. Living in hotels, looking for a lead.

For the first time in years, his beard was back, and his hair had grown longer than he liked. He hid it under a beanie, thanks to the cold weather. His clothes were limited to just the few that would fit in his backpack, and his weapons were wrapped up in a lacrosse bag. People on the street probably assumed he was just an overworked college student.

It wasn't far from the truth. Exhaustion dogged his every waking moment, and now that Erik was dead, he was at his wit's end about what to do next.

He stared out the window again, contemplating his next move, when something in the darkness snagged his attention. A woman, standing outside a restaurant, wrapped in a dark-red coat as she checked her phone. She was the only person who didn't look as cold as the people around her, too engrossed in the technology at hand.

His eyes lingered on her, the contrast of her olive skin against her dark hair. She could pass for a modern-day Red Riding Hood in that jacket. Her midnight-black hair was cut at the shoulders, giving a perfect frame to her heart-shaped face. Her tight jeans showed off shapely legs and a nice figure. In her free hand, she held a plastic shopping bag as she waited.

Then, as if some instinct compelled her to do so, she looked up and locked eyes with him across the street. Barcus felt his breath stall at the sight of her. He'd seen beautiful women in the years he'd walked the earth, but there was something ethereal about those painted red lips. When their eyes met, his entire body warmed from head to toe.

She was temptation in a red coat. The sight of her was much more appealing than searching for signs of Xanthus. But that wasn't why he was here.

It was lucky, then, that a young man approached from down the street and took that temptation away. Disappointment bit into his side at the sight. Boyfriend—of course she had a boyfriend. But then he watched as the guy pulled her into a nearby alley.

Barcus held his breath, his eyes unable to turn away. That was suspicious, *very* suspicious. Years of honing his senses to recognize danger had him moving before he could fully fathom the reason. This would only take a second. Just a second to check on the woman and then he could return to the task at hand. He tugged the lacrosse bag over his shoulder. The weight of the spear inside came as a welcomed presence.

He doubted it would even be needed; this was a mortal he was dealing with, after all. He would need to show some restraint.

II

AN ALLEY. REALLY? Allie had to stop herself from rolling her eyes. She wasn't so young anymore that a quickie on a side street was romantic. And doing so surrounded by dirt-colored snow with her back against an icy brick wall sounded *horrible*.

But the guy was really excited at the prospect of getting his rocks off. A new sense of urgency propelled Leo forward, his hand steering her deeper into the alley.

But she'd had enough.

Allie dug her feet into the ground. "I'm sorry, but I didn't sign up for this. I was thinking we'd do more of a Netflix-and-chill thing."

His harsh bark of laughter came as a surprise. "I won't be doing anything with you." He reached into the pocket of his hoodie and pulled out a long, elegant dagger.

Allie stared. "Are… are you mugging me?"

Original, but not entirely unwelcomed. Her night had been utterly boring with Celia's no-show. At least this way, she'd have a fun story to tell her sisters when she got home.

"Keep walking," Leo demanded. He was the least intimidating mugger she had ever met. Just from his height and body weight, he couldn't have been more than twenty years old. An amateur, really. He tried to put menace in his voice, but Allie could hear the faintest hint of a tremble.

He was nervous about something. Oh Mother, was this his first attempt to rob someone? She almost felt sorry for him.

"Do you want my wallet or something?" That was what a mortal woman would ask, but it was difficult to put even an ounce of concern into the question. First, Celia had stood her up, and now her one chance at a good time had gone and done this.

Why do the gods hate me? It was a rhetorical question, of course. The gods didn't hate her specifically; they hated everyone indiscriminately.

Seeing a mortal flaunt their fragile power was nothing new. And sometimes she liked playing the damsel, especially when there wasn't any real danger. It made it all the more satisfying when her attacker realized exactly what they were dealing with.

The second he made a wrong move, she would reach out and slit his throat with her claws. Her fingertips itched with the need to transform. This kid had no idea what he had gotten himself into.

Leo snorted. "Not exactly."

"Well, that is just vague enough to make me worry." Mortal women definitely did not use sarcasm in these situations, but hey—if he wasn't going to give it his all, neither was she.

"I don't want to hurt you, but I will if you don't cooperate."

"Yeah, I don't think either of those things is going to happen—"

He moved with a speed that caught her by surprise. Lightning fast, he slashed out towards her. Allie's reflexes took over, the sharp sensation of her talons growing out of her cuticles tingling as she blocked the attack. The bag of chips she'd bought for Ocypete fell to the ground with a loud crunch.

His knife swiped down, cutting the inside of her palm. Now that she faced the man head-on, she studied the expression on his face. His eyes went wide as he took in her claws, but there wasn't any surprise.

Interesting. Usually when her more monstrous side flared out, men went sprinting in the opposite direction. This guy steadied his stance and held his knife up in anticipation.

Ice hit her stomach as she realized what that meant. "You're not mortal, are you?"

Her eyes went to his chest. It was impossible to see a coin under his bulky hoodie, but there was no mistaking the implication. A hero.

Heroes hadn't been a threat since the establishment of the New World—when the Covenant between the heroes and unmortals looking for a fresh start in America had been written up. For years, those rules had made her people feel safe. Foolish of them, really.

It had been a while since she'd run into a hero, but if this was what they had to offer, then the quality sure had gone down. "Do you guys really have nothing better to do than wait tables and prey on unsuspecting women?"

Things had been bad for her kind since the Great War had nearly wiped them all out. Only recently had they crept out of hiding and begun to fully immerse themselves into life with mortals. It appeared the heroes were doing the same. But Leo's cruel chuckle dismissed that theory. "No. I snuck into that place to keep an eye on you. It's amazing what people won't question if you look like you belong somewhere. Isn't that right, harpy?"

He practically spat the word, as if it were the worst kind of thing he could call her. Allie's talons prickled with eagerness. His immortal blessing meant she couldn't kill him, but now she didn't want to. A quick death would be too good. "So, what do you want? To kill me?"

His dagger twirled between slender fingers in a fancy display. Men always thought such a demonstration was intimidating. But she'd seen drunken pirates do the same thing as a party trick. "No, my orders were to bring you back alive."

Orders? Oh boy, she didn't like the sound of that.

"I think you need to talk to your brothers again," Allie said. "We have a deal. You can't harm me unless I've attacked mortals. And besides the occasional scratched-up lover, I've been a good harpy."

"Times are changing."

"It's unfortunate, then, that you heroes still *insist* on being such assholes." Her talons would be enough to handle this. There was more than one way to harm a hero. It was a good thing her coat was red; things were about to get messy.

Before she could make her move, another pair of footsteps echoed down the alley along with a shout. "Hey!"

The boy jumped, his bravado failing as he turned, dagger poised to slice into the poor unknowing stranger who had stumbled across their scene. A cry of warning squawked out of Allie's throat, but it was too late.

A fist slammed into Leo's face.

The guy fell, hard. Sprawled out on the cold concrete,

eyes closed and unmoving. Allie's mouth fell open in surprise. *I guess the quality of heroes really has gone down.* What an anticlimactic ending.

"Are you okay?"

Her eyes flew up to meet the stranger and, wow—maybe it wasn't as anticlimactic as she'd thought. After a dozen lifetimes, mortals had all started to look the same. Each decade had its fads, its haircuts and fashion that men and women alike clamored to emulate, and for those brief moments in time, the people around her believed they were beautiful. But it was a fading beauty.

The man in front of her wasn't faded, though. He was an icon of classic masculinity, even with a dark-blond beard threatening to cover it up. It was present in his sharp nose and high cheeks. The lines of muscle that ran along his neck suggested that there were more to follow under his winter clothes. His handsome face twisted in concern as he looked her over, and it was then Allie remembered he'd asked a question.

Her hands flew behind her back, talons disappearing as quickly as the threat. "I'm fine."

The shock in her voice was real, her mind still trying to process what had happened. Not so much that someone had tried to attack her—men and women had done that a depressing number of times in her lifetime—but that a *hero* had attacked her.

Her heart was racing; her nerves sang with the need to fight and kill the unconscious man. But she needed the Good Samaritan to leave first.

"I saw him drag you off into the alley and came running. He didn't hurt you, did he?" Her savior stepped confidently over the body and into her space.

"Nope, just gave me a little scare." Allie held up her hands, perfectly human once again. Everything was normal except for the sharp stinging sensation burning the inside of her palm. The cut was still there. That was strange; usually such a minor wound would stop bleeding in a matter of seconds.

The man hissed at the sight of it. Before she knew what was happening, he took her hand and examined the cut. "That looks bad. I should take you to the hospital. It could use stitches."

"Don't worry about it," Allie said, recoiling from the touch. "It's fine, really." In a few hours, it would be as if nothing had been there at all. Being an unmortal didn't mean immortality, but it did mean she healed quicker than mortals.

"Well, would you like me to walk you home? It's the least I could do."

Aw, a gentleman. Something in her cooed at the suggestion. Even a monster wouldn't object to being taken care of after someone threatened her life.

New hope blossomed in her chest. Maybe her night wasn't completely lost after all. She could see the interest all men had when they laid eyes on her; it was doing vicious battle with the concern he felt.

"Thanks. I'd appreciate it. I've lived in the city for years and have never had that happen to me." Not this year, at least. She'd been mugged in DC roughly twenty-three times, but that wasn't so bad considering she'd lived in the city for nearly seventy-five years. Before that had been twice in Orlando, ten times in Pittsburgh, and twenty-five in New York. So many times, and never once had she been afraid, but now a shiver tingled up her spine. He might have been an incompetent hero, but her body remembered what it was like to face his brethren.

Usually, heroes didn't fall so easily. She was lucky.

Seeing her tremble, the man stepped closer, the movement slow but a deliberate show of comfort. "Let's get you out of the cold. I'll call the police."

"Thanks." A little part of her melted at how kind he was being. After such a shitty day, he didn't have to do much else to convince her to go home with him. "I'm Allie, by the way."

He flashed a bright, easy smile and gods, the way it lit up his face was a crime. "Barcus."

She froze.

Barcus. That was a strange name. It didn't belong in the world of skyscrapers and technology. It belonged in an ancient world long since gone. It was a name every unmortal knew and feared.

Her shitty day had just told her to hold its beer.

"No. Way."

His smile fell. "What's wrong?"

She pointed at the unconscious boy. "You're one of them!"

His face twisted in genuine confusion. "One of who?"

"Them!" she snarled. "You're a *hero,* aren't you?"

That perfect mouth fell open in surprise. "H-How do you know about that?"

He was looking at her in a different way now, trying to assess her. "Barcus," she repeated, "the Great Hunter of Artemis. The man who slayed all the water serpents in the Aegean and nearly hunted the great cats into extinction." Allie glared at him. They all knew the stories. Every hero had them, and every unmortal told those stories to their children as a warning.

Heroes were the *absolute* worst. They were cruel and killed without any provocation. All of them were to be feared, but none so much as Barcus.

Well, he didn't look so tough. She lifted her hand and let her talons flash out. They caught the light from the mouth of the alley, stretching her shadows and making it look like five pristine daggers attached to her hand.

His expression opened, not in surprise but in absolute disgust. "You're a—"

"A harpy," she said pointedly.

"A monster," he finished.

Ouch. She'd heard it all before, of course, but sometimes it was easy to forget what others thought of her kind. "You know that is a derogatory word, right? These days we prefer unmortals."

Barcus didn't react. He looked from her to the unconscious hero in guilt. "What did you do?"

Allie bristled. "I was just minding my own business!"

"Then why did he attack you?"

"He said he had orders. Care to explain that, Hunter?"

"That's nonsense."

"So now I'm lying?" she growled, feeling a twinge of satisfaction when he tensed as if expecting her to attack. "You know what, I've had a really terrible night, and this is just the icing on the cake. I don't need to take this. If you think I did something wrong, then you can finish what he started."

The anger on his face vanished, replaced by hesitation. You'd think she'd just asked him to kiss her instead of kill her.

He didn't move.

Well, she was *not* going to wait for permission to leave.

She unbuttoned her coat, then tore it and her sweater off in one quick movement, revealing the silk top underneath. Barcus jumped at the sight. "What are you doing?"

"If you're not going to attack me, I'm leaving." She kicked off her heels with exaggerated force. One sharp spike just barely missed his head. Usually, she'd be more careful and make sure such expensive shoes made it back home with her, but she wasn't going to risk getting closer to Barcus the Hunter. At least she'd almost hit him.

Her muscles began to shift with the thought of full wings catching the air underneath her. The prickle of feathers shivered down her spine and arms as human skin rippled into a cascade of black feathers. Full-grown wings replaced her arms, and her feet transformed into sharp talons that expertly picked up her clothing and her bag. The night air was chilly, but the blood in her veins kept her warm.

When she looked up, Barcus was gawking at her like she was a monster. Heat clawed up the side of Allie's neck. After all these years, it still hurt. *Icing on the fucking cake.*

The sudden sound of feet on pavement brought them out of the moment. They both turned around to find the mugger on his feet and sprinting away.

"Fuck," snarled Barcus.

Allie felt a growl well up in her chest as well. "You're letting him get away!" She pumped her powerful wings and prepared herself for flight. There was no way that man would be getting away after he'd tried to attack her.

"Wait! Stop!"

She was just off the ground when a body slammed into her, throwing her onto the concrete and pinning her in place. For a moment, Allie didn't know what had happened. She couldn't remember the last time she'd fallen out of the sky. She was sprawled on the ground, her breasts pillowed under her body like airbags, protecting her from the brunt of the impact. But then she felt the hard muscles grinding against her own, the large hands scrambling to pin her wings, the large... *other* thing that brushed against her ass, and it dawned on her.

The hero had tackled her!

A scream tore out of her throat as he crushed his body against her. "Get off me!"

"Only if you promise not to kill him," he answered through gritted teeth.

"Never!" She twisted in his grip and managed to turn around. It gave her better leverage, but it presented a new problem. She was up close and personal with those handsome, statuesque features the gods had blessed him with. Her fingers itched to scratch it all to ribbons.

"I can't let you attack him. He's my brother!"

"Your brother broke the Covenant!"

He froze above her, really listening to her for the first time. At the first sign of hesitation, Allie twisted her body, trying to throw him off-balance. Barcus retaliated by pressing down, using every ounce of his strength to keep her in place. Her nose was buried in the crook of his neck. With each breath, she inhaled the scent of the man on top of her.

Somehow the hero smelled like flowers and fresh soil tinged with gold, and damn if those weren't her favorite scents. His thick coat-clad muscles covered her entire body, protecting her from the winter cold. It would have been so easy to just lie still and beg for mercy. That would give her the best chance of returning home to her sisters, to Ocypete and Celia.

But she couldn't—mother of monsters, she could not

lie still against a hero when every instinct screamed at her to fight.

Heroes might be immortal, but they were still men. She raised her knee and buried it against the crotch on top of her.

She heard the air leave the hero's chest; his hold weakened enough for Allie to get the upper hand. Her wings transformed back into arms just in time to grab him and turn him on his back. She pinned his arms above his head, her body crouched on top like a bird of prey. A knee hovering above his jewels in a silent threat. "I'm going to go now," she panted.

He stared at her and then his eyes glanced down at her silk top and the cleavage that was mere inches from his face. "I can't let you leave." He sounded breathless and slightly in awe.

Allie tilted her head in amusement. "I wasn't asking."

"Neither was I." His hand opened, showing a small pile of dust. Before Allie could react, the wind took it and delivered it to her face.

She reeled back in surprise, cursing Zephyr's godsdamn wind. "What was that?" she demanded, even as her limbs slowed down and her body felt heavy.

The hero stood up, brushing the dirt off his knees. He looked totally in control. Curse him. "I told you, I'm hunting, and a hunter never leaves without his tools. I'd like to start over, Allie…"

His voice was growing muffled. Slowly Allie sank to the ground even when all she wanted to do was to rise, rise into the sky and return home. To her nest, to her sisters.

He'd gotten the upper hand. Damn heroes. They always had their tricks, and she had fallen for it.

"Allie…"

He was still saying her name. Not in the same way he'd said *monster*. This time it was softer, sweeter. Maybe the drugs were making her lose it.

As the dark edges of the night closed in on her, she could still hear his voice. But that couldn't be right, because she thought he'd said, "Allie, I'm going to need your help."

III

BARCUS HAD A problem. Well, several problems, but he couldn't think about the rest until he solved the one lying on the ground in front of him.

The woman was a problem.

No, not a woman. A monster. Daughter of Echidna. A harpy. It was pure luck he'd managed to catch her off guard. The legendary harpies were nothing to scoff at. Their ferocity had once earned them the title "Hounds of Zeus." Doing the gods' bidding by tormenting any man who dared defy the Lord of Olympus. She'd introduced herself as Allie; only now did he recognize the ancient name buried underneath. Aello, one of the known harpy sisters.

Seeing a harpy for the first time in years had rattled him to his core, and he certainly didn't remember them looking like *her*.

Heat scorched his face as he looked back down at the woman. Her winter clothes had been discarded in her attempt to fly away. Leaving her behind wasn't an option—not like this, and definitely not after she'd attacked a mortal.

Immortal. She had said the other man was a hero, like himself. But that didn't sound right. Barcus knew almost every hero in the Western Order, and he definitely did *not* recognize that guy.

One dead hero with evidence of a monster attack was odd, but witnessing another? Barcus couldn't shake the feeling that the two events were connected. Monsters and heroes had an understanding; the Covenant was supposed to prevent these sorts of things from happening. He had questions, and only the harpy could answer them.

"I'm sorry about all this," he whispered, reaching down to pick up her fallen items. Respectfully, he got to work dressing her, making sure not to let his touches linger too long. When that was done, he hefted the unconscious body up, draping her arm over his shoulder as she hugged his side. It wasn't the best look; bystanders might suspect she was a girl who had had too much fun and passed out. And that was the best option he could hope for. He groaned at the thought as he gathered her discarded shoes and bags, then started the trek back to his hotel.

Thankfully, the hotel was nearby. By all standards, it was elitist. The patrons consisted of old men who wore suits and severe faces, but Barcus's money was good enough to get him a large penthouse suite with a rainfall shower and a bed fit for an emperor.

They got up to his room without any problems, and he dumped the body unceremoniously onto the bed before staring at her.

She was still asleep. Without the wings and talons, she passed easily as a mortal woman. Innocent… harmless… but that was a disguise. He could never hurt a woman, but a monster… a harpy… that was something entirely different.

The Orpheum Powder he'd used could knock a lion unconscious for a few hours, but there was no telling how long it would affect a creature like her. When she did wake up, she was going to be mad as hell, and he was sure the front desk would not appreciate a screeching harpy making a scene.

Barcus contemplated his next move. He didn't have any Hephaestion Chains to tie the creature down, but he did have something else that would help. He moved to his aged hunting bag, tossed into the corner of the suite's living area. Inside was a mess of supplies.

An aroma of plant-based powders and balm clung to the bag. He could pick out each scent and its origin. There was more Orpheum Powder, some smoke bombs for when he needed to make a quick escape, and rope blessed by the cult of Artemis, right next to a roll of duct tape from Lowe's. Both were handy when hunting small game, but they'd be useless on a creature with the blood of titans.

Eventually, he found what he was looking for: olive-tree bark and plumeria, both in small glass containers, and another container filled with sand. The grains were from the battlefield of Troy, where gods and men had drawn lines dividing their camps. If it was good enough for gods, it would definitely work on a harpy.

He got to work quickly, crushing the ingredients into powder and sprinkling the sand, bark, and flower petals against the windowsill and bedroom doorway. He was just putting on the final touches when the woman made a small noise. Barcus froze, the noise finding its way deep into the subconscious of his mind. It was nothing like the screech she'd let out in the alley. It sounded like… a moan.

She's not human, he reminded himself firmly. *No matter how much she might look like a supermodel, she's a monster.*

Which meant she was dangerous.

It had been years since he'd seen any of her kind, but he still remembered the days of mud and sun. The cattle slaughtered by giants, the men lost to the tides of sea monsters, the soldiers carried away by harpies and torn apart in the sky.

You have a mission, he told himself firmly. *Remember why you brought her here. Remember the true enemy.*

Xanthus. It was possible he had offered the monsters an opportunity to strike back at the Order. Gods knew Xanthus was displeased with the way of the world. How the gods had seemingly disappeared, leaving their worshippers and patrons behind. The peace they'd fallen into meant there was little work for heroes these days, but that would all change if monsters started attacking unsuspecting mortals.

Barcus positioned his body outside the doorframe as he rolled different scenarios around. When her hawklike eyes opened, he watched the confusion skitter across her flawless features. This was the part of the hunt he'd grown to hate the most. The moment when his prey realized their plight and fear took over. When realization dawned on them that there was no way out and that they were good and thoroughly trapped.

His stomach squeezed in sympathy. He knew that feeling well and wouldn't wish it on anyone if there were an option.

But this was different.

He waited, but there was no fear on her face, only curiosity. The harpy looked around, taking in the large bed and shaded windows. Her confusion shifted to narrow focus as she turned her sharp gaze to him.

She pinned Barcus in place, taking away all feeling of control with just a single look.

"Listen," the harpy said slowly, "if you wanted to fuck me, all you had to do was ask."

⚬

The expression on the hero's face was priceless. Wide-eyed and sputtering, red crept from his ears down to his neck as his anger showed. "I do not want to fuck you!"

Allie threw back her head and cackled. "So, you brought me back to your hotel room, to your *bed*, for nothing?" It was easy to throw in a purr with the words. Her fingers creased the bedsheets underneath her and his eyes followed the movement.

It took just a second too long for him to pick his next words. "This is your cage."

Allie gave the room a sweeping look. "It's a very nice cage." One that probably cost a fortune by mortal standards, and was that wine on the nearby writing desk? Not bad at all, but there was nothing of real worth in the room. No gold embellishment or jeweled centerpieces. "I've been in better, but I've also been in worse."

The hero only needed a moment to gather his wits. "I need you to answer some questions."

Allie scowled. They were talking about this again? "I already told you, I didn't do anything wrong. Your brother attacked me for no reason."

"I find that hard to believe." Barcus crossed his arms over his chest.

"Believe what you want," she snapped back before giving the hero an obvious once-over. He wasn't wearing a coat anymore; now his muscles were on full display under a long-sleeved workout shirt that hugged his body just right. He looked even yummier than before. "The answer is no, by the way."

"No?"

"I've decided even if you asked to fuck me, I'd say no." She crossed her own arms and grinned at him. "Too much history between our kind. It would get messy."

His frown deepened, but he didn't look dangerous. Quite the opposite. When the gods had blessed him, they'd trapped Barcus with youthful features. Handsome features. Even displeased, he looked more like a perplexed puppy than a savage Doberman. That thought brought out a fit of giggles from her.

"What's so funny?"

"Oh, nothing," she sang, throwing her legs over the side of the bed. "Now, where are my purse and jacket? I really need to leave before my sisters get worried."

"In the living room," Barcus answered, inclining his head to the room behind him, where she could make out a small U-shaped couch and even a fake fireplace. Sitting on the cushions were her belongings.

"What a gentleman—you managed to grab all my things when you abducted me. I hope you didn't forget those chips I bought. Ocypete will be upset if I don't come back with them." Barcus didn't say a word as she approached the doorway. His stone-built body didn't move, either. Maybe he expected to fight her again. Well, she would be ready this time.

When Allie reached out to brush him aside, her hand passed through him. She gasped at the sight and took an involuntary step back. "What?"

The hero had the audacity to look smug. "I told you,

that room is your cage until I get the answers I'm looking for. I took the liberty of sprinkling it with a little recipe I learned that can trap any being inside a space of my choosing. I can step in"—he put one foot inside, playfully nudging her own—"but you can't step out. Doing so will turn you into nothing more than a spirit in this world."

"Witchcraft," she snarled, throwing a fist at the barrier, right in the direction of Barcus's face. It didn't hit him—it didn't hit anything—and his smirk remained infuriatingly in place. "Who taught you this?"

"A hunter never tells his secrets." He winked at her, cocky bastard. "But feel free to tell me all yours."

"I don't have any secrets," Allie growled. "I was just minding my own business when two arrogant heroes came and attacked me."

Oh, he didn't like that. His jaw locked in place, the earlier mirth gone. Something cold kissed Allie's spine at the sudden change. Her blood sang a warning. *Foolish harpy, this isn't just any mortal.* No, this was a hero, one nearly as old as she was and just as dangerous.

"One of my Order is dead," Barcus said slowly, "and I have it on good authority that a monster killed him. Now tell me, which of your kind would kill an immortal?"

Ah, so that was it. An immortal was dead and this hero thought he could capture her and have her spill all the secrets of her kind. No way. Allie crossed her arms and pursed her lips. *My beak is sealed.*

Barcus glared at her. "Do you know of a man named Xanthus?"

She didn't, but even if she did, he wouldn't be getting that information out of her.

"Fine. You'll talk eventually."

"I'm glad he's dead." She raised her chin defiantly as the hero's muscles tensed. She knew that would get a response out of him, and she hoped it would be enough to have him cross the boundary. If she could just get him to set foot in the bedroom, the ward wouldn't protect him. Then she could slit his throat and scratch his eyes out until he called it quits. All her hatred and venom seeped into her voice as she continued, "You still think of yourselves as heroes, but you're not. You were pets to the gods, and now you've been abandoned. You're just a bunch of murderers with nothing to do."

A dark shadow crossed his face at her words, and for a second Allie wondered if she'd gone too far, if he would kill her then and there. All the smugness and the humor were gone. The man standing in front of her was a member of Olympus's Order. All muscle and malicious hatred for her kind.

It had been a long time since she'd been face-to-face with such a warrior. Her hackles rose to meet his gaze, even as her talons itched to come out. She felt her body come alive, every cell reacting to the man in front of her.

To her surprise, though, he didn't say anything. With a shuddering breath, he closed his eyes and turned back to the couch. Ignoring her.

The door remained open between them, allowing the hero constant vigilance over her until one of them caved. The odds of that weren't good, though; heroes were stubborn, and if she intended to win this war of wills, she'd have to do better. Maybe she should just open the wine and enjoy it while it lasted.

Oh…

A wicked thought bloomed as her gray eyes took in the

wine on the counter, then shifted back to the open door. She could see Barcus, sitting on the large couch and doing his best to ignore her. Well, two could play that game.

She'd never made a hero beg before, but when a challenge presented itself, Allie always rose to the occasion.

⸘

Bringing the harpy back had been a bad idea.

Barcus couldn't concentrate. Not with her sitting just in the other room. The myths regarding harpies hadn't done them justice. For so long, men had warned of creatures with hag-like features, their resemblance to women visible only in their faces while the rest of their bodies took the form of vicious vultures.

Had any of those idiots ever seen a harpy?

They were beautiful. Sirens of the air, and just as dangerous.

Having her so close was a reminder of the man he used to be. Her words still rang in his ears. *"You're not a hero."* Did she know how close they were to the truth, or was it just a mind trick? Either way, her aim struck true.

He was playing a dangerous game, but hopefully one that would pay off. In the meantime, he returned to the gory details of Erik's apartment.

Now in the seclusion of his own space, he forced himself to stare long and hard at the disheveled state of Erik's room. The blood smeared across all the furniture, splattered against the wall and the ceiling. Barcus felt his breathing hitch as he stared at the gore. His fingers tapped nervously against his keyboard as he scrolled to the other pictures.

Despite the crime scene looking as if a monster had done it, he couldn't find the obvious telltale signs. There were no claw marks, no fur. *No feathers*, his mind supplied helpfully. Even with all the blood, all the furniture was intact. It was unlikely there had been a struggle. Had Erik been immobilized? Or had he simply allowed his death to happen?

Or maybe they learned how to kill discreetly, a dark voice whispered across his mind. They had certainly learned how to mimic humans over the years.

Again, he thought of the harpy, her belongings sitting on the couch next to him. A cell phone, heels, and a bag of potato chips. Things any woman would have on hand. It was certainly more normal than carrying a spear and a bag full of hunting equipment. If any of the maids actually cleaned his room, they might mistake him for a serial killer.

That dark voice laughed at the thought. *They wouldn't be wrong.*

"Gods," he sighed, rubbing his hands across his face, "get a grip."

There was too much to do, and too much at stake for him to be losing control.

Sleep sounded very good right about now. It had been a long day and an even longer night. His laptop clock helpfully told him it was nearly one in the morning. After the evening he'd had, of course his thoughts were spiraling. He needed rest.

The sudden sound of glass clinking broke him out of those thoughts. He was on his feet in an instant, head cocked towards the bedroom. Another delicate sound filled the suite, followed by a pleased little moan.

Frowning, Barcus grabbed his spear and inched towards the doorway, where the sight brought him to a full and complete stop.

Allie was lying on the bed, the tight jeans and soft-looking top gone to reveal black lace underwear and a matching bra with gold trim. She was lounging against the pillows, her hair disheveled. *Sex hair*, Barcus's mind pointed out helpfully. *That is sex hair and* that *is a come-hither look.*

He gawked as the harpy brought one of the hotel's water glasses to her lips. It was filled halfway with the complimentary white wine. Really, he should have expected this. "This is good stuff, hero," she hummed happily, smacking her lips. "You have good taste."

Despite himself, Barcus felt his lips twitch. "Help yourself. I wasn't going to drink it, anyway."

"What a waste." Her voice was all innocence, not a hint of the diabolical creature that lurked underneath. She took another sip and then leaned forward, the glass hovering right in front of her barely covered breasts, directing the eye to the point where flesh met cloth. She moved like a dancer, all grace and purposeful intent. Tonight's intent: to seduce.

"Are you ready to talk?" It was a miracle that his voice remained steady, unaffected by the sight before him.

"Talk? Oh, no." A wickedly beautiful smile flashed his way. "This is how I get ready for bed."

Gods! Barcus didn't know if he wanted to laugh or groan out loud from the words. She was laying it on pretty thick, but the show was a good one. The way she said "bed" was almost too much to take. He'd slept in that bed just the night before, alone among the plush king-size pillows, thinking about how the room was meant for two. It had been a long time since he'd shared a bed with a woman. So long. And now there was a beauty sipping wine in her underwear on his bed.

No, not a beauty. A monster.

He didn't dare move. He couldn't show how she was affecting him. It would give her all the power. *Just turn and walk away.*

"But," Allie continued, taking another sip of her wine, "I always sleep naked."

Barcus's cheek twitched at the words. He couldn't let her win. "Then sleep naked." His voice was not his own anymore; it was deeper, darker. He rose to her challenge and enjoyed the brief hesitation that flickered across her face before it set in renewed determination.

"Alright then." The glass clinked against the countertop as she slammed it down. Barcus thought it might shatter into a million glistening shards, but it held its shape.

Allie stood up, showing off her long legs and hourglass shape. He allowed himself to soak in the sight of her, the way her breasts threatened to spill from her bra, until the bra was suddenly gone. He was looking at a pair of the best breasts he'd ever seen. They were touched with the same golden complexion as the rest of her body, but in the middle of each breast sat a perky brown nipple just begging to be touched. She was aroused, but there was no way it was because of him.

Barcus locked his jaw in place before it could fall on the ground. Based on the way the harpy's eyes lit up, she knew exactly how she was affecting him. This was a game of chicken he didn't intend to lose. At least he wasn't the only one staring at the other in perverse fascination. His cock had grown hard at the sight of her, and the harpy's eyes were glued to it like it was one of the seven wonders of the world.

Barcus reached down, giving it a long sensual stroke. Two animalistic groans filled the space between them.

Allie licked her lips, contemplating her next move. "Why don't you come to bed, hero?"

His tongue dragged over his lips, pulling a single word along with it. "No."

"Where do you plan on sleeping tonight, if not in this bed?"

"The couch is fine for me. Thanks."

She frowned in annoyance. "Alright then, I guess it's time *I* went to bed." With that, she jumped under the covers. Her body wiggled under the bright white comforter; her hair became even more tousled, if that was possible. Her body was covered, thank the gods, but now there was a new problem.

Bed. Harpy. Bed. Allie. His mind could only process one word at a time.

He wanted to prowl into that room and pin her to the bed the same way he'd pinned her in the alley. The memory of their bodies pressed against each other, and the pleasure it had brought, drew his hand to his cock in search of relief. They could have a lot more pleasure if he just…

No. Barcus stepped back from the doorframe, just to be safe.

Allie grinned at him from a mountain of pillows and white fluff. Then, in a final power move, she dropped a pair of tiny black panties to the ground.

Barcus coughed. "You can't be serious."

"I am."

"You don't want me. You just want me to lift the spell on the room." The words were there to remind himself. An anchor for his own sanity.

Allie blinked innocently back at him. "Why don't you come in here and see for yourself?"

"No," he growled, reaching his limit. "I am done playing games."

He did what he should have done in the beginning. Turned and walked away. Not back to the couch where his makeshift bed was, but towards the hallway bathroom. Allie might have the large plush bed, but Barcus had the master bathroom, and right now he needed a shower. A cold one.

IV

T HE SMELL OF utter deliciousness woke her the next morning. Allie blinked herself back into awareness, the fog of sleep lifting from her mind slowly. Too slowly. The aroma of dark coffee in the morning wasn't anything unusual; she and her sisters had an unhealthy addiction to the stuff. But her keen senses picked up cooked meat and toasted bread, a full buffet of food.

This early in the morning? No one was that productive.

Her eyes snapped open as the memories of the past day crashed into her. At the same time, a low, husky drawl came from the nearby doorway. "Is Sleeping Beauty awake?"

She growled in answer, but sleep made the noise less of a divine threat and more of a grumpy rumble. After years of setting her own schedule, she wasn't used to being awakened before she wanted, and even then, mornings were her least favorite time of the day. Add to that a smug hero and the fact that she was stuck in a hotel suite, and the morning was shaping up to be one of the worst yet.

It still rubbed her raw that she hadn't managed to get

him to step foot into the room. She'd stripped down to nothing, and he'd liked it. There was no doubt about that. The fire in his eyes was the same as she'd seen in every mortal before him. The need to touch her, to claim her. But the moment he turned away, the game had changed in his favor.

Fuck. This was going to be harder than she'd thought.

With a groan, she picked herself up and glared at the man standing outside the doorway. Damn him. How was he up before her? He had been typing on a laptop when her eyes had inevitably closed last night, and here he was again, up at the crack of dawn. "Don't heroes sleep?" she asked, trying to mask her irritation.

Who knew what he had done while she had slept? Reinforced his traps? Set new ones? Plotted how he was going to torture her for information? Her eyes narrowed on the breakfast in accusation. *Bring it*, she thought. *I've been through worse.*

Granted, it had been a couple hundred years, but she wasn't so out of practice.

Barcus snorted. "Still as friendly as last night, I see."

"Am I still trapped in this room?" Allie raised an eyebrow at him and the clear line of dirt at the bottom of the doorway. "Then yes, and I don't see that changing. You are my enemy, after all."

"Because I trapped you here?"

"Because you are a *hero*," she snapped. Wasn't that obvious? "Heroes *kill* unmortals."

"Monsters kill heroes as well, and innocent people. The road goes both ways."

"We've stopped."

"My men have stopped killing as well, as long as no one

is breaking the rules." He gave her a pointed look before pushing the plate of food inside her room. "I got this for you. You should eat it."

His hand was back out before she had the chance to attack. Allie stared at the offering, considering it carefully. The hero sighed. "I didn't drug it. The kitchen downstairs made it."

She crossed her arms and sniffed just to be sure. No scent of any natural poisons or drugs, but it could be odorless. Barcus had proven that he was adept at mixing herbs. Best not to risk it. "I'm fine not eating."

"You'll get hungry…"

"I'm immortal, just like you. It will be awhile before I feel any pain."

He rolled his eyes. "Come on. I'm trying to make amends here."

"Then let me out."

His eyes darkened. "Alright. If you tell me everything you know about a hero named Eosphorus."

Allie tilted her head. It might still be Apollo's unholy hour, but she wasn't stupid. "That wasn't the name you said last night."

She watched his reaction carefully, saw the way his eyes widened just the slightest bit before the mask fell back into place. "Do you know him?"

"I don't."

A beat passed between them. Then another question: "And what about a man named Xanthus?"

Interesting, there was an unmistakable pitch in his throat. As if the syllables scorched his insides.

"No." She put as much conviction as she could into the word and held his gaze. With every molecule in her body, she ached for him to feel the truth in the words.

Let me go. I don't know anything. She just wanted to return to her sisters. If the gods would let her return to them unharmed, she would do anything. She would never again consider leaving their side. "It has been a long time since I've seen any of your kind."

"Alright." Barcus nodded and turned back to the living space of the main suite.

Panic jumped up her throat at the sight. Alright? What did that mean?

"Wait!" She scrambled to the edge of the bed to keep him in sight. He hadn't gone far, back to the couch where… dear gods, the mess had exploded overnight. More paper piles had appeared, taking up every cushion on the couch. How could he sleep with all those? *Where* did he sleep? She was beginning to suspect he just didn't.

Her panic surged as the severity of her situation hit her. What had she gotten herself into?

Barcus turned back at her cry, looking tired and just as unsure as she felt. Ever since she had heard his name, an image had been ingrained in her mind. Barcus the Hunter, the hero chosen by Artemis to hunt down every child of Echidna left on the earth. Every creature who had wronged the mortals of the surface. His legend threatened to shadow even Herakles.

But that man didn't stand in front of her.

That man wouldn't have kept her alive long enough to ask her questions. He wouldn't have gotten her breakfast. And he certainly wouldn't have looked at her with unquestionable lust sparking in those storm-colored eyes.

So, who was standing in front of her?

"Do you believe me?" Her words were barely a whisper, but they seemed to echo throughout the quiet suite.

"Yes." The reply was soft, unlike the man who uttered it. "But I still need to know about the other monsters in the city. And I think you have the answers I'm looking for."

"I can't tell you anything." Frustration coated her tone. She couldn't… she *wouldn't* betray the others like that.

"Maybe not now." Barcus's eyes darted away from her, his scowl back in place. "But we're stuck together until you do. So please, put some clothes on."

The words were like cold water on her anger. She glanced down, taking in the naked state she had slept in the night before. Embarrassment threatened to cloud over all other thoughts, but she tamped it down. There was nothing to be embarrassed about. Once she had flown across kingdoms as naked as the day she was born, her wings spread wide under the harsh, unflinching sun. She had been a fearless Icarus. Men who had dared to stare at her had had their eyeballs plucked out. She had not known the meaning of the word embarrassment then, and she would not let this hero invoke that emotion now.

Not after she'd seen the lustful glint in his eye.

"No." She tucked in her legs and straightened her spine, pushing her breasts out proudly.

Barcus let out a low noise of frustration. "What are you doing?"

"Waiting …"

"For what?"

"For my sisters," she announced smugly. "You see, they will be looking for me. We're never away from each other too long. When I don't return, they'll get worried and search for me. Is that what you want? Three harpies instead of one?"

This was a gamble. While it was true that every bone

in her body knew her sisters would eventually come look-ing for her, she wasn't sure how soon. After all, it was the weekend. She and Celia were known to go out and disap-pear for a day or two at a time, binge drinking and having fun with mortals and unmortals until Ocypete eventually called them home. And she didn't even know where Celia was. It would be at least another day or two until her sisters tried contacting her.

But he didn't know that.

What will the Great Hunter do now?

Barcus's face did not change. Not in fear nor in sur-prise. He only nodded as if in a dream and said, "Then we don't have much time."

"What?" The word came out as an undignified squawk. "Did you not hear me? *Three* harpies. Even you can't fight us off."

"Maybe not," came the calm reply. His words were flat in a way that sent a shiver down her spine. There was nothing in the words. No fear, no surprise—he was stone accepting the pounding rain. "But what can three harpies do to an immortal? What can one? You can attack me, but you cannot kill me. You cannot eat me, or turn me to stone."

Her teeth clenched in frustration. Damn him to the underworld, he was right. "It doesn't matter. I'll devote the rest of my life to torturing you. Just as we made King Phineus pay for his arrogance."

"Ah yes, I know the story well. You stole every piece of food laid before him so he could not eat. Phineus had to ask the Argonauts to help fight you off, and if memory serves, they did so successfully." A slow smile pulled at his lips with the jab. "But that doesn't matter. You see, as an immortal,

I don't need to eat. I don't need much of anything to keep living. Believe me, I know."

She didn't dare argue. Something had settled in his eyes, taking the spark away and making him look like a shade. This man wasn't afraid of her legend or her claws. Was he afraid of anything? Her throat clenched at the thought. This was what made an ancient hero. Fearless, even of death itself.

Barcus shrugged easily, settling back into his self-assuredness. "Plus, that all sounds like a lot of work for you. And you seem like you have a lot going on right now." He cast a meaningful look at the bag of chips she had purchased, sitting on the couch with the rest of her belongings. Heat flushed her face at the obvious sarcasm in his face.

Damn him. Damn him! She screeched, grabbed a nearby pillow, and flung it at him.

It disappeared as soon as it hit the doorway, vanishing into an invisible field. She couldn't even hit him with a pillow. Mother's maw! This was the worst kind of torture.

"Eat your breakfast, Allie," Barcus said in response. "The sooner you realize I have you cornered, the sooner I can set you free."

⌘

Maybe he had been too harsh to the monster.

Or too kind.

Kindness hadn't gotten him far in the past. But it was a habit that he couldn't shake, no matter how many times it bit him in the ass.

He shouldn't have given her the food. Or at least he should have used the food as a reward. The old him would have done that, but now, his mind felt muddy. The lack of sleep was taking its toll, and the harpy in the other room wasn't helping things, either.

Think, Barcus! Think! She knew something that would help him find Xanthus. Why else would that hero attack her?

That in itself was a mystery that needed to be solved. Because if she had deserved it, he needed to end her life now. But if she hadn't… then that was a larger problem. Heroes and monsters had been at peace for nearly three hundred years, and now all that seemed to be in jeopardy no matter how he looked at it.

She's not an animal, a logical voice spoke up among the fog of exhaustion. *Try reasoning with her. She probably doesn't want a war to break out.* History had shown that if heroes and monsters were attacking each other without reason, that was exactly what would happen.

With a heavy sigh, he grabbed a few pages of his notes and marched back to the door. It had been an hour since they had last talked, and the silence was making him anxious. When he peeked in, he saw her sitting on the bed, watching a television show where people decorated houses. She was dressed, thank the gods. He didn't know if his tired mind could take it if she was still naked.

Her eyes flickered over to him at his arrival. Those eyes that looked so much like the eyes of a bird of prey, sharp and full of intelligence. Barcus was caught under their intense stare. No turning back now. "We need to talk."

"I told you I have nothing to say."

"Then I'll talk," he answered gruffly. "This isn't about you, and as soon as I have answers, you are free to go. I give you my word."

She laughed. "Your word doesn't mean a thing to me. Heroes always lie!"

"Our word was enough when we made the Covenant," he shot back, voice stern but not hard. She already didn't trust him, and shouting wouldn't help that. He needed to approach this the same way he would an injured animal. More softness. He cleared his throat before finishing, "So it will have to be enough now."

The change in tone didn't help the way he'd imagined it would. The harpy's fingers drummed against her arm, nails growing ever so slightly. "Covenants and promises don't mean much when you look the other way whenever you want."

"I know," Barcus said through gritted teeth. "I was there when members from your clan, my Order, and surviving Mythos came together to make those commitments." That had been the first time he'd realized how few in number Mythos were. When he'd been granted his blessing from Artemis, the whole world had been Mythos, believing in the gods and making sacrifices to them. But as the years had gone on, those beliefs had been shunned. People followed new gods or followed none at all; it didn't matter. They were Aethos: those who didn't follow the old ways.

Allie's eyes widened slightly at that, not in surprise but in interest. "No one told me that. Why would the Great Hunter be there?"

"Because I was the one who called it." He held her gaze. "I came to this country like everyone else, looking for a fresh start. And I quickly realized I wasn't the only one. Mythos came here as well to hold on to their beliefs, and monsters—"

"Unmortals," Allie corrected again, but her voice was soft. "We came here to get away from your kind."

He nodded. The wars had done their damage to all of them. "That's why we needed a peace treaty."

The Dark Ages had been nonstop fighting between them. Eventually, the remaining monsters had gone underground or learned that to prey upon mortals made them prey as well. They'd stopped fighting, and mankind had finally begun to develop at a rate that had surprised them all. New religions had risen in power. The old ways had become nothing but memories kept alive by devoted Mythos families, and the gods had slowly but surely fallen quiet. When the new continent had been discovered, everyone had seen it as a fresh start, one without blood feuds and war.

Over the centuries, there had been so much blood on his hands. He'd needed to get away, far away. Living alone in the wilds of the New World provided that escape, but it wasn't until Artemis found him that he was able to regain his footing. She gave him a new purpose: to establish peace. The Covenant had been his attempt to make amends. To ensure such senseless killing never took place again. And now that peace was under attack.

Remembering it all now helped center him. He would not hurt another monster unless they were guilty. And in this case, the evidence was still lacking. He didn't know if Allie had attacked that hero or not, but if there was a chance that she hadn't, he owed it to her to find out. "I will find the hero who attacked you, and we'll get to the bottom of this. Justice will be served as the Covenant commands it, as agreed upon by our two races. You deserve and will be given a fair investigation. I swear to Artemis."

She bit her bottom lip, still looking displeased but unable to say anything else. The fact that she wasn't arguing with him for the first time in twenty-four hours was a good sign. Barcus held up the pages from his notes for her to see. "One of my brothers is dead and I believe a mon—I mean, an unmortal might have done it. Can you look at these pictures and tell me if anything stands out to you?"

That seemed to take her by surprise. "Why are you telling me all this? Do you not have any friends?"

He laughed at the absurd question. "I have friends." Friends who worried too much about him and whom he cared for deeply in return. Men to whom he couldn't reveal the truth of his latest undertaking for fear that they would insist on joining him. "I just… prefer to work alone."

The harpy didn't look convinced. "Fine." She blew a silky strand of hair out of her face and moved to the edge of the bed. "Hand it here and I'll give it a look."

Victory sang through him like an epic poem. He held the notes out, hope swelling in his chest. He realized his mistake the moment her fingers curled around his wrists and not the papers. There was no time to brace himself against the doorframe before the harpy pulled him into her cage.

He fell forward with no grace. Nearly face-planted into the bed before he managed to roll to the ground and caught himself. But it was too late—the harpy was on him. He felt her strong thighs straddle his hips and her hands pin his to the floor. His papers went flying, crinkling as they wrestled for control. It was an odd reversal of their first encounter together. He was trapped, this time without his spear or his hunting tools.

Panic seized him, immobilizing his arms and limbs. It was only a few seconds, but those precious few seconds were enough for the harpy to get the upper hand, her talons flashing out and digging into his arms like daggers. Out of the corner of his eye, he could see that wasn't the only thing that had transformed. She was a completely different creature now. Black feathers tracing up her arms, glistening like wet onyx. The long legs he had been admiring earlier were gone, replaced with ones hooked like those of a bird of prey, sporting deadly claws that threatened to tear his skin like paper.

This was the true form of a harpy. Deadly, powerful, and still… beautiful.

The word took him aback for a moment, but no, it wasn't a mistake. The way her feathers caught the light made him want to stroke them. Her golden skin hadn't changed, and now it rubbed against him. Her breasts hung under his nose like two perfect bells. He still saw the woman who had captivated him.

The talons tightened on his arms painfully once again, and he realized she had said something. The ringing in his ears faded out, and her voice echoed around the room, hard and commanding. "Lift your spell and I won't tear your arm off."

He knew she couldn't kill him, not with claws alone, but that didn't mean she couldn't hurt him. Torture wasn't a foreign experience; prolonged pain, an enemy to hiss at and hate. Memories filled his gut like hot coals. He remembered the many years of self-loathing well and never wanted to experience it again.

His chest tightened as if her claws were leaking venom into his blood. Years of training had taught him to control fear and never show it. But something was off. Ever since he'd started searching for Xanthus, he'd felt fragile, like a glass statue instead of one made of stone.

"Get off me," he growled, bucking against her.

She countered with her own weight, the strength in her body a reminder that she wasn't mortal. "I tried playing nice."

"So did I," he hissed back. "I guess that makes us both fools. Now. Let. Me…" He reached down deep to growl out the words, but it was hard. Every syllable scraped against a lump in his throat, threatening to tremble. He almost did it too, but he lost the last word. A faint quiver hit the word "go."

He shouldn't be afraid, but he was. Gods, he was.

Of what, he didn't fully know. But she saw it, and instead of pouncing on him like a vulture on a bleeding carcass, she hesitated. To cover it up, he fought harder. Letting his fear feed his adrenaline. Her grip slackened and he threw her off.

Black feathers fell around them in the chaos. They both scrambled to their feet at the same time, but she stood between him and the doorway. A storm cloud of emotions darkened her face as she dug her heels in.

Standing, he felt the fear recede, just enough that his thoughts became clear again. He didn't have claws or his trusted spear, but he had other things at his disposal. The harpy had taught him that last night. Anything could be a weapon.

"You won't overpower me so easily this time, hero," Allie hissed at him. "This time it's just you and me. Man versus Harp—UPH!"

A hard-thrown pillow cut her off. Barcus didn't hesitate to throw another, but this time Allie was prepared. Her claws reached out and batted it away with ease, slicing into the soft fabric and sending white plumes of goose feathers everywhere. Winter snow exploded in the room.

"Are you serious?!" she squawked in surprise—a noise he was quickly learning meant her guard was lowered. Barcus took the opportunity to rush the door. He jumped to the right and she followed him, but the cover of feathers hindered her keen eyesight. It was too easy to spin on his heel and fake her out. He rushed past her and leapt through the ward. His foot colliding with the coffee table in the living room, he collapsed onto the sofa, smacking his jaw against the armrest. Gods, it hurt. Pain laced up his foot, but neither would leave a mark for long.

He was free. That was the important part.

Behind him, Allie's curses filled the space, and more feathers erupted. Another pillow fell victim to her anger.

He stared at the doorway, his breath coming out in heaving pants. A trembling hand ran through his hair, combing the goose feathers from his locks. They fell like fluffy snowflakes, all except one. A single black feather landed in his lap. Hesitantly, he picked it up.

What just happened? His body felt electric from the sudden fear and excitement. Highs and lows so abrupt he was still reeling. A madman's laugh bubbled out of him as the harpy screeched.

He was losing his mind. Clearly and truly. Bringing the harpy back really had been a mistake.

A LLIE WOKE UP to the sound of Madonna's "Material Girl" jingling across the room. She groaned into her pillow, her hand reaching out blindly towards the nightstand to grab her phone, but it wasn't there. Her eyes snapped open, taking in the foreign room that surrounded her as the events of the night before came crashing back. "Shit." Her head sank deeper into the soft feather pillow.

In the other room, she heard the hero groan his annoyance. "What is that noise?"

"My phone!" she called back. "Can you bring it here?"

There was rustling from the other room, and a few unmistakable curses in Greek, before Barcus appeared in the doorframe, phone in hand. He looked even yummier in the late-morning light. Shirtless, draped only in a pair of baggy gray sweatpants that hung low on his hips. If he had looked like that last night, Allie might have been too dumbstruck to win their little game. The same frown was pursed against his lips, though, as he waved the phone in the air. "Do you think I'm dumb?"

"What do you mean?" She scrubbed a hand across her face and gave a loud yawn. The ringing had mercifully stopped.

"You want me to give you your phone? So you can… what? Tell your monster friends and family to come kill me and let you out?"

She stared at him, her hand cradling her cheek as she tried to keep her eyes open. "Actually, I was just thinking it was polite to answer the phone after I've been missing all weekend, but that plan sounds good, too."

"I'm not giving this to you."

"Material Girl" started up again. Allie huffed in annoyance; that was definitely one of her sisters. "Look, it doesn't matter. Either way, it's a win for me. My sisters are going to worry if I don't answer the phone. Eventually, you'll have three shrieking harpies hunting you down to the ends of the earth." She let the threat hang between them for a moment before offering, "But if you give me that phone and leave now, we can avoid all that."

"I have a better idea." Barcus jabbed his thumb at the glass screen and held the phone up to his ear. "Hello?"

Allie's fingers dug into the comforter. This was going too far. She didn't want this man talking to her sisters and telling them lies. She clutched the covers to her body and hurled herself to the door, trying to put an end to the conversation before it even began.

A wickedly beautiful smirk nestled on Barcus's face as he stepped away from the doorframe and carried on the conversation. "Allie is in the shower right now. I can pass a message on to her… Yes, I'm her boyfriend."

She screeched and tried to grab the phone from his hand, only for it to disappear into the ether past the doorway. Barcus raised a brow at her and mouthed the words, *"In space, no one can hear you scream."*

Space had never met a harpy. She inhaled a lungful, ready to shatter windows if need be, when Barcus's brows suddenly dipped in concern. "Miesha?" he repeated out loud, eyes searching her for a reaction.

Her blood ran cold. Miesha was one of Celia's employees. If she was calling, then something was wrong. Maybe with the business, maybe with Celia. Her fingers clutched the blanket tighter to her breasts against the new chill in the room. Then Barcus's voice cut through her shock. "Actually, Allie is available now. Here, let me pass the phone over to her."

To her amazement, his arm reached out, passing the phone safely into the room. Allie stared at it, then stared at him, her silence asking a single question. The smugness was gone from Barcus's face, replaced with quiet concern as he pressed the phone towards her. Not good, if a hero was giving her that look…

She snatched the phone out of his hand and turned so he couldn't see any of the emotions written across her face. "Hello?"

"Allie?"

"Speaking." She ran her hands through her messy hair, trying to sound normal.

"This is Miesha—I work with your sister."

"Yeah, hi, Miesha." She remembered the young unmortal, a gorgon whose frizzy black hair was home to a snake or two. Celia only hired unmortals at her company to help them learn new skills and adapt to a continually changing world. Their community was small enough, even in the city, that she knew all the gorgons and satyrs. "What can I do for you?"

"Well, I was wondering if you've seen your sister. She didn't come into work this morning. Usually, she calls if she's going to be late, but—"

"Celia's not at work?"

"No, and I tried calling her a million times. Is she at home?"

The chill became a blizzard, turning her entire body numb. "I… I'll check and call you back."

She didn't even wait for a reply before hanging up and checking her messages. Still nothing from Celia. Her fingers trembled as she scrolled to her sister's number and hit dial. An eternity passed as she waited for someone to pick up. In the end, Celia's chirping voice mail greeted her and urged her to leave a message.

A growl worked up Allie's throat as she hurled the phone to the floor. Anger and helplessness filled her veins as she paced the room, the white comforter trailing behind her like the robe of an empress. "My sister is missing…" The words came out slowly, without any bite to them. They didn't feel real, and they wouldn't feel real until she could get out of this damn room and check every place Celia usually lurked.

"I'm sorry." Barcus's voice was soft. There was pity in the two words, and she hated that.

Her pacing stopped and she locked eyes with him. "I need to get out of here and look for her."

Barcus crossed his large arms over his chest in a defiant stance. Allie braced herself for the refusal, air trapped in her lungs as she planned the best way to tear the room apart in order to make her escape, when he said, "Alright."

"Alright?" she repeated, waiting for the punchline to follow it. Nothing came. "You're going to let me go?"

"Of course," he said, stepping closer to the doorframe. His foot inched towards the threshold, where the sand and herbs formed a solid line for her confinement. "But you have to promise to help me as well."

"I don't help kidnappers," she told him firmly.

"And I don't help monsters." His reply was brisk, with no room for argument. When she opened her mouth to dispute the name, he quickly added, "But seeing as you're not a monster and I'm not a kidnapper, we should be able to help each other, right?"

Oh, he was good.

"Fine, I'll help you. But first you let me out. I have a few places I need to look for Celia before—"

Barcus shook his head. "No, I'm coming with you."

That stopped her short. "No, you are not. I can't bring a hero to my house. To my sister's workplace! There are…" Allie cut herself short, unwilling to tell him that other unmortals worked there.

"Either I come with you or you don't leave at all. I'll go out searching for all the clues I need by myself. I'm a good hunter. I'll find my answers eventually." The last words hung between them like a promise. A beautiful, threatening promise.

Allie considered her options. Stay locked in a room for gods knew how long while her sister was missing, or show their belly to the beast. Where they lived, where they worked—exposing not just her and her sisters but other unmortals as well. Instincts she hadn't exercised in decades flared to life, warning of impending danger while screaming for her to take action.

She gritted her teeth. Ocypete would be furious if she knew what was being considered. Heroes had hunted them for years and had slaughtered so many of their brothers and sisters. Even after a couple of centuries of peace, they couldn't be trusted, no matter how handsome.

In the end, it was really no choice at all. She couldn't stay here without knowing where Celia was, and she had to see Ocypete to make sure the nest was safe. Being careful wouldn't give her the edge in this situation. She needed to be clever in order to protect the life they had built. "Alright, you have a deal."

Barcus nodded and scuffed the line of sand with his foot, disrupting the spell. The room seemed to heave a sigh of relief as it rejoined the mortal realm, but besides the sudden lightness of the air, there didn't seem to be any other telling marks that things were back to normal. Slowly, Allie stepped to the doorway.

Barcus's body still stood guard outside of it, a towering golem made from marble and steel. Only a few inches separated them. It would be so easy to reach out now, to have talons instead of human fingers, to see who would truly prevail—immortal or unmortal.

He didn't flinch as she raised her hand and held it past the doorframe, inching closer and closer until it hovered against the pulse in his neck. She could hear it clearly. It was the only thing that broke the illusion of what he was. Just a man, not a god or an icon. With all the stories and legends, it was easy to forget that heroes had all been just men once.

Her fingers itched to touch him, but that felt taboo, like petting a stray dog. You never knew if it was rabid or not, and she didn't care to take the risk. She was already risking too much.

With that, her hand fell and grabbed hold of the door-knob just outside. Barcus's brows crumpled as she shooed him away. "What are you—?"

"I need to get dressed," Allie said, making sure to keep an edge to her voice. It was best they both remember what she was and what he was and why they needed to keep their distance. "No more peep shows for you." Her eyes dared him to argue the point before she slammed the door in his stupid, handsome face.

❦

Barcus huffed a cloud of frigid air as he followed Allie down the brick sidewalk in Georgetown. Everything was gray, the color of a corpse. He much preferred the constant summers of home, where it might get cold, but snow was never a worry and the ocean always sparkled. Just thinking about it made his heart ache. But he was here, in the cold, wet city, accompanied by his worst enemy.

The harpy was agitated since he'd stopped her from flying. He'd threatened a spell that would molt her wings, and even though no such thing existed, it had scared her enough not to try. They took a taxi, pressed together in the confined space as they crossed the Potomac River. As soon as they reached the other side, she suggested walking.

He knew the signs of fear when he saw them. He couldn't forget the vulnerable way she had clutched that comforter to her chest as she'd talked to Miesha. As if her heart couldn't take the news.

Barcus knew what that feeling was like. He remembered so many years ago when he'd heard Argos had disappeared. The heartbreak he had felt at losing not just a member of the Order but his true brother in arms. Together they had searched obsessively for Argos, using every skill in their arsenal to divine where his friend had been taken.

There was a bottomless desperation that consumed a person when a loved one disappeared. It had left Barcus feeling powerless for the first time in his life. The gods had refused to answer their pleas; both Hestia and Artemis had never given them a clue about Argos's location. And the Great Hunter had been unable to find any trace.

Maybe that was why he'd shown empathy for the harpy. Why he'd offered her freedom instead of keeping her locked away.

He shook those thoughts away and adjusted the lacrosse bag on his shoulder. "So your sister has a job? I didn't realize your kind—"

She stopped short and stared at him. "Be very careful how you finish that sentence, hero."

Well, now he felt like an ass. "I just haven't seen your kind for so long, and the few times I did..." He trailed off, not knowing how exactly to tell the woman how he had killed cyclopes partaking in human trafficking or the recent animal shifters on Circe's island.

Allie shoved her hands deep into the pockets of her jacket and led the way past the boutique shops and morning yoga studios that peppered the street. "We can't all keep doing the same job century after century," she said sarcastically. "What was it you said you do again? Hunt?"

It burned his nerves to admit that she was on to something. Pride fueled the men of his Order. All had once been the greatest fighters or tacticians the world had ever known. Too many of them were clinging to their days of glory, even though those days were long gone. Barcus could only account for a few who had settled into each new century with a new day job and a life that resembled normalcy.

Barcus had yet to manage it.

"Well, if you insist on a modern-day profession, you could say I am a detective," Barcus offered. "It sounds a little more formal, but a hell of a lot sexier." Not that he cared if this woman thought he was sexy. But the joke seemed to make the right point as Allie was smiling again. "What is it you and your sisters do?"

Her lush lips pursed as she considered what to tell him. He saw the questions running through her mind before she came to a decision. "Celia runs a graphic design studio, and Pete writes history books."

"And you?"

Silence. Barcus grimaced as he realized he'd crossed a line; usually he was good at small talk. A little interest and the right question often led to people sharing more information than they should. But Allie was different from his usual suspects. Everything he said to her was taken as some kind of attack, meant to be countered or parried.

It was a surprise when this time she allowed the question to break through her defenses. "I'm trying to figure that out right now."

"Ah, so terrorizing the city locals isn't your scene anymore?" he asked. "Shame, because you could put those wings of yours to good use. I hear vigilantes are in this decade."

Allie laughed, tucking a strand of black hair behind her ear. "That has never really been my scene."

"What was, then?"

She preened at him, looking secretive and mischievous and damn sexy as she said, "Jewelry thief."

"Why am I not surprised?" Now that she mentioned it,

they had passed several high-end jewelry stores, and Allie's eyes always lingered on them as they passed. There wasn't a doubt in his mind that the harpy could afford the gems; she probably had a collection back in her nest that would make the store owners gawk.

Allie turned down a street lined with identical brick buildings that had been converted to host a variety of different businesses. She opened the door of the third one on the left. Soft heat wrapped around them when they entered the front doors, touching their skin and seeping into their frozen limbs. He followed Allie up to the second floor, where two elaborate Doric columns framed the entrance. A sign written in elegant cursive welcomed all to the home of Classical Design.

Walking in, Barcus felt like he'd stepped into the workplace of an interior designer instead of a graphic designer. White chairs and desks sat in uniform lines across concrete floors, each accented by pink and yellow accessories. It was all very… feminine. A small collection of potted plants sat in the sunlight under a window, still thriving despite the harsh winter outside. Some of the company's designs hung on the walls, ranging from congressional campaigns posters to events hosted at the Smithsonian.

Five young women looked up from their computers at their arrival. One stood up and waved them down to her desk.

"Miesha," Allie greeted her warmly, taking the girl into a hug.

"Oh, thank god you're here." Miesha was a small woman with large fashionable glasses set in front of her almond-shaped eyes. Her hair was what Barcus assumed women wanted when they talked about volume. The brown curls were blown out and coiffed in a deliberate way. He was admiring them when something poked out of the dark curls.

He reared back in realization, gritting his jaw before an unheroic noise could escape. A snake! A snake was poking its head out right beside Miesha's ear, and if he didn't know any better, he'd say it was rubbing its head affectionately against her cheek. As he stared, another poked out from the other side, confirming his suspicion.

This woman was a gorgon!

And he had met her gaze.

Yet he wasn't stone, and neither was Allie. The two women were conversing in quiet tones, neither cautious in how they handled each other.

"Tell me everything," Allie urged, showing no fear as her eyes looked beseechingly at Miesha.

Miesha nodded slowly, her gaze turning from Allie to Barcus, who looked towards the floor. Damn training. "Um… you brought a friend?"

"Oh, him." He couldn't determine the tone of Allie's voice. If she wanted to get rid of him, this was the perfect way. You couldn't kill a member of the Order, not with a normal weapon. But a gorgon didn't need weapons. They could turn a man to stone for the rest of his life. Just one look and he'd be another decoration for their strange studio, with plants hanging off his arms. Barcus gritted his teeth, realizing how stupid he had been. He never should have trusted a monster.

"He's my boyfriend." The admission cut off the spiraling train of thought. It surprised him so much he looked up, catching the amusement across Allie's face and the interest on Miesha's.

"The one I talked to earlier?"

"Yep. He's a Mythos, but he hasn't interacted much with our kind," Allie explained easily. She gently grabbed his arm and gave it a soft pet. "It's okay, honey. Miesha has special glasses that prevent her from turning people to stone." There was a slightly patronizing tone to her voice when she talked to him, but the explanation eased his fear. Just a little bit.

Miesha was still staring at him, unsure. "I guess I'm a little surprised you came."

"Why is that?" Barcus asked, despite Allie giving him a look of warning.

"Well… it's just… Allie, are you sure you want him to be a part of this?"

They both straightened at the question. If Allie needed an opportunity to cast him aside, this was it, and the silence from her end wasn't very reassuring. Barcus prayed she remembered what he had promised her and that the bargain was enough to hold strong even now.

"Yeah," she said with a heavy sigh. "Yeah, I think he can help."

Questions danced across Miesha's face at that, but she nodded dutifully and urged them to follow her to the room at the end of the floor. The gorgon kept her voice low as the other women worked, clearly not wanting to cause any more commotion. "When I came in this morning, the doors were unlocked. Celia almost always gets here before me, but when I went to her office to say hi, I found something… disturbing."

She opened the office door and showed Allie and Barcus in. At first glance, nothing looked out of the ordinary. A large desk sat untouched at the far end of the room, with family pictures and a fancy art pad sitting in the middle. "I tried calling all morning and she didn't answer. Have you heard from her at all?"

"No," Allie answered softly, studying the room. "We were supposed to meet up for dinner the other night and she didn't show. I thought she was just working late and forgot."

"She was still here when I left on Friday." Miesha worried her bottom lip.

Barcus moved deeper into the room, alert as he searched for anything that seemed out of place. Finding clues was always easier when he had a baseline for what was considered normal. A coffee cup left unattended, a coat still sitting on the rack. These could all be indicators of trouble if he knew what to look for. Everyone left a footprint, even a digital one, but Celia had left none of those things. The room was bare, as if she really had left for the night.

Which meant he would have to rely on older methods. Searching for broken branches and markings had been how he'd hunted in the past. His eyes moved down to the hard concrete as he circled the room, then stopped. "Allie…"

She was by his side in an instant, taking in the sight. Two long scratches marred the concrete floor, scratches that didn't look like any claw marks he'd ever seen. No, the cuts were too shallow. They belonged to a short sword. And they were still clear, not worn away by time or footsteps.

Fresh. His mind clung to the word. Right next to the marks, hidden under the desk, were three speckles of red. Allie knelt to scratch at the substance, digging a little bit under her fingernail before bringing it to her lips. Her eyes closed against the taste. "It's blood…"

"Oh, Mother." Miesha exhaled, bringing a hand up to her mouth. "What do you think happened?"

There weren't enough clues to tell them what happened before or after, but it couldn't be a coincidence that a hero had been here the same night Allie had been attacked.

He looked up in time to meet Allie's intense gaze. She made the same connection.

"Mother's maw, it was *him!*" A promise of violence and hatred filled the accusation.

Miesha jumped at the slur. "Who?"

"The hero."

"You ran into a hero?" the gorgon squeaked, eyes growing wide. She looked like the mere mention of a hero was enough to send her scurrying for cover. Ironic, given that she was one of the creatures heroes feared the most.

"More than ran into one," Allie growled, her body tense like a creature about to pounce on its prey. Barcus held his breath, unsure of what she would do next. The presence of his spear burned against his back. If she attacked him out of anger, he would have to defend himself. But that would mean exposing who he was in front of a gorgon. It would mean death.

A growl of frustration seethed between her teeth. He and Miesha watched, bracing for whatever Allie would do. Talons, blood, feathers. All he could think about was the poor pillows she had slaughtered the other night. Here, she had the perfect fleshy target to attack. Him.

He prepared himself for an eruption, but instead he watched, dumbfounded, as the harpy turned on her heel and marched out of the building.

She was on the warpath. No doubt about it. *And there is nothing more dangerous than an angry harpy,* Barcus thought, chasing after her. Earlier, he had thought they had been making good progress in the strange partnership between them. Now he could see that progress literally marching out the door.

Behind them, Miesha called out, "Wait, Allie! Should I tell Ocypete?"

Allie visibly bristled when she turned around. "No, never ever do that." Her gaze met Barcus's when she said, "I'll handle everything."

LLIE COULDN'T HOLD it in any longer. As soon as she stepped foot outside, she let out a screech of anger that shook the earth. The sound still vibrated in her rib cage as she paced the sidewalk, her mind spinning with the newfound knowledge. Her sister was gone, kidnapped by the same hero she had let get away.

No, that wasn't right. *She* hadn't let him get away.

Her eyes fell on Barcus, leaning against the brick exterior and watching her with a cool gaze. "You let him get away!" Her anger cut through the air like a blade ready to strike. It was as if the goddess of vengeance had possessed her body.

His muscles tensed as he sensed her anger. "No, I didn't know—"

"Bullshit. Zeus should strike you now for that lie!" She glanced up hopefully, but the cloudy skies held no hope of lightning. She cursed again. "You'd think Zeus would do me *one* favor after the thousands I did for him."

"Allie, I had nothing to do with Celia's disappearance.

Why would I have let you out of the hotel if I was trying to capture you both?"

She hated how sensible he sounded. How heroes acted superior to everyone else. They never knew real fear and never had to worry about being hunted down like animals. Anger worked its way up her throat, threatening to come out in another inhuman screech. She bit it back, but heat bloomed behind her eyes. Damn him. Damn all of them.

"Your brothers have done something with my sister," she snarled at him, taking the man in with new eyes. Hard to believe that just that morning she had been admiring his chiseled looks. She'd even allowed herself to think he wasn't that bad. Fool! He'd locked her in a bedroom while his kind likely tortured Celia. Worse, she could be *dead*.

The ground tilted at the realization. These were heroes, men who killed unmortals without rhyme or reason.

She stalked towards him, pushing herself into his space. "What do they want with her?"

"I don't know." Fear dilated his pupils. He was too well trained to show it on his face, but the eyes always betrayed one's true feelings. *Good, he should be afraid.* There was barely an inch between their bodies, and her keen hearing could pick up the sudden uptick in his heartbeat and the way his breathing wavered the tiniest bit, just on the edge of panic. Interesting. "I'm telling you the truth," he pushed on. "I'm trying to figure that out as well. But I think we have a common enemy."

"Enemy?" She laughed. "Now you call them your enemy?"

He raised his chin. "If they are hurting your kind unprovoked, they are breaking the Covenant and they will pay. This I promise you."

The anger in his voice caught her off guard. Everything he had just said was wrong. Heroes were loyal to each other, no matter what. They always played the role of good guys while her siblings were cast as the monsters.

Barcus didn't look away from her. "You need my help if you want to find them and your sister."

She laughed. "You asked for my assistance just this morning. I don't need your help. You need mine."

"You're right. I need your help."

The ease with which he said those words irritated her to her core. Heroes didn't need unmortals—or at least they would never admit it out loud. But here he was, easily offering to help her and receive her help in return. She didn't know what to say back. All she knew was that she was standing too close, the sharp metallic smell of his golden coin making her nose itch.

Stepping away from him was harder than she thought. Her feet staggered one step and then two. Allie forced her mind to focus on other things besides the open look on Barcus's face. "I need to speak with Ocypete. She'll be worried about me... and Celia."

"I'm coming with you."

"No," she cut him off, but the word wasn't as hard as she meant it to be. "No, I could lie to Miesha about who you are, but I can't do that to Pete. She'll ask too many questions. If Celia and I don't show up today, she'll go out looking for us."

"And how do I know you won't just leave?"

"If you let me do this alone, I swear I'll come back to the hotel before tomorrow night. Then you can help me find my sister."

He didn't correct her. The man knew when to pick

his battles. "Fine. I'll see if I can track down that hero in the meantime."

"Good." Allie's talons tingled with the need to slice that boy's scrawny neck, but that would have to wait. They needed answers before blood. She patted down her hair and adjusted the scarf around her neck. It was time to go back home, and she didn't want to look like a complete mess in front of her sister. Every hair out of place felt like a dead giveaway to the truth of her whereabouts. Out of the three of them, Pete was the smartest. The fewer questions, the better.

A firm hand touched her elbow, begging her to turn around. She didn't, not even as Barcus's low voice creased the back of her neck. "I have something for you."

"What is it?"

A white piece of plastic flashed in front of her face. She snapped it out of the air and glared at it. "A room key?" Her eyes shot up, demanding an explanation. "Don't you think this is moving a little fast?"

He ignored her joke. "I asked for a separate room just in case you agreed to work together. I didn't want you to feel trapped in that room after … it's your choice, of course."

He'd done that for her? It was oddly considerate, not to mention a gamble. She clutched the card to her chest. "It's not a cage if there's a key, right?"

"That's not what I meant." His voice was barely audible.

"I know." There was no more fight in her. She checked the card, where the room number and Wi-Fi were printed in elegant cursive. "Same floor as your room."

"I figured it wouldn't hurt to be close…" He didn't finish that sentence before shaking his head and saying, "Be careful. If you don't come back, I'll look for you."

She nearly shivered at the words. Her mind didn't know how to translate them. Threat or kindness. If she didn't know any better, she'd almost think he was protecting her. She wasn't used to getting that from anyone but her sisters.

Her own surprise was the only reason she replied, "Don't worry, I'll see you at the hotel."

It was a promise, then. There was no getting out of seeing him again, but maybe that wasn't so bad.

✍

Their nest wasn't far from Celia's business.

For the harpy sisters, Georgetown had been the perfect place to settle down in the big city. The college side had the nightlife Allie enjoyed, resources for Ocypete's research, and good clientele for Celia—everything was within arm's reach. But today she didn't notice any of the charm. It was a brisk walk to her cobblestone street, fear driving every step.

Allie's stomach sat in a tangle of knots. She was worried about Celia, worried about Ocypete, and even more worried about her new partnership with Barcus. *Mother, please let this not be a mistake*, she prayed as she opened the front door. If it was, she couldn't risk involving Ocypete. Allie would gamble with her own life, but never her sisters'.

As soon as the door opened, she heard her name being called. "Allie? Celia? Which one of you is it?"

"It's me," she called back. Relief sang through her at the sight of her sister stepping out of the kitchen, still dressed in her pajamas. Her frizzy, dark hair was pulled into a large bun on top of her head. No doubt this was the first time all morning Ocypete had stepped away from the kitchen table and her open manuscript. She looked the part of a studious author, complete with an open energy drink in hand. "Where have you been?" her sister huffed. "I have been texting you and Celia all morning! You totally flaked on bringing my chips home. I was about to go looking for you."

Allie gave her sister's clothes an appraising look. "You were?"

"Well, maybe in another hour or two." Ocypete took a sip of her drink, giving Allie's clothes a lingering look. "Isn't that the outfit you wore the other night?"

"It is," Allie said, shedding her winter accessories onto the nearby coatrack. "I was out having fun. You should try it sometime."

"Ugh—no, thank you." Out of the sisters, Ocypete detested mingling with mortals the most. A waste of time, she called it; they'd all be replaced with new ones in a day. Which was why her job as a reclusive history writer fit her personality so well. "So where's Celia?"

"Oh, she messaged me the other night and said she would be out of town for a while," Allie answered, heart in her throat. It felt awful to lie, but what other choice was there?

Ocypete clicked her tongue in disapproval. "Would have been nice of her to tell me."

And that was that. No follow-up questions. No suspicion. Trust made even the worst kind of lies easy to swallow.

"Well, it isn't like you had dinner waiting for us," Allie pointed out.

"No, but I did want to watch *Buffy* last night and I felt bad without you guys there." Ocypete gave a wistful sigh. "Celia's work really is taking a lot of her time. I can't remember the last time we had a Slayer Sister Night."

Allie swallowed hard. Of course, Celia had an excuse

to be out and busy. Ocypete had a job as well, and Allie…
she had nothing. Her life was filled with sleeping till noon,
spending the days in front of the television and the nights
out in the same old bars. It was tiring having nothing to
do but see the same sights around the city. But a job wasn't
her style either. Working from morning to evening, serving
mortals. There was nothing about it that sounded fun.

Centuries ago, she and her sisters would travel to every
corner of the world, adopting new personas, new lives.
Things had changed so much within a few decades that it
felt like an ever-changing kaleidoscope.

From Greece to Northern Africa, to Constantinople,
and finally to Europe. She'd been mistaken for a goddess
and a princess, and for a brief time in France, they'd played
the roles of angels. It had been exciting. She had been exciting. A creature with no limits who did what she wanted
when she wanted it. At first it had been so exciting to be free
of Zeus's leash, but when the heroes had started hunting
down every unmortal who dared to show their true colors,
they'd been forced to hide.

Gods, that had been so many years ago. And in that
time, she and her sisters had become… domesticated.
Working daytime jobs, doing menial errands. Ocypete
and Celia seemed so content with it all, but a squirming
need to do something else continued to grow in Allie's gut.
Unwavering, unstoppable, demanding she throw caution to
the wind and do something more with her life.

That had been why she'd wanted to talk to Celia
that night.

The idea of leaving the nest was a daunting one, but she
knew Celia would support her. It hadn't been long ago that

their youngest sister had confided in her about a dream to start a graphic design business.

"*You don't think it's a step down?*" Celia had asked, her toes wiggling against Allie's thigh.

We used to feast with the gods—of course it's a step down, she'd wanted to say. But Celia was the youngest of their trio; she hadn't gotten to enjoy all the pleasures of working for the gods. By the time she was fully grown, the Romans had been moving eastward and the old ways were beginning to disappear. Ocypete would prefer if they interacted as little as possible with humans, but Allie had seen the way Celia's eyes lit up when a mortal paid her a compliment. Or the way she fawned over their new technology and styles. Working with humans was their reality now, and Celia was embracing it.

How could she fault her sister for that?

"*You'll be amazing at whatever you want to do. All those years of experience will put you head and shoulders above the mortals.*"

Celia nudged her with her elbow. "You're my sister. You're supposed to say that."

"True." Allie grinned. "And I would definitely lie to you to protect your feelings."

Her sister laughed. "But you forget, I can always tell when you're lying."

She could, but that also meant Celia knew she meant every word. They had cuddled closer on the couch as the commercial break ended and the night's episode of Love Mansion *came back on. Allie was ready to crack another joke about a terrible chest tattoo on one of the male love interests when Celia spoke softly beside her. "I'm going to do it. Even if I have to sell my silks and jewels. I'm going to start my business."*

"And I'll support you."

"Even when I tell Pete?"

"Especially when you tell Pete."

Their older sister wasn't as open to change as Allie. It had taken the promise of two full weeks of sister movie night and the purchase of some expensive reference books to convince her to let Celia move forward with the plan. Allie's job during those two weeks had been to uphold the peace in the household.

But that had just been Celia starting a job in the city. If Allie approached her family with the idea of leaving, without any kind of backup, it would be inviting another Great War in their house.

And if Celia was gone, she would never find the strength to leave the nest.

She closed her eyes against the thought and shook them away. No, Celia was safe. She just needed to be found. "We'll have a sister night when Cee comes back. Deal?"

"Sure." Ocypete shrugged. "Did she mention when?"

"No clue." But hopefully soon. Allie wouldn't last long with all this worry seeping into her bones.

Ocypete grinned. "Then I'll just start the new season of *Project Runway* without her. I need something mindless to give my thoughts a rest." She turned and started back to the kitchen, where a pile of books sat open in disarray and the dull glow of a laptop reflected on the walls.

"Ah, the life of a writer sure is hard," Allie called after her.

"Don't be fussy. You can watch it with me if you want."

"Can't. I have work to do." Allie started up the stairs before she realized her mistake. But Ocypete's yelp from the kitchen brought her to a full stop.

"You're doing work?" Her sister's head poked out of the doorway again, her eyes wide. "What is this? Did Celia rope you into her business?"

In a way. Allie waved off her sister's surprise. "It's nothing for you to worry about. Just trying something new. I'll let you know how it turns out."

Ocypete's gaze narrowed into a scrutinizing look all big sisters had perfected. "Alright, but on the next sister night you are telling me everything."

"Sure, sure!" She couldn't take the stairs fast enough, jumping two at a time up to the second floor.

There was no way she was going to tell Ocypete about the last few days. That conversation would not go well. *"Hey, Pete, remember when I said I had work? Really, Celia was missing and I lied about it so I could help a hero find her. Funny, right?"* If there was anything Ocypete hated more than mortals, it was immortal heroes.

Down the hall, she could see into her own room: door ajar with large portions of the floor obscured by piles of clothes. Celia's door was closed, as always. Being the youngest sister, she coveted her privacy and hoarded the space like a sphinx guarding a treasure. Behind that closed door might be something that would tell Allie where she was. Allie marched across the hall and opened Celia's room without knocking.

It was pristinely clean, almost a miniature doppelgänger of her office space: a neat white desk sat in the corner with her work computer and framed pieces of art hung in creative patterns across the walls. Seeing the perfection of the room snagged the last bit of hope she'd clung to. The last time she'd seen Celia, they had all been clustered in the kitchen late on Thursday evening, seeing each other for the first time all day. Her sister had been dressed for work, blonde hair pulled into a perfect bun, as she'd poured a healthy amount of wine.

Allie had hoped there would be clues, but she couldn't bring herself to disturb the scene. How could she? When Celia did come home, she would want everything to be in order, precisely where she'd left it.

She allowed herself to linger among the room's pastel colors, inhaling the flowery perfume that clung to the floorboards after years of use. An ache throbbed against her heart as the weight of the situation settled over her. There were no clues here. Nothing she could use to find Celia on her own.

If she was going to find her sister, she needed Barcus. But everything in her screamed that he was trouble with a capital T. The key he had given her burned in her back pocket. He'd threatened to look for her if she didn't come back.

No, not threatened. The words had been too kind to be a threat. She'd seen genuine concern on his face when he'd wished her well. He'd actually been worried about her. And that made her heart do an embarrassing little flutter.

Heroes did not worry about unmortals. Especially heroes known as the Great Hunter.

Barcus alone had killed hundreds of them in the Great War. Allie swallowed as she recalled the stories about him: a hero in golden armor carrying a black-tipped spear, with soulless eyes and Artemis whispering in his ear. One of the only men alive who had earned Artemis's approval when it came to the hunt.

None of that matched the man who'd held her captive for the last few days.

The Barcus of legend would have killed her without a

second thought. He wouldn't have listened to her plea to find Celia. And he certainly wouldn't have set her free. There was no golden armor, no magical spear, no soulless eyes. If anything, he had too much going on behind those piercing blue eyes. Guilt and pity. Compassion and cunning. Desperation and loneliness. "Fuck." Her fingers scrubbed at her eyes. She couldn't think like that. She turned and stormed to her own haven. A messy whirlwind of color and junk food littered the space, but it was home. She needed to think.

Stripping out of the soft sweater and pants she'd been wearing for three days, Allie threw on a pair of jeans and a long sweater dress that hung down to her thighs. She sighed, pulling her hair into a high ponytail and completing the transformation from night owl to homebody. Ocypete wasn't the only one who could rock comfortable clothes. When winter brewed its snowiest days across the Potomac, she preferred to stay inside with her sisters, fuzzy socks on their cold talons and a hot cup of coffee in hand.

If she was going to do this, trust a hero and spend gods knew how long searching for her sister, she needed to be ready.

It took a moment for her to dig out an old gym bag from under her bed. The tag was still on it and it was full of dirty laundry. Allie dumped the contents and began packing. Fresh clothes she could easily slip out of if she needed her wings, warm scarves for the cold nights, Celia's perfume in case Barcus could work his magic and track her. Drawers opened and banged shut as she searched her room for anything else that would be useful. Her eyes lingered in consideration on her underwear drawer. A girl always needed a fresh pair on the go, but her fingers only seemed to be drawn to pieces that were all lace and very tiny.

There had been no one to wear such pieces for before; they were only to boost her own self-confidence. Now she couldn't help but look at the underwear and wonder what kind of expression Barcus would make if he saw it. The memory of his wide-eyed surprise that first night came to mind. It had been so much fun torturing the hero. Could she make him falter even more? Or maybe…

Maybe she could get that flash of lust to stay on his face.

Ugh. What was she doing? *You should be ashamed*, she told herself, but threw the garments into the gym bag, nonetheless.

The loud ping of her phone broke her out of her internal struggle. She reached into the back pocket of her pants and checked the text message.

All the air squeezed from her lungs. It wasn't a message; it was a picture of the hotel where Barcus was staying. She recognized the glamorous exterior, the iconic white columns in the entrance that made it look like you were walking among the national monuments. In the picture, she could barely make out a man's figure entering the building. It was Barcus, judging by the familiar bag slung across his shoulders.

It was unclear if the image was a threat or something else entirely. All Allie knew was that it had been sent from Celia's phone.

VII

BARCUS HADN'T EVEN taken off his coat when there was a knock on the door.

His body froze at the sound. For a full breath, his feet refused as his mind worked to assess his surroundings. *It could be Allie*, he reminded himself, and if that was case, he should go and answer as soon as possible. He didn't want her to be discouraged and walk away.

Unless… she had returned with her unmortal friends, ready for revenge. It was impossible not to consider a scenario where he opened the door and faced a battle.

What if it was Xanthus?

That thought was enough to turn his insides to ice. He wasn't ready to face Xanthus. Not now. Not like this.

Another series of quick annoyed taps fell against the wood. He gave the room an appraising look, taking in the mess from Allie's stay. The bedroom looked as if the harpy had thrown her own private party, and the living room was just as bad. His notes and belongings lay scattered on every available surface. If he was attacked, his research would be ripe for the taking.

Stupid, stupid. He wasn't prepared, and something like fear dug its claws into the tender muscles of his throat. Threatening to suffocate him.

You are pathetic. Heroes don't shy away from battle. The words from his darkest nightmares crawled into his ears, filling him with shame.

Move forward. You have to move forward, another voice countered. A feminine one that would always calm the inner demons.

The mantra was from Artemis herself when she had dragged him out of the depths of isolation.

Still, it took every ounce of his strength to move a single foot forward. And then another. He moved to the door and cautiously checked the peephole. It wasn't Xanthus and it wasn't Allie. He was looking down at the top of a stranger's head, or the top of someone's hat. All he could make out were bright flashes of red and gold.

A stranger. He felt his muscles recoil at the realization. Instinct took over as he quickly grabbed his spear from its case. His fingers twisted the two parts together as more knocks fell on the door. "I'm coming," he growled. When the spear was at its full length, the weight of it heavy in his hand, he felt ready to open the door.

Barcus did so cautiously, opening it just a crack to take in the visitor. "Can I help you?"

"We need to be quick; she'll be here any minute." A small body pushed the door open, stepping into his space without invitation.

They didn't get far. Barcus's hands struck forward, a trap just sprung. The black tip of his spear came down fast, stopping just a hair away from the man's neck. No, not a man. Now that the door was fully open, he could see the stranger was younger than he'd first thought, dressed in a ratty Capitals hoodie and jeans. When the guy looked up, his hood fell back, revealing pale-blond locks that fell just past his ears and the scattered stubble of a beard that refused to grow. His eyes gave a wide, impressed look at the spear.

He shouldn't look impressed. He should be terrified. Barcus's hands shook at what he had almost done.

"Wow, nice to meet you, too," the guy said, eyeing the weapon when Barcus didn't lower it, "but I'm not the enemy here." Slowly, his hand inched to his collar and tugged the hoodie down so Barcus could glimpse the golden chain around his neck. Attached to it was a glimmering gold coin.

A hero. All at once Barcus fully recognized the young man in front of him, recalling the vibrant red hoodie in a dark alley and the crack of bone when Barcus's fist had slammed into his nose. There was no sign of the fight on the guy's face, though, thanks to the divine blessing that had been given to all heroes. But he was much too young and too clumsy to be a hero.

"That has yet to be decided." Barcus's voice was low and dangerous, and only then did hesitation cross the boy's eyes. Glancing down the hall to make sure no one was witness to their scuffle, Barcus grabbed the kid by the hoodie and dragged him into the suite.

He stumbled, arms flailing about and head swiveling to take in his surroundings. The guy might have the coin of the Order, but he didn't move like any hero Barcus had ever met. He was too slow. It was all too easy to pin him against the wall, one large arm pressed against a thin neck before another word could come out.

Barcus stared at the face before him and didn't recognize it. Just to be sure, his gaze slid down to the guy's neck, to the golden coin that rested there. Zeus's face stared back at him, identical to the icon on his own coin. It was shinier than any of the coins he'd seen in recent years. Newer. Hard to believe his own coin had looked like that once. "Who are you?"

The guy croaked, his face changing from pale white to cherry red. Barcus quickly loosened his hold. It was easy to forget his own strength sometimes, especially when his adrenaline buzzed so loudly everything else fell into the background.

Gasping for air, the guy reached his hand up to rub tentatively at his neck. The familiarity in his gaze was gone now, replaced with caution. "I'm Leo. Leo Di'Legulia."

"Alright, Leo, nice to meet you. Now why don't you tell me why you attacked the pretty lady the other night?"

Really? That was the first question he was going to ask? There were so many that boiled against the surface of his mind, but all he could think about was this rookie had attacked Allie. The expression on Leo's face questioned the logic as well. "Isn't it obvious? She's a monster!"

"Unmortal," Barcus corrected. "And we have made a covenant with them. One that strictly says we do not engage unless they kill mortals."

Leo's brows creased. "Oath? What oath?"

"You don't know?" That wasn't a good sign. Barcus searched the kid's face. He was young, no doubt... but how young? "When did the gods bless you?"

"Fifty years ago."

Barcus blinked in surprise. He had thought the youngest had joined their Order just over two centuries ago. This guy was practically a newborn babe. How was it that Barcus didn't know about him? He talked to the Eastern Order and the Central Order annually, and they kept extensive records of their history and members to prevent something like this from happening. More frightening was how untrained the kid was. He didn't even know their most basic laws. "Who took you as an apprentice?"

"Regan took me in," Leo answered, voice unsure. "He asked me to watch the harpy, see if she would lead us to more of her kind."

"You attacked her," Barcus corrected.

"Only because she wouldn't listen to me." Leo's face pinched. "I thought maybe if I could take her down, the other heroes would show me a little more respect. What does it matter anyway? Heroes have always hunted monsters."

"We used to." Barcus twisted apart his spear with ease, but kept the pointed tip trained on the younger hero.

Regan. He didn't know anyone by that name either. His stomach rolled at the implication. As the years carried on, the apprenticeship between old heroes and new became more necessary. The gods blessed men who weren't familiar with the old ways. Men from all over the world who served bravely in the new wars or did deeds deemed worthy of Olympus.

Looking at Leo, Barcus thought the boy didn't look like he had a single ounce of warrior's blood in him. He was handsome, but surely not handsome enough to catch Aphrodite's eye. Barcus had seen men so beautiful even he would fall to his knees if they had asked. Leo wasn't one of them. Too scrawny, too young. There was something about his eyes; they still had a bright innocence that hadn't been carved away by a millennium of pain and war.

"What else did this Regan teach you?"

"How to fight," Leo answered and then added, "with a weapon." As if there was any other way to fight. He reached into the pocket of his hoodie and pulled out a beautiful dagger, one that looked as if it was ten times older than the boy holding it. Barcus recognized the *kopis* immediately, the short blade curved forward like a wave, perfect for cutting clean through flesh and bone. The handle was decorated to look like the roaring maw of a lion. A slender hand could easily slide between its teeth to grip it.

Giving such a gorgeous weapon to someone so inexperienced was blasphemous. Daggers were already difficult for the unskilled warrior. They required one to be close to the enemy, to have excellent reflexes, and to know the exact point to cut. Giving a new hero such a weapon and then sending them off to engage a harpy was irresponsible at best. For one as unskilled as Leo, it was practically a death sentence.

"Let me see that. You're holding it all wrong." Barcus reached for it, but Leo snatched the dagger back, holding it close to his heart.

"Don't!" The newbie bared his teeth. "He gave this to me."

"Who? Regan?" Barcus scoffed.

"No," Leo answered. "Lord Xanthus."

Allie rushed to the hotel as quickly as she could.

Not because she was worried about Barcus. No, she doubted anyone could wipe that smug look off a hero's face. Her heart was only pounding from the exertion of flying across the Potomac without being seen and then hoofing it the rest of the way. Gods, she hated running; it took too damn long and made her sweat. Eventually she spilled into the hotel lobby, where she lingered long enough to search the crowd for Celia.

The text message had been both a relief and a burning question, one propelling her forward with newfound hope. Barcus was wrong. Celia wasn't in trouble. Her sister was safe. She was free.

But then, why had she not come home? Why would she send a cryptic message with a picture of Barcus's hotel?

Mother, why couldn't she have typed a quick text instead? A simple *trust him* or *don't trust him* would have been great. But Celia hadn't texted her anything else, not even when Allie had unleashed a flood of concerned messages back.

There was no sign of her sister in the lobby, which meant she was already gone or…

Allie's chest tightened as she made a beeline for the elevator. The sound of her heartbeat thundered between her ears as she contemplated what awaited her in Barcus's suite. Chances were good someone was going to be dead. She just hoped it wasn't Celia… or Barcus. She wasn't done torturing him quite yet.

At the ding, she was out and racing down the hall. There was a noticeable lack of the screams one would expect if a hero and harpy fought. But Barcus could have used the same tricks against her sister as he had on her. Allie's fist practically dented the door when she banged on it. "It's me! Open up!"

Barcus answered quickly. A cloud of exhaustion marred his perfect features, but it cleared up at the sight of her. "You came back."

He was unharmed. Joy and confusion strangled her at the realization. Then the anger came back. "Where is she?"

"Who?"

"Celia…" Allie pushed into the room, stopping short when the smell of olive bark and fresh plumeria filled her lungs. The same smell she remembered when she had woken as a captive in the room. Her gaze fell on her old cage, where a fresh line of powder lay across the doorframe. But Celia wasn't on the other side.

A young man sat in the bedroom, spine ramrod straight and muscles tense, like a creature caught in the sight of a predator. She instantly recognized the halo of curls and the sheepish smile. "You're the creep who tried to attack me."

His chin tilted in the smug defiance that heroes wore like a shield. "I can still take you, harpy."

Barcus had found her attacker. He'd imprisoned his fellow hero.

She forced herself not to look too deep into that turn of events. Keeping her face impassive, she turned to Barcus. "What is he doing here?"

"He came to warn me that you would be coming." Barcus was leaning against the counter of the room's kitchenette. "And apparently he was right."

"How did he know I was—" The question trailed off at the sight of a familiar pink iPhone case sitting next to Barcus's hand. Her breath caught in her throat. "That's Celia's phone."

"I know," Barcus said quietly. "I found it on him."

The phone confirmed the worst of her fears. All the hope that had filled Allie drained at the realization. Her sister was gone, in the hands of the heroes. She cursed, whirling on her attacker. "And you kept him here as a present for me? Good. I'd really like to repay him for the other night."

The hero tensed at the underlying threat, eyes round as they looked towards Barcus for protection. With a sigh, the older hero straightened. "It's alright, Leo. She doesn't really mean it."

"Yes, I do. He knows where my sister is and he's going to tell me everything, or I'm going to cut off every finger and toe."

"Down, girl. I'm not going to let you torture him."

The words felt like a betrayal. After the promise he'd made just that morning, he was choosing his brother over her. "You don't get to decide that," she growled. "He attacked me, remember? He had my sister's phone. He's clearly broken the Covenant, and he deserves to pay."

He held her gaze, and once again she saw the swirl of too many emotions hidden behind his eyes. "You're right," Barcus finally conceded, keeping his voice low, "and he will pay, but right now Leo's our best chance of finding your sister. He has vital information we need if we want to track these guys."

"Or he could lie to us!" Allie sneered.

"Like I would reveal anything to a shrieking harpy," Leo shot back.

Allie turned back to Barcus, eyebrows raised in silent reproach. *See?*

Barcus stared them both down with the patience of a saint, or a man who was used to preventing stabbing incidents on a yearly basis. "Fine. If you really think that will get us answers, I'll let you do what you want."

The admission caught her off guard. A retort had been primed and ready to cut him down, but here he was, surprising her again. "You don't mean that."

"I do. The Covenant dictated heroes would be the ones who delivered the punishment, but that hardly seems fair, does it?" A hurricane of pity and compassion clouded his gaze; the same emotions he'd shown her were now being given to this oath breaker. "I will let you be the one to carry out the punishment, but first let me be the one to question him."

"Why?" Her heart was still pounding, but it was impossible to tell if it was from anger or surprise. She had never expected Barcus to give in to her demands.

She watched the hope flicker in his eyes. "If one of us has to be seen as a monster for this, I'd rather it be me."

It doesn't matter, she wanted to cry. *He already thinks I'm a monster.* Except it did matter. It mattered that Barcus wanted to protect her against that image. That he was willing to bear the brunt of hate from his own ally than have her do it.

Allie stared at the man in front of her, trying to find the Great Hunter from the legends. But all that stood before her was Barcus.

And she wasn't sure exactly who that man was anymore. But, gods, she wanted to know.

"Alright, if this doesn't work, we try things my way."

"Sounds good to me, partner." Barcus rolled his shoulders and took a deep breath. Before her eyes, he transformed. The soft-spoken man who'd greeted her with a smile disappeared and a shadow crept over his features.

Leo straightened, sensing the sudden shift in the air as well. He was doing his best to hide his fear, but the whites of his eyes had the same round terror of a captured animal. "Traitor! You're helping the enemy."

"Let's be clear. *She* is not the enemy. Your boss is. After what you've done, she has every right to hurt you. And I would let her, as was agreed upon in our Covenant. The only reason you are unharmed right now is because she's allowing it, but that can change. Understand?"

Leo glared at him. "They warned me about you. I should have listened."

"They?" Barcus prodded.

"Lord Xanthus and the others. They said you used to be one of them, but you grew too soft." His eyes fell to Allie, and there was such hate in them it nearly turned his gaze black. "Clearly they were telling the truth. Heroes are supposed to hunt monsters. Not befriend them."

"Xanthus broke our laws in his pursuit of unmortals, and because of that, I've vowed to kill him. If you stand with him now, you will fall to the same fate."

Leo stood eye level with Barcus, but there was no comparison between the two. They were both heroes, but Barcus was in another category altogether. He towered over the rookie, pushing out a confidence that Leo couldn't seem to match. "You can't do anything to me. I'm immortal."

A harsh, unrecognizable laugh tore from Barcus's lips. "Immortality means endless suffering. If I will it, when this city no longer stands, you will remain in this room. A virtual spirit that time will forget. No water, no food, no light. Such simple things, but a century without them will break a man worse than any medieval interrogation method."

The quiet way that he growled those words was its own form of mastery.

This was Barcus. The Great Hunter.

And she was afraid of him.

"It's naive to believe heroes can't be killed just because we're immortal." He grabbed one of the papers from the couch and held it up. Allie gasped at the gruesome sight laid out in it. Blood and broken furniture, and a man's crumbled body lying on the ground. "Did you know a hero by the name of Eosphorus?"

"No…" Leo blinked at the picture, just as surprised by the carnage in its frame. "Is that him?"

Barcus nodded. "And he's dead now."

"Because of her kind," Leo snarled.

"No." The word crashed into the room like a cruel bark. "No," Barcus repeated. "I thought so, too. But now I'm beginning to think someone else might have had a hand in it."

Leo's eyes widened. "What? *Me*?"

"You are the one attacking unmortals without provocation. Are you trying to prove something to Xanthus? Is that what you're doing?"

"No!" The young hero staggered back, tripping over his own feet in the process and falling to the floor. If they had been in a real fight, he would have been dead. And he knew that. In this exchange, Barcus held all the cards and all the power.

"Prove it to me and I'll let you live," Barcus said. "Tell me what you know about the other harpy."

The young hero stuttered, his confidence shattering in the presence of a real threat. Fear could be a powerful motivator—there was no need to raise a weapon when one could break the enemy with a few carefully placed threats. No longer was Allie the only monster in the room.

"She's safe. She's safe. They need her alive for now."

Allie sagged at the news, but Barcus wasn't done yet. "For now?"

Leo shook his head. "I—I only know that they need her alive for the ritual tomorrow."

"Ritual?" Allie whispered, dread seeping back into her lungs, giving no time for the relief to settle. A catalog of old ancient festivals and celebrations flashed in her mind, but nothing in mid-February came to mind. "What ritual?"

A glare was sent her way, as if she'd asked the world's stupidest question. "Tuesday is the commemoration of Lord Xanthus's immortality. He promised to achieve greatness once again. To make the world how it once was, with us on top."

"That's a thing you heroes do?" Allie asked, looking towards Barcus.

He didn't get a chance to answer. Leo had regained his confidence, reveling in something that the others didn't know. "The old Order didn't, but the new one does."

"Old Order?" Barcus scowled at the boy, the muscles along his neck taut from holding back a thousand different curses. "How many are in this new Order of yours?"

"Enough."

"How many?!" The burst of emotion caused even Allie to jump. She'd never heard Barcus shout, not even in their most heated arguments. He lunged forward, and for a moment she thought he would barrel into the room and strike the boy.

Leo clearly thought the same. A shout tore from his lips before he raised his arms in defense. A coward's position. "I don't know. I swear!"

Barcus clutched the doorframe, panting hard as he took in the young hero. There was a wild look in his eyes, one Allie hadn't seen before. He reached up and pawed at his face, easing away the tension and fear that had hardened his handsome features until all that was left was lingering regret.

"Fuck." He growled the curse at no one in particular, and before Allie could ask, he turned on his heel and marched into the balcony's frigid air.

VIII

LEO'S PROTESTS CUT off behind her when Allie slammed the door closed. Good riddance. She didn't know how much longer she could stand to hear the hate spewing from his lips.

The balcony was cozy in size, big enough for two chairs to overlook the frozen Potomac. She found Barcus leaning against the glass railing and staring down at the snow-covered ground below, gaze unfocused.

Not even the sound of the door banging shut woke him from his thoughts. It was strange seeing him so quiet after what she'd witnessed inside. She was almost afraid to disturb him, unsure if she would be the next focus of his dark threats. But Barcus had had his chance to threaten her, to attack her, back when they'd first met, and he never once had. He'd been patient and kind, even when she had been the one to push.

She inhaled the cool air greedily and said, "That went well."

He didn't have a jacket on, but that didn't seem to

matter. Barcus rocked on his heels, detaching from the railing inch by painful inch. "I took things too far, didn't I?"

"No." She didn't care about sparing his feelings, only the truth of what he had done. "You got us answers." Celia was alive—there was some comfort in that—but now they knew for how long. A day. That wasn't much time. Plans to go back inside and conduct her own interrogation already began to form. They needed more answers, but something about the line of questioning had shaken Barcus to his core. "Would you really leave him in there for all eternity?"

Barcus huffed. "No. I could, but no one deserves that fate."

"Maybe he does," Allie offered. "He's a bit of a douche."

"He's young, untrained, and brainwashed. He doesn't know what he's saying." And by the far-off look on Barcus's face, the hero was blaming himself for all that.

Allie settled closer beside him, offering her body heat against the frigid air. "Tell you what. I've decided I won't torture him for now, but I'm going to need you to fill me in here if we're going to work together. What was that kid talking about?"

One of his big hands stroked his bearded jaw, pulling the skin tight and trying to wipe the exhaustion away. His other hand extended to her, the picture from before out as an offering. "This is why I'm here. Why I kept you in this place. Eosphorus—Erik, was murdered not long ago. And I thought unmortals were involved." He took a deep breath of the frigid air then and shook his head. "But I was wrong. It was heroes all along."

The admission sounded like it had been pried from his very soul. Allie might have once basked in hearing those words from Barcus, but somehow none of that seemed to matter anymore. "I knew Xanthus had a few who were loyal to him, but I never thought he would try to take it this far."

"What are you saying?" Allie asked. "Don't you know this Xanthus guy?"

"I have known Xanthus my entire life." He gave her a meaningful look that encompassed centuries. "We were brothers. Both in the Order and in mind. But then everything went wrong. He isn't the same man I once fought beside."

She licked her lips. There were so many times in so many centuries where things had gone wrong. For heroes, for the gods, for her and her sisters. She almost didn't want to know what he meant by the phrase, but a part of her yearned to understand. "What happened?"

"Xanthus and I knew each other when we were still mortals, dreaming of glory. We came from different backgrounds. I came from the island of Iolcus. Xanthus was born in Lacedaemon."

"A Spartan," Allie breathed.

Barcus nodded. "Our paths brought us together when we were searching to become heroes. Xanthus was blessed by Ares, the god all Spartans honored, and he was known throughout Sparta as a demigod on the battlefield until he decided to give it up."

"Why would he do that? Don't heroes live to honor the gods?" *And don't Spartans live to fight?*

A bitter smile grew across Barcus's face. "You never realize when you accept immortality what that truly means. There is greatness, but there is also sacrifice. As heroes, falling in love or starting a family means we risk watching our loved ones die before our eyes. But Xanthus still wanted that. He couldn't see why heroes couldn't have it all. He married and started a family. He was happy until the war of the Peloponnese broke out. All of Greece participated."

"I remember," Allie said. "Greeks fighting Greeks."

"Heroes fighting heroes," Barcus added quietly, voice rasping over the words. "Artemis asked that I fight for Athens and our friend Argos did the same under the request of Hestia, but Xanthus was Spartan born and raised. He was their best general, and all Spartans knew that when war came, they must pick up their shields. But Xanthus didn't answer the call to arms. He'd grown soft in his love for his family. Ares himself demanded he fight, but Xanthus refused."

Allie went still. She knew exactly what happened to men who refused a god.

The man who had kidnapped her sister did not deserve her sympathy, but Barcus looked shaken by the memory. She touched his arm gently, willing that look away. "You don't have to continue."

"No, it's important that you know exactly who we are up against. Xanthus… Ares slaughtered his entire family in retaliation and gave him no choice but to fight. The moment he took up his sword, the war fell out of our favor. It was a blessing I never had to face him on the battlefield. But the loss changed him. His purpose for being a hero died with his wife. His trust in Olympus was gone. All he had was Argos and me.

"Then Argos went missing and Xanthus and I both went mad with grief. For a hundred years, we searched everywhere for him. We even went to an Oracle to try to find him. We believed Argos had been taken by unmortals in retaliation for the previous wars."

"Did you ever find him?"

"He was taken, but not by your kind," Barcus said. "Turns out he was imprisoned by Circe."

Gods—Allie felt the cold air suddenly take hold of her, eliciting a shiver. She'd heard of the sea witch and how she'd gone mad after Odysseus left. Years of isolation could break any mind, even that of an immortal like Circe.

"We didn't know, and the years we spent searching were like returning to the Dark Ages." He looked down at his feet. "We fought every chance we could, looking for answers, killing everything we thought had a role in his disappearance. Eventually, I couldn't do it anymore."

"Why?" She wasn't surprised by the idea of Barcus killing aimlessly, but the admission that he had stopped was new. She'd never heard of a hero who'd just stopped fighting before.

"I just couldn't do it, the fighting… the blood. I knew what we were doing wasn't right, but he refused to quit even when I pleaded with him and we fought." A dry, bitter laugh cut from between his lips. "He walked away that day, from me and from the Order."

"And now there's a rogue hero out there who has my sister! What does he want with her?" She kicked the railing in frustration, easily bending the steel with her strength, but it did nothing to quell the emotions bubbling inside.

"I'm not sure."

"Mother's maw," she whispered, taking everything in.

Celia was still alive; above everything else, that was what was important. But Leo had attacked her as well, which meant—

"Gods, I have to go warn the others."

"Others?"

"There are more of us in this city, remember? If they

attacked me and Celia, then other unmortals aren't safe." Without another word, she turned and stalked back into the warm hotel room.

"Shit," Barcus cursed, following in close step. "I'll go with you."

"That would be a very bad idea." For so many reasons. How would she explain that heroes were possibly hunting them down while she was accepting help from one? It wouldn't go over well.

Leo was leaning against the edge of the door, trying and failing to look casual as he watched them. At their reentrance, he stared at Barcus in awe. "She didn't kill you…"

"Of course not," Allie huffed, moving to the hotel door. "What do you think I am, a *monster?*"

"Allie," Barcus called after her, his voice booming across the room with authority that made her skin prickle. There was the hero she knew. The one who had looked at her with eyes lit with fire.

Her feet came to a stop and she turned to find him slinging his spear bag over his shoulder. "I said I'm coming with you. If there are heroes out there hunting your kind, I can help."

"And what about him?" She nodded to their captive, who kept opening his mouth as if to protest and then closing it, a perpetually confused look set on his face.

Barcus gave the kid a pitying look. "I'll call someone to pick him up."

"What?" Leo demanded. "You're going to *leave* me here?"

"Yes." Barcus's eyes narrowed on him. "Think about what we talked about. By the time we come back, maybe you'll be willing to give us some answers."

"Traitor," Leo hissed, but Barcus's back was already turned.

Allie couldn't believe it. With those words, he really had picked her over his brothers. She didn't know how to feel about that. Except that when he turned his attention back to her, ready to leave, she couldn't find an excuse to argue against him.

IX

THEY WERE GETTING close now. Steam wafted from nearby Chinese restaurants; a few mortal children hugged the walls as they talked and smoked. No one glanced their way, not on this street. The buildings were more run-down, the houses less pristine. Any tourists that ventured into the area stood out like a sore thumb, which meant, of course, that Barcus stood out.

She stopped suddenly and turned to the man trailing behind her, taking in his lacrosse bag and expensive coat. "Alright, first we need to lay down a few ground rules."

His brows arched up. "About what?"

"I'm about to take you into our local den. You're going to see some things no hero has ever laid eyes on before. You have to promise not to go all… hero on me. Got it?"

He frowned at that. "Are you doing something I wouldn't approve of?"

"What? No." She glared at him. "Nothing illegal and nothing that breaks our side of the oath." *Unlike your brothers*, she itched to say, but she managed to refrain. She gave herself a mental back pat at the self-control. "I just need to make sure you won't attack anyone."

He nodded. "I promise."

"And when we go in there, you need to take off your coin."

"What?" His hand instinctively reached for the object. Her eyes followed the movement, primal instinct homing in on the shiny item. The sight of the aged gold metal brought back fond memories. A coin that old was impossible to find these days.

She'd heard that the coin was special to heroes, but that was all she knew about them. It must carry some magic, a blessing from the gods.

"You can't wear that where we're going," she told him sternly. "Everyone will know immediately what you are, and we won't get any information. Take it off and play like you're a Mythos."

His frown was still in place, his fingers rubbing the golden ridges of the coin in contemplation. There was no way he would agree, and when he didn't, she would be free to go about her work without him. She could finally be alone and—

"Alright," he said, taking the chain and lifting it from around his neck.

Allie faltered. "What?"

He didn't reply, but held the chain out to her without hesitation. "You take it."

"You're serious?" she asked, shoving her hands deep into the pockets of her coat to keep them away. But they were aching from the offer. It was too good to be true. For sure, it was a trap.

"This isn't a trick. Consider this a peace pact between

the two of us. You guard my secret and I'll make sure none of your friends know you're willingly working with a hero," he said, offering a small smile.

"Alright…" If he was insisting, she wouldn't hesitate to agree. Her fingers snatched the metal chain before he could rethink the offer. It was still warm from his skin. A soft aura pulsed from the coin when her fingers closed around it, just a hint of ancient magic that called goose bumps to her arms. It reassured her in a way nothing else had in years. She smiled, slipping the chain into her pocket.

When she looked up, Barcus was staring at her. Not at his precious coin, but *her*. The weight of that gaze made her stomach take flight. She squashed the glow of pleasure, quick and mercilessly. Now was not the time to make googly eyes at a hero. Celia needed her. The others needed her. "Come on, let's go."

They swung around the back of an old foreign antique shop. It was closed even though the sun was still up, but through the window they could see a collection of Afghan rugs and chipped statues. Allie went around to the back alley to a simple, red-painted door. Any Aethos would take the doorway as the back exit for the shop owner. They wouldn't know what had made the scratch marks that marred the wood.

Barcus was a trained hunter, though; he stared at the grooves. No doubt he knew exactly which creatures made them and how dangerous they could be. Allie gave him a knowing smile. She knocked once, then extended a single talon and dragged it down the middle.

The door opened with a jolt, revealing a stout man whose beard wrapped around his chin like a leather strap. A single big eye blinked at them. "Harpy."

"Jo," she greeted. "You going to let us in? It's freezing out here."

His eye moved to Barcus, taking him in with interest. "You brought a mortal? You aren't usually the type."

"I promised to show him a good time." She threw a flirtatious glance at Barcus, who returned it with ease. They were getting good at holding up this lie.

Bad idea. The words lit like a headline against her mind. She pretended not to notice his gaze lingering for a moment too long.

Jo sighed. "Alright, alright, but only because we could use the business." He stepped back, and Allie pushed in. As they stepped past the threshold, the small cyclops gave a mock bow. "Enjoy the sights and delights, mortal."

Allie rolled her eyes. "He has to say that to everyone."

Inside, the space was as large as a coat closet. Only an iron staircase offered them an out, down into the depths of the building. Shimmers of white light danced up from below the metal frame, enticing all to come down. The faint sound of a lyre and laughter grew louder as Allie led the way.

"You bring mortals here often?" Barcus asked behind her.

"Don't give me that judgy tone. I know what you're thinking."

He laughed. "What am I thinking?"

But Allie wasn't laughing. "Every community needs a place to unwind and just be themselves," she told him. "This is that place for us. If there are still Mythos and even Aethos who want to be exposed to something different, why not let them join in? We don't hurt anyone. Anything that happens here is fully consensual and secret." She couldn't help throwing in a teasing tone at the end, painting an image of what to expect.

He blinked at her, wearing the same unguarded look he had in the hotel. "I just had no idea."

"So, there are still some wonders in the world." Gods, it was fun to rattle him. For a brief, glorious moment she almost forgot why they were here, together. But as they reached the base of the stairs, it all came back.

Allie stepped aside to see Barcus's face when he laid eyes on their little wonder.

Being an immortal hero, she knew he had seen his fair share of amazing sights, which made it even more satisfying when the man was left speechless.

"Wow." True awe spread across his face as he took in the underground cavern.

"Welcome," Allie said, "to Tartarus."

"Is that some kind of joke?" The question came out before he could think better of it. But she couldn't be serious. This wasn't Tartarus, at least not the real one. A single set of iron stairs under the city couldn't lead to the infamous depths of the underworld.

And besides, no one wanted to *go* to Tartarus. Zeus had banished the titans there; the gods sent the worst humankind had to offer to its depths for punishment.

A death without honor wasn't the worst-case scenario for a hero—Tartarus was. Stuck in never-ending torture by the furies and the creatures that lurked there. They said the titans enjoyed sucking on the bones of dishonorable soldiers, and, oh…

Allie leveled him with a look at the same time the thought occurred to him. *Artemis, take me.* Of course unmortals would find comfort in such a place. Some of them were descendants of the giants that the Olympians had exiled. Most unmortals shared direct blood with the mother of monsters, Echidna, and the titan Typhon.

"Tartarus might be hell for you and your precious mortals, but to us, it is a second chance at life once we go there. Like one big, happy family reunion."

What could he say to that? Nothing. There was nothing he could say that would make up for his offense.

It was just as well. Allie didn't wait for a response before leading the way into the lair. "This way."

Barcus couldn't remember the last time the modern world had surprised him, but Allie had done it. Tartarus could have easily fit the mold of mortal luxury. Smooth marble lined the floor of the cavern-like space, catching the light from an ornate chandelier that hung above it all. Blood-red silk draped down from the chandelier's arms, stretching to every corner of the room. He had to tear his eyes away from it, the color too stark. It reminded him of the photos on his computer, of a battlefield covered in blood.

The joy he had felt only a moment ago flickered as a dark shadow blanketed his mind. The sensation wasn't anything new; he recognized it as a sign of too much stimulation. His senses were going on high alert.

Danger, his muscles screamed. *You're putting yourself in danger.* He was surrounded by creatures who would kill him if they knew what he was. The prickles of a migraine started building at the base of his skull.

Barcus brushed it off as nonsense. There were mortals here with unmortals, all perfectly safe. People sat next to creatures of all sizes, sipping wine and popping desserts into their mouths. The music that filtered from a nearby sound system wasn't anything he knew. But he recognized the lyre under the hypnotic electrical beat.

They walked past a deep fountain carved into the floor with a pool of water surrounding it. Nymphs huddled at the edge, their feet in the water as they talked and looked down at their phones. A centaur stood at the outer edges, looking bored as a mortal talked to him, and a full-bodied sphinx prowled beside a companion who carried her drinking bowl.

Allie led him to the large bar that took up half the length of the room. The biggest dryad Barcus had ever seen was behind it, stocking the shelves for the night. The shirt he wore hugged his broad chest, and his hair had been pulled into a small bun on the top of his head. The only thing that set him apart from a mortal was the brown pieces of bark that extended out of his skin just along his cheekbones and the slightly pointed tips of his ears.

At their approach, he looked up, ethereal green eyes widening in recognition. "Allie, haven't seen you in a long time. Are your sisters here?"

One of Allie's genuine smiles answered the question. "No, Oak. Ocypete is at home like always."

"That girl." The dryad shook his head with a laugh. "You need to bring her out more. We miss her here, not that we don't mind having you."

"I brought a new friend instead. He's a Mythos," Allie supplied. "You remember Princess Io? He's from her bastard's bloodline."

"Sorry to hear that," Oak said with a grimace. "So what are we drinking tonight?"

"Couple of the usual, hold the lotus."

"Just a water for me," Barcus added. Allie's dark eyes glanced at him, unsure what to make of the decision.

Oak pulled out two glasses and skillfully pulled together the drinks.

Allie looked around to see if anyone was listening. "Look, we need to talk to you."

"Alright, but it's going to have to wait till after the rehearsal."

"Rehearsal?" Barcus had been under the impression this was just a local hangout for unmortals. What would they need to rehearse?

"Oh, we put on shows here twice a month. Mostly old plays, but occasionally we have open mic nights. I'll have to help backstage and—" A tall, muscular centaur tapped the bar impatiently on the other end, catching Oak's attention and giving him a look of warning. "I'm on the clock."

She was shaking her head before he even finished the sentence. "That doesn't matter. This is more important."

"Maybe to you, but ever since you got fired, Cal has been on my ass," Oak affirmed with a nod to the centaur. "I actually want to keep this job. You'll have to wait."

"Oak," she tried again, voice firmer, but the dryad was already pulling off his apron, ready to head off to do whatever job the centaur had for him.

"I'm sorry, Allie. Afterwards, I promise."

"Fine," Allie huffed. "We'll stay. What show are they rehearsing, anyway?"

"*Ajax.*" Oak grinned.

Oh no.

Oh yes. That sinister voice cackled.

"Should be a good one. They got Dynarios to play Ajax. I love that guy. Can make a Bronze Man cry, that one. We'll chat later, yeah? I'll find you." The bark on his eyes moved when he winked in promise.

"Yeah, yeah," Allie huffed, her feathers ruffled.

They watched as Oak darted off to tend to the production.

Barcus took his drink in hand. He could see the dejected look on Allie's face as she stabbed at one of the fruits in her cocktail. "We have some time to kill—why don't we talk to the other unmortals around here? See if they know anything."

"Yeah, we should do that." She took her drink, sipping it gingerly as they turned back to the surrounding space. "Are you sure you don't want anything?"

He shook his head. "I haven't had alcohol in nearly a century."

"A hero who doesn't drink?" She tilted her head, staring at him in that inquisitive way that reached into his soul. "Are you sure you're alright?"

That was a loaded question, one he'd received a hundred times from concerned friends. The response was instinctive at this point. "Of course." He sipped his water and focused on the crowd around them. Taking note of every creature, the way they laughed, the ease in their bodies.

Allie's body settled beside his, their arms brushing together, allowing him to share in her warmth. "If this is all too much for you, you can leave."

It was another out. A second opportunity for him to leave if he wanted to. And gods did he want to. The headache grew by the second, banging against his temples. But if he did that now, she would think it was because of the repulsion he felt at her kind, and he couldn't have that.

All he had to do was last a little longer.

Barcus downed his water and started for the theater. "Come on, let's go see what we can find out."

⚬

The unmortals in Tartarus greeted them warmly. Well, they greeted Allie warmly. Barcus was surprised to see her open up to the creatures around them, pulling them in for hugs and asking about their lives. These unmortals weren't just Allie's friends; they were her family.

Her eagerness to come to Tartarus and check on them made all the more sense. He watched with rapt attention as she worked the crowd, choosing her words carefully as she asked pointed questions—whether anyone had noticed anything weird. Whether they had been attacked.

Each unmortal looked amused before shaking their heads. Only one cyclops asked, "Why? Did something happen to you?"

"Someone tried to attack me. Emphasis on the *try*."

It was the perfect opportunity to see if her announcement invoked some kind of spark in the other unmortal. But the cyclops merely laughed, revealing a mouth of pointed teeth that shined like daggers. Barcus felt his muscles flex for the umpteenth time at the sight, the tension curling like a snake about to strike. "I can't remember the last time someone tried that with me. I don't think I have it in me anymore to fight back. What's the point? They can't kill me."

Allie's smile grew tight. "Well, if you ever run into trouble, Telas, you let me know. I'll do the fighting for you."

One large eye closed in what might have been a wink. "You are too kind, harpy," he said before excusing himself.

Once he was out of earshot, Allie let out a frustrated sigh. "Nothing. Not a single clue."

"There are still plenty of people we can talk to," Barcus encouraged. As the evening wore on, more unmortals filled the lounge, though it wasn't nearly as many as he would have anticipated. He watched the cyclops join a group of nymphs and dryads lounging across plush couches. Everyone looked well at ease; he only wished his own body would get the hint. It didn't matter that he knew there was no threat—his body was strung tighter than Eros's bow. His muscles were beginning to ache from all the tension.

Barcus hummed, his eyes falling on the sphinx he'd spotted earlier. The woman's head on a lioness's body. Her fur the color of Egyptian sand and her claws on full display as she flexed them against the tile. Yet the man next to her did not look afraid.

It was a strange sight, but then again, he was standing next to a harpy.

"So," he prodded as Allie searched for their next victim, "how is it that mortals are allowed in here?"

"We wanted a place where we could be ourselves and relax. Recently we started allowing mortals in so they could"—she bit her lip, considering her next words carefully—"accept us."

"Are you planning on making yourselves known, then?" The last time unmortals had lived freely on the surface, the world had been chaos. Monsters and men had fought at every opportunity. Back then, there had been the need for heroes to keep the peace. Times had changed, but that didn't mean there wouldn't be chaos if they decided to show their fangs again.

Allie shrugged. "Probably not. Most unmortals don't want to deal with the hassle. It's easier to hide."

"But you don't agree."

"I would like to give everyone a choice. Right now, it doesn't feel like we have one."

She did a good job hiding her thoughts, but he knew Allie was different from other unmortals. She flew across the city at every opportunity. She reveled in who she was. He'd learned that when she'd unashamedly walked around the master suite, beautifully naked. Speaking of which…

His eyes lingered on the fur, the reptilian eyes, the hooves. All small things, but it made them stand apart from mortals, nonetheless. Then he looked at Allie, standing next to him in her soft sweater and jeans.

She frowned at his stare. "What's wrong?"

"Everyone else has dropped their disguise, but you haven't."

"I'd love to, but I know it would make you uncomfortable."

"Me?" He barked in laughter before realizing she wasn't kidding. *Shit.* She honestly thought that. "I wouldn't mind."

"You're a… you know. Hanging out with unmortals isn't really your thing, so I'm trying to look mortal." She refused to meet his eye, instead watching the nymphs splashing about in the fountain.

Well, that made him feel like crap. He didn't mean to make her feel that way. It had just been so long since he'd met a harpy or any of her kind, and most of those interactions had involved him nearly getting eaten.

He touched her arm, and to his surprise, she didn't snap at him. "I'm sorry. I want you to feel comfortable." It wasn't her kind that made him uncomfortable—it was a hundred other things. Things he didn't dare burden her with. Things he didn't fully understand himself. But Allie didn't look convinced. He tried again. "The other night, I wasn't able to see your true form because of the darkness. I can't remember if your feathers were raven black or crow black."

An absurd squawking sound erupted from her. "Are you kidding me? There isn't a difference between those colors."

"You think?"

"I know."

He hummed. "I'm doing my best here to remember, but I just can't. Maybe I should see it again."

"You are being ridiculous, you know that?"

Was that a blush blooming across her nose? Barcus stared in utter fascination at her face, feeling his nerves settle for the first time since he'd stepped through the doors. Without warning, the skin of her arm shivered under his touch. Allie shucked her sweater, revealing a loose, silky tank top underneath. Goose bumps erupted along her arm, rippling and shifting. In seconds, her skin was covered in a sleeve of smooth black feathers, and an angel of darkness stood beside him.

It was amazing how her expression changed with the freedom of her transformation. Her face softened and there was a new glow about her. A pleased groan spilled from her lips as she stretched her wings. One that went straight to his groin. He wanted to hear it again.

"That feels *so* much better," Allie cooed before glancing his way. He saw now it wasn't just her wings that had changed, but her eyes as well. The birdlike sharpness was there in her expression as she gauged his response.

This was the first time he had gotten to see the full details of her other form. He made sure to be obvious as he looked her up and down. Eyes lingering on her wings, her talons, the slender bones of her shoulders. He was not afraid of her—no, it was quite the opposite. He was fascinated. "I'm glad. I'm sure your friends would wonder if you didn't transform."

"Right." Allie drew out the word before inclining her head to the edge of the room. "Come with me. I think there are some more unmortals this way."

He followed her to where four large columns held up the ceiling. Two columns on each side framed a sudden drop in the floor. The lounge burrowed deeper than he'd first imagined. Instead of floors leading up, it buried itself underground, as if digging towards its namesake.

Once they reached the edge, he saw it. "It's a theater," he said breathlessly. An amphitheater of lush, red-cushioned seating. At the bottom sat a stage.

"You were expecting something else?"

"No, it's just… I haven't been to the theater in a long time."

"Same. There was a time when my sisters and I came here to see the old plays performed every chance we got. No matter how many years pass, the classics never change."

Barcus could understand that. Once every decade, he would pick up a bound collection of Aeschylus or Sophocles and be transported back to a different life. Back to the festivals in Athens when he'd been young and so hopeful.

A few creatures dressed in flowing ornate chitons were on stage, darting between the curtains, laying out scenery and shouting directions for the stagehands. It wasn't exactly like he remembered the plays of the past, performed out in the hot sun while the audience sat on hard stone. The stage was set high, using the red curtains from the lounge to carry into the space, giving it the appearance of an expensive opera house. It was hard to remember that this place was buried under a run-down antique shop.

Maybe it was the elegant tile, or the stonework of the columns. Maybe he was getting used to the sights of unmortals standing next to mortals, or hearing the laughter of the nymphs. But in that moment, he finally felt at peace.

"Do you perform new plays?"

"Sure we do," Allie answered. "A few decades ago, Ocypete even wrote a play. Back when she was trying her hand at fiction writing."

"I didn't even know a place like this could exist."

"Well, that's kind of the point. This has been our little secret." Her hand fell against her pocket where his coin lay hidden. Her voice became a soft whisper between them. "Everyone would lose their mind if they found out I brought a hero here. Understand?"

"Of course." He nodded, though there was nothing for her to fear. He could think of a dozen of his brothers who would feel the same sense of awe as he did in the space.

"For what it's worth," Barcus said, his words stopping the harpy in her tracks, "I don't think it's stupid. Trying to figure out where we all fit in this new world. Judging from this, I think you unmortals are doing a better job than us heroes."

Her smile was small but real, and he basked in it. "Thanks…" She looked as if she wanted to say more but couldn't figure out what. Only when she turned away was she able to find her voice again. "Come on, let's take a seat."

❧

He couldn't remember the last time he'd been to a theater performance. Maybe the last Dionysian festival in Athens. All he remembered was that the wine had poured freely, and he had drunkenly played *kotabass* with Argos and Xanthus until sunup.

"They cycle through the classics all the time," Allie explained. "Krone says it's good for morale."

Barcus froze. It had been a long time since he'd heard the name of one of the monster's generals. His head swiveled around, searching the room for the man's unmistakable dark mane. "Krone? He's here?"

"No. He doesn't come by very much anymore. Why?" It wasn't a real question; she and every unmortal in the den likely knew the story. That didn't make it any easier to hear her say, "I think everyone here would pay good money to see the last Nemean lion meet the Great Hunter."

Guilt swelled in his throat at the memory. Once, lions as large as cattle had roamed the Mediterranean. Offspring of the great Nemean lion. They had killed livestock without remorse and run off worshippers from temples. He'd hunted them at Artemis's request. It had once been a source of pride, but now he felt nothing. Nothing except the headache beating at the back of his skull.

"Yes, well, I'm not his favorite person."

Allie laughed at that. "Then we have that in common. The lion isn't my biggest fan either."

"Why? Isn't he your leader?"

She snorted at that. "Leader? Not since the wars. Now he's just a cranky old cat who likes to think he's in charge." An odd look passed across her face. He caught signs of her trying to look at him out of the corner of her eye, but unwilling to stare. As if she had just realized something. "You fought in those wars, didn't you, Hunter?"

There was that old name again. He knew she used it to make a point, and it stuck hard.

He couldn't remember what had started the first Great War, only that mortals, immortals, and monsters had all fought. Cities and heroes had rallied to put an end to the unstoppable hunger of monsters. The earth had been stained red for hundreds of years; truly, they'd earned the name Dark Ages.

When the Crusades had begun and humans had ventured east to fight for their newfound religions, the Order had joined them. By that time, the monsters had taken refuge in the desert sands and rural mountains, but still the fighting had continued. There had been a time when war brought with it great honor, but not those wars. Unmortals no longer presented the same threat, but fighting was the only thing heroes knew how to do.

He didn't want her to think of him like that. He'd done more in his life than just kill, and he would continue to do everything he could to make amends for the past. "I did. But I do not fight anymore."

"Do you really think you can stop fighting?"

He expected to hear the doubt in the question, maybe even disbelief. He'd heard it all before from his brothers as well. "A man can only take so much bloodshed, even an immortal."

But Xanthus had kept going, searching out any army that would take him. In his darkest moments, Barcus regretted the decision to stop fighting. If he had stayed, maybe Xanthus wouldn't have carried so much hate in his heart.

That was part of what had driven him to advocate for the Covenant, to establish rules and allow for healing between their groups. Mortal, immortal, and unmortal. He had hoped it would be enough to ease the ever-present guilt churning him inside out, and for a while, it had been. But one good deed could never make up for all the pain he was responsible for.

Allie made a small noise of understanding. It seemed he'd answered her question. But she didn't know the whole story, and leaving her to draw the wrong conclusion seemed wrong.

"I'm not being naive. There have been times when I've needed to fight, to protect the people I love, to save mortals from harm. I'll work to keep the peace as much as possible, and if there isn't a choice, I'll do what needs to be done. I believe our job is to protect, not kill."

"And if your brothers don't feel the same way?"

He'd asked himself this same question a thousand times. The ache in his scar was a constant reminder of the last time one of his brothers hadn't agreed. "Then I will fight for those who need me." Another question burned in her eyes, one Barcus knew without her uttering a word. "No matter who they are."

Allie's gaze darted back down towards the stage. Her voice, when she found it, was barely a whisper, as if she didn't expect him to hear it. "I don't know what to think when it comes to you anymore."

Not for the first time, he realized they had more in common with each other than he had originally thought— for he did not know what to think of her as well.

X

SOPHOCLES WASN'T HER favorite playwright, and *Ajax* wasn't her favorite play, but among her kind, it was a fan favorite. Any play where the hero came out on the bottom deserved a standing ovation.

After the death of his friend Achilles, Ajax was driven mad by the gods. He set out to slaughter King Agamemnon for wronging him in the distribution of Achilles's armor, but instead, he slaughtered a pen of cattle. When he awoke from his madness, guilt at what he had planned to do crippled his heart, finally driving him to kill himself.

Oak was right—Dynarios made a great Ajax. His giant's blood gave the appearance of the towering hero Ajax had been. His voice boomed across the stone theater as he cried out, cursing the gods. A few cheers arose from the crowd as he picked up Hector's sword, intent in his eye.

That was when Barcus stood up and excused himself quietly.

The sudden departure broke Allie from the scene's spell

as she watched him slip back up the stairs, disappearing over the edge to the main floor.

Onstage, Dynarios pretended to impale himself, and a loud cheer rose from the crowd that had gathered. As the director came onstage to give him notes, he broke character and bowed with a flourish, causing another cheer. But Allie wasn't interested in joining them, not when her own hero had just slunk off to do gods knew what.

Barcus hadn't made it far, stopping just at the top of the stairway to lean against a stone column. His eyes were closed, and a green tint colored his features.

The usual sharp remark poised itself on the tip of her tongue, but something about the way his body was slumped triggered alarm bells in her head.

He hadn't noticed her yet, which was strange considering his earlier rapt attention. Allie casually dragged her foot against the tile as a dead giveaway. It worked. His eyes snapped open in alarm before focusing on her. At once, the tension in his body eased, but something was still wrong.

"Hey, are you alright?"

Within the span of a single breath, he collected himself. One minute, Barcus was a man, vulnerable and shaken—and the next she was looking at the stoic hero of tales. "I'm fine."

"You don't look it." The look in his eye was the same as he'd had during their fight in the hotel room. Wild. Panicked.

Barcus was a man of legend, one whose name struck fear in the hearts of her kind. He hadn't hesitated in volunteering to come with her, but she'd seen fear overtake him like a disease at the oddest of moments.

"I just..." He ran a hand through his hair, searching for an explanation. "It's not my favorite play."

"Did you know him?" She knew some heroes were millennia old. They had fought at Troy, or aided Herakles in his trials. Those men were the most dangerous, with experience in battle that matched even her own. They remembered a world in its most primal state. Many still acted like nothing had ever changed.

Barcus shook his head. "That was well before my time. But… we all know the story. It makes for a good warning."

"About what?"

He scrubbed his large hands over his face, looking a hundred years old. "That war can make even good men do terrible things."

There was nothing she could say to that.

Allie looked around. No one had noticed them yet, but they would. If an unmortal came over, they'd know immediately that something was wrong, and from there they would easily figure out exactly who Barcus was.

They needed somewhere private where Barcus could recover from this panic attack.

That was the word for it.

It struck her so suddenly and with such truth that Allie almost forgot who she was looking at. It was almost as if she was looking at a mirror of Ajax. And if there was one thing she had learned from the play, it was that heroes could be dangerous when blinded by fear.

She made sure to approach him slowly, her wings slowly reverting to human arms so she could softly guide him. "Come with me."

He complied without a word, and she tried not to let that freak her out too much. With an arm steadying him, she led him to the bar. Barcus shook his head slightly. "Alcohol isn't going to help me."

"I didn't offer you a drink," she said, remembering the way he'd shied away earlier. "I'm just offering you privacy so you can freak out."

"I'm not freaking out." His voice was cold. The hard edge tried its best to convince her and himself, but she wouldn't be fooled.

She made sure her own tone was soft as she moved her hand to cup his chin. "I'm sorry. I didn't mean that."

Lifting the divider, they walked through the familiar space behind the bar and into the back storage room, one of the only private spaces in the lounge. "This is where I always used to hide when I wanted to avoid work."

Barcus gave a dry laugh as he sank to the floor, back pressed against a crate of wine. "I would think you'd make a great bartender. Easy on the eyes, always quick with a comeback, and"—he glanced at her arm before easing her grip away—"you have good instincts for when others are in trouble."

She fell to the floor beside him with a sigh. "I wasn't bad. I just… hated the work. There wasn't anything satisfying about filling people's drinks and gossiping night after night. It wasn't for me." In the past, she had given advice to world leaders and philosophers, so standing aimlessly, waiting for customer to pick which cocktail to order, had driven her crazy. When she'd tried to talk to her sisters about it, they'd encouraged her to find a different job. One with a power suit and lots of money, or maybe one selling precious gems. On paper, they sounded like the perfect thing for her, but none of those suggestions felt right.

"Of course not," Barcus said. "You're a harpy."

"What's that supposed to mean?"

He held up a hand, showing no ill intent. "I only mean

that you're a girl who likes her freedom. Am I right? Harpies have always been the terrors of the sky and wind. But in this new world, you can't be that. It must be hard, trying to change into something less."

Yes. That was exactly it. She loved the convenience of the modern world, but she didn't want to change for it. She wanted to hang on to what made her an unmortal, what had once made her appeal to the gods. Pretending to be a human felt like a lie, one she couldn't live with. Not even Ocypete understood that.

But Barcus did.

She studied him in the dim storeroom light. She'd seen panic attacks on television before, but never in real life. He looked like the world had tipped over from a simple play. No. She shook her head. The play wasn't the problem; it had merely been a catalyst. Her throat tightened. If she was going to rely on Barcus to find Celia, she needed to know what was wrong.

"Do you want to talk about it?"

Silence followed the question. Impatience nipped at her nerves, but she tamped it down. Barcus didn't need her to lose control, not now.

When he did answer, it was as if he were muttering to himself. "It's been getting worse."

"What has?"

"My…" He waved his hand in the air, searching for the right word and coming up with nothing. "I don't know what to call it. It is as if Phobos possesses me, twisting my insides and making me useless. I've been pushing through it, but…" He licked dry lips, once again looking lost for words.

Allie waited, letting his confession sink in. Phobos,

child of Ares and Aphrodite, and the harbinger of fear. It didn't make sense that he would torture one of the chosen heroes. "I always thought heroes didn't feel fear."

A brittle chuckle escaped him. "Yes, I used to believe that as well. But it is a lie. Everyone feels fear, and to pretend not to will drive a man mad. Believe me."

Mad. The word rang with a deafening echo. Ajax had gone mad, the gods and his own anger fueling his madness and driving him to commit suicide. But that wasn't Barcus. The man huddled next to her didn't seem to have an ounce of rage in him. He was considerate, for a hero. Kind, even. Did he not see that?

"You are not mad." The conviction in her voice surprised even her, but she believed it. She knew it in her *soul*. How could he not see the same thing?

"Not yet." Barcus met her eyes, and in them she saw the same tired expression. For the first time, she realized she was talking to a man who was pushing his own limits.

"I can barely look at blood these days without feeling ill. What kind of hero does that make me?"

The confession surprised her. Suddenly, things made so much sense. The lack of sleep. The wild look that had come about when they'd first tangled.

"Is that why you stopped fighting?"

"Yes. I was sickened by what happened in the wars. And when Argos went missing, I thought I could work with Xanthus to get him back. Track him down by hunting unmortals. It didn't take long before I could barely hold my spear. The nightmares…" He let out a shaky breath, his eyes closed, and he looked like he might be ill again. "I couldn't do it anymore, so I was useless to Xanthus."

Allie recalled what he'd said in the hotel. She knew how

the story ended, and her heart ached to see how it pained him. "He didn't help you?"

"There is no greater crime to a Spartan than being a coward. That's how he saw me."

She wanted to ask what he meant by that. The need burned her tongue, but he had already given her so much. Maybe too much. If she were a lesser unmortal, she would use this knowledge to her advantage.

But she wouldn't do that. She couldn't do that.

This thing between them shouldn't exist, but it did, and even though she didn't fully understand it, she didn't want to do anything to harm it, either. Barcus offered hope that something could finally change between their kind. He said he wanted to help them, and Allie was finally beginning to believe that.

His body shifted as he took one deep, muscle-shuddering exhale. "I'll be fine. The sooner we finish this, the better." He moved as if to stand, but she gripped his shoulder and pushed him back down.

"Stop pushing yourself," she told him firmly. "We still have time before rehearsals are done, and you look like shit."

A weak smile broke out on his handsome face. "Ah, there she is. I was beginning to wonder why you were being so nice to me."

"Hey, I can be nice. I'm not a total heartless bitch." Her lips twitched in response. If he was joking, then that must mean he was feeling a little better.

That got a laugh out of him. "No, you're not," Barcus agreed. "You are nothing like I expected."

The tension in his body lifted, and things felt lighter between them. Allie couldn't look away from him. Now that the shadows had been chased away, he looked more handsome than usual. As if he truly appreciated every moment when his fears didn't bog him down.

Suddenly, she was very aware of how close together they were. Huddled between two giant crates of wine, their shoulders pushing against each other.

When she'd worked at Tartarus, this had been her favorite place to take handsome unmortals and mortals for an impromptu makeout session. She and Oak had developed a secret language anytime either of them wanted to take a break. It worked out well until Krone had found out and fired her. Now those memories hit with distinct clarity.

Then Barcus reached out and she didn't flinch away. Instead, she watched in quiet fascination as his hand inched closer, tucking a strand of black hair behind her ear in a touch that was almost too gentle to catalog.

Her keen senses could hear the still-frantic rhythm of his heartbeat as hers raced to match it. She should look away; if she continued to stare at him, she would probably do something they would both regret.

But she didn't move away. Instead, she leaned forward, curious to see what he might do next.

Barcus licked his lips. "You're a lot nicer than you want me to believe."

"Tell anyone and I'll kill you."

He laughed at the non-threat. Compared to the ones she had seethed at him days ago, it was nothing. And they both knew it. "You're brave," he whispered. "It makes me want to be brave, too."

His body leaned forward, eyes flickering down to her mouth and... oh, Mother, he was going to kiss her.

Allie felt her body freeze even as pulses of electricity thrummed to her head. This wasn't their earlier game of chicken. This was something else. The chicken had evolved into an emotionally confused harpy. She felt lightheaded, giddy. She *wanted* him to kiss her.

She wanted him.

The familiar clang of the door broke the spell. Allie reeled back, putting as much space between herself and Barcus as possible. The warmth of his breath disappeared, and she had just enough time to realize he had almost kissed her when Oak's voice boomed out. "Alright, lovebirds, I need to see twelve inches between you two."

Allie swung her gaze to her friend, who stared at them smugly. "Allie, you know how management feels about using the storeroom as a makeout spot."

There was no use denying it. She couldn't exactly explain that Barcus had been feeling unwell, and Oak wouldn't believe her anyway. She feigned embarrassment, tucking a stray piece of hair behind her ear. The same strand of hair Barcus had so tenderly touched just moments ago. "Is the rehearsal over?"

"Yep, the crowd is thinning out and I still need to close up, but I have some time for my favorite harpy."

"Please, we all know Ocypete is your favorite harpy," Allie said, trying to distract the dryad from the obvious tension in the room. She pulled herself to her feet and put space between herself and Barcus as he did the same.

We came here for a reason.

"Oak—" Allie cleared her throat, "—Celia is missing."

"What?" The warmth slipped from her friend's face. His brown skin turned ashen as the news sank in. "What do you mean?"

"I mean, she's been gone for three days and no one knows where she is. Miesha called me when she didn't show up. Something is wrong." Saying the words out loud to someone besides Barcus felt like a weight had been lifted from her. Suddenly, it wasn't her little secret, but with that relief came a wash of fear. This was real. This was happening. "Have you heard anything?"

Oak hesitated at the question, and dread pooled down her throat. *He knows something.*

His long fingers nervously scratched at his scalp as he collected his thoughts. "Allie, I'm so sorry…"

"Oak," she said slowly, "if you know something, please tell me. I'm going crazy here."

His eyes fell on Barcus. "Are you sure you wanna have this discussion in front of the Mythos?"

"I can leave," Barcus offered without pause. Allie appreciated the gesture, the respect it showed both her and Oak. She might have once accepted it. But at the idea of facing bad news, she suddenly didn't want to be alone.

Her hand reached out, gripping his to keep him in place. To his credit, Barcus didn't react.

"No, it's alright. He's… helping me."

Oak's brows rose at that, a question evident in the look. *Just how serious are the two of you?*

Allie gave him a hard stare back. "Tell me everything you know."

"Alright, but it isn't much and you didn't hear it from me. Krone will kill me if he finds out I told anyone."

Her breath caught in her lungs at the implication. "Krone knows?"

Oak nodded slowly, his voice dropping low as if the lion were nearby. "Last week a siren who was a part of the show disappeared."

She felt her chest constrict, thinking of all the sirens she knew. "Which one?"

"Seraphina."

She knew the name. Seraphina with her colorful mermaid's tale, who had a laugh like a bell. Unmortals fell over themselves for her, but she was always talking about a Mythos boyfriend at home.

"What is Krone doing about it?"

A look of apology twisted Oak's features. "He told us not to worry about it."

Anger washed over her at the news. "Someone is attacking unmortals and he didn't tell anyone?"

Her anger took both men by surprise. Barcus squeezed her hand—whether in warning or reassurance, she wasn't sure. Oak's eyes widened in surprise. "What makes you think we're being attacked?"

"Because I was attacked the other night by a hero and I think he's doing the same to other unmortals. Isn't that enough?" Her voice broke under the weight of her anger, and she didn't care. "Something has to be done."

Oak wouldn't meet her gaze. "I'm sorry, Allie. I don't know what you think I can do."

Had he forgotten what he was? What she was? They were more powerful than the average human, ageless and timeless. Oak's admission felt like an echo of what she was becoming—a creature who had forgotten what it meant to fight, to protect. Well, Oak might be happy working his mundane job and ignoring the signs of danger. But she was not.

"Oak, I need some help. Let the others know something is happening. Tell them to watch their backs."

He shook his head. "I'll talk to Krone, see what he thinks."

Something in her shattered. That would take too much time. Who knew what would happen while they argued about whether unmortals were really in danger or not? She stepped back, unable to stand next to him a moment longer.

"I'm sorry, Allie. I know that isn't what you want to hear."

"No, it isn't." She had come here to warn her friends, but Krone knew something, and he'd decided to keep it a secret. If he had told them last week that Seraphina was missing, maybe Celia would have come straight home that day. Maybe Allie would have thought twice about meeting her for dinner and making them both easy marks.

"You may trust Krone with this, but I can't. I am going to find my sister and Seraphina. Tell him that when you see him and tell him if he doesn't come clean about this, I will. The unmortals in this city deserve to know."

The look on Oak's face was one of pure dread at the idea, but she didn't care.

Allie stormed out of the room before Oak became a victim of her ire and before he saw how much his words had hurt her. Out of all her friends, she had placed all hope that he would understand her fears. That he would stand up with her.

Now a new reality settled over her shoulders. The only person who she could trust to help her was a hero.

XI

"LOOKS LIKE IT'S just you and me."

She'd been determined to continue to search for Celia after Tartarus, but she had no idea what direction to go, and arguing with Oak had drained her. Her fear and anger had been enough to drive her ahead, but now she was spent. Emotionally and physically. Returning home and coming clean to an inquisitive Ocypete was not an option. Her sister would just side with Krone, as usual. Allie needed to think, to rest, to put herself back together again.

So here she was, alone with a hero. The hotel key Barcus had given her burned a hole in her jeans pocket as they rode up to the top floor. Barcus shifted quietly next to her, only the cheerful elevator jingle between them.

Allie sighed, running a hand through her hair and giving it a hard pull, hoping to jostle some sense back into herself. "I must be crazy for coming back here with you."

"Not crazy," Barcus said finally. "There's a lot we have to do."

We.

On the outside, he was taking this all very well. But she'd seen the cracks in his armor tonight.

The elevator dinged and he stepped out first, giving her his back. It was a nice back, but showing it to her was another sign that he was exhibiting weakness. His guard was completely down now, as if he didn't care at all that they were enemies.

Were they still enemies? She gritted her teeth as she noticed how pale his complexion still was. She shouldn't care, but her fingers wanted nothing more than to reach out and give him some sort of comfort.

Oddly enough, she could use a little comfort as well.

Her room was in the opposite direction from his. She strolled down the plush carpet, ready to cut all ties for the night and retreat to the comfortable silence of her own space. There, she could think about everything. She could come up with a way forward.

But Barcus followed, his steps keeping a careful distance behind her as they marched.

"Afraid I'll fly the coop?" Allie asked over her shoulder, but even she recognized the usual jab was lacking venom. She cleared her throat and stopped at the door with her number on it. "You don't have to escort me to my room."

"I just…" His voice trailed off as if he didn't know how to finish the sentence. "I wanted to make sure you were alright."

A dry laugh croaked out of her throat. "Alright? My sister is missing, my friends are in trouble, and there's a homicidal hero running around the city." She turned and found him standing all too close to her. Her nose was level with his broad chest, and she could hear the rapid flutter of his heart beating between his ribs. It was the same erratic tune from the storeroom, one that revealed his hidden anxieties. She risked glancing up and found a face made of stone.

He was trying to hide it from her, but that only made her question the fear more. "Are you alright?"

"Not at all."

"At least we're on the same page then." She reached for the key and unlocked the door with an easy swipe.

The door opened. One glance inside and her heart dropped. Darkness greeted her, along with a room that was not her own. A room with none of the comforts of her nest or her sisters. Suddenly, the idea of being alone wasn't so appealing. For hundreds of years, she hadn't been alone. There had always been Celia or Pete to keep her company when something was wrong. To complain to or seek encouragement. But they weren't here.

"Do you want to come in?" she asked casually.

Barcus hesitated. She would have thought less of him if he hadn't, but it was only a second before he nodded. "I do. Thanks."

Allie moved into the room and flicked on the light switch. The suite layout was slightly bigger than Barcus's, but maybe that was because there wasn't a mess of papers littered everywhere.

The living space had floor-to-ceiling windows that showed the snowy cityscape and a full kitchen, with a glass tabletop and a bottle of wine calling her name.

The door clicked softly behind him and she heard the metallic lock of the bolts clicking into place. She turned, half expecting him to have wised up and retreated to the safety of his own room to check on their prisoner.

But no… there he was. More handsome than any hero had any right to be. His expression cautious but hopeful.

He was waiting for her to make the first move. Allie smiled, watched how his muscles slowly relaxed. *The man really should learn not to let his guard down*, she thought, and then… she pounced.

It only took two steps before she was in his space, their chests pressed against one another, her nose brushing against the underside of his chin. Barcus startled, backing against the wall where she used her strength to pin him in place. His heartbeat rioted next to her ear.

Neither of them moved. She recalled his quick movements in the alley, the way he had subdued Leo. If Barcus wanted to, he could do the same to her. They would be back to square one, fighting with no possible winner.

"Looks like the tables have turned," she purred. "Now I have you trapped in my room. You made a big mistake coming in here."

"Did I?"

She'd heard his voice tremble in fear earlier, but there was no sign of that here. Barcus looked resigned, as if this moment had been predicted by the gods and there was no use fighting it. Her fingers curled around his thick wrists, but he didn't fight back. He stood perfectly still, waiting to see what she would do.

She frowned at the thought. There should be some fear. Some emotion in him. This was her chance to get back at him for everything he had done to her. Didn't he see that?

"Why aren't you afraid?"

"You've had more than enough chances to attack me and you didn't. Why now?"

"Because I'm angry," she snarled.

"I know," Barcus said calmly. "If it would make you feel better, you can slash my throat."

Her stomach rolled at the suggestion, even though she had made that very threat to him only a few days ago. Why? Why did the thought suddenly paralyze her? Why had she invited him into this space?

She knew the answer—deep in her gut, she knew. His smell penetrated her senses, the same way it had in the storeroom. Her gray eyes searched his face, but he was still waiting. Waiting for her to make the first move.

He licked his lips, and she followed the sight like a hawk.

Allie couldn't help herself; she leaned in and pressed her lips against his. To her surprise, his lips parted to receive her. A fierce need to take advantage of the vulnerability took hold. Her tongue darted out, looking to break past his defenses, but he was already opening up.

It was a blessing from the gods that they hadn't kissed in the bar. If they had, she didn't know if she would have been able to stop.

A pleased noise escaped her as she deepened the kiss. Barcus's hands twitched within her grasp, so she let them go, too preoccupied with the battle raging between their tongues to care what his hands were doing. But then she felt them, skimming down her sides, brushing against her ass and pulling her closer like she was all he needed.

Maybe she was.

Maybe this was what they both needed.

Barcus pushed forward and pulled her up, lifting her in one clean athletic feat. Allie kept her lips pressed against his, unwilling to break the kiss as she hooked her legs around his waist.

He moved as if she were nothing, following the wall to the door that could only be a bedroom. His foot closed the door with a loud bang, sealing them further into a prison of their own making.

The slam jostled them both, breaking the kiss. Allie panted as she stared at the man holding her, her dark hair falling around them like a curtain. "I'll give you one last chance, hero," she told him. "Last chance to walk away."

This was a bad idea. They both knew it, but if they were going to make one of the biggest mistakes in the history of the gods, she wanted to hear him say it.

Barcus stared at her, his lips still wet from the savageness of their kiss. "I could never walk away from a woman in need."

She pulled Barcus close, her breath mingling with his. "I suppose I could accept your help this once."

His large hands laid her gently on the bed before moving seamlessly to assist in lifting her sweater. All the while, he planted kisses on every piece of newly exposed skin. Allie ached to lose herself into a tousle of arms and clothing, but Barcus's touch set a different pace. Slowly, tenderly, he sank to his knees before her, like a mortal in the midst of worship.

Seeing him like that trapped the breath in her lungs. Never, in a millennium, had she seen a hero so content to be on his knees. He pushed her leggings down with care, eyes drinking in the sight of soft skin that lay beneath.

And Allie watched him. Watched as he stripped her down to her bra and panties with the care of an artisan. It was strange to remember that Barcus was a trained killer. And so easy to disregard that fact while in the throes of passion.

Allie's hand moved under his chin, tilted it up to get a better look. His blue eyes were dark in the room, clouded over, but this time it wasn't with memories of the past. It was with lust. The past had no room between them. Not now.

"Come here," she said, urging him to his feet with just two fingers. He followed wordlessly, giving her all the power. Following her lead. His eyes raked over her body, taking her in as if she were a creature he'd never seen before.

She tugged on his shirt, pulling him closer. "This needs to come off. I want you now."

"Patience is a virtue."

"Maybe for noble heroes like yourself—" the fabric tore under her eager hands, "—but I am a creature without morals."

Barcus didn't argue as he lifted both sweater and shirt over his head and—*mother's maw*—revealing a set of broad muscles that she'd admired since the first time they met. The jeans came next, allowing her to feast on the sight of sculpted muscle and an even more glorious cock.

She now understood where the beauty of marble sculptures came from. The perfect proportions, the shapely arms. They must have had heroes pose for those iconic depictions, because Barcus was Herakles-made flesh.

The only imperfection was the smattering of scars that decorated his skin. Most old and faded from a time before immortality had blessed him. But there were some more prominent. The scar on his collarbone was the worst of the bunch. It cut low, the pale white line stopping just above his heart.

"Like what you see?" The question lacked the usual confidence Barcus exuded. It was quiet, unsure.

Allie put her mouth against the edge of the scar in a gentle kiss. He tensed at the contact, body as taut as Artemis's bow. At any moment, he was prepared to run. His subconscious was probably telling him the same thing hers was: *This is a big mistake.*

Her hands fell against his hips, anchoring them both in place. "I've seen worse."

"You have."

It was not a question.

Only unmortals knew the life she and her sisters lived. A life that had started in the deserts of civilization and brought her here, to a modern city, with so much at her fingertips but so little to do. Only unmortals knew the strength and troubles that came from starting life over and over. The strange loneliness that came from years of reinventing yourself and how exhausting it could be.

As she looked into Barcus's eyes, it was clear he was plagued by the same bone-deep weariness.

Allie pushed down the emotion that rose up with that thought. Her fingers traced the outline of the scar. "If I have any complaints, it's that you're too perfect."

He rolled his eyes. "Do all harpies use flattery to get what they want?"

She grinned. "Flattery did get me all the jewels the French royal family had to offer. Is it working?"

His hard cock pressed against her, reawakening the nerves of her body. Allie moaned as she shifted in his arms, causing the two to rub against each other. Barcus's grip tightened. "Make that noise again."

With excruciatingly slow movements, he laid her across the bed. The hair of his naked legs tickled as they pushed her thighs open.

"This reminds me of something," Allie panted, remembering the way his body had pinned her down that first night. The lightning bolt of pleasure that had prophesied this moment.

"I'll admit I've never had a woman squirm so much to get away from me before," Barcus said, his tongue grazing her breasts as he lowered her bra straps around her arms, giving the illusion of bondage.

"I don't need the foreplay, hero…"

"I know what you need."

Because he needed it, too. An escape from the harsh reality of the world around them. A touch of comfort that could only be found in the arms of another person.

His fingers trailed down from her navel to the top of her panties, where one large digit slipped into the folds. Allie gasped at the sensation, slow and probing but *so* good.

"More…" She wanted more. Needed it. She needed to get fucked. Not this slow, careful devotion.

But Barcus wasn't listening. He was too entertained by her breasts. His hot tongue tortured her with languished swipes across her nipples, bringing them to brown peaks. His mouth moved down, down the sternum of her chest and her stomach before kissing each hip. Allie sucked in a breath of anticipation when his mouth fell just along her panty line.

Then the warm finger between her folds disappeared.

Her hands tangled in his hair. "Come on, hero, I need you to fuck me."

Barcus's hot breath hit the skin of her thigh as he looked up at her and damn if it wasn't the most attractive thing she'd ever seen. A hero's head near her cunt, his eyes dilated with lust. "Mmm." His moan went straight through her. It was a noise that said he was enjoying this agonizing pace. "If I fucked you, I wouldn't have time to do this," he said, flicking a finger against her clit.

Her body arched at the sensation, and a breathless

"*yes*" tore from her lips. He did it again, stroking two fingers between her folds and conducting a spark of pleasure through her that soon ignited into a fire.

It would be too easy to lose herself to the heat of him. To let him take her away and forget. But then his voice broke past it all, a quiet whisper that sounded like an echo in her ears. "Besides, I need this, too. Let me just take care of you."

Why? Why do you want to take care of me? But more importantly, who was taking care of him? She had seen that haunted look in his eye in the theater. Knew he needed this just as much as her. Slow and steady love was not a distraction.

Passion, fire, and people shouting in the streets were the kind of lovemaking that made a girl forget. Whatever misplaced sense of chivalry made him think she needed this more was wrong.

And she intended to show him.

⤎

There was something about the woman under him that made Barcus want to touch her all day. He wanted to take his time, tease her the same way she had done to him in the suite.

He wanted to show her that Artemis's Hunter could do more than destroy; he could be gentle as well.

Her moans urged him on as he licked at her clit. Two fingers worked inside her entrance, stretching and thrusting at the same pace as his tongue. His other hand splayed across her flat stomach, holding her in place to ensure she surrendered to his speed. Slow and steady. The longer he could milk this moment out of her, the better.

His mind had been about to burst on the way home from the theater, still full of Ajax's screams and the information that monsters had gone underground and that someone was hunting them.

No, not someone.

Xanthus.

He was here in the city. He had to be. The tracks were there. Barcus just needed to follow them until they eventually led him to the confrontation, when his worst nightmares would be made real.

The nails in his hair suddenly sharpened, scratching his scalp as they transformed into talons.

Before he knew it, the weight between them shifted. The legs wrapped around his waist skillfully flipped him over, maneuvering their bodies in one swift movement, so Allie was suddenly on top of him. Gravity took hold, grinding her hot sex against his erection. She grinned down at him. "You need to stop thinking."

"I'm not…"

"You are," she interrupted. "And it is distracting you. Most ladies would find it insulting. Luckily, I'm not most ladies." To emphasize the point, she reached down and gave his cock a long, sensual stroke.

Any protest died on Barcus's lips. His eyes rolled back, head falling against the mattress as all thoughts fell away to heat. A noise caught between a groan and a blissful "*yes*" escaped his lungs.

The woman on top of him preened. "That's better."

He watched as she brought one delicate talon against her lace panties, tearing the fabric easily. Barcus felt his mouth go dry. A new desire to have been the one to rip the panties overtook him, but there was no time to argue the point. Not tonight, at least. Not when Allie lifted her hips and used her hand to guide his cock towards her entrance and then—*oh sweet gods.*

They groaned in unison as she sank down.

This was what they needed. Their minds falling deeper into the dark depths of pleasure. Sweet, blessed pleasure. Barcus closed his eyes and just allowed himself to feel her heat. When he rolled his hips, she gasped, gray eyes flying open. "Oh gods, Barcus…"

Hearing her say his name in that tone broke him. An overwhelming need to hear it again propelled him into action. Barcus rolled his hips, grinding against her, faster and faster. He was mesmerized by the way her breasts bounced and how her dark hair fell across her face.

She was just as lost as he was, her head thrown back in pure ecstasy. "Fuck, more! More!"

His lady was asking for it, and he would give it to her. Barcus deployed the same trick she had used on him, leaning up to grab a hold of her and then twisting their bodies so he was once again on top. She squeaked and then moaned when he thrust into her, harder and faster than before. He thumbed her clit, teasing the aroused head of her sex with precise fingers.

She gasped with each thrust. "Mother—" The curse broke off into a delicate spasm as she came. The muscles tightened around him. Her fingers clenched the sheets under them, tearing holes into the soft fabric.

She was lost to the pleasure, and soon Barcus followed after her. His own climax sent him falling down a well that wiped his mind clean of all thoughts as he roared his completion and fell on top of her.

He didn't know how much time passed after that. Only

the sounds of their panting breaths filled the room. His body was half on Allie, half tangled in the bedsheets, but he didn't care. Not when her fingers were running so tenderly along his scalp.

Exhaustion threatened to pull him under, but he fought it until his arms wrapped around her slender waist. He kissed the nearest piece of skin, thanking her the only way he knew how.

It was inevitable that sleep would take him, but when it did, the nightmares didn't come for the first time in months.

In fact, it was the best sleep Barcus could ever remember having.

HELEN HAD EXPECTED more upon her grand arrival in DC. Trumpets blaring, clouds parting… something more than just a piece of gum stuck to her boot. After all, this was it. Her first steps on an actual quest.

But there was no fanfare when she exited the Metro at Dupont Circle. Only tall buildings and roads that stretched out in every direction. The biting cold was a shock after the too-hot Metro ride, but she welcomed it with a deep inhale. She dragged her long coat tighter around her body, pressing the short sword at her waist against her hip.

After a long morning of travel, she had finally made it. Now she just needed to find Barcus.

When Eolis had received the phone call, they'd all been shocked. It had been months since anyone had heard from him, and now it turned out he was in DC.

He was so close and hadn't bothered to call. The realization burned, but she forced herself to shake it off as she stared down Massachusetts Ave.

So close, yet she couldn't remember the last time she'd made the hike down from Annapolis. Traffic and a long train ride usually deterred her from the trip. She wasn't nearly as familiar with the city as she would have liked; the larger Metro stations and the landmarks were easy, but the address Eolis had written down wasn't familiar.

She checked the path her phone laid out and started walking. Eolis was supposed to be the one on escort duty. He'd been the one Barcus had initially called. But unfortunately for both heroes, she'd been there when Eolis had answered, and Helen had seen the opportunity for what it was.

She liked to think sniffing out adventure was a sixth sense. Barcus's disappearance and this new request seemed like just the opportunity she was looking for.

Her nerves danced in anticipation. It was always fun to meet new heroes. Men who had a thousand stories, who had seen and done things she could only dream about. Maybe this guy would need her help to appease some god. A chance for her to do something great, to prove herself and accomplish a quest that would ensure her a place in the Order.

From Dupont Circle, she followed the directions on her phone. The closer she got, the more suits crowded the sidewalk. Men and women off to work in their thousand-dollar outfits. Some were already on their phones, talking to an associate before they even set foot in their workplace. Putting on her dark sunglasses, she strolled past expensive coffee shops and banks that looked more like ancient landmarks than modern-day businesses.

Helen knew a temple when she saw one; she'd lived right above the ruins of one all her life. Even as a child touring the city with her mom, she had seen the city for what it was.

One big-ass monument to the gods.

The opulent statues and grand architecture, every piece of marble an homage to a way of life that was thought long dead.

Finally, the Atlas Hotel stood before her. It was a stunning building, twice as wide as anything else on the block and just as tall. Its dark glass walls stretched high from the ground, while a large globe sat suspended between the two towers of the hotel. She gave a low whistle of appreciation. The life of a hero was nothing less than glamorous.

Walking in felt like stumbling on a hidden oasis in the middle of winter. She admired the lush greenery inside and the sand-colored tile. Suit-clad businessmen speaking in different languages surrounded her on all sides, occasionally checking their Rolexes for the time.

It was clear from first glance she didn't belong in the hotel. But she would not let this building make her feel small. She was on a mission. A *quest*—her insides thrilled at the reminder. An errand for the actual Order of Olympus.

This was her big break.

A man at the front desk watched as she marched across the wide space, heading towards the elevators. Normally, a place like this had great security; even the elevators wouldn't work unless a person was equipped with a room key. But she had everything she needed and then some.

Before he'd left, Barcus had been her mentor. Teaching her the types of weapons heroes specialized in and the tricks taught to them by the gods. He had shown her everything the followers of Artemis had taught to him. The potions, the Hephaestion Chains, the long-lost recipe for Greek fire.

There were so many artifacts that had been blessed by the gods. Barcus hadn't had the time to explain all of them, but Helen had been more than happy to do trial and error in the time that he was away.

That was how she had found the key.

She grabbed the small handle and brought it out of her pocket. Its appearance was simple. No jewels or carved figurehead adorned the small shape, but when her fingers closed around it, she felt a sizzle of energy that could only be magic. And that magic meant no door was safe from her.

It was still unclear to her which god had blessed the item, or which hero had used it, but it certainly was helpful. At home, the key had successfully unlocked her mother's shop, a damaged padlock on an old boating shed, and on one occasion her car door when she had accidentally locked her keys inside. Now she just had to pray that it would work on the elevator.

She pressed the key against the card scanner and pushed the button. When the light turned green, a squeal of joy eeped out of her throat. *Thank you, magical key.*

The desk clerk was still watching her, waiting for any excuse to call security. She did her best not to pay him any mind. At least not until the elevator doors opened and she stepped into the large metallic space. Once inside, her lips peeled back into a victorious grin that could be seen across the hall.

Easy work for a girl who was going to be blessed by the gods. If she couldn't get past hotel security, she had no right to try to be a hero. Warm assurance pooled through her. After over a year of training, of wishing, of fighting with her mother, this was it. Her first mission.

Sure, Barcus wouldn't be thrilled to see her, but

if she played her cards right, she would be blessed before summertime.

The elevator chimed at her destination. Nothing could stop her now. *Immortality, here I come.*

⁘

"Don't forget our agreement."

"Yes. Yes." Allie waved him off with her sweater before pulling it over her head. "You catch more senators with wine than water. I promise to behave."

He flashed a lazy grin from the bed. "I don't think that's how the saying goes. Just try not to provoke him the way you did with me those first couple of nights." The warning was a joke, but she heard the distinct edge of jealousy in the undertones.

Allie grinned. "You ask too much of me, hero."

He hadn't moved yet. Instead, he seemed content with the comforts of the bed, sprawled across the pure-white sheets and watching her get dressed. They took their time getting prepared, coming up with a plan to use against Leo while the warmth of the sheets cocooned them. She could still recall the soft touch of Barcus's fingers as they ran up and down her arm. It was such a thoughtful gesture, one that had made her body tingle with pleasure. In those predawn hours, his attention had been all hers.

Now an undeniable hunger filled his gaze. One that told her he wouldn't be opposed to another round.

The idea sparked a shiver of excitement through her. She made sure to slow her movements for his enjoyment and took the time to admire him back. There was no telling when she would get another chance, and by the gods, he was handsome.

Under the cover of darkness and cloth, they'd exchanged memories that most living creatures would consider things of fiction. At first it had just been to take her mind off her sister, but as time had gone on, it had acted as a strange reminder that they both came from the same roots. Suffered from the same struggles. Believed in the same gods.

Immortal and unmortal.

Last night, none of those things had mattered.

The fact that a hero would be so gentle with a harpy… it shouldn't happen.

It *wasn't* happening. Not really.

He was using her just as she was using him. She needed to remember that, but in the meantime, they had an understanding. An agreement. There was no point in fighting each other when fucking was so much more fun, plus it helped ease the stress of everything else.

Allie shook the last of the afterglow away with the thought. It was time to remember what she was doing here in a hotel with a hero instead of at home with her sisters.

Once dressed, they stepped out of her room and headed towards his own suite. Barely a step away, Allie sensed that something was off.

Not between her and Barcus. No, the hallway wasn't right.

The doors. She could hear someone talking, but the hallway was empty. Her ears picked up two voices, their tones muffled, but one she recognized as belonging to the young hero they had captured.

Barcus felt it as well. His body tensed before he sprinted forward towards his suite. Allie jerked at the motion, caught off guard by his sudden speed. The delay cost her precious seconds before she started after him. "Hey, what—"

Barcus threw open the door to his room.

It wasn't closed. Someone was in his room.

She cursed, bursting in just as she heard Barcus shout, "No!"

A high-pitched squeak echoed behind the shout as he tackled a figure to the ground. Allie's attention zeroed in on the doorframe where Leo stood, still trapped.

The young man's face was pale as he stared at Barcus. "Don't hurt her!"

Her?

Barcus froze before pulling abruptly back. His large body completely covered the smaller one underneath. Allie could only make out slender limbs and long black hair.

A girl.

She wasn't fighting back, either. Instead, she lay completely still as Barcus tried to calm down. His voice trembled when he finally spoke. "Helen?"

"Hello to you, too." The girl actually laughed as Barcus scrambled to his feet.

When she stood, Allie was finally able to get a good look at her. Dark bangs curtained her eyes as the rest of her hair draped over her shoulders. Several glittering piercings caught the harpy's attention. Young, athletic and totally, completely *mortal.* No scent of god's blood, no coin around her neck. *So how does she know Barcus?*

"Helen." Barcus said the name the same way he used to say Allie's—in a tone of total exhaustion. "I almost—" He stopped himself short and tried again. "What are you doing here?"

"You called for backup." Helen's dark-painted lips twisted into a smug smirk. "I'm here to help."

Barcus pawed at his eyes and sighed. "I expected Eolis or Hector. Not you. Where are they?"

Helen's smile remained in place. "I left before them. Figured I could spare everyone the extra effort. All you needed was someone to escort a newbie hero, right? Should be a piece of cake."

Barcus hissed an ancient curse. "I'm going to kill them."

"You can't, remember?" the girl sang. "Now, Leo was telling me you're under a siren's spell. Is that true? Do you need help?" Excitement vibrated through the question as her eyes flickered around the room, quickly landing on Allie. "Is she a siren?"

"I'm a harpy," Allie offered, unsure what to think of this strange new arrival.

"A harpy!" Helen squealed. "That's so awesome! I've never met a harpy before. Never met any monster, really."

"Unmortal," she and Barcus corrected in unison. Their eyes met across the room, and despite all the noise and the turn of events, Barcus didn't look so tired anymore.

His attention quickly zeroed on their captive again. "*Leo*, huh?"

Leo's face paled under the scrutiny, nearly matching his hair in color. He stepped away from the doorframe, retreating deeper into the room that had once been Allie's prison. Helen wasn't at all concerned about the silent treatment; she was more than happy to fill in the gaps.

"He told me you left him for dead." She gave the prisoner another look. "If this is the kind of treatment you give your fellow heroes, maybe I don't want to be one anymore."

Allie startled at the realization. This girl wanted to be a hero? But there were no female heroes. The last had been Atalanta, but that had been before the age of the Order.

Yet Barcus acted as if her statement wasn't a surprise at all. He continued on in his line of questioning, his tone hard. "And you were going to let him out?"

"Well, not unless you told me I could. I'm not stupid. But I did lend him my ear for a bit." She leaned over and flashed an assuring grin at their captive. "See? I told you it would be alright."

Allie turned to Leo, who looked on at the whole exchange in horror.

"Helen." Barcus drew out her name with a familiar exasperation. "You can't be here. Go home."

"No way." She shook her head, allowing the morning light to glint off numerous piercings. "By the looks of this, you're investigating something pretty serious." Her eyes scanned the surrounding mess in the room, hungrily taking everything in. "This could be the big break I'm looking for. I am *so* not leaving."

Barcus turned towards her, his expression pleading for a suitable excuse. But Allie shook her head. "This is your problem, hero, not mine."

His eyes narrowed. "Next time your unmortal friends ask, I'm not denying anything."

A cackle bubbled out of her lips. "Joke's on you. Because if this all works out, you'll never be in the same room as my friends ever again."

"Wanna bet?" His head gave an innocent tilt, one that challenged her in every kind of way. "I think I'll be in the mood to see a play soon."

Her amusement died instantly. "I hate your guts."

"Oh, you two are adorable," Helen commented, looking between them like they were her new favorite show.

"No!" A shout crashed through the lighthearted

moment, along with the sound of the bedroom television hitting the ground. Leo stood over the broken pieces of metal and plastic, his chest heaving from the outburst and his face pale.

"No, you shouldn't *like* her," Leo sneered. "She's the enemy. She's a monster!" A fist slammed against the doorframe. His hateful gaze focused on Allie. "Watching the two of you makes me sick. I hope your sister screams in pain when she's offered as a sacrifice."

Allie thought she'd heard it all before, thought she could take it, but the mention of Celia brought her up short. Before anyone could make a move, Barcus was in front of her, his spear in hand. In an instant, he transformed. The storm playing across his features made him almost unrecognizable. This wasn't the man she had slept with the night before.

No. The man protecting her now was the Great Hunter, and right now, his ire was focused on Leo.

He was not a good man.

Most heroes weren't. They all committed terrible sins under the guise of righteousness and law. For so many years, he'd tried to move past those horrible memories. He'd tried to convince himself it wasn't true.

In the end, he'd had to swallow the painful truth of the world.

That a hero and a good man could not be the same person.

Nothing proved that more than the moment when he pulled his weapon on a fellow member of the Order. A rookie hero, a young man naive in the way of the world.

This was a new low.

This was something Xanthus would do.

He nearly recoiled at the thought. *"Do you really think you can give up fighting?"*

No. But he'd told Allie he would stand against his brothers if it meant doing what was needed. What was right. But his body had other plans. A paradox pulled at his muscles, half of which remembered what it had once felt like to leap into action in order to protect. The other half seized at the very idea of his spear slicing a man's neck open.

Barcus pushed the doubt aside. The careful plans he and Allie had concocted that morning were out the window. Now he needed to be the Great Hunter once again. He needed to steel himself for whatever came next.

"You will not speak to her like that," he growled. "We've given you more than enough time to decide if you want to help us or not. You will tell us where we can find Xanthus. If you refuse, I'm going to have to hurt you."

Bend, he prayed. *Don't be prideful. Just tell me what we want to know.*

But Leo did not break. Instead, his eyes turned to steel. "Do it. Show me you aren't a coward."

Coward. That was exactly what Xanthus had said to him all those years ago. No matter how much time passed, no matter where Barcus was in life, hearing it again brought him back to that temple in Turkey where they had come to blows. Where Xanthus had used the newly formed *Theres* Blade to carve a wound on his immortal body and leave him for dead.

Barcus felt something inside him break.

Maybe it was his own exhaustion at days without sleep, or the memory of Ajax's screams, or his own realization that he would need to break this rookie down if they were going to get any answers.

Protect or retreat. It was the same dilemma as always. He couldn't think past the thundering of his own heartbeat.

I can't do this anymore. It wasn't the first time those thoughts had entered his mind; it wasn't even the hundredth time. Barcus had hoped that after all these years he was strong enough to push past it, but as his anger faded, he realized there was no fight left in him.

The younger hero's eyes flashed, recognizing the weakness for what it was. "All you do is throw meaningless threats. I know you can't really hurt me." He nodded towards Barcus's hands, which held the slightest tremble.

Fuck, now even his own body was betraying him.

Barcus turned away, unable to face the younger hero. Needing to gather his thoughts. He could feel Leo's smirk of triumph and Allie's concern follow him to the window. A gray day stretched out, offering no comfort.

When a gentle hand brushed against his arm, it took every ounce of strength not to jerk away. His eyes snapped over, finding Allie. Her features were soft, free of judgment, and somehow the panic that had been crawling up his throat died down just a little bit.

"Please don't ask me if I'm okay." People always did that, and every time he struggled with the answer.

She nodded. "Let me do the rest of the talking. He won't be so smug when I'm done with him."

He looked at the woman beside him. She would do anything to get her sister back, anything to protect her people. And in that moment, that devotion was pointed at him. Yet the idea of her interrogating a young hero made his stomach roll. Not because he didn't believe she could do it; not because she didn't deserve to get answers.

If she tortured Leo, it would solidify exactly what the young hero thought of her. Any blood shed between heroes and unmortals would only breed more violence.

Before he could say anything, though, Helen's voice entered the fray. "Why are you protecting him?"

At first, Barcus thought the question was directed at him. His head snapped up, a protest poised and ready, when he saw it. Her question wasn't meant for him; it was directed at Leo.

His heart thumped against his chest at the sight of her standing so confidently in front of another hero. Argos had confided in him late one night about the shared blood between Helen and Xanthus. Such a secret was one of the reasons he'd kept his distance while on the hunt. Barcus hadn't wanted her exposed to any of Xanthus's poisonous thoughts, and he intended to keep it that way.

Without a second thought, he moved forward, but Allie's fingers tightened around his wrist, keeping him in place.

"If he tries anything, I'll be quicker than you," Allie whispered, eyes fixed on the two. "In the meantime… let her try."

Helen looked fierce as she stared Leo down. The stare was as fierce as that of her mother, who sent heroes scurrying with just a look. But ferocity wasn't enough.

Leo's attention was focused on her in return. His anger subsided just the slightest bit. "Lord Xanthus is one of the greatest heroes of all time. He took me in when I had nowhere else to go."

"That man you are protecting is not a hero. If you stand

with him, then neither are you." It was so easy for her to say those words. The truth Barcus couldn't bring himself to face for years until he'd finally stood against his friend. He watched as Helen continued on, her voice even. "He has broken the Covenant, turned on the gods, destroyed lives."

"He has his reasons." Leo's response came quick, too quick. Like a child fumbling with an excuse. His throat bobbed as he swallowed and found a gentler voice for the girl standing before him. "Helen. You said you wanted to be one of us; Xanthus can make you one. Once he becomes a god, it would be easy."

Greed flared in Helen's eyes, bright and impossible to miss. Along with it was the unmistakable glimmer of hope. Then her dark eyes narrowed, and whatever strange friendship had flourished between her and Leo died a sudden death, crushed under the heel of her boot. "I would rather take the place of Prometheus than rely on that man for help."

"Helen—"

"No." She didn't retreat. Her voice boomed with a steadiness that made men feel small. "That man you're protecting is a liar! Xanthus uses his status as a hero to gain trust and then leaves a path of destruction behind. Everyone is a means to an end to him, including you. He sent you to fight a harpy and another hero without any backup? They must know you're missing. I bet he hasn't even sent someone to look for you." Her brow arched. "Maybe they think you're dead. Do you think they'll mourn you?" Leo's face paled as he realized the truth in her words. Helen drew a sharp breath; she was not finished. "Sucks to be abandoned, doesn't it?"

"He wouldn't abandon me. I've been nothing but loyal to him."

"He abandoned the gods who gave him immortality," Helen snapped back, her voice harder than Barcus had ever heard it. And underneath that stone, he recognized the hurt she tried desperately to hide from the world. He'd always thought she was ignorant of Xanthus's real role in her life. But whether she knew the man was her father or not, it didn't matter. Xanthus had hurt more than enough people to warrant such pain.

"He abandoned all the mortals he swore to protect," Helen continued. "He abandoned his best friend. You are *nothing* to him."

"You—" Leo's teeth gnashed together. The wicked gleam in his eyes extinguished, leaving only a man shaken to the core.

Leo whirled and Allie leapt forward, her movement as fast as wind. Without a thought, she grabbed the girl and pulled. But Helen resisted, catching her hand on the doorframe and digging her feet into the carpet, accidentally breaking the seal.

Soon Barcus's brain caught up to his eyes. Leo hadn't lunged at them. He'd turned away, not to strike out but to hide his shame. His slender shoulders shook as an internal battle waged itself inside. Barcus felt pity for the youth in that moment. It hadn't taken much to break him, but Helen had known the right thing to say, the only thing that connected all the victims of Xanthus. The overwhelming sense of betrayal.

"The National Art Gallery." Leo's voice fell like water, barely able to hold form. "They're holding the ritual at the gallery tonight."

Allie didn't look convinced. "That's one of the busiest museums in the city. How does he plan to do that?"

"The museum is having a gala; other members of the Order will be there."

Other members of the new Order, of Xanthus's Order. Barcus tucked that piece of information away. He wouldn't just be facing Xanthus tonight, but other men as well.

Allie's talons flexed. "You better not be lying."

"I'm not," growled the rookie.

Allie looked ready to direct another threat his way, but Barcus touched her arm. "He's telling the truth."

She stared at him, a hundred questions lingering in her gaze. But how could he tell her what he saw in the kid's hunched shoulders and trembling voice? He wouldn't pretend to know everything Leo had endured in his years with Xanthus, but he did recognize the look in his eyes now.

He held his breath, hoping his words were enough for the harpy. Unsure if the fragile trust between them was still intact. A sigh of relief exhaled from his lungs when her talons receded.

"Tonight doesn't give us a lot of time." Her lips pinched in concern and all Barcus could do was nod.

"It's enough time to come up with a plan."

"No," Allie announced, taking him by surprise. "No, I need to go."

XIII

"GO? GO WHERE?" Barcus asked as he watched Allie pace the length of the room. So much had changed in the last few hours; he could feel the tension between them easing and tightening with each passing moment.

Allie ran her fingers through her black hair. "I have things I need to do. If the gala is tonight, that doesn't give me much time to prepare."

"Allie, we should do this together."

"No." There was a finality in the word, and she refused to meet his eyes when she uttered it. "No," she repeated again. "I have to go find Krone before tonight and let him know what's going on. And then I have to make sure Ocypete is safe. I think… I think it's best if you handle your business and I handle mine from here on out."

He could feel Allie holding back because of it. "Let me at least walk you out."

"Always such a gentleman." He could see she was

tempted by the offer until her gaze fell behind him, towards Leo. "But what about…?"

Helen laughed in response. "Don't worry about him. I'm acting bodyguard until Barcus can fix the seal."

"You?" Leo stared at her.

"Me." The single word dared him to say more.

"Let's go," Barcus sighed. He could feel an argument brewing between the two and the beginning of another headache because of it.

It was a relief when they stepped out of the room. When it was just the two of them again.

Allie turned and pinned him with her dark eyes. "Aren't you going to tell me not to get in any trouble while I'm out?"

"What's the point? You're going to do what you want, anyway." She preened, as if he'd found the right answer to an unspoken question. "But," he continued, "you should take this." He pushed a piece of paper into her hands. "Reach out to me if there's anything I can do to help."

Her brows scrunched in confusion at the note before her lips popped into a surprised but pleased "oh."

"Hero," she drawled, "this is your phone number."

"Yes."

She was grinning now, a bright, beautiful, mischievous smile. "You wrote it down? How old-fashioned of you."

He couldn't make heads or tails of her expression, but felt a jolt of pleasure when she tucked the paper into her pocket.

"Just so you know, what happened last night won't be happening again. It was a onetime thing," Allie continued.

"I… I wasn't trying to imply anything—"

She shook her head. "Sure."

"I'll be there tonight," he vowed, bringing them both

back to the moment. The real reason they were together, in this hotel. Not to exchange numbers, but to find Celia. To find Xanthus. "Our goals are intertwined. You don't have to do this by yourself."

He watched as she reined in her emotions, slipping on a cool mask of indifference. "This is unmortal business, Barcus. We can take it from here. Besides, who has ever heard of a hero helping unmortals?"

"I helped you earlier, didn't I?" he asked. "We helped each other."

Her jaw tightened, and he could see that had gotten a reaction out of her. Yet she refused to acknowledge it. "Be there if you want. It will make no difference to me."

She was pushing him away. The sting of that realization wasn't nearly as bad as the way the harpy had shredded his hope. Hope that they might be able to have each other's backs. Hope that maybe, just maybe, heroes and unmortals could finally work together.

Barcus forced himself not to reach out when Allie stepped away. He watched until she disappeared in the elevator, and then he watched some more, hoping she would step out again.

When she didn't, there was nothing left to do but to head back to his room. Inside, two pairs of curious eyes stared at him. Barcus felt his mood sour. "Yes?"

"You deserve death for fraternizing with the enemy," Leo huffed.

"I approve of her wholeheartedly," Helen beamed.

Barcus rolled his eyes up to Olympus. *I know I've done terrible things, but do I deserve this?*

⚶

Leaving Barcus behind was a necessity. It gave her more room to maneuver in the world she knew well, and their trip to Tartarus had revealed a gap in knowledge that needed to be filled.

Krone knew something and he was keeping it a secret. Not just from her, but from everyone.

He had better have a damn good reason; if not, Allie was considering giving the cat an unscheduled neutering.

Her anger carried her all the way across town to the Mount Pleasant district. She glanced down at the address Oak had texted her. The dryad had supplied the information with a skull and crossbones emoji. A not-so-subtle warning, really.

In the entirety of her time in the city, she couldn't remember anyone calling for a private meeting with Krone. To her knowledge, no one had even visited the man's house before. Doing so felt like an unspoken taboo, one of the last dangers hidden in the modern world.

Unlike heroes and mortals, unmortals did not elect a leader to lord over them. Krone's position was established based on one thing. Power. And unmortals respected power. He was one of the oldest of their kind, part of an elite group. With that status, Krone didn't have to govern. His presence alone was enough to keep unmortals in place. Most of the time he stayed out of sight, only showing himself to make sure they were all assimilating well before slinking off again. He'd been a terrible boss and made for an absent leader, but people followed him without question. People like Oak. People like Ocypete.

Bundled-up families strolled past, and dirty snow was piled high near the road, but the sidewalks were clean and well kept. It was a neighborhood well-off families and professionals liked to call home.

Krone was a man of legend among their kind, the last descendant of the great Nemean lion who Herakles had hunted. But this was the last place she would have expected to find him.

Apartments slowly blended into single-family townhomes until a familiar set of numbers lined a historic brick townhome. Allie looked down at her phone, then back up to the house, and back down to the address again.

The house was Krone's, despite the overwhelming normalcy dripping from its iron-tipped fences. But she knew better than most that appearances were always deceiving.

When she knocked, no one came to answer.

A subzero breeze pushed against her body, urging her to turn around and go back to her warm home and the one sister who still waited for her.

It was tempting, but Allie remained planted on the doorstep.

She had come to talk to Krone and she intended to do just that. He had a job working as a security expert for high-paying mortals and government officials, in addition to owning Tartarus. Sometimes that job kept him out late.

An hour passed. And then another. She sat on the steps to the doorway, staring at her phone as she watched the time tick by.

Dimly, her mind wandered back to Barcus. Their last conversation had not been ideal, but it had been necessary. The more time she spent with the hero, the deeper he burrowed under her skin. She was getting too close, trusting him more than was healthy. Now that she knew where Celia was, there was no reason for their partnership. Not anymore.

But when she closed her eyes, all she could see was that haunted expression he'd carried after talking to Leo. Allie played back the conversation in her mind. One second Barcus was in full control, acting every bit like the fearless Hunter stories had described him as. And the next…

He was touching her. Looking at her as if she was the only bright spot in the world. She didn't hate the way he looked at her. He'd been there for her last night when her emotions had burned through each other like an inferno. Frustration, anger, and then… lust. Barcus had taken it all in stride, meeting her in the middle and giving her the best godsdamn sex she'd had in centuries.

Mother's maw, she'd slept with a hero. And she'd liked it.

"What are you doing here?" The gruff question knocked her back into the present. She looked up to find Krone hovering outside his iron gate, his features shadowed by his long, dark locks. One hand rested in the pocket of his coat while the other held a bag of Chinese takeout. The smell of cigarettes and coffee encased his clothing, a lingering residue from wherever it was he'd been.

Allie brushed aside her lust-filled confusion and rose to meet his annoyance with her own. "Waiting for you to get home. Where have you been?" She stood as he stalked up the walk, moving out of the way before he could step on her to get to the door. She'd seen him do more for less.

His large shoulders shrugged. "Work. It's something most people do."

"Most mortals, you mean."

"Unmortals need it just as much as humans. Psychology

has proven that getting up every day with purpose is good for a person's psyche."

Her feathers ruffled against the comment. She knew he was right and it chafed against her pride. Knew Celia had found joy and confidence with her business the same way Ocypete enjoyed putting her knowledge to good use and upstaging human historians.

And what did Allie have?

A comfortable couch. A giant flat-screen television and the occasional sister's night. But it wasn't *enough*. The itch to do something had been gnawing at her for months now. A nine-to-five job wouldn't fill that hole inside of her. She'd wanted to rediscover *herself*. But that was before Celia had gone missing.

"I need to talk to you."

"About what?" The door opened and he was already pushing through. She only had one chance to snag his attention before the door slammed in her face.

Allie steeled herself for what might come next and said, "Unmortals are missing."

Krone stopped midstep. One breath passed before he jerked the key out of the door. A harsh crack echoed in the courtyard. "This should probably be handled in private."

She bit the inside of her cheek at his lack of denial and what it meant. "I agree."

"Then come inside." He pushed the door open farther. By all appearances, it was a friendly invitation into the lion's den. But she wasn't stupid.

"Only if you promise not to kill me, no matter what I might say."

Krone's brows rose at the demand, but it was a necessary precaution. Danger oozed off the unmortal like a miasma. It had been centuries since she'd laid eyes on his true form, but the memory of it remained etched into her core. The Nemean lion of old was truly a monster in sheep's clothing. It would be foolish to let a few centuries make her forget that.

"Fine, fine," came a growl of annoyance. "I promise not to kill you." He moved forward, leaving the door open in his wake and switching on the lights. Instantly, the house looked more accommodating, and Allie followed. As she passed the threshold, the metal of the door handle caught her eye. A jagged crack split the steel down the middle.

"I'm going to eat while you talk," Krone called back as he disappeared towards a kitchen area. "You can wait in the sitting room."

She looked to the alcove on her left. There was nothing shiny or new in the apartment that she could see, no sign of the riches that Krone must have stashed away. The furniture looked decades old, as if Krone had put in the effort to decorate once but couldn't be bothered to update the design. She assessed her sitting options between a vintage leather sofa that might have been from the seventies and an armchair covered in flowery fabric.

The only ornate thing in the room was a beautiful oak sculpture that outlined the fireplace. Three lions, all male and roaring their approval as they crawled along the wood. Almost appearing as if they were coming out of the wall itself.

Allie stared at the piece as if it were a gemstone. She allowed her fingers to dance inside one lion's mouth, feeling the sharp canines that had been cut into the wood.

"They aren't missing," Krone's gruff voice said, suddenly too close.

Allie jerked away from the fireplace and found the lion getting comfortable in the flower-patterned armchair, a pair of wooden chopsticks in one hand and a takeout box in another.

She hadn't even heard him move into the room. A man of Krone's size usually carried some weight when he walked, but his lion stealth clearly carried over to human form.

It took a moment for her to recover enough to ask, "What do you mean they aren't missing? Oak said a siren disappeared just last week."

A long piece of lo mein muffled his answer. "They aren't missing. I know exactly where they are."

There was no concern in his voice. Not even an ounce of worry. Her body fell onto the firm leather sofa as she considered what he meant. "Where are they, then?"

Krone lifted a brow as he chewed slowly. She waited, fingers drumming against the couch's arm as he swallowed his food and continued, "Why do you care?"

Allie straightened, feeling the sting of the words as if he had sunk his teeth into her. "Because they are our friends, Krone. They are our family. If something is going on, everyone else should know about it."

"And like I said, nothing is going on," Krone continued, dangling noodles above his mouth. He swallowed the soy sauce–drenched strings with a lick of his lips. "Let me ask you a question. Why do you think our numbers keep decreasing? Even with three centuries of peace, the lounge feels more and more empty every time I go down there."

They were losing numbers? For years, she'd believed it was just her imagination that their numbers seemed smaller. She'd chalked it up to the daily monotony of living amongst the mortals. People got busy, fell out of touch. Now all that felt so naive. "What aren't you telling me?"

"It's not me who isn't telling you. You would rather stay at home than face our reality. It's too hard to keep up the disguise. Too constricting not to run free. A satyr came to me just last month asking to leave. And before that it was a family of centaurs. No one has to ask my permission to leave, and I won't tell anyone they have to stay." His hazel eyes met hers as he put the empty Chinese food box down on the table. "Unmortals are growing tired of this world. They are returning to the underground."

She frowned at the news. "Why would they do that?"

"A number of reasons," Krone sighed, lifting his large hand to list them off. "They can be themselves down there, live amongst our own kind, embrace our more primitive nature." He wiggled his brows suggestively. "I heard the furies were offering jobs to those who wanted to torture souls. Doesn't sound like a terrible gig."

"I can think of a million reasons why the underworld is horrible," Allie snapped back. "There's no light, no fresh air, no comfort. You're surrounded by dead people. Gods, they don't even have the internet."

"I heard they were working on getting it," Krone said. "Besides, there are plenty of reputable creatures who live down there. Clearly it isn't all bad."

He's not concerned, she realized, horror squeezing her rib cage. *Which makes it all the easier for the heroes to hunt us down.*

"No, you're wrong." She felt her hands grip the couch, talons digging into the soft leather. There was only so much she could take of this nonsense, and he needed to know it. Krone lifted a dark brow, a look that could be either a warning or an encouragement to continue on. Allie did her best to swallow all anger and appear calm. "Celia is missing.

Has been since last Friday. She wouldn't just leave without telling me or Ocypete."

A muscle twitched in his jaw—the first crack in his mask of emotions. He hadn't been tracking that news. She plowed on, unwilling to lose the momentum or the upper hand. "Something is going on, Krone. Celia wouldn't just leave without telling me and Pete. Then there's the siren who disappeared from the play."

"Who told you about that?"

"That doesn't matter. Krone, the heroes are behind this. At least, some of them are. And I have it on good authority that they're planning something for tonight. We need to—"

He held up a hand, cutting her off midsentence. "Don't be ridiculous. The heroes wouldn't dare try to pull something like that off. To do so would mean war again. And even if they did"—he leveled a dark glower at her—"I would know."

A ball of ice dropped in her gut. He didn't know—worse than that, he thought this was a joke. "I'm telling you right now, something is happening."

Krone's large shoulders lifted in a shrug. "I'll look into Celia tomorrow if it will make you feel better."

"What? No, tomorrow will be too late. Krone, please just trust me."

"Trust you?" he barked. "I couldn't even trust you to manage a bar for eight hours without sneaking off."

"This is different," Allie pressed. "This is about my sister, about protecting our kind."

He shook his head. "Can't help you. I have an important client paying me for security tonight. The best I can do is look into things tomorrow."

She couldn't believe what she was hearing. He was

using his mortal job as an excuse not to help. Everything he said might have been true about the old Allie, about her being lost, listless... lazy. But something within her cracked upon Krone's refusal. For so long she'd been unable to think of what would fill the hole inside of her; now she knew what to do.

Krone had forgotten his duty, so she would do it.

Protect her sister. Protect all the unmortals. At any cost.

Krone leaned back in his chair with the careless attitude of a house cat. "Now, is there anything else I can help you with?"

"No." Such a simple response, and she managed it with the cool detachment.

"Good." Krone waved her off as he grabbed for another white cardboard takeout box. "Now get the fuck out of my house."

XIV

"YOU LOOK AMAZING."

Allie turned, surprised to see Ocypete leaning against her bedroom doorway. "You don't think it's too much?" She motioned at the pale-lavender dress draped across her body and the necklace she'd been fiddling with.

Ocypete's eyes drifted up and down with a critical eye. "I would probably lose the bracelet."

Allie hesitated. The elegant gold cuff on her wrist caught just the right amount of light, and it was one of the few items she still had from the Romans.

Ocypete rolled her eyes, stepping carefully into the room. "You're lucky one of us has fashion sense."

"Do you still?" Allie teased, earning a glare of warning. Ocypete had been able to predict fashion trends a decade away. Now it was a miracle if she got dressed to sit in front of her computer. But as her sister neared the mirror, she raised her hand and plucked an amethyst ring from her finger. "Here, put this on instead."

Saying no to a new gem was not something Allie had ever done. She took the offering with a quiet "thanks."

Something eased in her as the ring slipped on her finger. It would be the closest thing to having her sister with her tonight, whether Ocypete knew it or not.

"Where are you going that has you dressed up so nice?"

"There's a gala at an art museum. Figured I'd go upstage some fancy art collector on what's what."

They both laughed at that. Ocypete's hands absently soothed her black curls, helping them fall just right along her shoulders. "Well, you'll upstage everyone in that gown. I hope you have fun."

Temptation burned in her throat, along with the truth regarding the night's plan. For the hundredth time, she considered telling her sister everything. It would be easier if Pete was there beside her, fighting together like they used to do. But when she opened her mouth, the truth didn't come out, only a vague invitation. "You can come with me if you want."

Ocypete was already shaking her head before the question even finished. "My deadline is in two days, and besides, I don't have a dress."

Lies. She had dresses, ones that people would kill for. But if Pete was going to pretend that she didn't have anything to wear, then Allie was going to pretend like she didn't need any help.

"Why don't you wear this as well?"

Her sister picked up a gold chain from the dresser. Barcus's coin sparkled in greeting. Without a hero's neck to hang on, it seemed Ocypete didn't recognize what the item really was.

She wouldn't be caught dead wearing that thing. The

very idea felt intimate, as if it would allow Barcus to lay claim to her. Besides, the enemy would pick her out in a second. "It's a little too simple, don't you think?"

"Simple is sometimes better." Her sister shrugged, putting the coin down and heading for the door. "Just let me know if you're going to be late again tonight. I'll be up, anyway."

"Alright," she hollered back, checking the dress over once again. There would be no flying tonight, and if things came to a fight, well, she was realistic about what would happen to the dress. Still, trading a dress for her sister would be more than worth it.

Satisfied, she grabbed her clutch and put in a request for an Uber. Before stepping out, she grabbed the coin off the dresser and shoved it into her clutch. She had every intention of returning it to Barcus if she saw him tonight.

When, her mind supplied helpfully. *You will see him again, but this is the last time.*

⟩

Barcus stared at the grand building in front of him. The lights outside brightened up the exterior of the museum, engulfing it in a heavenly glow. Women and men strolled in, wearing black ties and shimmering dresses.

This wasn't just a gathering for heroes; this was a gathering of the city elite.

He'd bet his spear that the majority of the people walking in had no tie to the ancient world. It was risky for Xanthus to hold any kind of meeting here. But he doubted the other man cared. One did not become a hero without taking risks.

His hands smoothed over his own newly bought suit.

He'd spent plenty of time in the company of kings and queens, but he'd never tried to be one of them before.

"You look great," Helen encouraged from the driver's seat. "But if you don't stop fidgeting, I'm going to take that suit and walk in there myself."

"If you do, the deal is off," he growled, giving her a look of warning. She had outright refused to return to Maryland with Leo now that she knew Xanthus was nearby, and Barcus hadn't been able to convince her otherwise.

Xanthus was a cloud hanging over her head as much as Barcus's, but he refused to let her get involved any further. Tonight, she would be acting as his getaway driver once things were finished. He just prayed she stayed in the car and out of trouble while he was gone.

"Remember, stay here and keep guard. If you see any other heroes…"

"We'll text you," Helen said, her fingers already fiddling with the radio on the dashboard.

In the back seat, Leo rested his head in the palms of his bound hands. "I was supposed to be in there."

"Sorry, kid, don't trust you that much." The young hero had been an ideal captive, quiet with minimal fighting. Helen made a fine warden for their prisoner, but if she decided to act tonight, she would no doubt drag Leo along for the ride.

"Do. Not. Follow. Me. In," Barcus repeated for good measure. "If I'm not back by morning, you two are to go get the others. They'll know what to do."

"You shouldn't go in there alone," Helen pointed out.

It was an echo of his words to Allie earlier. A barely concealed plea for him not to do anything stupid. And though he'd ached when Allie had refused his assistance, he now understood why she had done what she had.

Xanthus was his problem, his responsibility. He would face the other man alone and dole out the punishment he deserved.

He didn't need anyone else's help. Not Eolis or Hector, not Helen or Leo. Xanthus would have men with him, but Barcus could handle that. He had to be able to handle it. There was a reason he was the leader of the Western Order.

"Just trust me." His grip tightened around an overly large umbrella sheath. His sports bag and spear wouldn't do for this event. Tonight, the *Theres* Blade needed to accompany him amongst the mortals. He'd had the sheath specially made to conceal it, blessed by a patron of Hephaestus. The sword should make it through security undetected. But the disguise did give the appearance of the oddly shaped umbrella.

Barcus marched towards the building, a storm of emotions brewing inside him. He kept his focus on the task at hand. *One foot in front of the other, find Xanthus, and—*

He stuttered to a halt.

A woman was ascending the stairs, her lavender dress almost transparent against the bright lights, amplifying the dark silhouette of her curves. Curves he knew all too well. He recognized Allie by the way she walked, with a confidence no woman could gain in an ordinary lifetime.

Other men were looking at her, too, their wives grim-faced with envy. To the men without dates, she was an easy target. One was already at her elbow before she even reached the door.

Jealousy surged through him at the sight. That mortal

didn't know her. Didn't have the right to even look at her. Barcus picked up his pace, taking the stairs two at a time.

He slid silently against Allie's side and touched her arm, startling her out of the conversation. When their eyes locked, there was relief in hers, but only for a second before those elegantly dark brows rose in a question.

"Darling, I told you to wait for me," he said.

Allie answered with a dazzling smile, returning to their invented relationship with ease. "Sorry, honey, I was just so excited." She turned to the man who'd been talking her up and tilted her head. "As you can see, I already have an escort, but thank you for the offer."

She took Barcus's hand, allowing him to escort her up the remaining steps. He was surprised that she had chosen to go with him rather than blow them both off, but a ball of warmth settled in his gut at how easily they fell into the charade of a fake relationship.

"Were you waiting for me?" he asked as they strolled up the steps.

"Not at all. I was scoping out the area."

"See anything?"

She nodded to a group of men ahead of them who stood off to the side, laughing and smoking. "The man on the right is one of your brothers."

"Really?" Barcus had to force himself not to stare, but a quick glance confirmed his fears. "I've never seen him before."

Allie nodded. "His coin was attached to his cuff link."

A spot unnoticeable to Barcus or other humans, but to a harpy whose eye tracked shiny objects, it was nothing. He took the opportunity to stroke his thumb down the side of her hand. "Does he know what you are?"

"I don't think so. He has a particularly stupid look on his face."

Barcus bit back a smile. "Good."

Silence followed his assurance, but he could feel her eyes on him. Staring at him. He wished he could do the same, just to drink in the sight of her in that dress, but he kept his eyes set ahead on the line forming at the entrance. "I thought you would be here with Krone."

Allie's grip stiffened on his arm, her fingers digging into the soft fabric of the tuxedo. "He didn't believe me."

Barcus bit back a curse. "I'm sorry."

"It doesn't matter. I don't need him."

"Ah, so you still plan to go in there alone?"

A pause followed the question, and Barcus half expected her to step away, to distance herself once again. Instead, she redirected the conversation. "Are you going to be able to fight without a weapon?"

"I have my weapon right here," he said, holding up the umbrella.

Her painted lips pursed in an unamused line. "*That* is the worst disguise I've ever seen."

"What? No, it isn't. This was specially made by a hero who apprenticed under Hephaestus. It will work."

"If that thing works, mortals are bigger idiots than I thought."

They approached the doorman, and Allie took out a ticket from her clutch.

Barcus froze. *Shit, tickets*. He hadn't thought about tickets. The man waved her through before casting an expectant look at Barcus.

His hands dug deep into the pocket of his suit as if

looking for the imaginary ticket. "Sorry, hon, I think I left my ticket at home."

He waited, expecting a snarky comeback before Allie disappeared into the throng of people and music that waited inside. She wouldn't think twice about leaving him behind again. Not when she was so close to finding her sister.

Yet the harpy didn't move. Her gray eyes rolled to the ceiling in exaggerated annoyance. "I swear you would lose your balls if they weren't attached."

The doorman balked at the statement as she reached into her clutch and took out a second ticket. "Here, now can he come through?"

"Of course. Enjoy the gala," the doorman stuttered, stepping to the side to allow access.

"What just happened?" Barcus whispered as they walked past security.

Allie nodded to his umbrella. "Humans are idiots."

Laughter and music greeted them upon entrance, the sounds echoing just out of reach. He could see partygoers crowded in the main atrium under the golden light of a massive chandelier.

"You didn't have to help me."

"I know that, hero. I had an extra ticket in case Ocypete wanted to come. It's no big deal."

It was all too easy for them to fall into the same rhythm they had before. After the night they had shared together, he had been afraid things wouldn't be the same between them. And then she'd left and he'd prepared himself to take on the task of fighting Xanthus alone.

She would never know how much it meant to be by her side tonight.

Before they fully entered the crowd, Barcus pulled

them into a nearby alcove filled with portraits of museum founders. Partygoers walked past it, not sparing it a second glance—not when there was champagne and company a few steps ahead.

"What are you doing?" The question came out barely above a whisper. As if her tongue didn't dare risk attracting anyone's attention.

"I just wanted a moment alone before we get in there." Before either everything went to shit or they accomplished what they had come to do. Either way, this could be his last chance to speak with Allie alone. He pressed close to her side, testing to see what she would do. When she didn't jump away, he whispered, "You look beautiful tonight."

His fingers brushed against the straps of her gown, where he picked off a single black feather before letting it drop to the floor.

"I can clean up when I need to. You don't look half bad yourself, except…"

"Except?"

She slipped something into his palm. "You're missing something."

He felt the familiar tingle of power before her hand pulled back, revealing his gold coin.

Barcus sucked in a breath. "I honestly didn't think you would return it."

"Why? Cause harpies like shiny things?" There was no bite to the words, only a sigh of resignation. "I don't need any extra attention to come my way tonight."

His fingers closed around the necklace, feeling the metal warm at the contact. His nerves quieted at the sensation, and for more reasons than one, he whispered, "Thank you, Allie."

"Don't mention it." She held up a finger, cutting off the next words out of his mouth. "Seriously. If word got out that I gave that back, others might ask for the same thing."

Barcus couldn't help but laugh. "Other men gave you jewels?"

Her eyes flashed. "Oh, honey, you don't even know."

There it was again—a flash of something between them.

His thumb stroked over an enlarged jewel on her ring finger, and he saw her body shiver in response. Interesting.

"Shall we?" she asked, her mask of cool indifference firmly in place. Without waiting for a response, she took his arm and together they stepped into the rotunda. As the gallery's main entrance, it was a grand room, with a domed ceiling that reached well above their heads. Black columns circled around them. Their dark onyx stone stood out against the gold-painted walls. Men in black ties and women in richly colored dresses chatted as waiters moved about the floor with champagne flutes and plates of hors d'oeuvres.

Barcus felt his muscles tighten up. Hidden among the sea of bodies was the enemy. They all blended together, making it impossible to tell which was which.

It hit him then that for the first time in centuries, he was in the same building as Xanthus. It had been so long since he'd last seen the other man. And now he could be any one of the black tuxedos surrounding him.

The room around him tilted, his shoulder bumping hard against Allie. Her hand steadied him as her voice cut through the nonsense of his frantic thoughts. "Barcus, breathe. Focus on something else."

"Like what?"

Allie hummed thoughtfully next to him, the heat of

her body pressing closer. "You could tell me how your little captive is doing?"

"Leo is doing well. Still pissed about me…er, grounding him."

Allie laughed at that. "Then we have that in common."

"It seems you have more in common with heroes than you originally thought."

"It seems that way."

"Keep talking," he urged, feeling the numbness dissipate. Air was coming back to his lungs easier now, his panic ebbing away. "It's helping."

"Alright, what else to talk about… maybe you should tell me how much you've been craving my body ever since last night."

His cock throbbed at the suggestion. She was just teasing him, of course, but if only she knew the truth in those words. Seeing her again tonight made it difficult to think of anything else, but as the memories came back, he found they pushed away the suffocating fear.

"Or maybe…" Her lush voice drawled on as she pretended to contemplate a new topic, but then her feet came to an abrupt halt. A small gasp escaped her throat. "Maybe we should talk about that?"

In the center of the room sat a large fountain, and on top of it was a bronze statue of Hermes himself. Wielding winged shoes and donning a helmet of rusty metal, the god looked to be in mid-flight to deliver an important message, or more likely, off to cause trouble.

Still, the sight of the Olympian messenger could only mean one thing.

"I think we're in the right place," Barcus said.

Allie nodded, her eyes fixed on the statue. "Small wings for a god. Bet other parts are small as well."

Barcus choked back a laugh. "That's blasphemy. I'm sure Hermes won't stand to have his manhood insulted."

"Please, the gods haven't been seen in decades. I doubt they're listening now. Besides, if they did decide to grace us with their presence, they might as well do us a favor and smite Xanthus." Allie looked to the domed ceiling as she waited one breath, then another.

Barcus held the air in his lungs as he waited as well, watching as a slow grin crawled across her mouth. "There. Nothing. The gods have completely and utterly abandoned us. We must make our own way tonight."

She wasn't wrong. He'd known for years that the power of the gods was waning in the modern era. Once, the entire world wouldn't dare act without the blessing of Zeus or his brood; now only a select few followers believed the old gods existed. Argos had managed to summon Poseidon in his time of need, but these days, the great god of the sea was preoccupied with the dangers of pollution and changing sea levels.

Even Barcus struggled to recall the last time he had spoken to Artemis. For her, the rules of the hunt had changed too much. Forests decreased in size, and men paid for the thrill and used weapons that required no skill. It disgusted the goddess, but where she might have once punished those who were ignorant about her ways, there were now thousands of mortals defiling the forests. One day Artemis had just stopped fighting back and disappeared into the woods.

It was strange to think that after ruling the world for so many years, the gods could simply vanish without any fuss. Many years ago, not a day had gone by when he hadn't given Artemis an offering or joined her on a hunt. She'd helped him at his lowest point when he'd nearly given up on life. Maybe it had been foolish, but he had thought of her as a friend.

"It looks like the gala is about to start," Allie observed, bringing Barcus out of his thoughts.

He looked around and noticed the crowd had thinned significantly. The group was making their way down the west wing, where signs helpfully guided guests to the garden courtyard.

Allie moved to follow, but he held her back. "If the gala is in the western corridor, I doubt Xanthus will be there. He would want to be as far from mortals as possible."

They both turned to the only other option the circular room offered—the eastern hallway, blocked off by a large velvet curtain with no one standing guard. A sliver cut in the middle of the curtain showed a stark white hallway. As they stared, a shadow passed by, causing the curtains to flutter.

Barcus felt his nerves electrify at the sight. "That's where we need to go."

He sucked in a deep breath, forcing himself to count to ten. As he exhaled, his anxiety leveled. Its presence still made the blood pound between his ears, but it was… manageable.

The rotunda was nearly empty, yet Allie stayed by his side. "I'll go by myself if you'd like. You don't have to do anything more."

"No." His fingers curled around the umbrella sword. She didn't have a clue what kind of monster they were up against.

Xanthus would see just another harpy, a creature to kill without hesitation.

But to Barcus, she was so much more than that.

"I'm ready."

"Good," Allie said. "As much as it pains me to say this, I think I could really use your help."

XV

THEY MOVED DOWN the eastern hall, past sculptures of Roman figures and Grecian goddesses that lined the pearl-white walls. The statues looked classical enough, but they reeked of new stone.

Another black curtain blocked the next galley. Barcus signaled for them to pause as he peeked through the fabric. Allie stretched out her senses, trying to pick up anything that would lead her to Celia.

She heard the rumble of the party down the west corridor, the clinks of champagne glasses and the high-pitched laughter and chitchat. Behind it all, she heard a dull undercurrent of music that didn't match.

"All clear," Barcus said, pulling the curtain back. "Quickly, before someone spots us."

They ducked into the next room. Another fountain sat in the middle; two bronze cherubs stood on top, frozen mid-play. The fresh smell of flowers assaulted her nose as she looked upon the man-made garden. There were no other pieces of art. No sign of rogue heroes. Scanning between the greenery, she found three doorways on each side of the room.

"Where to now?" Barcus asked.

Allie closed her eyes, focusing on the noises she had heard earlier. It wasn't all from the gala, she realized. The steady beat, now recognizable as drums, came from somewhere else entirely. "Below," she said. "They're below us."

She made her way across the room and pushed hard against the easternmost door, opening it with a slam that echoed across the stairway. Barcus made a face but followed silently. Together, they descended to the ground floor two stairs at a time.

The noise from the gala drifted behind them as the drums became louder. With each step, her adrenaline spiked to match the fast tempo. They walked down a long hall lined with marble busts older than anything on display upstairs. Some were figures they knew well. Pan's leering grin gave nothing away of the danger that lurked ahead. A sign pointing them in the direction of the next hall read, "Garden café." But another dark curtain hid the threat that lay beyond it.

Allie's hand was already grasping the thick cloth when Barcus caught it. "We need to be smart about this before we act."

Her face pinched in disagreement. "If they're hurting my sister, you won't be able to stop me from killing them."

"Maybe not," Barcus said, peeling it back enough so they could peek out. Behind it lay a courtyard full of warriors, at least twenty total, all wearing pristine tuxedos with weapons dangling from their hips. He visibly flinched at the sight. "Gods…"

"There are so many." Fear coated her throat, threatening

to come out in a childish squawk, but she fought it down. Her eyes scanned the area, noting where every man stood and what he held as a weapon.

There were too many for her to take on alone. These men were immortal, after all. She could stun one or two, but it would be impossible to take them out before the others were on her.

Then she saw them. Five bodies lay on the ground, tied up and struggling—a familiar blonde head of hair among them. The air in the room suddenly grew too hot as Allie gasped, "Celia."

Dread seeped into her stomach as she did the math. Five unmortals, twenty rogue heroes, and only she and Barcus stood against them.

Even for an immortal, those odds weren't good.

⁂

They were horribly outnumbered. Leo had said there were other members of the new Order, but Barcus had never believed there would be so many. Every lead he'd followed on Xanthus had mentioned five or six men. This, however… this was too much.

Barcus struggled to think of the last time the odds had been so grim. A hundred battles came to mind. Each one had been its own struggle, but he'd had his brothers by his side. And that had made all the difference.

Maybe he should have waited for Eolis and Hector. Even just two more heroes would have made a world of difference. But he'd focused on Xanthus, on his own need for redemption. He'd imagined this fight would come down to just the two of them, and that had been a dire miscalculation.

"Barcus." Allie's voice cut through his panic, bringing him back to the task at hand. He blinked away those swirling thoughts to find her staring at him with concern. Her hand braced against his forearm to steady him. "Barcus," she repeated, "can you do this?"

"I honestly don't know." The words were out before he could think better of them. Heroes didn't voice their doubt, but looking at the sea of heroes, men who were trained in the same skills as he was—well, it was better to be honest.

"I know." Her eyes flickered back to the group before returning to his face. "Don't worry. You don't have to face them alone."

He studied the creatures tied up on the floor. One was clearly Allie's sister from her white wings and birdlike talons. Next to her lay four other squirming unmortals. Barcus spotted two satyrs and an unmoving hippocampus. The last was the missing siren; the gag around her mouth gave her identity away. Without it, her siren's song would have made the surrounding men crumple to their knees.

Barcus sucked in a breath, realizing he recognized the face attached to the siren's body. "Allie…"

"What?" she whispered back at him.

"That siren…"

Allie took a moment to study the unmortal's face before nodding. "Yeah, that's Seraphina."

Seraphina. She looked exactly like the drawing he had seen in Erik's notebook. He'd thought the old sketch had been of his wife, but there was no mistaking it now. "Shit," he hissed, feeling a new sense of shame crash against his focus. "Shit, I've had it all wrong."

"What?"

"The claw marks in Erik's room weren't from his

attacker. They were from *her*. They must have kidnapped her, too, and Erik was trying to save her."

Allie jerked, her hand nearly tearing the curtain down. "Are you saying *they* tore that hero to shreds?"

The memory of those photos threatened to tunnel his vision, but he pushed it down. There was no way to do that to another immortal. Not without the right weapon.

He felt Allie huddle closer to him. Felt the fear prickling her skin. The need to reach out to her tingled along his fingers. But that would only make her feel weak, and he didn't want that.

"We need to wait for an opportunity to grab your sister and the other unmortals, then get out. If possible, we won't engage." This was a fight they wouldn't win.

"What does an opportunity like that look like?" she asked.

He honestly didn't know. Sometimes instinct just told you. "We'll know it when we see it."

She nodded, standing still beside him. Trusting him. He felt the inner voices quiet as he stared at the woman by his side. In her eyes, he saw the same fear and anxiety reflected back. Usually he was alone in his fear, but tonight they were in this together. Allie was relying on him, trusting him. There was comfort in that.

"Welcome, everyone, to a very special event!"

A new voice cut through the crowd, and ice pierced his heart. Barcus knew it well—to this day, he woke up in a sweat from nightmares of that voice taunting him.

He didn't dare move, but Allie did. Still crouched low, she pulled the curtain back a little farther. "Is that him?"

He tried to turn, but the movement felt wooden. He had known this would happen when he'd taken on the mission. Had known he would eventually come face-to-face with the past, and still he had agreed to find the lost hero.

Xanthus.

The man stood out from the group gathered around him. Experience hung over his body like a well-worn cloak. He had discarded his dark suit jacket from the gala and rolled up the sleeves of his white button-down, showing off powerful forearms.

His hair had grown longer, hanging over his shoulders in dark locks. There was no weapon that Barcus could see, but Xanthus didn't need one, not with his army acting as circling sharks.

Barcus felt the sword in his hand grow hot. He gritted his teeth and gripped the handle harder, using the pain to sharpen his focus.

The chatter cut off abruptly as the men turned to their leader. A sharp smile fixed itself on Xanthus's face. He didn't care that there was a mortal gathering happening above them. Didn't seem at all bothered by the noises of their captives wiggling on the ground next to his feet.

"Tonight, we will achieve our long-awaited goal." He waved a hand down to the unmortals and his voice held an air of triumph as he announced, "Soon you will witness the birth of a new god."

"What is he talking about?" Allie hissed, but Barcus barely heard her over the cheers that statement evoked.

He'd seen this before.

Again. It was happening again. This was the ritual Leo had warned them about.

Phobos's claws dug into his chest, burrowing into his lungs and holding the air there as realization dawned.

How had he not realized it sooner?

Xanthus moved through the group, letting his fingers skim over the greenery before settling his hand on one of the nearby columns. He sucked in a deep breath, one that shuddered on release. "Ah, yes. The stones in his building are ready as well. Ready for a sacrifice they haven't seen in a millennium."

One of the heroes stepped forward. The gold coin around his neck appeared blood red under the fire's light. A sharpened sword in hand, the blade's curved steel perfectly sculpted to hack off a creature's head.

The grin that cut across Xanthus's face as he took the blade was full of teeth. "This blade has spilled the blood of hundreds of unmortals. Tonight it will kill its thousandth, transforming it into a fully divine weapon. One that will make even the gods quake in fear."

A roar of approval filled the chamber. Men banged their swords against the tile in a clang that sang of war and death.

Barcus felt his stomach heave at the announcement. A blade that had killed nearly a thousand unmortals? That was double the amount it had taken to make the *Theres* Blade. It might not be divine, but the *Theres* Blade could do any number of amazing feats—kill an unmortal, end the immortality of heroes, even injure a demigod. But it could not kill a god.

This new weapon would be different, though—more powerful. More dangerous.

Xanthus took the sword and walked over to the hippocampus. Outside of water, the creature was like a discarded doll. The usually glistening skin of the water horse looked dry to the touch. Its fishlike tail flapped uselessly. A crazed look flickered in its eyes when it saw the sword.

"Barcus?" Allie touched his shoulder, but he didn't

respond. His eyes were trained on the weapon, mouth painfully dry.

Again.

Without hesitation, Xanthus lifted the horse's head and said, "Number nine hundred and ninety-six."

And then he slit its throat.

After years on the battlefield, Barcus knew that blood did not gush from a throat wound. Not the way movies would have one think. Instead, it ran down the neck the same way water leaked from cracks in the wall. Pooling slowly but still able to cover the bare skin within seconds.

It was an awful way to die. They could hear the noise of the hippocampus choking on its own blood from their hiding place.

Barcus closed his eyes and sent a silent prayer to the gods for the creature.

Beside him, Allie's entire body trembled in rage. "He—he killed her."

They both knew what that meant for her sister. Barcus's eyes snapped open, his hand reaching to steady the harpy's rage.

But it was too late.

She let out an unholy shriek that ricocheted off the walls. Barcus felt the noise cut through his ears like a blade, but so did the other heroes, who doubled over in surprise. Only Xanthus stood unfazed. His attention fixed on his next victim.

Feathers burst from her arms in an explosion of fury. Allie took to the air and sped towards the small army. The men drew their swords at the sight of her, ready to impale.

Barcus shouted in warning, but at the last minute, Allie veered to the side, her talons hooking into one of the men's shoulders. He screamed as she flung him across the room. His body hit the stone wall with a force that would have left a mortal man with broken ribs, but the hero scrambled to his feet a second later, eyes bright with anger.

There wasn't enough room for Allie to soar upward, but she proved that flying wasn't her only deadly skill. Even on the ground, she was a force, moving as fast as the wind. Her talons carved into any man who got between her and her sister.

Their cover blown, Barcus charged into the fray. He didn't need his mind to do the work of a warrior; the body knew exactly what needed to be done.

Swing, duck, tackle, stab. There was no time to take in the faces of his opponents; best to think of them as strangers rather than men who were part of the Order. When the *Theres* Blade struck, its victim did not get up. It was impossible to tell screams of pain from the screams of battle. The noise pounded behind his eyes, making him see double for a second. But his body kept moving, striking down those that got between him and Xanthus.

Then Allie shouted his name. His brain snapped back to attention and his focus wavered. His eyes found hers across the room. She had a man pinned under her talons, but her eyes were looking elsewhere. Barcus followed their line of sight to Xanthus, standing a few feet away, his sword against the next unmortal's neck. The male satyr had tears streaming down his face. His lips were moving in a rapid prayer that none of the gods would hear.

A welcoming grin broke across Xanthus's face as he ignored the chaos around them. "Barcus! I didn't think I'd ever see you again."

"Xanthus." The name carried an invisible weight from his lungs as he expelled it. "What are you doing?"

"Just finishing what we started all those years ago." Xanthus gave an easy shrug, as if that explained it all. "We were told five hundred would be enough, but that turned out to be a lie. A thousand should work, though." The edge of his sword pressed against the satyr's throat, enough for a light cut.

Ice encased Barcus at the sight. "Please, think about this—"

Disgust twisted Xanthus's features. "There it is, the same weakness I saw three hundred years ago. Heroes do not beg, Barcus." The blade sliced deep into the unmortal's neck. "Nine hundred and ninety-seven."

Allie screamed from where she stood and made to charge him when a sword was thrust into her left wing. Her battle cry turned into a wail of pain as she fell. Barcus's heart stopped beating at the sight.

At Xanthus's feet, Celia struggled at the sound of her sister's scream.

Xanthus looked between the two harpy sisters before his gaze fell back on Barcus. "Are you on their side now?"

"There are no sides, Xanthus," he hissed, stepping closer and eyeing the blade at Celia's throat. "Only those who need protection and those who wish to harm them." The noise of battle was nothing compared to his own blood thundering in his ears. He stared at Xanthus; they were so close. He could see that the other hero remained untouched by time. Yet the deep. maniacal grin was unrecognizable.

"Protection? Don't you remember what these monsters did? How many lives they took!"

"And we did just as much damage to them." Barcus could barely hear the words coming out of his mouth; he was too focused on Xanthus. Only a few more steps and he could counter.

Xanthus shook his head. "It doesn't matter. The world won't be safe until they and the gods are wiped from the planet." He moved to grab Celia, but Barcus was already moving towards him, sword held at the ready.

Xanthus paused at the sight of the blade. "Is that my—"

He swung down, ensuring Xanthus either let go of Celia or lost his hand. The man chose his hand, dancing back enough to put sparing space between them. For the first time that night, Xanthus's self-assurance wavered.

"Where did you get that?"

"An old friend of yours," Barcus growled. "I promised her I'd use it to kill you."

The men around them laughed. They knew the arrogance of immortality; the gift from the gods ensured that death was a difficult thing to come by. They didn't yet realize that Xanthus wasn't laughing or that the men Barcus had cut down with the sword weren't getting up.

Xanthus regained his stance, the weapon used to cut the throats of two innocents gripped in an iron fist.

Dully, Barcus was aware that his hands were shaking. Blood from the fallen unmortals crept towards his foot, their bodies still twitching with their last breath. He tried to shake it off, and it was then that Xanthus moved.

His sword swung down, but Barcus managed a parry at the last moment. Xanthus fought like a bull, charging forward and using his shoulder to knock Barcus off-balance. Stumbling backward, Barcus tightened his grip on the *Theres* Blade, but another blow was already coming.

The steel bit into his upper arm with such force it vibrated throughout his entire body. He fell, and to his horror, landed right next to the dead satyr. The creature's blank eyes stared directly at him. The blood… it was *everywhere*: his weapon, his clothes, his hands. That dark-red color stained his vision, making it impossible to think of anything else.

Barcus froze. His mind shattered as he stared death in the face.

He was supposed to save them.

He was supposed to save so many.

But he'd failed.

He heard Xanthus laugh from far away, the tone a mocking echo of the words he had once thrown at Barcus years ago. "Such a shame. It seems you're even more of a coward than the last time we fought."

Allie screamed something, but he couldn't hear the words. His eyes swept the room until they found her struggling to dislodge the sword from her broken wing. She was surrounded. The men around her grinned as they watched her struggle.

"Because we have a history, I won't kill you," Xanthus said, stepping over him and reaching for Celia. He picked her up by her blonde hair, her body fighting against him with every ounce of her strength. Allie screamed, calling out to Barcus and her sister. Begging him to do something.

But he couldn't move.

"Nine hundred and ninety-eight," Xanthus said.

And then he slit the harpy's throat.

Allie was dying.

It felt as if the sword had cut across her own neck. She screamed, yanking her wing hard enough to tear the flesh free from the sword. Agony ripped with the skin, but at least she could move. Her feet stumbled under the pain, and she fell to her knees next to her sister's unmoving body.

Oh gods. Oh gods. Her eyes blurred with tears as she tried to keep the blood at bay. It was too late, though; the life was gone from Celia's eyes. Her spirit had gone down to the underworld.

A noise escaped her, one that cracked the stone beneath their feet as it tried to reach the realm of the dead. All over, she hurt. Her body trembled from the pain of a broken wing and a broken heart.

Lights filled the room, then a sharp contrast from the darkened garden. Someone called out, "The police are here!"

Xanthus straightened, looking only slightly ruffled from the fight. A muttered curse fell from his lips before his gaze fell on the harpy sisters. He stared for a long moment, and she could see the temptation to try to get one more kill in before leaving. Allie tightened her grip on her sister's corpse, ready to attack anyone if they approached.

"I hate to leave when we're so close."

Her skin crawled; anger she would have expected, even disgust. But Xanthus didn't see her as a monster, nor a woman, but only as a means to an end. Before either of them could make a move, Barcus was there, his body planted firmly in front of her. He was still trembling, even as he raised his sword.

That sword.

She couldn't look away from it. Every unmortal knew exactly what the *Theres* Blade was. The weapon had become legend after it had been created with the blood of her people. So many stories surrounded the sword, but she'd never thought for a second she'd actually see it. And to see it in the hands of a man who'd promised to help her. A man she *trusted*.

"You're not a god yet, Xanthus," Barcus growled, his voice unrecognizable.

"Do you think you can stop me? I just need two more sacrifices." Xanthus's eyes lingered on Allie. "And I have an army at my disposal."

"Maybe, but all I need to do is cut off your head to put an end to your grand plans. It doesn't matter if I die in the process, as long as I take you with me."

Allie swallowed hard. Xanthus had them right where he wanted them, but he still hesitated.

Barcus wasn't afraid of death, but it seemed Xanthus was.

She watched as the man's face twisted in fury. "There's always next time." The threat was followed by a piercing whistle as he called his dogs to yield.

And to Allie's disbelief, they just… walked away from the bloody scene.

XVI

PEOPLE WOULD TALK if she was seen coming home in the starlight hours of morning. No, home was out of the question. One nosy mortal neighbor catching sight of her would be trouble. And the hotel would call the police on them the moment they stepped inside.

They needed somewhere safe. A location where they could hunker down and regroup.

So, she took them to the theater.

Jo didn't answer the door when they knocked. Instead, it was Oak, his face pinched in annoyance. "This is the second time in a week," he started, before registering their bloodstained clothes. "What—"

"Is Krone here?" Allie asked, pushing past.

"No, he isn't. What is going on? Is that… is that blood all over your arm?" Barcus followed behind her, Celia in his arms.

No. She shook her head. Celia's *body*.

The thought threatened to pierce the icy numbness that had encased her body since they'd escaped the museum. Allie forced the wave of emotions down and focused on the task at hand. She did not think about the trail of blood that followed them as she stalked down to the stage. "Put her here."

Barcus laid her out at the foot of the stage. Under the bright lights, her wound was on full display. Her blonde hair was caked in blood, and the gash across her throat was a gaping wound. Blue eyes that had always been so bright now gazed blankly at the ceiling. Allie's stomach twisted at the sight before she closed the lids.

Oak paled. "Is she…?"

"Dead," Allie said, her voice splitting the word in two. "Can you… can you call Ocypete for me? Tell her to come here."

He nodded slowly, green eyes still taking in the sudden carnage. Without warning, his arm wrapped around her shoulder, careful not to jostle her injury. The act of comfort felt like a balm of relief, and it took every ounce of her control not to break down then and there.

Allie closed her eyes and turned away. "I need to go clean up…"

"Of course. You can use the dressing room. I'll go get a medical kit," he said before jogging off to make the calls.

Allie turned to the others in their small gang. Helen had been unusually quiet the entire drive to the theater, and even Leo hadn't made a single pointed comment. Barcus was busy attending to the other two unmortals they'd saved; both looked on the brink of tears. Seraphina especially was sobbing hard, clinging to him as if he were her new savior.

It pained her to leave Celia, even for a second, but she needed to step away. "Can I trust you with her?"

"Of course," Helen said. "Nothing will happen. She's safe with us."

Safe. Allie nearly laughed at the word. They weren't safe. Not anymore.

She limped down a nearby hall at the base of the stage. It was a mess from the last performance. Props and trash littered the floor. The women's dressing room was no better, with costumes thrown about in disarray. A single chair was the only thing free of theater props. Allie collapsed on it. Her breath and body shuddering once she was finally alone.

One large mirror covered the wall, making it impossible not to catch sight of her reflection. All the glamour and shine from earlier in the evening was gone. A creature stared back at her with feather-covered arms and a blood-stained face. "What a mess."

Celia had tsked those same words when she saw the junk food littered around the living room. Allie never used to think twice about being what others would consider a mess. She'd never thought those words about herself before.

Now, she was the very definition of it.

A large T-shirt covered in makeup sat on the counter, and a pair of old sweats lay on the floor. *They'll have to do.*

The sweats were first, but they weren't easy by any means. Allie used her uninjured arm to shimmy into the baggy pants.

Next was the shirt. Her eyes darted down to her injured wing, still speckled in feathers and blood. There was no easy way to do it. The arm ached like a bitch. Already she could feel the nerves working to mend themselves, but the trauma of the wound made the healing process slow. She wouldn't be able to revert it to human skin, not for a while. It was sheer luck the bone wasn't broken. The sword had impaled muscle and torn through feathers. Both healed faster than fragile bird bones.

It had been so long since she'd been injured that it took a moment to do the math on how long the healing would take. A week? Maybe two for her feathers to grow back fully. But at least they would grow back. The sword had been nothing special, nothing like the *Theres* Blade Barcus wielded.

Her heart clenched at the memory.

That blade.

Before, it had just been another weapon collecting dust in Barcus's bag. One she never looked too closely at until it was too late.

Why hadn't he used it on her those first days? It would have been so easy for him to threaten her with it. But he hadn't.

Because Barcus wasn't that cruel.

She'd thought she knew the truth of Barcus. How he despised killing, how he was too trusting in some respects and too guarded in others. For a brief moment, she had actually believed that he had changed. That he could be an actual good guy. But that sword had been created from the death of her brothers and sisters, hundreds of them. And he had wielded it without remorse.

A light knock on the door. She glanced at the mirror and saw Barcus standing just outside the threshold.

"How are you doing?" His voice was tentative in a way that was unrecognizable.

She held his gaze in the mirror. "Well, let's see. My arm is useless, my sister is dead, and her killer is still running free. So, I'd say I'm doing just great."

His eyes shifted down to the shirt in her hand. "Here, let me help you."

"No." She thrust every ounce of herself into the word.

Begging him, pleading with him not to come closer. She didn't need his comfort. There was nothing he could say or do that would make her feel anything. A numbness had seeped into her veins. One she feared would never go away. "I don't need any more help from you."

His skin was pale in the glass, face a stark white, but he obeyed her command. He always obeyed her, no matter the pain or discomfort it caused him.

Emotion tightened in her throat, along with a thousand accusations she wanted to scream. It would be best to be quiet. To keep all those things unsaid.

But she was hurt.

And she wanted someone to feel just as broken as she did.

"You've had that sword this entire time." She spun in the chair and glared at him. "Do you know what that thing is?"

"Yes." Despite the ashen look on his face, his voice carried no remorse. No apology.

Her throat clenched around the anger boiling inside, lacing each word with fire. "Of course you do. You're the Great Hunter. You probably love having that weapon, knowing how others fear it."

"No." He stepped forward. "I only need to use it to kill Xanthus—that is what I promised. I know what that weapon is capable of, and I hate it with every fiber of my body." His hand reached up to rub at his collarbone, where a stark white scar bit into his skin.

Sympathy rose within her like a wave. This wasn't his first time fighting Xanthus. This wasn't his first time *losing* to him. He'd told her that before, when he'd told her about those dark days searching for Argos, killing in search of his friend.

But the sympathy did not extinguish her anger. There was something Xanthus had said back in the museum. A piece of the story Barcus hadn't told her before. *Just finishing what we started all those years ago."*

"Did you help make that weapon?"

His eyes widened at the accusation. "Allie—" He started moving towards her, but she backed up. Her name was not a denial. All she had to do was look at his face to know the truth.

"I get it now. Why you're so eager to make amends towards unmortals. It's because you killed us to make that… that…" She couldn't finish the thought; it was too horrible to consider. "Funny how you didn't mention any of that when you were spinning me pretty tales about how you don't kill anymore."

"I don't," he urged. "You need to know—I was there when the *Theres* Blade was created, but I didn't do any of the killing. That's the truth. I couldn't. I—" His voice broke in shame, and she wanted so badly to believe him, but there was no going back to how things had been between them. The trust, the spark—hell, even the attraction—she crushed it all down and latched on to her hurt inside.

"You didn't stop it, either," she snapped back.

She watched the muscles of his throat and jaw clench and unclench as he tried to use more of his apologetic words against her. When he did speak, it was as if glass had cut him from the inside out.

"I know I messed up. Back then and now. There isn't a day that goes by where I don't think about that. At the time, I thought what we were doing was the only way to find Argos. Xanthus said it was. I didn't realize until it was too late that it was never about finding Argos for him, but creating the perfect weapon. I know you hate me for using it, but that blade is the only thing that can kill Xanthus. If I must use it to avenge the souls used to make it, I will."

"You couldn't even do that!" Allie shouted. "You said you would stop him and you didn't."

His face hardened. "I know. I'm sorry."

"Sorry?" she snarled. "Sorry doesn't do either of us any good. My sister is *dead*."

He winced under the force of the last word. As if she had landed a physical blow. Finally, some emotion. Some hurt. She wanted him to feel the same hopeless pain that had invaded her body.

She stared him down. "You just stood there and watched as he slit her throat. You froze."

"Allie, I—"

"You really are a coward." It was the worst thing she could have said. The worst insult one could call a hero. She knew that and still it slipped past her lips. The ultimate way to hurt him. And it felt good until she saw the way his muscles tensed and the way it left him speechless.

The conversation came to an abrupt end when a loud animalistic growl interrupted them. Allie tensed. She would recognize that sound anywhere.

Krone.

The lion's large body pushed past Barcus, his hard feline eyes zeroing in on her with murderous intent. "You…"

Uh-oh. Instincts took over next. She was backpedaling before her mind could conceive of the actual threat. Makeup and chairs clattered to the floor as she scrambled to get away as quick as possible.

All she knew was that the man in front of her, the

creature in front of her, could kill her if he wanted. And she was already injured. Weak. Vulnerable.

Allie's back hit a clothing rack, preventing any kind of escape. There was nothing she could do except close her eyes and wait for the inevitable.

Poor Ocypete, she's going to lose two sisters in one day.

She'd expected sharp teeth to slay her, but nothing came. Allie opened her eyes in time to see Barcus holding Krone by the arm, the muscles of both men strained under an invisible test of strength. A cold command fell from the hero's lips. "Don't you come near her."

Krone's brows narrowed. "What's this? Are you protecting one of my unmortals?"

Allie's heart stuttered to a halt at the words. There was no way he was protecting her. Not now. Not after everything she'd just said to him.

Barcus's lips twisted into a snarl. "If you intend to hurt her, then yes. Can't you see she's injured enough?"

"What?" A new voice spoke out as Ocypete pushed into the room, dressed in baggy pajama bottoms and a loose coat. "Allie's injured?"

A sob escaped Allie at the sight of her sister, and her own tears started flowing. "Oh, Pete!"

Ocypete moved without hesitation, blowing past the two men and opening her arms for Allie to fall into, immediately noticing the bloody sword wound. "Your wing…"

"I'm fine. I'm fine." It wasn't true, but she didn't want to worry her sister any more than she had already. All the secrets she'd carried were overflowing and with them the guilt.

"Ocypete, step away from that traitor," Krone growled. "She's brought a hero here and endangered us all."

Maybe it was the blood loss, or the constant thrum of pain, or maybe it was the adrenaline still pulsing in her system, but Allie felt a hysterical cackle bubble between her lips. *"I've endangered us all?* I told you Celia was missing and you did nothing! I said unmortals were in danger and you didn't want to tell anyone."

Another growl thrummed in the room. Krone's beard bristled, rising like the hackles of a cat. "You moved without my permission. I told you to stay out of it and you worked with a hero instead."

"She was helping me," Barcus spoke up in her defense. "I forced her to help me with Order business."

Panic seized her as Krone's anger refocused on Barcus. The statement was practically signing his own death sentence.

"Are you sure you want to say that, hero?" Krone spat in anger.

"No," Allie cried out. "Stop it. I don't need you to protect me." She glared at Barcus through her tears, angry at herself for showing such weakness and angry at him for being such a willing sacrifice. She didn't need a hero, not now.

She watched the muscles of Barcus's jaw work, locking his emotions in place. A vindictive sting of satisfaction filled her at the sight before she focused back on Krone. "I chose to work with Barcus. He was the only one who would help me when you refused. Seraphina and that satyr would be dead if I'd waited for you." She stared at the lion, the man they had chosen to be their protector. The man who was the strongest among them. "Am I wrong?"

"I took it seriously enough with the information you provided." Krone's lips twitched. He looked ready to lunge. "If you had been honest with me about what you knew, if you had trusted me—"

"Stay back, Krone," Ocypete hissed at him, curling closer against her sister, a thousand questions likely buzzing around in her mind. But she didn't retreat. Gods bless her. She wasn't going to take his side in this. "She was hurt fighting to save Celia, while you don't have a scratch." Her voice dripped with violence. "If you threaten her, I'll make sure everyone knows exactly who it was who protected our people tonight."

Krone took in the small force that stood before him: a hero and two harpies, undeterred by his intimidation tactics. Eventually, he crossed his arms over his chest. "Fine, we'll continue this conversation once you're bandaged up. You"—he nodded towards Barcus—"can leave, hero. This isn't any of your business anymore."

"I'm afraid it is," Barcus countered. "The man who did this was a hero, and it is my responsibility to stop him."

"Ah, so your men break the Covenant, and you think I'll sit by and let you fail at catching them." Krone flashed his canines. "I don't think so."

"You can punish Xanthus's men however you deem fit, but I will be the one to stop their leader."

"Like you stopped him tonight?" The jab was effective, shutting Barcus up and letting Krone bulldoze over him. "You've had your chance to solve this; now it is mine. The Covenant has been broken, and if you don't leave now, I will use your blood as payment. If you return to this city without notifying me, I'll consider it an attack."

Barcus swallowed hard at the ultimatum, but Allie could see that he didn't have the energy to fight back. Krone was too angry to reason with, and Barcus too worn down from the night's events.

Slowly, he nodded and moved towards the doorway,

but not before turning and pinning her with one last look. One that reflected all the hurt and exhaustion pulling at Allie's own subconscious. She'd been the cause for some of that pain, and still he could look at her like she was the only thing in the world that mattered.

He bowed his head at Ocypete in quiet reverence. "Please, take care of her…"

Ocypete straightened, her hold on Allie tightening. "Of course."

And with that, her hero walked away.

XVII

HER HOUSE USED to be a place of laughter and smiles. Now it was a prison, complete with her own personal guard.

"How do you watch this garbage?" Oak asked, rolling his eyes at the family on the television screen. The DNA-test results had just been announced, sparking a heated argument between a pair of siblings.

Allie watched in morbid fascination. "This is my morning ritual. You can either clam up and accept it or leave."

The bark along his brows narrowed. "You know I can't do either."

Allie rolled her eyes. Oh, she knew it well. Krone had given her a harsh tongue-lashing, but even he didn't have the heart to do anything more than confine her to the property until Xanthus was caught. Oak had been more than happy to comply when ordered to watch her, as it gave him an excuse to see Ocypete every day.

"It's not so bad." She watched the siblings continue their shouting match with a sense of longing.

After a week of danger and peril, her life had become a thin caricature of what it used to be. *Jerry Springer* in the morning. Court TV in the afternoon. And reality television at night. Just like old times. Except nothing about the last two weeks was normal. Her prison was a constant reminder of how incredibly fucked up everything was.

Celia should be the one sitting on the couch next to her, laughing at the couples. A familiar pang twisted in Allie's chest at the thought. She managed not to let her discomfort show, focusing entirely on the television. It was a vast improvement from the week before, when the pain had been so intense she could barely crawl out of bed.

There was nowhere in the city to build a pyre for the dead. Instead, they'd buried Celia under the icy dirt in a small cemetery outside of the city. Her sister was closer to the underworld now than she was with her family.

Ocypete hadn't talked to her since the funeral. There had been no questions about the gala, or Barcus, or even why Allie had kept it all a secret. No screaming. No crying. No comfort.

Only silence.

And that had hurt most of all.

Her sister had never, in a thousand years, given her the silent treatment. Allie knew what that silence meant, knew that Ocypete blamed her for Celia's death. And why wouldn't she? When Allie lay alone in bed, the blame encased her like a second blanket. Grief and guilt threatened to drive her insane, more so than Springer's audacious drama.

In her stronger moments, she refused to take the burden of that loss alone. There was only one person who was to blame. And that was Xanthus.

But without Ocypete to talk to, those moments were few and far between.

Oak didn't argue any further, turning his attention down to his phone. "If my siblings and I fought over such trite things, we'd never find peace."

"That's because you have a hundred siblings," she pointed out.

"More like a thousand," Oak corrected. Dryads and nymphs were all related in some form or fashion: cousins, half-siblings, full siblings. They considered each and every one family, but that left little time to grow close to any relative. She'd seen how Oak interacted with his family. It was more like the politeness of old acquaintances meeting for a high school reunion. Would she and Pete turn into that?

Her head tilted back, trying to get a casual look at Pete's room, where the door had remained shut since yesterday. She bit the inside of her lip. No, she couldn't let that happen. Celia wouldn't want that. If it took years or decades, she would do everything possible to make sure this didn't break her and her sister.

"You should try talking to her."

She rubbed at her arm, pretending to nurture an old ache. "She doesn't want that."

"You two will get through this. I know it. And once you patch things up, you can start traveling like you planned."

She swallowed hard, remembering nights in the theater when she had griped to Oak about her need for more, even when she couldn't pinpoint what the more was.

He'd been the first one to know about her aspirations of independence; he had even planted the seed of travel in her head. Now here he was again, encouraging her. The nerve.

What had she been thinking? Leave? And do what?

She'd be horribly lonely without Celia and Pete there to keep her company. "I could never leave Pete alone. Not now."

She curled against the cushions and tried not to think about it. Her life wouldn't be any different from what it had been before. Any hope of leaving had died with Celia. Those short few days with Barcus had been full of worry and dread, but she'd also felt alive. Something she had lost over the years had awakened in the search for her sister. The once-great harpy who could strike terror had protected those in need. At least that was what she'd thought.

Xanthus's sword had put a swift end to that dream. But the loss of the dream hadn't hurt nearly as much as the death of her sister.

After everything, her plans of leaving the nest now seemed frivolous.

Oak's rough hand patted her thigh in sympathy, and she rewarded him by changing to the food channel.

A few minutes in, Ocypete stepped out of her room. Her brown eyes passed over her sister without familiarity. "Oak, would you mind reading these pages for me? I need an outside opinion."

"Oh… sure." Oak's head swiveled to Allie, projecting a question her way. *Do you mind?*

Of course she didn't. But Krone's command to watch her at all times had been punctuated, word by word, with a low growl. She certainly wouldn't tell the lion if Oak stepped away for a few minutes.

Her phone buzzed, dragging Allie's attention downward. A familiar name filled the lock screen, causing her heart to feel something other than pain for the first time all day. Her fingers curled around the hard plastic, tilting it out of view. "I'm not leaving the house anytime soon. I promise."

A bright grin flashed across his face before he leaped off the couch to Ocypete's side. But her sister didn't move. Deep brown eyes stared at her, silently judging. As if she knew the name that glowed on her phone. Allie held her breath, waiting.

Finally, Ocypete's attention broke and she returned to her office, a happy dryad trailing behind.

Allie waited a breath. Then two. Enough to ensure they wouldn't be returning anytime soon before giving the phone her full attention.

It hadn't been a hallucination. Barcus's name flickered up at her along with a text. Eager fingers tapped on it, bringing the conversation up. There she could see all the messages that had come before this one. Nearly one a day without fail, even though she refused to type back.

Allie, I'm so sorry.

What happened?

Just checking to make sure you're okay.

Is there anything I can do?

And so it went. Nearly two weeks of texts where he checked in on her and offered updates on his ongoing search.

He must know she wasn't okay, not enough to talk to him, at least. But the memory of the broken look on his face after she'd called him a coward haunted her as much as Celia's ghost. She shouldn't have said those words to him.

She scrolled to the latest text. Her heart stopped at the message in front of her. No check-in. No words of comfort. Barcus was trying a new tactic to draw a reaction.

I'm back in the city.

"Idiot," she hissed at the phone. Back in the city? Did he

have a lead on Xanthus? Was he going to fight him alone? If Krone knew, it would be trouble. Her finger itched to type back a remark, but she pushed down the urge. Not out here.

Springing to her feet, she raced up the stairs to her bedroom. A bundle of dirty laundry nearly tripped her up before she fell on the bed, eyes glued to the screen of her phone, reading the message over and over.

Not answering wasn't an option anymore. If he was back, she needed to know why. Her curiosity grew by the second. And dammit, that was probably what he'd planned all along. The man knew her better than she'd thought.

It didn't take long before her fingers were typing out a reply. *What brought you back?*

It was ridiculous how fast her heart was beating when she read his reply.

You.

Liar, she typed back.

And Xanthus. But I'm not leaving until I know you're alright.

Her nerves sang to life. She reread the last sentence for good measure. Excitement, fear, and relief all combined in a confusing swirl of emotions. It was strange after so many days of feeling nothing. She wanted to hear his voice. To talk to him. To know he was okay. Her thumb brushed against the call button, ready to give into temptation and—

"Aha!"

Allie jumped at the noise, stashing her phone under the pillow before she turned. Her sister stood in the doorway and then...

She. Stepped. Into. The. Room.

Pete's anger should have been enough to keep her far, far away. But it appeared that wasn't enough anymore.

Allie immediately straightened. "Pete? Where's Oak?"

"Reading my chapter downstairs. Bought us a few moments alone." She took another step into the room, carefully avoiding the piles of trash. Within seconds, she stood within reach of the bed. "Now, fess up. What were you doing in here?"

"Nothing."

Ocypete glanced to the pillow where Allie hid her phone. "I know you're hiding something. Again."

"I—" Guilt clogged her throat, preventing any excuse from forming.

Again. She was doing it again. Keeping secrets. Just like she'd kept her meeting with Krone a secret. Just like she'd kept her desire to leave a secret.

The second of hesitation was all Ocypete needed to lunge for the pillow, knocking the phone to the floor.

Everything seemed to happen in slow motion after that. Allie watched as her sister picked it up and scanned the texts. "Is this… that hero?"

All protest died on her tongue. Keeping secrets was what had gotten her into this mess to begin with. If she was going to repair their relationship, it was time to come clean.

"He's been texting me. Just checking in…"

"It looks like a little more than just checking in." Ocypete's brows rose in a silent question.

"Well, I haven't been engaging with him." *Much.*

"I can see that." Her eyes glanced down at the phone again, reading the messages there. "Is he still looking for Celia's killer?"

"It looks like it."

"If Krone finds out, we'll both be in trouble."

Allie swallowed hard. "Yeah."

With a sigh, Ocypete tossed the phone back before plunking down on the bed next to her sister. If Allie closed her eyes, it would be easy to imagine the two of them gossiping and sitting together under different circumstances. Like they used to before Celia's death.

"You're… not going to tell Krone, are you?"

"No. I'm not." Pete bit her bottom lip, staring down at the carpet as she sorted through her feelings. Allie waited patiently, still reveling in the fact that her sister was here, talking to her. Finally, she said, "I don't like being mad at you."

"I don't particularly like it when you're mad at me," Allie answered honestly.

Ocypete smiled a little at that. "I miss you… and Celia."

"I know." Emotion welled behind her eyes, but she fought it down. "I miss her, too. So much."

"I wish you had told me she was missing. I feel like I could have helped. I *would* have helped."

"Pete, I'm so sorry—" A raised hand cut off her groveling midsentence. There was a lot she wanted to say now that they were talking to each other again. Her regret that she'd been selfish in her pursuit. How a night didn't go by where she didn't cry over their fallen sister. But she bit all that back. Pete deserved time to air her grievances.

Her sister took a shaky breath. "We don't have a lot of time. I gave Oak a long chapter, but he'll come looking for me soon. I wanted to say I would have helped you, but I know why you made your decision."

Allie blinked. "You do?"

"Yes, I… I probably would have just waited here for all the answers to come to me. I wouldn't have searched for her like you did. I definitely wouldn't have trusted a hero to help find her."

"You don't know that," Allie interjected, giving her sister a reassuring squeeze. "You are the best flier among us. You were amazing!" Like a dark angel, her older sister's devotion to protecting their roost had always inspired Allie. "Maybe if I'd told you, you could have searched by air."

Pete sighed at the memories. "Gods, I was such a different person back then." A shake of her head sent her black curls bobbing. "But I'm not her now. And I'm okay with that. I've put those days behind me. But you have always been protective of us."

"It wasn't enough." Saying the words aloud for the first time brought a flood of emotions that cut off anything else she'd planned to say.

Ocypete took her hand, nodding in understanding. "It was enough. You and that man saved two unmortals. They would have died that night, too."

Allie was about to speak up again when she saw a flash in her sister's eyes. A promising glint. "Now let me help you."

"What?" Allie breathed. "Why are you helping me?"

"Because I don't think it's fair that Celia's murderer is free while you're imprisoned up in here. Allie…" Her sister held her gaze. "No matter what Krone says, you are not a screwup. You are the first unmortal to befriend a hero in a thousand years."

Heat scorched up her neck at the praise. *I did more than just befriend him.* "It doesn't matter," she said out loud. "I trusted the wrong hero."

Pete clicked her tongue. "Of course it matters. I saw

the way he looked at you. The way he stood up to Krone. I'm not blind, sister. That hero cares for you, doesn't he?"

A lump in her throat prevented the answer. She wasn't blind either. She'd seen the way he'd looked to her when Phobos had grabbed him, like she was his guiding light out of the darkness.

"Because of you two, we now know there is a danger to be aware of," Ocypete continued. "Maybe, if we had worked more closely with heroes in the beginning, we would have been able to save more of our kind." Her voice grew quiet, eyes glued intently to the phone. "Do you trust that hero of yours?"

The question caught her off guard. Did she trust Barcus? He had asked her that question so many days ago while they'd argued over Leo.

"Do you trust me?"

"Only a little," she had teased back. But that hadn't been the whole truth. With each passing moment, he'd proven her trust wasn't misplaced. He'd given her a part of himself that no one had ever seen, and she'd done the same that night in a dark hotel room when it felt like the world had been utterly against them both.

She'd thought he could take Xanthus easily. But he'd never told her that. It was her own imagining of Barcus that created those assumptions.

Barcus the Hunter.

Barcus the hero.

Barcus, the man who needed her help just as much as she needed his.

"I do," she whispered.

Ocypete nodded. "That's all I needed to know. Alright, I'll help you escape."

Allie sputtered at the sudden exclamation. "How?"

"Easy. I'll distract Oak while you slip out. Just don't tell me where you're going. I can't guarantee I won't crack under pressure."

She wouldn't, of course. Allie remembered how her sister had stared down Krone in that costume room. But she understood that any additional information might put the people she loved at more risk.

Allie gave her sister's hand a reassuring squeeze. "Thank you."

Pete shook her head at the protest. "You're not the only harpy sister who would do anything for her family." Her eyes trailed down to the travel magazines that littered the floor, the pages creased from years of use. Together, they both looked at the pictures that filled every available space on the wall. Pictures of the three of them from all over the world, before they had finally settled down.

There were so many memories in those photos, but none from a time before the camera had been invented, when they'd lived across the ocean in a land that felt both like home and like a strange dream.

"Someone needs to bring Celia's murderer to justice, and Krone can't do it on his own. If anyone can help, it's you and that hero."

Allie nodded, letting her sister's comfort roll over her. It didn't feel real to hear those words from someone else. But there it was. Ocypete believed in her. Believed she could be the one to chase down Celia's murder. And Barcus…

He'd frozen once against Xanthus. But she would never forget how he had thrown himself in front of her, even when his arms trembled. He'd saved her that day. And without him, she wouldn't have been able to save those other unmortals.

And she had called him a coward.

She needed him.

She missed him.

Ocypete wrapped an arm around her in a tight embrace, and Allie buried her face into the crook of her neck, memorizing the scent of coffee that clung to her sister's skin. "Thank you."

"Just do me one favor," Pete whispered.

"Anything."

They pulled apart. Her sister's dark, owlish eyes were focused on her with the same dark intensity that not even Krone could stand against. "When you find the bastard who killed our sister, you won't take him on by yourself. Call me. We'll end him… together."

Her inner harpy puffed in pride at the words, at the thirst of vengeance she saw in her sister then. She had forgotten, in the comfort of mortal life, what it felt like to hear the war cry of another harpy. Even if that cry was just a whispered promise, it rang between the two of them. Her fingers tangled with Pete's in answer.

"Of course."

A loud knock on the door broke the spell of the moment. Allie was already on her feet. "Were you expecting anyone today?"

"Please," Pete scoffed, "when have I ever invited anyone over?"

That was what she feared. Krone would have told Oak if he was making a visit, which meant there was a stranger at the door.

"Stay back. Oak and I will handle this." She silently

prayed it would be Xanthus or one of his men; then she could put an end to this once and for all.

Pete followed close behind her. "I thought I was the best flier around. If it's Celia's murderers, I'll gut them on the street."

Pride swelled inside her as they marched down the stairs to the first floor. Oak was huddled by the door, one hand raised to stop them on the stairway landing. "You might want to come and see this, Allie."

"Why?" She was already moving, pressing her body against the door to peek out of the keyhole when all the air left her body.

"Who is it?" Pete asked.

Allie didn't have time to answer. Her fingers were quick to undo the locks and fling the door open. There on the steps of their small brick home stood Barcus.

"Sorry to intrude, but this couldn't wait."

XVIII

BARCUS BRACED FOR the door to slam in his face, but the longer it stayed open, the more time he had to take in the woman behind it. She was a sight to behold. Safe, whole, and not entirely displeased to see him.

"Why—how—?"

"I'm a hunter, remember?" He punctuated the word by holding up a single black feather.

Allie stared at it. "Is that one of the feathers you plucked from my sweater?"

All those days ago. Barcus nodded; he'd held it close as a reminder of the harpy just in case they never saw each other again. When the time had come, it had been exactly what he needed to find her again. Tracking spells were no easy feat, but Artemis had been smiling on him in this instance. Another week and the feather would have lost its effectiveness.

He paused, giving her a moment to process his presence. To rage and scream or to slam the door closed if need be. When she didn't, he asked, "Do you mind if I come in?" He'd done his best to ensure no one had followed him to the harpy's nest, but that didn't mean their conversation was meant for mortal ears.

Allie glanced behind her, where Barcus could see a dark-skinned woman and the dryad from Tartarus. He vaguely recognized the woman from the night of the gala. So much had happened, but he would never forget the way she had swept into the room and provided Allie comfort when he could not.

Her sister.

The woman nodded, much to his surprise. "If he says it can't wait, then we should hear what he has to say. Don't you think so, Allie?"

Familiar gray eyes focused on him with all the intensity of a hawk sizing up a meal. Judge and jury for his intentions. After their last conversation, she had every right not to trust him. He'd failed in his promise to her. If the gods had allowed it, he would have never shown his face to them again. But they weren't so lucky. If there was any hope of righting the wrongs of the past, he had to speak to Allie.

She was still staring at him even as she said, "Come on in, hero."

Thank the gods. He swallowed his relief and followed her in. "I won't be long."

"Take as long as you need," the sister said, crossing her arms, "but I hope you don't mind that Oak and I eavesdrop."

"Of course not." This was intended for them as well. He moved forward and extended his hand. "We haven't been formally introduced. I'm Barcus."

"The Great Hunter." Her brows rose in surprise. "You are my sister's hero?"

"He's not *my* hero," Allie said with a grimace.

Her sister ignored the words and took Barcus's hand. "Ocypete. It is nice to finally meet you."

Allie ushered them all into the living room, where Barcus took a seat on the couch. To his surprise, Allie took up the spot next to him. His hands rubbed against the smooth cushions, looking for a distraction. It wasn't a surprise when they found another dark feather lying against the cream-colored cushions. He picked it up, unable to hold back a smile.

Allie grimaced. "Sorry. My feathers are still coming in after the gala."

That caught his attention; any amusement he felt died instantly. His eyes swept over her, lingering on the arm that had been sliced that night. "You're still hurt?"

"Don't worry. I'm fine." She lifted her arm, showing off the unblemished skin. "I just need another week for my feathers to heal. That's all."

"I'm glad." This close, he could get a whiff of her perfume, a flowery odor that reminded him of the sunlit woods. The smell brought back a spell of memories, both good and bad. He clung to the good ones the same way he had for the past two weeks. It was hard as hell not to stare at her, to touch her and reassure himself that she was alright. Having an audience helped grind those urges to a halt. Ocypete sat cross-legged on the love seat catty-corner, poised and ready to move if he should do anything she didn't approve of.

"You shouldn't have come here," Allie said softly beside him. "If Krone finds out, Xanthus will be the least of your worries."

"Krone has been ignoring my calls for weeks now. I had no choice."

"No choice?"

There was no hint of skepticism or distrust, only patience. Barcus nodded. "Allie, I know when Xanthus is going to strike again and I'm afraid he's going to come after you."

A blanket of shock fell over the room, quiet enough that all could hear the softest rip of fabric. Looking down, he saw Allie's fingers tearing the fabric of her soft pajama pants at the sound of Xanthus's name. Calm resolve tempered her voice as she asked, "When?"

"We suspect he's waiting till the first of the month to conduct the ritual."

"Ritual?" Ocypete repeated. "For what religion? Not even Zeus required a sacrifice of unmortals."

"His own. The Order has come to believe Xanthus has broken away and started his own subsect. A hero cult dedicated to himself."

"How do you know it's the first?" Allie asked. Barcus could already see the concern burning behind those gray eyes. It was only two weeks away.

"Leo told us," Barcus explained. "As the cult is dedicated to Xanthus, so are the days of the ritual. The day he gained his status of hero. The day he won at the battle of Aegospotami. He has his pick of dates. The man has triumphed in hundreds of wars."

"Why?" Allie asked. "Why would Xanthus start his own cult?" She pinned him with the question and it felt like a test. She was looking for a reason to trust him, to believe him.

Barcus took a deep breath. He'd known it was coming, had been preparing himself to give this answer for days now. That didn't make it any easier, but he owed her the truth. He owed it to all the unmortals.

He looked at the faces around him, the lives of people who were now reaping the havoc of his misjudgment. "For years, I thought he hated unmortals, but it isn't just your kind. It's the gods themselves Xanthus hates. Ever since the death of his family, he's had nothing but contempt for them, and their disappearance has only validated that hatred more. That's why he set out to make the *Theres* Blade."

The faces around him turned to stone at the news, but it was Allie who spoke up. "He wants to kill the gods?"

He nodded. "But the *Theres* Blade isn't strong enough to give him the satisfaction he desires. It can kill lesser immortals, but not an Olympian."

The words rolled over Allie, her face ashen at the realization. "He's trying to make a new weapon. That's why he's killing unmortals again?"

"He must have discovered the secret to making such a thing. If he could accomplish it, it would raise him to a status no hero has ever achieved." Xanthus's words from that night echoed in his head. *"The birth of a new god."*

Ocypete's brows narrowed at the news. "You heroes really think you're something special, don't you?"

It wasn't disagreement—the harpies knew the power of a cult. Several heroes had been raised to demigod status because of their followers. But none of those men had been strong enough to kill an Olympian. If they had, there would have been chaos, amongst mortals and in Olympus.

Power was not set in stone. Zeus had once overthrown his father to rule over Olympus, but that had been a long-fought war between the Olympians and titans. The entire earth had shaken under the strain. If someone tried to do the same thing now, the world would be shaken to the core. Everything would change.

He turned to the woman beside him, fighting back the urge to touch her. Their fragile bond had been broken two weeks ago, and he didn't deserve her comfort. All he could do was try to assure her of the truth. "I couldn't stop him from creating the *Theres* Blade, and I'm sorry for that. Please, let me help set things right."

A kaleidoscope of emotions skittered across her face. "I've… never heard a hero apologize before."

"I'll apologize every day of eternity. I'll grovel for your forgiveness if it means you'll listen to me now."

"Alright." Her entire body straightened in anticipation, as if the next words spoken would decide both their fates. "I'm listening."

His relief was painful, but not any more so than what he said next. "Xanthus will target you, Allie. You were the one who got away at the gala. I know him. He won't let that stand. Not when he's this close to finishing his weapon."

He watched the way the news sank into the room, how both Oak and Ocypete's bodies tensed. But Allie didn't flinch; she didn't cower. He must have played this moment out a thousand times in his mind, and her reaction was just as he'd imagined. The slow curl of her lips, the flash of anger in her eyes. "Good. Let him come."

After seeing firsthand the destruction Xanthus could weave and after losing her sister, she was ready to face him again. He swallowed his own panic at the thought and focused on the balloon of pride he felt at knowing this woman.

She was so strong. Stronger than most heroes he knew, but he couldn't risk her life. "Allie, we have two weeks until the first of the month, and we still don't know where he's hiding. If we give him the advantage again, it could mean your death or"—he peeked at Ocypete—"the death of another loved one."

"Then what do you want me to do?" Allie asked, frustration creeping into her voice. "I can't just leave."

"You can," Ocypete said, speaking up for the first time. Her voice was steady but commanding. Barcus saw the effect those words had on Allie, the way her mouth clicked shut in surprise. "We talked about this, Allie. If it means life or death, you should go with him, at least until we can figure out where this Xanthus guy and his cult are hiding." Her gaze fixed itself on Barcus and it held the same predatory look he'd seen from Allie. Where Allie reminded him of a raven, her sister was a different kind of creature. A predator with unspeakable intelligence hidden behind those intense eyes. "You asked me to protect my sister, but I'm the one who needs to hear that same promise from you."

There was something truly terrifying in the way Ocypete spoke. It wasn't a question, but a command, one that promised unending pain if he didn't follow through on it. And it was a promise Barcus found he could make, *would* make, without a second thought. "Your sister means the world to me," he said. "I swear to make sure no one ever hurts her again. Including myself."

Allie shifted next to him, her lips parting in a quiet gasp. It might be awhile before she fully trusted him again, and that was okay. He deserved that, but he would not leave her to fight this battle by herself.

"I won't leave Ocypete." Allie shook her head. "No. If they target me, they might go after my sister as well."

"I know." This he was prepared for. "She can come along as well."

"What?" the sisters repeated in unison.

Barcus turned to Allie, who wore the same perplexed expression. "I will not force you if you truly do not want to come, but Allie, let me help you with this. Please." He'd played this out a thousand times in his head as well, but that didn't make saying it any easier. What if she didn't believe him? What if she still didn't forgive him? He would deserve it, but if he didn't do everything in his power to protect this woman, it would be his greatest regret.

To hell with what-ifs. To hell with fear. He reached out for her hand and she met him halfway, grasping his fingers as if they were the only thing anchoring her in this world.

A sigh of relief broke past his lips. "I can't afford to lose you."

"Oh," Ocypete gasped from the love seat.

"Whoa," Oak hummed right next to her.

Allie's expression crumbled slightly, showing the only sign of vulnerability since he'd stepped in the door. She worked to put the mask back in place, but it was too late. He saw it then—the loneliness she'd been holding back, the love that he had thought was only reserved for her family, was now pointed at him. "Alright, where are we going?"

He couldn't hold back a grin. "How would you like to see the home of the Order?"

XIX

I T WAS A strange sensation, watching DC fade in the car's rearview mirror. The irony of the situation sank into Allie's gut like a cannonball. She'd been starving for a change, so eager to leave home, and now she was finally getting her wish.

Guilt and excitement bubbled in her stomach as she glanced at Ocypete. Her sister was being eerily quiet about being uprooted, her brows knit together as she stared out the window, no doubt worried over Oak. The dryad had volunteered to stay behind in order to talk sense to Krone and any other unmortal who would listen. *He will be fine*, Allie reassured herself. Even as they'd left, Oak hadn't seemed concerned about Krone punishing him. Which had been a relief. If anyone could talk sense into the lion, it was Oak.

Barcus was a good driver. He seemed to know all the shortcuts and back roads to take to avoid the East Coast traffic. It was easy to get caught up for hours on end on the popular highways, but Allie noticed the way he glanced at the rearview mirror. Constantly vigilant, checking to ensure they hadn't been followed.

Around them, the trees stood tall as dense forests hugged the side of the road. Before long, the Chesapeake Bay came into view; boats and historical houses signaled their proximity to the quaint town of Annapolis. Barcus took the Bay Bridge, and Allie stuck her nose close to the glass as she looked down towards the frozen water below. The Chesapeake looked beautiful in the winter landscape. Gone were the boats that littered the waters during summertime, but from the bridge, she could see the spiraling white buildings of the Academy and the mansions situated against the water.

She'd forgotten how much she loved the area, the small islands that seemed to speckle the bay and the people who had become adept at boating to make their livelihoods. It all reminded her of home centuries ago.

The other side of the bridge had bigger houses. Mansions, really, with large gates blocking private roads. Barcus drove past them all, taking the car downhill towards the water, where homes with personal docks sat at the ready. When he finally pulled into a driveway, Allie knew they had arrived. The entrance gate had two stone Pegasus statues sitting on limestone pillars.

The Order. They were at the home of the Order. Something no other unmortal had ever seen. They would be the first. Maybe Ocypete hadn't been wrong in her earlier praise. Maybe what the world needed was for hero and unmortal to finally put their differences aside.

One of the pillars bore a metal plate that read "Elysian Pointe" both in English and in Ancient Greek.

Allie snorted to herself. "Is that what you call this place?"

Everyone knew of the Elysian Fields, a special place in the underworld reserved only for heroes. The stories made it sound like heaven, all white clouds and champagne fountains, while Tartarus was nothing but rock and darkness. Ever since heroes had gained immortality, legends of the Elysian Fields had faded away. Now it seemed they had established a new Elysium.

"It's better than calling it the Maryland Base." Barcus hit a code on the intercom, and with a digital beep, the iron gate swung open.

The driveway yawned before them. At least an acre of wood surrounded the house before a brick-lined mansion peeked out. There were traces of the old culture built into the architecture—the vaulted roof overhanging the entrance, the white columns, and hundreds of hyacinth plants blooming up the walkway despite the midwinter freeze.

This place is touched by the gods, she realized, staring at the flowers. But she also recognized the impressive modern build of the mansion. Eight windows lined the front of the house, top and bottom, indicating endless rooms and plenty of light. A second brick building sat off to the side with five—no, six garage doors. Each one no doubt filled with an impressive vehicle.

Barcus brought the car around a fountain, where an iron statue of Herakles looked down in solemn determination. He cut the engine and turned towards the two harpies, trying to gauge their reaction. Allie made of show of rolling her eyes. "You heroes sure are show-offs."

"It's how we get all the pretty immortal ladies." He winked. She scoffed, but felt the smile pulling wider. She had *missed* this.

Together they strolled up to the door, where Barcus grabbed an elaborate brass door handle that placed the knob into the claws of a perched eagle. He held the door open and welcomed them in, as if it belonged to all of them. As if it were home.

The inside was just as grand as the outside. Stark white marble floors and crystal chandeliers. Allie tried not to stare at the sparkling glass, but her eyes were drawn to it. *Pretty*, her instincts cooed before Barcus pulled her away.

"I need to show you the progress we've made in the last two weeks."

The words were like diving into an icy lake. Barcus didn't have to say anything more to remind Allie of why she was here. To help find Xanthus and kill him. Two weeks was plenty of time for them to regroup, and now the clock was ticking again.

Barcus led the way to what he referred to as the crown jewel of the mansion. The library.

He opened the double doors with exaggerated flourish, revealing a room with a high ceiling and two floors of solid bookshelves. A spiral iron staircase connected the levels and a grand oak table sat in the middle of the room, covered from end to end with piles of paper. It appeared Barcus's mess of notes had been transferred from the hotel to a grander location.

A happy squeal escaped Ocypete at the sight. Her sister moved to the nearest bookshelf, fingers trailing over the old spines, while Allie glared at the thousands of pages before her.

She hated reading, hated research even more. When it came to those hobbies, Ocypete was better suited to be of help. But the clue to Xanthus's cult was hidden in those pages. She took in the pages of work set before her. The library wasn't beautiful—it was a challenge, one she would have to endure.

Three men were already in the library when they walked in. An olive-skinned man appeared from behind a pile of books. A look of mild irritation decorated his handsome face. "Finally, you're back."

Another hero, Allie's mind supplied as she took in the gold around the stranger's neck. He stood to greet them, showing a body smaller than Barcus's, stouter, but no less fit. The other two seemed to wake up from where they had been dozing on the plush sofas. One Allie immediately recognized as Leo, but the other was a stranger with a large bushy beard and fluffy brown hair pulled back into a ponytail.

"Ah! Guests!" The bearded one stood up with a surprising burst of energy. His towering height would make even Krone seem small. One look and Allie knew what this man was—a goliath, a fighter kings had once hired to win their battles. The grin on his face was nothing but welcoming, though.

"Ladies, this is Eolis and Hector. They've been helping me these past couple of weeks. Eolis acts as our unofficial librarian," Barcus explained.

Eolis laughed. "Yes, well, the last time I left someone else in charge of priceless documented history, everything went up in flames."

Barcus raised a hand for a poorly veiled stage whisper. "He's still a little bitter about the Library of Alexandria."

"Bitter is the wrong word." Eolis gave his fellow hero a pointed look. "I still wake up cursing the name of that idiot."

Allie pushed down her nerves and extended her hand towards him. His grip was unsurprisingly strong, but the shake remained friendly. If he knew she was a harpy, there was no sign of it.

The giant was next and already taking her hand in greeting. "It is good to finally meet you two."

"Um… right back at you." Allie held her breath as she watched Hector greet her sister with the same warm welcome.

"And you already know Leo." Barcus inclined his head to where the younger hero still sat on the sofa, glaring at them.

Allie pursed her lips. "What exactly is he doing here?"

"Training," Leo said as he lay back across the length of the cushions. "And helping."

"Doesn't look like you're doing much to help."

Barcus touched her arm in a gentle warning. "Leo has agreed to learn the ways of the real Order and assist us. Hector will ensure he doesn't cause any trouble."

They looked back to the goliath, who was happily chatting with Ocypete. She'd seen the same enthusiasm when Helen had first met her. There was no sign of hesitation or sign of disgust because of what they were. Even Ocypete looked taken aback.

"We've never had unmortals here before—we need to have a proper welcome," Hector was saying enthusiastically before cupping his hands together in a thunderous clap. "I know, a feast! We should have a feast!"

"Hector," Barcus called, "we don't want to overwhelm our guests. They only just arrived."

"Yes, and that is exactly why we should feast together. Surely you didn't just invite them here to work." Hector grinned when Barcus had nothing else to say. "Don't worry, I will leave you all to your research and make the preparations. It will take some time and coordination. No doubt Claire will want to be involved." He took Ocypete's hands again and gave a polite bow before whisking out of the library like a man on a mission.

The second he was gone, Leo sagged in relief. Even Eolis shook his head with a smile. "I think he was looking for an excuse to leave."

"You know how he gets." Barcus smiled.

But Allie's mind was still reeling from the introductions. Four heroes. She was in the room with four other heroes, and so far, no one had killed each other. More importantly, these heroes knew they were unmortals. "You don't mind?" she blurted, interrupting the conversation between Barcus and Eolis. Both turned to her, and she managed to finish the thought. "You don't mind that we're… harpies?"

"Well, it was strange when Barcus first made the suggestion," Eolis admitted, "but we've seen a lot of strange things these past couple of decades. Besides, you're victims of Xanthus as well. That means we have a common enemy, and we could use all the help we can get."

"What can we help with?" Ocypete stepped closer to the table, her gaze swooping over the notes scattered about.

"We'll start with this…" Barcus grabbed a pile of papers and laid them across the table.

Allie and Ocypete gathered for a closer look as Eolis started to explain, "We've spent a majority of the last two weeks reading the notes of a deceased hero who worked with Xanthus. It has shed some light, but these notes are a mystery. We can't make out the language he wrote in."

Familiar aged papers stared up at Allie. She'd caught

glimpses of them in the hotel room but never spent time fully examining them. Until now. Now the elegant script formed letters that weren't English nor any ancient language. At least not a mortal one.

Ocypete drew in a breath beside her. "That's…"

"Uranides," Allie finished.

"Uranides?" Barcus repeated. "I've never heard of it."

"You wouldn't. It's the language of the elder gods," Ocypete clarified. "The titans. And when they fell, it became the language of the unmortals."

"How would a hero know it?" Barcus asked, casting a look at Eolis. "No one in the Order knows anything like this."

"Maybe not in your sect, but Xanthus requires all his men to learn it," Leo clarified.

All eyes turned to where the younger hero had been quietly eavesdropping on their conversation. A prickle of anger twisted up Allie's spine at the sight of the young hero, still lying on the couch.

"If you knew what it was, why didn't you tell Barcus before?" she growled, stepping towards the younger hero until Barcus's grip held her steady.

Leo met her accusing tone, and she saw the hatred that still burned in those dark-blue eyes. It seemed not all the heroes were open to having unmortals under their roof. "It's none of your business, but they've had me busy with… other things."

"Training," Barcus clarified. "Proper hero's training. I didn't think Leo would be able to help with these files, so I didn't ask. It's my fault."

She could see he was regretting that assumption now, and even worse, that he was beating himself up about it.

Allie took a deep breath to ease her own inner rage and tried to focus. Being mad at Leo wouldn't solve their problems. "How well do you know Uranides?" she asked.

Another shrug. "I'm not fluent, but I have a rudimentary understanding of the language."

"Why would Xanthus teach this language to his followers?" Barcus asked.

"Maybe because he knows none of you read it." A smirk curled Leo's lips as he stalked across the room and picked up one of the pages.

A deep frown scored itself across Eolis's face as he turned to Barcus. "They're using it to tell their members apart from others in the Order. It's brilliant."

"It's alarming is what it is." Barcus didn't look nearly as thrilled by the discovery. "He's put meticulous thought into this, and we've been caught completely unawares."

Allie watched as he rubbed his whitened knuckles, hiding them from view. "This is progress, though," she reassured. "Pete, Leo, and I can help with translating the notes. They might have the key to where Xanthus is, right?"

She dared to touch his hand, a gentle brush of fingers to jog him out of whatever thoughts consumed him. He blinked hard, taking in her words with a nod. "Yes... yes, that will be a huge help. Eolis and I will continue to pore over the map of known attacks."

"I can help with that, too," Allie offered, raising her phone. "It might have been easy for Krone to ignore you, but he wouldn't dare ignore a call from me. Especially when he finds out I'm not in the city anymore."

That got a smile out of Barcus. "I think I'm beginning to love your crafty side."

"It's delightful, isn't it?" Allie grinned back.

◈

Watching Allie navigate her call with Krone was an eye-opening experience. For one thing, the damn lion answered the phone. Barcus could hear his angry growls from across the table. But his harpy held her own. "Have you made any progress?" she asked, at which the growls fell silent. "That's what I thought. I'm not playing these games anymore, Krone, and neither is Ocypete. The heroes have information. If they share it, will you answer my questions?" A pause, but Barcus saw Ocypete's lips tilt up. Allie nodded and snapped her fingers. Eolis was quick to grab her a pen and paper.

In that moment, Allie transformed before his eyes. The sly harpy turned into a commanding presence; it was like she'd been giving orders for centuries. Not long ago, she'd confessed to him that Krone thought she was lazy and weak. What a fool.

Allie was a conduit of information flowing between Krone and the heroes, marking the map as they went. It took hours, with the two bickering in between. Krone didn't have the research laid out before him, and he didn't have Barcus's notes. He wasn't nearly as prepared as Allie, who'd carried the problem with her for days. But he did have information, news from the unmortal community. Various attacks, unmortals missing without a word to their friends.

Before they knew it, night had fallen outside, and they had more information than they had started with. Allie promised to call again the next day, and even Barcus heard the grumble of approval that came with agreement. She ended the call and collapsed across the table. "He talked a lot, but it will be hours more until we can see if any of this information is actually useful."

"But you did it so well," Ocypete assured, hugging her sister's shoulders. "I told you you'd be great."

Allie's face softened at the encouraging words, as if she'd never heard them before. Barcus felt his heart twist; she looked so tired, but she was giving it everything she could to protect her people.

While she was doing that, he would have to ensure someone was taking care of her. "It's been a long day for you two. Maybe it's time we all go to bed. I'll show you to your bedrooms."

Leo perked up at the dismissal and was gone before anyone else could suggest otherwise. Times like these worked as a reminder that Leo was still young, but more than that, he was different from the other heroes Barcus had trained. A man who had not been born in the age of war, but one of the few heroes made in the modern age. He'd noticed the difference in the hotel. Xanthus had taught Leo the importance of honor and glory, but those traits did not drive the younger hero's heart.

That was what had saved Leo that day in the hotel.

It would take time, but Barcus was excited to see the type of hero Leo would become. To see the reason why the gods had chosen him.

The sleep that loomed across Allie's features pulled back at the mention of bed. She got up and moved towards Barcus, but her sister was lost to the depths of the page she was reading. "Pete?"

Ocypete shook her head. "I don't mind staying up. I think I can finish this tonight if I have some coffee."

"We have some," Eolis offered from one of the plush armchairs. He was still staring at the map, a frown puckering his lips. Barcus knew that look. His friend would be up until early morning poring over the information.

"Eolis," he called. The other hero's head snapped up as he blinked the sleep from his eyes. "Don't stay up too late."

"Yeah, yeah…" He still would, of course. Who knew, maybe he and Ocypete would strike up a friendship over their love of research.

"Will they be alright?" Allie asked as Barcus steered her towards the door.

"Eolis prefers to work late into the night. Let him pore over the information Krone provided. His ability to consume information is why we've made so much progress."

She ducked her head, the next question coming out in a soft whisper. "Then why didn't you ask him to help you in the beginning?"

Shame knocked in his chest. "For the past two weeks, I've been asking myself that same question. I felt like Xanthus was my responsibility to bear alone. My last great quest. We heroes were always instructed to handle quests on our own. Relying on friends and family only got them hurt."

The hunt for Xanthus had made him realize things he'd been trying to ignore for years. That he wasn't the same man who'd accepted a blessing from Artemis all those years ago. He wasn't even the same man Xanthus had left behind. He had changed and he needed to learn how to compensate for it. "Once I asked Hector and Eolis for help, things got better. And now that you and your sister are here, I feel like we're heading in the right direction. If you hadn't stepped in, we would have never gotten all that information."

She sighed. "Nearly three hundred years after the Covenant and we finally figured it out."

"Figured what out?"

"That unmortals and heroes can actually work together."

They strolled along the marble floors past antique lamps lining the hall, their light guiding them as they moved to the east wing. Everything was quiet. That was the only reason he felt brave enough to say, "Your words really did a number on me a few weeks ago."

Her body went rigid beside him, as if she were about to run. He threaded his fingers between hers and gave a reassuring squeeze. "Barcus, I'm so sorry."

"No. You were right. I failed in doing the one thing I told you… I told everyone I would accomplish. And I failed because I'm not the man I used to be. When I came back here, I reflected on that. On how we both insisted on doing things by ourselves. I wouldn't have found out about the cult if it wasn't for you. So I figured maybe my brothers could help me as well. Eolis has been a huge help, but there are still some things we couldn't figure out."

Allie nodded as if she knew the rest. "That's why you brought me here."

"That's not the only reason." He didn't dare look at her expression, and thankfully he didn't have to. "We're here."

Two French doors stood in front of them. Elegant crown molding surrounded the shape of the entrance. Allie eyed the brass knobs, lips curling in approval. With a nod from Barcus, she opened the doors. Inside was a room that made their hotel suite look like a cheap motel room. Barcus turned on the lights, illuminating a quaint sitting room, complete with an elegant vanity and paintings of the European countryside. The walls were painted a soft golden yellow that flowed into the main bedroom area.

Allie walked through it silently, her eyes large and

mouth open. The glasswork of the chandelier, imported from Italy, did not go unnoticed by her keen gaze.

In the bedroom sat a king-sized bed that would make even Hector look small. A blood-red silk robe was laid out on the bed, the same color as the jacket she'd worn the first night he'd laid eyes on her.

Barcus watched her find her words, taking delight in the fact that he had finally been the one to make the harpy speechless.

"Barcus… this is wonderful."

"This is your room."

She turned to him, mouth still open. "My room?"

"Remember what I said in the city? I'm not going to trap you anywhere. You are free to come and go as you please. You may go anywhere in this building. No one will hurt you." It was important that she knew this. Important that she knew that everything that had happened between them in the city didn't have to be the same here. She'd agreed to help them, but she wouldn't be a prisoner like she had been at the hotel.

In the few days he'd known her, Allie had discovered more about him than any of his brothers. She'd helped him with his panic, with his mission, and for that, he would never be able to thank her enough. Giving her the revenge she deserved and the freedom she craved felt like a good starting point.

She looked stunned. Her mouth kept opening and closing before she turned back to the room.

"I'm just down the hall." He stood by the door, watching as the glamour of the room captured her attention. She was happy and that was all that mattered. "If you… um, need anything."

She must have been tired because she didn't say any-thing else. Barcus itched to pull her close before they parted ways for the night. But the last thing he wanted was to make Allie feel like she owed it to him. To feel like she had no option but to be by his side in the house. Right now, all he wanted was for her to feel comfortable. To feel safe.

Which was why he left with nothing more than a part-ing, "Sleep well."

THE ROOM WAS beautiful. But it wasn't what she wanted.

When Barcus had suggested going to bed, a variety of different expectations had played through her mind. None of them had involved actually sleeping. She'd imagined his room, his own large canopy of blankets and pillows. A place where they had the opportunity to take their time exploring each other's bodies.

Instead, he'd given her a personal suite and left her… alone.

Damn him. The hero was too thoughtful for his own good.

Allie appreciated the sentiment, but this time he had completely misunderstood what she needed. She didn't want to spend another night by herself. Not after his beautiful promises. Not when their last night of passion still haunted her.

She eyed the red robe on the bed, knowing exactly what she wanted.

The robe draped over her naked body perfectly, fitting every curve and revealing her long legs. Allie glanced at herself in the mirror, a slash of satisfaction filling her at what reflected back.

Barcus didn't stand a chance.

She hoped.

Her feet fell hard on the plush carpet of the hallway as she marched down it once again. Only one door had a line of light shining through the bottom. She knocked politely, not wanting to be too abrupt, but after a second thought, her fist pounded against the wood.

It opened quickly after that. Barcus stood before her, dressed in a pair of gray sweatpants and nothing else. An obvious erection tented the loose-fitting fabric, making her mouth water. Mother's maw, he looked delicious.

"Hi." He licked his lips, sounding breathless. "Do you need something?"

"Yes." How could he not know what she wanted? What she needed. "You."

"Me?" he repeated. "But I thought—"

"Whatever you thought, it was wrong." She stepped forward, not pushing into the space as she might have once done but leaving room for him to deny her if that was what he wanted.

His eyes took her in from head to toe, taking in the scarlet robe. Desire ate away at his tired eyes as he stepped back. "Come on in."

His room was smaller than her own. Dark and cozy, with a roaring fireplace near the bed. Allie cocked her head. "I see you were expecting company."

"Not at all," his voice came from behind. "I was just about to fall asleep."

"Don't lie to me. I can see your erection, Barcus." She turned and gave it a meaningful look. "Were you going to take care of that yourself when I'm right down the hall?"

Barcus blinked, seemingly taken aback by the question. "I thought you weren't interested—" He stopped himself, licked his lips, and tried again. "I mean, I thought you weren't interested in pursuing anything after that night."

"Hero," she tsked as she stalked into his space, "if I wanted to sleep by myself, I would tell you. I have been honest with you about all my wants, haven't I?" She leaned forward, her breasts brushing against his chest.

"Yes," he breathed, eyes dipping low.

"Has there ever been a time that wasn't true between us?"

"No." His throat bobbed on a swallow.

There. No denial. No pushback. If he was sick, or tired, or not interested, he would tell her. But that hitch in his breathing, the pounding of his heart—it was all the evidence she needed. His body was screaming for her.

She grabbed his cock through the soft fabric of his sweats, feeling the bulge of hard skin fill her grip. Barcus groaned. "You have done plenty for me today. Let me show you how much I missed you."

"Allie…"

Slowly, she sank to her knees, eyes tilted up to watch his expression as she did so. Barcus let out a soft curse as she nuzzled his crotch, inhaling his musky scent. She felt herself grow wet in response. "Gods, you smell so good. And I bet you taste like a feast." Eager fingers tugged at his pants, pulling them down and freeing the cock from its prison. There it was. Just as beautiful as the first time she had seen it, but now it was up close and personal. Allie couldn't wait any longer. She licked at the soft skin of the head, already crowning with precum.

Hands twined themselves into her hair as Barcus hissed, "*Fuck.*"

"Ah, so this is the weakness of heroes," Allie mused with another tentative lick. "Their cocks. Clearly we've been doing things wrong all these years."

"There is a time and place for your teasing."

"Here and now," Allie sang back before taking him deep into her mouth.

Whatever Barcus had been about to say, it fell away to a string of ancient curses—some of which she'd never heard before. Allie hummed in approval as each lick pulled another delicious noise from her lover.

Amazing. She'd forgotten what it felt like to hold such control over a man. To grow excited by giving pleasure rather than receiving. Allie opened her mouth wider, taking him deeper. The tip of the head brushed against the roof of her mouth. She lathered it as much as she could with spit, moving her tongue up and down the length of the shaft.

"Tell me what you want," she whispered between mouthfuls. "Tell me what you need."

The hands in her hair twisted, urging her to pick up the pace. "I-I want to commit this image to my memory so the next time the nightmares stir back up, I can fall back on this moment."

Thrust.

"You. Asking for me."

Thrust.

"You, on your knees in my room."

Thrust.

"You, begging me like I'm something you need."

You are what I need. She tried to say the words, but Barcus's grip wouldn't let up. All she could manage was a low hum that vibrated throughout his dick. They both groaned. This was primal and rough, and they fucking loved it.

For the first time in years, Allie gave the control back to her lover.

This was what they were. Give and take. Equal partners in the act of pleasure. She was happy to lose herself to the sensations assaulting her. The taste of him, both salty and sweet. The smell of him, as if she were outside in the woods. All of it affected her keen senses like no other man had, making her head spin with pleasure.

She could hear every little noise he made, even the frantic patter of his heart. Together, it was an orchestra that filled the small room. The music of their pleasure built up within her, tingling her nerves from throat to clit. Gods, she was going to come just from sucking him off.

But before that, she was going to make him come.

She heard Barcus grunt above her, the fingers pulling hard enough to edge on the brink of pleasure and pain. "Yes, darling. Like that. I'm going to—"

The claim broke off into a guttural whine as he spilled himself into her mouth. Allie loosened her throat and swallowed it down. Her lips smiled against the head of his cock. There was a power in this unlike anything she'd felt before. Other unmortals could make a hero speechless by turning him to stone, or casting a spell. But she had managed to make him bow to her in a completely different way.

Barcus felt something for her, and gods help her, she felt the same way.

Her hero stood tall after the storm of his climax, the fingers in her hair pulling gently upward until their lips were only a breath apart, where he claimed her. Tasting himself on her lips. She moaned, her mind spinning and her unclaimed pleasure crying out in anticipation of what was to come.

Yes!

The mattress caught her in its softness as Barcus guided her back. Allie stretched out across its grandeur. He removed the robe carefully, like she was a precious package. For a moment she lost herself to the press of silk sheets and the golden glow of the room, which reminded her of days gone by. But the sensation of his fingers slipping between her folds kept her anchored in the now. In this moment.

"Yes." He relaxed on the exhale, fingers moving easily within her. "Allie, I need you." She reached out to caress his cheek, and his lips found her fingers, gifting each one with a soft press. "Tonight, no memories will take either of us."

He pulled his fingers out, and a cry escaped her at the emptiness. "Barcus, please!"

"I know what you need," he said, leaning down and slanting his mouth over her own. "It's alright, darling."

She threw herself into the kiss. *I need you!* The thought pulsed within her with every heartbeat. *I love you!* She felt the declaration rattle the bones of her ribs, but for some reason it stalled.

"I know," he murmured, as if he understood.

Then his cock was pressing against her entrance and sliding inside with a slow, burning pleasure that made her forget how to speak. They breathed in a sigh together, and if she listened hard enough, she could swear that their heartbeats were in sync, beating the same frantic rhythm.

One large hand gripped her hip while the other splayed out against her pussy, the thumb finding the swollen nub buried within it. He began to thrust, flicking her clit with each movement and sending a firestorm across her nerves.

Allie cried out, bucking against the sensation, thrusting back as hard as she could to take all of him. "Yes, Barcus!"

The familiar quake of an orgasm built within her. She gasped in warning, eyes flying to meet the gaze of the man on top of her. Barcus was smiling, staring at her in a way that was only meant for the two of them. That melted her heart and made it swell at the same time. His free arm cradled her against him, never breaking the cadence of their lovemaking until she felt her body crumple under him. His name fell from her lips with each tremble. "Barcus… oh, Barcus…"

And he held her, shaking and breathing just the same, his lips moving against her dark hair. "I love you. I love you."

"I… I…" Something firm lodged itself in her throat. She licked her lips, slowly coming down from the rush. Returning to the quiet of the room, the crackle of the fire, the weight of him on top of her, inside her. She reached for him, bringing him down for a long, lingering kiss.

"Can I stay here tonight?" The question made her feel like a hatchling, but the look on Barcus's face, warm and so, so happy, reassured her.

"Of course."

She snuggled against him, feeling the exhaustion from the day press against her like the weight of the world. Barcus draped a blanket over their naked bodies, and she felt herself drifting, but not before hearing his last words. "You can stay here for as long as you like."

XXI

"OUT OF ALL the places you showed us yesterday, I think I like this room best of all," she announced, watching as the sky outside filled with cotton candy-pink clouds. It was predawn, and soon they would have to get up and return to the library. But for now she could lie in bed with her lover and pretend all was well outside, that they were just two people basking in the morning glow after a wonderful night of sex.

Barcus's chest rumbled under her. "I've barely showed you anything of this place."

"Maybe so, but my decision remains final." Her eyes roamed out the room as if proving her point, taking in the fine craftsmanship of the fireplace mantel and the large windows that looked out onto the bay nearby. The building had had renovations made to its historic structure, but not so much that it had lost its smells. If she inhaled deep enough, it felt like she could sense a hundred other people who had once lived in the mansion. Their furniture, their aftershave, even some of the food once baked in the massive kitchen.

"How long have you lived here, Barcus?"

A pause hung between them as he picked his words. "Longer than most."

"Do you have another home?" As much as she admired Elysian Pointe, the mansion didn't feel like Barcus's style. Surely he had a place elsewhere that he called home. Who was she kidding? Of course he did. Barcus was a hero. "I bet you have a house in every country."

"I only have one other house. But I haven't been there in a long time," he answered.

"That sounds nice. What's it like?"

"You don't want to know."

"Try me." Not only did she want to know, but she was also hungry for the information. To know the kind of place Barcus called home. Not a headquarters. Not a hideout. But home.

He didn't immediately answer. Allie lifted her head from his chest to find him chewing thoughtfully on his bottom lip. She cringed, realizing too late that the questioning might have brought up memories better left forgotten for her hero.

Why was it every time she felt like they were making progress, something from the past propelled them back?

Because you both have long, complicated pasts, idiot, she told herself, *and long, complicated pasts mean lots of baggage.*

"You don't have to—"

"No." He shook his head and offered a gentle smile. "I would love to go back to it someday. To take you there if you'd like to."

"Take me where?" she asked, snuggling closer.

"Vermont. That's where I made my home."

"You made it?" She grinned at the idea. "That's very old-school of you."

He shrugged off the praise, but a sheepish grin broke across his face. "It's just a log cabin. Nothing fancy. I haven't been there in years. By now the wood has probably rotted."

"A cabin?" she repeated, unsurprised. It was exactly the kind of place where she could imagine Barcus living. "If you made it, it must have been…"

"1710, when I first got here. Give or take a few improvements over the years." His smile fell. "You should know, Allie—when everything fell apart with Xanthus, I didn't know what to do. I felt alone… broken, so I did what everyone did back then…"

"You came to America."

"I ran away to America," he corrected, and she could hear the unspoken "like a coward" floating between them. Barcus blinked a few times, chasing away whatever thoughts plagued him. His hand drew her closer for warmth, and Allie complied, offering her presence as an anchor before he continued talking. "As soon as I arrived, I went as far away from civilization as possible. I built the cabin in the mountains and stayed there for twenty years."

Her breath caught on a swell of pity. "By yourself?"

"I didn't trust myself to be around anyone. It was just easier that way."

"For how long?" How long had he lived in self-isolation? In the wilds of a country that offered none of the comforts of home? No friends, no family. Just the thought of it broke her heart.

"Fifty years. I didn't know how to make amends for all the wrong I did, so I tried to get back to my roots. Only kill when it was necessary. Only hunt when it was needed. I made these promises to myself before I realized—"

"Realized what?"

"I couldn't do it anymore. I couldn't even stand to skin a rabbit without feeling ill. I grew hungry, but I couldn't die of starvation. I was lonely, but no one ever died of loneliness."

"What changed?" Because something must have. The man Barcus described… she couldn't fathom him being the same hero who stood before her. Who unmortals feared.

"Artemis came to me."

She balked at him. "The goddess of the hunt?"

"The one and only. She appeared in my small, simple cabin and didn't bat an eye. She came to America for the same reason we all did. For a new start. The land was wild here. The game practically untouched. She found refuge in the wild… and then she found me. Her once-favored hero, now a half-starved hermit. Do you know how I gained my immortality?"

Allie blinked, not expecting the question, and surprised that she didn't really know the answer. "You killed a lot of unmortals?"

"No. Nothing like that. I had never even killed an unmortal when I went seeking a quest from the goddess."

"Then how—"

"I challenged Artemis." A wry smile curled his lips. "I was the best hunter in our village, and I sought Artemis out and challenged her to a hunt. And she accepted."

Interest piqued, Allie leaned forward. This was one legend few had ever heard, and she would cherish it like the treasure it was. "What happened?"

"My quest lasted three months. First, I was turned into a dog and asked to hunt one of her great golden hares. Then I was turned into a stag and told to avoid her hounds for three weeks. My final challenge was as a man. I had to hunt and kill a lion before the goddess."

"And you did it?"

He grinned, moving between her legs. Allie spread them wide, welcoming him between her curves. "Yes."

"But no man—"

"I wasn't a man."

"What?"

"I had already killed a lion when I was a stag. I knew Artemis would accept a challenge to hunt against a mortal, so I suggested the lion. When she accepted, I pulled out the carcass."

She squawked a laugh and pushed him away. "And she didn't kill you?"

"Surprising, I know. But I think I impressed her after the first two challenges."

"So she likes you?" Allie teased.

"Enough that she made a house call to my cabin to kick my ass back into gear," he sighed, leaning against her. And Allie welcomed his weight as her own. "She spouted some nonsense about how this world still needed the Order. How we didn't have to live like we did in the past and… well, I liked it. I wanted to help make that dream a reality, and she told me that unmortals and mortals were ready to make it come true."

"And that's how you helped form the Covenant."

"Really, I just showed up. Me and a few other heroes who were just as lost as I was. They turned to me for guidance, and that's how I found myself in charge of the Western Order."

Allie snorted at that. "Very diplomatic of you all."

"I know." But his smile was back, and she didn't have the

heart to tease him anymore. Instead, her hands smoothed his short-cropped hair. "But I've liked it."

"They are lucky to have you," she said.

Barcus's eyes were trained on the ceiling as he hummed in reply. "Maybe. I don't know much use I've been these last couple of years. Maybe if I had done more, our men wouldn't have felt like they needed to join Xanthus."

"Don't say that." Allie sat up and forced his bright eyes to meet hers. "Barcus, you are exactly the kind of hero this world needs. One who can admit when he's done something wrong. One who wants to fix things. If those men left, it isn't a reflection of you. You don't need heroes like them."

He blinked at the forcefulness of her words, and even Allie had to admit she was surprised by the truth she felt in them. But she would be damned if they spent a moment of their time together mourning over men who didn't give a damn about protecting the innocent.

Slowly, a wide smile pulled at Barcus's lips. His arms pulled her on top of him, and before Allie could protest, he kissed her deeply. Gods, the man was a great kisser. His tongue could be used as a weapon against the right enemy.

Allie found herself useless against it, melting into his embrace as a fire of lust encased her.

"You're right," he breathed, tangling his fingers in her hair. "Fuck them."

A fire was back in his eyes. One Allie was beginning to love. She pushed her hips down against his hardening cock. Delicious friction tingled across her nerves as she grinned. "No, hero, fuck me. Right now."

⚘

Both Eolis and Ocypete were still in the library when they walked in. A stack of thick leather-bound tomes surrounded them like a wall. Four different cups of coffee and a bowl of cereal sat in scattered piles across the oak table, making it impossible to tell how long they had been working.

Barcus stared at the sight in disapproval. "I told you to go to bed."

Eolis waved him off. "I will once the caffeine runs out. In the meantime, come look—I feel like I've made a lot of progress on our map."

"What are you eating?" Allie asked as they approached the table. "Chocolate milk in cereal? Aren't you a little old for that?"

His thin brows narrowed in confusion. "This isn't chocolate milk. It's cold coffee."

Barcus groaned, but Allie couldn't hold back a laugh of surprise. "You're kidding."

"Not at all." As if to illustrate the point, he took another mouthful. "It isn't bad."

"Don't knock it till you try it," Ocypete agreed, raising her own bowl.

"You're both heathens," Barcus said, falling into a chair. "Now why don't you tell us what progress you've made."

"Right." Eolis set his bowl aside and directed them to the map, now covered entirely in a rainbow of pushpins. "Once we put Krone's information together with what we gathered, I found a pattern. We have three distinct locations here. Green marks where unmortals live or frequent. Red is locations where we know an attack took place."

"And what does the blue represent?" Allie asked, taking in the colors speckled across the map. There hadn't been any blue yesterday, but now it outnumbered every other color on the map. In a few locations, the blue cropped up close to where unmortals lived, but more alarming were the speckles that overlapped with red.

Eolis grinned at her, as if he'd been waiting all morning for that question. He tapped a finger against a nearby notebook. "Your sister's translations really came through. These represent buildings Erik worked on as an architect."

"Erik," Barcus mumbled, moving to grab one of the notebooks from Eolis's hand. He flipped through the pages until he stumbled upon a photo, tinted brown from age. In the center sat a skinny man with glasses and a crooked nose. He looked like an academic type, with a young face but eyes that spoke of a truer age.

"Yes, I managed to lay out a few of the projects he worked on from his notes and drawings," Ocypete sighed, eyes sweeping over the map once again.

Allie studied the map, noting the familiar streets and building names. The National Art Gallery was highlighted with both a red and a blue pin. A cluster of blue and red pins hovered nearby. All were public areas, places where crimes were known to have taken place in the past. Union Station and a fancy grill off Fifth Street. It was hard to believe the deceased hero had had a hand in so many of the city's landmarks. Nearby, the Lincoln Memorial and the Congressional Library were both blue, with no other colors nearby. The latter sparked something in her memory.

The library—she'd been there before, with her sisters.

It can't be. She checked the other blue-pinned locations just to be sure. The Capitol building, the US Treasury building—yes, it was all here.

"You're sure this Erik guy built these buildings?"

"Well, he orchestrated them, planned them out, and got the resources. It's all in his notes."

"In Uranides?" Allie asked for clarification.

"Yes…" her sister said slowly.

"I know what's special about them."

"You do?" Eolis and Barcus stared at her.

She ignored the surprise in their voices and turned to her sister. "Pete, remember when you took us on the tour of the city that one summer because you were researching turn-of-the-century influence?"

"I can't believe you remember that." Ocypete blinked, but as the shock wore off, a newfound realization took its place. She looked back down at their notes, then back to Allie. "*Oh…*"

"What?" the heroes asked.

"I was doing research into scared sites. DC is known to have the largest collection of them in North America," Ocypete said.

"And now we know a hero working for Xanthus had a hand in creating them," Allie finished.

"I've never heard of a sacred site," Barcus said, turning to Eolis, who wore the same blank look.

Ocypete waved a hand towards the map. "All the buildings highlighted in blue used material blessed by the homeland—either in their staircases or in the main structure of the building. If what you said is true, your hero installed all these locations with ancient material blessed with the presence of the gods. All it takes is a single brick or stone from a temple to infuse a place with old magic. It doesn't have to be much, but unmortals can feel it."

"Fascinating," Eolis breathed. "What do they do?"

"Sacred sites are used mostly to get closer to the gods.

In the old days, mortals would make sacrifices at the temples, but now those locations are little more than debris. By using pieces in buildings here, a location can become closer to the gods." Allie didn't dare take her eyes off the sheer number of sacred sites laid out before her. As she spoke, the significance of Xanthus's plan became clear. "Making them the perfect place to perform a ritual."

Both men started at the information. Barcus was the first to recover. "Each time we killed for the *Theres* Blade, it was always at an ancient site. I knew he was conducting a ritual, but I never thought twice about why the location mattered."

"Which means Xanthus will likely look to conduct his next sacrifice at one of these sites," Eolis assured.

"Bingo." Finally, they had the clue they had been looking for. And they'd done it together. Her relief and pride almost eclipsed the overwhelming reminder that Xanthus would try to kill again. She just hoped they could stop him before that.

"I'll ask Krone to keep a watch at these sites, but we'll have to be careful. We don't want Xanthus to catch on that we know something."

"Tell him he won't have to do it alone," Barcus said. "I'll call for backup. We'll have men staked out at each site. It would be ideal to catch Xanthus before the next ritual, but if we can at least keep him from making a sacrifice, that will buy us more time."

"Does this mean we can go home?" Ocypete asked. Allie half expected to see hope in her sister's eyes, but there was a pleading tone to the question. A small cry of disappointment.

When Barcus shook his head, an odd sense of relief

pulsed through her. "I don't think that would be wise. Krone will ensure all the unmortals are safe, but Xanthus will still try to target you two. If you stay here, it will deny him the one thing he wants most for the ritual."

Only a few more days until the first, Allie reminded herself. They could do that. Keep a low profile and help Krone from afar. She would not complain about the extra time with Barcus—who knew how long these moments would last? Allie refused to think about how her chest tightened at the thought.

She wasn't ready to leave either. Not yet.

XXII

ALL THEY COULD do now was wait for an update from Krone or one of Barcus's heroes. While Ocypete nested in the library and Barcus dealt with Order business, Allie occupied herself by exploring the house.

Doing so had become her own personal game as she tried to piece together the lives of the heroes she now lived beside. She took in the luxury that decorated every hallway: antique vases, ancient artwork, random period pieces from the past centuries. All priceless, but none had the sparkle of gems that Allie coveted. She'd managed to uncover a variety of strange rooms in that time. Most were glorified storage spaces stuffed with weapons and discarded boxes. The place could likely house twenty heroes, maybe more, and she made a note to ask Barcus about those men later. There was still so much she didn't know about them, like how they had adjusted to the modern world and where they were now. After a few days, she'd only seen the four heroes in the large mansion. And after all the glamour of Elysian

Pointe, men had still chosen to follow Xanthus and his cult. She was beginning to wonder if maybe the Order wasn't as powerful as she had once thought.

Allie pocketed the question for another time. For now, there was one last room she hadn't explored in the eastern wing, and curiosity thrummed in her veins at the idea of what lay inside.

She knocked politely before pushing the door open. A large sunroom stretched before her, filled with leather couches and a glistening chandelier. Even at night, the room sparkled. It was instantly her favorite.

The young hero stared at Allie in open-mouthed horror, his paintbrush just inches away a canvas.

So… this was his room. The one he retreated to when he wasn't being harassed into training by Hector or grumbling in the library.

They stared at each other until Leo's anger unfurled across his face. "What are you doing here?"

"Exploring," she answered easily, bracing herself against his ire. "What are you doing here?"

"That's none of your business," Leo growled like a defensive animal as she stepped farther into the room. After nearly a week in the same house, she'd learned to ignore his irritation. The hero could bark all he wanted, but he wasn't dumb enough to make a move against her.

An eclectic collection of canvas paintings covered the walls, catching her eye. The skill of the paintings drew her closer. Most were portraits. She spotted Hector and Barcus, and a few nameless women in a variety of poses. There was even one of Pete's face, highlighting the hazel speckles of her eyes as she stared off into the distance. Then one made her stop, and a small gasp escaped.

"That's me."

A woman with beautiful black wings, silhouetted by the moon. Dancing among the stars were two more figures. Her heart clenched. Her sisters.

As soon as he realized she'd spotted his art, Leo jumped from his stool and moved to block her path. "That's nothing."

She whirled, pinning Leo with a look. At first, she mistook the red hue that colored his face as anger, but his wide, innocent eyes suggested something else entirely. He looked away, stammering over an explanation. "Don't get a big head. I just... I... sometimes I see things and they stick with me until I paint them on the canvas... It isn't..." He couldn't even finish the words.

"It's beautiful."

His head jerked up, looking as if he hadn't heard a compliment before in his life. Or maybe... in a very long time.

"Thanks." He rolled his shoulders and stood a little straighter.

She turned away from the painting, unable to look at it any longer. Swallowing hard, she tried to embed lightness into her tone. "So, shouldn't you be training with Hector?"

Leo ran a hand over his blond curls, looking too young. "He's distracted with a project from Barcus."

"Does Barcus know?" Allie let the question hang between them. She wasn't stupid.

He paled at that. She laughed, waving off the fear. "Don't worry, I won't tell him."

He has enough to worry about.

"Good," Leo said. "Thanks."

"Thanks?" Allie felt a thrill of victory from the word.

His defenses rose again, as high as the walls of Troy.

"Yeah, now can you go? This is the first time in years I've been someplace where I can relax and actually paint."

She didn't move. "I had no idea you were a painter."

He didn't reply. Just dunked a brush in a cup of water and eyed the colors in front of him.

"Is this what you did? Before you became an immortal?"

His mouth twitched down and she was sure he would snap at her. But he didn't; his hand moved across the canvas with singular focus. It was the first time she'd seen him so intent on something.

"Which god was it? Was it Athena? They say she always appreciates good art."

Leo sighed, mumbling something in… Italian. Yes, that was definitely an Italian curse. Oh, this was fun. Teasing heroes was quickly becoming one of her favorite pastimes. "What was that? I didn't hear you."

"Aphrodite," he said, casting his voice across the room. "Aphrodite turned me into this."

Turned me into this. That wasn't how heroes usually talked about their blessing. They puffed with pride before launching into an exaggerated tale of their quest. That was how she had found out Hector had retrieved Hephaestus's steel leg from Hermes, who had stolen it as a jest.

But Leo was tight-lipped, offering no sign of wanting to continue his story. He wore a look she recognized from all her time with Barcus.

Pain.

Fuck, good job, Allie. You've done it again.

"I'm sorry. I shouldn't have pried."

"Why even ask?" He started moving again, painting red across the lips of his figure. Where his movements had been easy before, they now seemed stiff. "You don't care."

"Sure I care," she protested. "It might explain why you're such an asshole."

He laughed. "I was always an asshole, even before I was made immortal. It's a prerequisite of art school."

"Is it a requirement for Aphrodite to give you immortality as well?"

"No. I'm just that good." She could hear the smirk in his voice. There must have been hundreds of girls in the past who had swooned at that smirk. Hell, even she had fallen prey to its charms upon first glance.

Allie scoffed, and it was all the encouragement he needed to continue. "Really. I didn't want immortality. I had no idea things like this even existed. One day I'm in the studio, making my own painting of Aphrodite, when the goddess herself appears out of nowhere. She said no one had ever made such a likeness, and she wanted to reward me."

"It doesn't sound like you thought it was a reward…"

He frowned at his painting. "I didn't ask for this. Any of this."

It was easy to forget he was just a young man when the gods had blessed him. Not unlike the other heroes, but also completely different. Leo had not trained for battle; he hadn't sought out quests or dreamt of victory. His greatness came from his keen eye for beauty.

"Barcus said I should apologize to you."

The confession caught her off guard. Allie could only watch as he considered his next words. Forgiveness wasn't easily doled out just because someone asked. It would have been easy for him to shrug off the attempt at an apology and never bring it up again. But Leo didn't make the easy choice. He met her gaze and pushed on. "Look, I know I tried to kill you and all. I… thought I was with the good guys and now it turns out that was wrong. I made a lot of dumb decisions and I'm trying to do better from now on. So… I'm sorry."

Wow. Allie couldn't believe what she was hearing. If someone had told her weeks ago that Leo would actually apologize to her, she would have laughed. But here he was, not threatening her or trying to kill her, but apologizing.

It wasn't because of her. She'd done everything in her power to tease the hero.

This was all Barcus.

He'd seen that small fragment of goodness in Leo when Allie could not. He'd seen the goodness in her when others hadn't.

"Apology accepted."

Leo nodded before returning to the age-old tactic of totally ignoring her, but Allie caught a glimpse of the relief that crumpled his face. It was easier to focus back on the painting than acknowledge that they had just shared a moment of understanding.

She took one last look at the winged creature in his painting, the bright moon and the power of her silky black wings. Was that what Barcus saw when she allowed herself to transform?

Beauty and death wrapped into one creature. For so long, she'd forgotten how others saw her kind. The word *monster* was thrown around so carelessly, but she didn't see a monster in that picture. She saw something godly.

It was a rare moment when she saw something she wanted and let it slip through her fingers. Committing the painting to memory one last time, she did just that and left Leo to his paintings.

❧

"Where are we going? The party is the other way."

It felt strange to be having a party while Xanthus was still free, but Hector had insisted, and she didn't want to offend the giant man. The feast would be a welcome break from the hours they'd spent researching every sacred site in DC, and she was ready to eat, but it seemed Barcus had his own plans to take her mind off things.

"Maybe I just want you all to myself for a little while."

"If that was the case, why aren't we going to our room?"

He didn't correct the phrase, and a thrill of possessiveness sang in her heart. *Our room. Our home. Our life.* Those things felt more real every day.

"There are more rooms in this place than just the bedroom and the library. And I'd like to show you something."

Allie pouted, eyeing the large portraits that hung around them. Expensive oil paintings of heroes doing what heroes did best—fighting. She recognized a few of them based on context: Achilles shining brightly with his golden shield, Bellerophon on his black-winged Pegasus, Perseus staring down the kraken. All were cast in a glow of glorified battle, blood speckled across their faces and weapons in hand. She noticed Barcus didn't pay the paintings any mind. He walked with purpose to the end of the hall, where two black porcelain statues of Kerberos sat against a wall. Each of the three heads had sharp canines bared in a snarl of warning.

Barcus put his hand on top of one of the heads in a loving pat. "Good boy." In response, the stone statue groaned and the wall next to it slid open, revealing an undiscovered stairway.

"What is this place?" Allie asked, trying not to look impressed. Plush carpet covered the floor as efficient lighting led them down into the depths of the mansion. It looked nothing like the secret passageways she was used to. Where were the wet stone walls? The torches to light their way? It didn't even have any cobwebs. Considering the men who lived in the house, she bet Eolis made time to dust every inch of the mansion at least once a week. Even the secret staircases.

Barcus only beamed with pride as he led the way down. "Consider yourself lucky. Very few get a tour of our treasury."

"*Treasury?*" Her heart skipped at the word. There were legends about the great treasures of heroes. Gifts and gold that extended back to the dawn of civilization. Allie couldn't believe her ears. She, a harpy, was being shown the greatest collection of treasures in the world. She had to be on her best behavior, but her fingers itched with the need to know what was there. If she hadn't grown to care about him so much, if this had only been a few thousand years earlier, well, she wouldn't be making the same promise.

Her head whipped around, taking in the enormous space they walked into. Three large iron chandeliers hung above their heads, catching everything in their light. All around them stood shelves, each a different size in grandeur but breathtaking, nonetheless. To her left lay a pile of ancient weapons. To her right, a collection of terra-cotta vases. Her eyes didn't know where to look first.

"It's a lot to take in," Barcus agreed. "Every time I come here, I find something new that's been forgotten."

"It's all yours?" she asked, stepping farther into the room.

"No, we tried to divide the space up so everyone has their own real estate. Come on, I'll show you my wing."

"You have a *wing*?" Her voice hitched as she followed. Every step on the treasury's stone slab floor echoed back at them. The farther they walked, the more she saw how disorganized it was. They passed several weapon stands, each different in the items they held. A small table displayed coins of all sizes and heritages under a glass panel. There was even a pile of Renaissance paintings lying on the floor.

The treasury wasn't just one room, she discovered, but many different ones. Once, when she'd lived in Europe, she and her sisters had taken up residence in an abandoned castle. Its basement had had a similar structure to it. Little alcoves with stone archways sectioned off the floor. Back then the rooms had been used for the help—one to do the cooking, another for laundry. Here, the men used the different spaces to divide their years of spoils.

When they came to Barcus's room, there was no sign, no nameplate that distinguished it from the others, but she knew it on sight.

Everything that Barcus was sat scattered throughout the space, from the collection of spears placed carefully on their pikes to the large vase, unadorned and chipped, set against the wall. A peasant's vase from a life before immortality. A set of boar tusks the size of a child's bicycle hung on the wall, alongside various animal skins. His hunting trophies were the predominant items in the room, but they weren't the only things.

On a table, there was a shield with a golden stag painted across the front. The creature's head was bent low, ready to spear its enemy before the killing blow could take it down. Typically, it was an image of unmortals that decorated a soldier's shield, an icon used to strike fear in the heart of their enemies. Barcus didn't have that. His shield told every man exactly who he was—Artemis's Great Hunter. That alone would make his foe tremble.

She wanted to rifle through it all as a child might tear through Christmas presents. But this room was every moment of Barcus's life, every adventure he'd been on, and every victory he'd enjoyed. They deserved time—time where she could take in the items and give them proper adoration. Time to memorize the things Barcus cared for so much he would hold on to them for centuries.

Next to her, the hero shifted from one foot to another. "I told you," he said quietly. "I'm only good at one thing—hunting—and this is what it's gotten me."

"That's not true," Allie said, tearing her eyes away from the treasures. Barcus's brows knitted in confusion, a protest already posed on his tongue, but she gave him a look of warning. "It's not, Barcus. You are good at so many things. At leading, mentoring, making people feel important." *Making people feel loved.* She didn't say the last part out loud, but there was no need. "You can't hang those things on the wall, but you don't have to. I've seen it."

He closed his eyes as if allowing her words to wash over him, and when they opened, there was a fire in them that made Allie's knees weak. "I bought you here for a reason, Allie. Over here." Barcus moved towards a small wooden box that looked so plain among the precious souvenirs. The box sat in the middle, made from old elm wood. Allie glanced at Barcus, silently asking permission, and with a nod he granted it. Eager fingers fell upon the box, cradling it, feeling the smoothness of the wood and the weight. It was surprisingly heavy. Allie opened the box and bit back a gasp.

A collection of jewels consumed the light of the room, reflecting it back in a pristine, shimmering rainbow. Beautiful gold earrings and a necklace with a blood-red ruby. There were so many chains and bracelets, all tangled together. A little love and care would allow her to see them in their full glory again. "If you treat them so poorly, they will be of no use to you when you need them."

"I've had no use for them in centuries. I doubt that will change."

Allie cooed to the metals, plucking a bundle of tangled necklaces up before she caught sight of what lay beneath them. A ring, golden like the sun, with an Adonis flower blossoming on each end. In the middle sat the largest obsidian stone she'd ever seen. The inky blackness of the gem reminded her of the winter nights. If she stared at it long enough, she could see the stars themselves reflecting back.

"Where did you get this?" In all her years, she'd never seen anything like it. It was in immaculate shape, only slightly aged from years of neglect. It shined so beautifully. A little cleanup would make it the envy of the world once again.

"An Italian princess gave it to me a long time ago," he answered. "Do you like it?"

"I love it." Her fingers caressed the petals of the flowers.

"Then it is yours."

There was nothing that could tear her attention away from the ring, except those words. Her head jerked up, meeting Barcus's eyes. He was staring at her, a small smile tugging at his lips. "Wha—what did you say?"

"It is yours," he repeated. The words hadn't magically changed. "All of it, if you want it."

The declaration stole the wind out from under her wings. She was falling, hard and fast, towards the ground. She stared at the man next to her, the ring still clasped between her fingers. "You don't know what you're saying."

"I do. In a thousand years, I've had no use for these treasures. I can barely look at my mementos from war. I don't need it, Allie. Any of it."

"I don't want your charity," she said firmly, watching his expression.

"This isn't charity."

"Then what is it?"

"Isn't it obvious?"

She didn't think Barcus could surprise her anymore. After nearly a month with the man, she thought she knew his brand of heroism. But then he dropped to one knee in front of her and Allie felt like he'd landed a fatal blow to her gut. "I believe tradition states I should be on the bended knee when I ask permission."

"You want to marry me?" she squeaked.

Marriage! She'd never considered it before. Unmortals didn't get married. The thought of being tied to one person for a hundred years was suffocating, much less till death and all that. She could feel her feathers bristling under her skin, but not in fear. They trembled under an entirely different emotion.

Barcus shook his head. "It doesn't have to be like that. I'm asking if you want to share this life with me. As partners."

Partners. The ring felt hot in her hand. Yet her fingers curled tighter around it. "For how long?"

He shrugged. "For as long as you'll have me."

She didn't want to fall into the same trap as before, tied to one space because of duty and obligation. And Barcus knew that—he always seemed to know what she needed to hear, what she needed to do, even when that didn't make sense to everyone else. And he was giving her the freedom to decide. Gods, she loved this man so much. This hero.

There was only one answer she could give.

She threw the ring at him.

⌁

It flew across the room, a golden star across the sky, and pinged against his chest. Confusion poured over him, overpowering any sense of hurt. "What was that for?"

Allie was in front of him before the question finished, her hands cupping his cheeks, urging him to stand. He did so slowly, feeling her body curl closer against him as he took her in his arms. He would be forever surprised by how featherlight her body was. "You seem to be under the wrong impression."

"And what is that?"

Her head tilted up, allowing him a full glimpse of her hooded eyes and those lips—perfectly shaped like Eros's bows. "You think I'll only agree if you give me something shiny to persuade me. I don't need that ring, Barcus, or any of it. If I have you, I'll be happy."

Happy. Gods, he'd given up on being happy centuries ago. He'd resigned himself to a life where love would blip in and out like a star, only felt through the lens of someone else. When he'd found Argos, there had been a brief moment of happiness before the search for Xanthus had pulled him away.

Now it was different. He'd thought happiness would diminish the weight on his chest, but somehow it pressed harder, making his heart throb with each beat. He sucked in a breath of air, but even that was a struggle. "Is that a yes?"

Allie nodded, red lips curling into a smile. "Yes."

He'd forgotten how painful hope could be. How it filled a man with enough joy to make him high and with enough dread that if it were ever taken away, he would truly go mad. For now, he buried his nose into her inky-black hair and thought of nothing else but her. When the memories of the past came back to haunt him, this would be what he would think about. This would help keep him sane.

"I love you," he said.

She didn't tense as she might once have done. That was the old Allie. Her muscles melted against him instead. "I love you, too," she breathed, eyes wide.

Their lips met for an air-swallowing kiss, one that made the room spin. He could stay like this forever, wanted it more than he could remember wanting anything in the world. But eventually, the kiss had to end. Allie was the one to pull away first, his hand still cupping the back of her head as they stared at each other.

"Are we crazy?"

"No," he said in a soft voice. "For the first time, I don't feel crazy at all."

Allie grinned and bent down to retrieve the ring. "Can I still keep this?"

"I thought you said you didn't need it."

It slipped onto her left hand as if it had been crafted for the finger. "I don't, but now that I've gotten my point across, I don't want it to go to waste."

Barcus laughed, taking her hand and bringing the ring

to his lips. "It looks great on you. Help yourself to all the jewels. In fact…" A wicked idea burned at the edge of his mind, making his cock go instantly hard. "I'd like to be the one to put them on you."

Her brows dipped in confusion. "Alright…"

"But first, these clothes are in the way." His hand slipped under the thick fabric of her sweater, skimming over the smooth skin underneath. Allie's eyes widened, her mouth falling open in a soft moan.

"Oh?"

"Yes. You see, some of these jewels are from the third century. Queens and kings wore them. They really need to be the center of attention, and they can't do that lying against synthetic wool."

Allie moaned as his hand inched higher, cupping her breasts. "You make a good point."

"I know. Now undress for me."

The command elicited a lovely shiver out of her as she obeyed without any fight. But the fire he loved so much sparked those gray eyes. First, he lifted her green sweater up and over her head, then the deep-cut camisole that lay underneath. Barcus ate up the sight of her slowly revealing herself to him. The pale swell of her breasts, the perfect lines of her waist and hips. She discarded each article of clothing with a little flourish that made him chuckle.

"What next?"

"Next?" He strolled towards her and saw how her body reacted, tensing in anticipation of his touch. But she would have to wait. He walked past her towards the jewelry box, its contents still on display and ready for him to pick the first decoration. It was an easy decision—a gold necklace with a slender snake carved into the chain caught his eye.

He held it up for her to see. "This was one of the first treasures I collected. Found in the ruins of a Cretan castle."

Greed flashed across Allie's face. She moved to step forward, but Barcus shook his head. "No. Don't move. I'll put it on you."

"Alright," she agreed with a breathless sigh.

He moved behind her and brushed the ends of her shoulder-length black hair aside, showing her beautiful neck. When the chain touched her skin, her entire body trembled as if touched by a cold breeze.

"I'd like to think this once belonged to a princess. Maybe to Ariadne herself before she fled with Theseus."

"How did you come to find it?"

"I was asked to search the labyrinth for the bones of fallen heroes. I found many things there—weapons, helmets, coins… all belonged to men. Except for this." He turned the clasp and admired his work. The serpent's slithering body sat along the ridge of her collarbone, two red ruby eyes gleaming up.

"When was this?"

"Centuries after Theseus. But it was only right to honor those who were not granted immortality like myself. We found a few bones, burned them and buried the ashes so that they could safely navigate to the underworld." He turned back to the box, searching for the next piece, but not before catching the knowing smile on Allie's lips.

"That was nice of you."

"It was my duty."

"You're always doing that. Thinking of others."

He pulled out two large earrings set with onyx stones. He held them up for her approval, and she nodded. "Is that not what a hero is supposed to do?"

"Only the real ones."

There she went again. That tone with those complimentary words. It was almost like they were back to sending cruel jabs at one another, but he knew better now. He moved close, tucking a piece of black hair behind her ear as he carefully slipped the earring in place. Doing so brought their bodies together. From this vantage, he could see every breath she took, every pore and goose bump peppering her arms. "Don't move…" he whispered as a reminder.

"Then you better hurry up."

He finished the second earring, deliberately taking his time with the clasp. "And why is that?"

"Because I'm ready to lie across that table and have you fuck me."

He hissed, the image burning itself into his mind. Her sprawled out before him among the gold and silver, her black hair fanned out as emeralds and rubies peeked out between the strands.

The offer was too good to pass up. He bent down, pressing his lips to her neck expectantly. Allie keened; her knees buckled, but Barcus was there to steady her. He was done with this foreplay. "If that is what my harpy wants, it's what she'll get."

He lifted her up effortlessly and laid her out on the table, among the chaos and jewels. She didn't complain. Allie was a woman who thrived in a little havoc, and that extended to their lovemaking. His hands roamed the curves of her body, and her hardened nipples reached up to meet him, begging to be played with. "You have amazing breasts. The best I've ever seen."

He rubbed his mouth against the tender skin, tongue swirling around the areola. Allie squirmed against the touch, and it was delightful.

"Hey! If you love them so much, you have to be gentle."

"No one said anything about being gentle," he purred with a nip. She gasped, all complaints gone as his tongue circled the tip. He felt her long legs wrap around his torso, drawing them closer and grinding their bodies against one another.

Barcus grinned, fingers already trailing low until they dipped into her wet folds. "Gods, you are so wet."

"And impatient," she moaned.

He couldn't deny that; it was one of the many things he loved about her.

Love. The word echoed again in his mind as he leaned forward and licked her clit. He loved everything about this woman. The feeling was so strong it was like a shot of adrenaline to his body. He'd forgotten what this kind of passion could feel like. This was flint and steel scraping against his heart, setting it on fire. And he needed to show her what she did to him before his entire body went ablaze.

His hand held her hips in place as he lapped at her juices. Fucking her on the table with just his mouth. Allie cried out, his name falling from her lips like a prayer, and it was the most wonderful thing he'd ever heard. Barcus let his fingers move down, dancing against her entrance before plunging one finger inside. She was so wet and so ready for him that it didn't take long before he slipped a second digit in as well.

Her hands were suddenly in his hair, tugging him up for a sloppy, wet kiss. She tasted herself on his tongue and shivered against him. Something cold slithered around his wrists. When he looked down, Allie had wrapped a slender gold bracelet there. One end around him and the other around her wrist.

Interesting. It would be easy to break the chain, but the challenge of fucking her while it held them together was even more promising. He flipped her over in one quick move and pulled his cock free with one hand. When he sank into her, their groans filled the walls of the treasury.

Sometimes he forgot his own strength, and sometimes he forgot that the woman underneath could match him. Neither had a reason to hold back. Each thrust made the table rattle. Jewels fell to the floor, but the chain around their wrists held true. His muscles contracted, climax rearing its head and taking them both and turning them into monsters, Barcus roaring like a minotaur as Allie shook the walls with her scream.

His body still shaking with aftershocks, Barcus fell on top of his lover. Allie shifted to look at him, the hand with the onyx ring reaching up to touch his cheek. Quiet fell in the treasury, a moment where they could exchange soft words and even softer touches.

"Hero." Allie panted the word, holding it out as if there was more she wished to say, but the only thing that came was, "My hero."

"Yours," he couldn't help but agree, finding her hand and letting his thumb stroke across the onyx ring. "Forever."

XXIII

"ALLIE! THERE YOU are!"

Walking into a party full of guests and food after being fucked on gold was a first for Allie. She looked up just in time to see Helen bounding towards her, wearing an adorable black dress and leather jacket. The girl already had a bottle of beer in hand, meaning she'd been there for some time.

Damn, she was late to her own feast.

"Sorry, I … uh, couldn't decide what to wear."

"What happened to you?" Ocypete asked, drawing the attention of the entire room.

Allie self-consciously pulled at her sweater, ensuring that not a single feather was out of place. "What do you mean?"

"I mean, you look like you just got—"

"It smells delicious in here!" Barcus announced loudly, waltzing into the room two minutes after Allie, like they'd agreed. He took in the guests that filled the large kitchen with exaggerated awe. "Argos! Claire! So you're the source of this amazing smell."

A woman Allie hadn't seen before turned from the stovetop, her honey-brown hair pulled into a messy bun that miraculously didn't have any food in it despite the chaos of dishware surrounding her. "Hello, Barcus. Hector told me you might need a professional for this meal."

"Feast!" Hector and the man named Argos corrected with glee, clinking their beer glasses in good cheer. Allie had heard so much about the hero Barcus considered a dear friend, but the man at the table didn't look much like a hero. He had the rugged good looks, yes, but there was no coin visible. Eolis and Leo sat nearby, both nursing glasses of wine, which they raised in a quiet salute.

Love warmed Claire's face. "Yes, yes. Feast."

"Come sit with us, you two!" Hector said, standing to make room. "Dinner is almost ready."

Argos followed suit, dutifully moving towards his wife to take instructions on what to place on the kitchen table. Allie stood beside Helen and her sister at the kitchen's grand island, a decision she quickly regretted when the two pinned her with nymphish grins. As the men eased into their own conversation, the young girl leaned over the granite, widening her eyes expectantly.

Allie raised her brows back. "Yes?"

"So where were you really?" Helen asked as Pete hid a smile behind her wine.

"Oh." This was a conversation she hadn't expected. She hadn't seen Helen in weeks, but the girl seemed comfortable picking up with her like they were the oldest of friends. She had such confidence after only a few measly mortal years. Allie was compelled by it. But she knew the pressure that came from having two sisters hounding her for information, and she stood strong. "Barcus wanted to talk to me about something."

"And what was that exactly?" Helen rested her chin in the palm of her hand and tilted her head in an "I'm listening" gesture.

"Helen, it's rude to ask people about private conversations. You should know that," Claire admonished. "Don't mind her. Would you like anything to drink?"

"Wine would be nice," Allie said.

Claire grinned. "Coming right up. I like those earrings, by the way."

"Thank you. Barcus gave them to me," Allie said, tucking a piece of hair behind her ear to show off the full glory of the earrings. She just so happened to use her left hand, revealing the onyx ring to her audience.

Helen's eyes widened. Claire grinned as she placed a wineglass in front of Allie. "Well, look at that. Should I be giving you my congratulations?"

"Oh, it's nothing formal," Allie said, looking down at the ring. "Barcus just had these gathering dust in the basement. I'm taking care of them for him."

"Right," Helen drawled. "By the way, you have a few pieces of gold stuck in your hair."

Allie combed her fingers through, and sure enough, a small piece of metal fell out.

"Well, I approve," Ocypete said, reaching out to pull the hand closer for inspection.

Claire's mouth curved into a smile with a thousand secrets as she expertly cut into one of the largest steaks Allie had ever seen. Within seconds, it was carved and plated with the rest of the food, completing the elaborate spread. "Alright, boys, time for your feast."

Hector let out a boisterous cheer, and Claire ushered them to the table. Allie sat down in the open chair beside Barcus, taking in the spread before them and—wow, it really was a feast. Delicious juices were still leaking out of the lamb, steam rose from the skin of fresh vegetables, and homemade pita bread accompanied a bowl of hummus. Claire listed the other platters, enough to feed an entire army. "Chicken risotto and some shrimp orzotto. I've been trying to perfect it for the restaurant. Let me know what you think."

"You made all this?" Allie blinked. "Today?"

Claire laughed. "I'm a chef. I've grown used to cooking a Thanksgiving feast for these guys on last-minute notice."

Argos laughed, taking his wife's hand and kissing the top. "You are a wonder."

Allie watched the two in fascination. Argos, the hero who had become a mortal for his wife. One glance and she could see how he'd made such a difficult decision. The two were head over heels in love. If she squinted, she might still see Eros's arrows sticking out of their backs.

When Hector had enthusiastically announced a feast only five minutes after meeting her, she had felt nothing but dread; she'd imagined awkward dinner conversations with heroes who couldn't hide their disdain. Yet the people here had shown nothing but kindness to her and her family. Even Leo remained civil.

Laughter fell easily as they reminisced with old stories and new. It reminded her of a real family dinner, and with that thought, her stomach hollowed with want. She'd forgotten the comfort of family.

Allie prepared herself for the overwhelming grief to encase her anew. And it did, but it wasn't as suffocating as it once had been.

As Eolis spilled into a story chastising Hector about leaving his weapons around the house, something brushed her arm. Barcus's hand twining with her own fingers, his thumb caressing the onyx with love. He leaned over, voice low so that no one would overhear. "Are you having fun?"

"Yeah." She shook off all somber thoughts and returned to the now. "Who would have thought—unmortals and heroes sitting at the same table."

He squeezed in understanding. "Not me."

We did this. The realization thrummed through her, and with it, a sense of accomplishment. Pete had been right— she'd sold herself short when it came to her and Barcus's relationship. Together, they were building a bridge not even the Covenant could manage. Hope for the future blossomed in her chest, along with an overwhelming sensation that this was only just the beginning. "After we take care of Xanthus, we'll have an even bigger celebration," she whispered. "One with unmortals, heroes, and even Mythos."

He laughed beside her, but didn't disparage the dream. "You're starting to sound like a hero."

"I guess you've been rubbing off on me," she purred, leaning in to swipe her lips against his own. It didn't matter that her sister was right there, or that there were other heroes surrounding them. No one uttered an objection, and it was glorious.

XXIV

TIME FLEW BY too quickly in the warmth of the manor. Before she knew it, the day before the ritual arrived. A new tension seeped into the walls of the house. Hector seemed to disappear after the festival, diving deep into training with Leo. While Argos and Helen seemed to spend more and more time around the house, both eager to help in any way they could, Allie and Barcus spent their time going over the plan again and again as the morning sun bathed their bodies in a reassuring glow.

Krone had encouraged all the unmortals to leave the city limits, while Allie and Ocypete made the effort to check in with each and every person. Doing so took most of the day, but knowing everyone was accounted for was a source of unending relief.

Xanthus hadn't captured his next prey. Without an unmortal, he wouldn't be able to perform the ritual.

Barcus had men patrolling the sacred sites, on call in case anything should occur. But no one had reported anything out of the ordinary. Tomorrow, he would go into the city with Eolis and Hector to meet up with Krone. She and Ocypete were ordered to stay at Elysian Pointe by all members of their small group.

The idea of him leaving her behind had chafed. She had imagined them fighting together. But she understood Barcus's need to take on Xanthus and to see that battle to the end. He would have other heroes. He would have Krone.

He would be alright.

As night descended upon the house, there was still no update from the lion.

"We should go to sleep," Barcus said softly before pressing his lips against her forehead.

Allie squirmed closer against him, her limbs draped over his firm body like a second blanket. Barcus's fingers absently played with her hair as they both lay hopelessly awake. "I'll go to sleep when you do."

He laughed and she joined him. That was not going to happen. Their nerves were a bundle of anticipation. Not even vigorous sex could untangle their emotions. All they could do at this point was wait and hope. Hope that the day would come and go without bloodshed and without a ritual. If Barcus had to fight, she would pray to whatever gods would listen to keep him safe.

"I don't mind staying up with you," Allie whispered. The moments they'd shared were the few bright spots for her. Moments when she could finally relax and feel something besides mind-numbing anxiety. Hours where they memorized each other's bodies and where they talked about their pasts without any judgment. She'd grown used to someone by her side in the morning, waking her with delicate kisses. The idea of having that taken away reinforced her resolve to stay up.

"No one has called with an update," Barcus urged softly. "Come on. Let's—"

The harsh vibration of her phone cut him off. Allie glanced down and saw Krone's name flashing up. Her throat tightened as Barcus let out a quiet curse. "I have to take this."

She sat up and put the phone on speaker so they could both hear the news. If Krone was calling, there was an equal chance the news was good or bad. "What's up?"

Something brushed against the receiver, muffling the noise. She thought she heard a pained gasp before a man's voice answered. "Ah, there you are."

At first, Allie didn't recognize the sardonic tone, too calm and far too familiar. Her body knew, though. Ice chilled her blood as realization struck. "Xanthus?"

"Good to know I made an impression."

Barcus pulled himself up, immediately on alert. Hot anger pooled into her, melting away the fear. Her talons sharpened against the phone's glass screen. "What are you doing with Krone's phone?"

"He let me borrow it. Since the city suddenly seems sparse with unmortals, I had to find an alternate sacrifice for our little gathering. The last Nemean lion adds a poetic touch, don't you think?"

Oh gods. Krone.

Xanthus had Krone, the oldest and strongest among them. She could only imagine how that fight had gone down and how much blood had been spilled.

She met Barcus's gaze and held it long enough to be assured that he wouldn't speak a word. It didn't seem like Xanthus knew they were together. That the heroes and unmortals were working as one. And that gave them an advantage.

"You still need one more sacrifice," she breathed. "One Nemean lion won't be enough."

"Well, I do have a dryad here, but he isn't quite what I had in mind."

Oak!

A wave of righteous fury crashed into her, threatening to consume her from the inside out. They'd underestimated their enemy—how desperate he was to kill again. It had been naive to think he would wait until tomorrow night to strike. Midnight was only a few hours away, which meant the day of the ritual was upon them. Stupid, stupid.

Her mind spun as she tried to think of a way to regain control of the situation.

It took every ounce of strength to keep her tone calm as she asked, "What do you want?"

"Isn't it obvious? I made a promise and was disappointed to find that you weren't available. So I guess I'll just have to make do."

Next time.

She closed her eyes, remembering how he'd cut Celia's throat on the count. How he'd stared at her like she was just a piece of meat. Barcus's warning.

Allie was the one unmortal who had gotten away. Xanthus wanted *her*.

"Tell me where you are. We'll make it a date."

Barcus straightened, a frown of disapproval etched on his face. Allie shook her head at him, knowing this was what needed to happen. They needed to find Xanthus, and if using herself as bait was the key, then she would do it.

"You are so easy, little harpy." Laughter echoed over the receiver, a sound that started genuine but ended in a cold purr. "Alright, I'll see you at Tartarus."

XXV

"THIS IS THE second battle we've been dragged into in two years," Hector said. "If I didn't know better, I'd say that's a rather bad omen."

"Second battle?" Allie asked, following the goliath with the rest of the group. The house had gathered quickly when Allie had called for them, all the heroes armed with whatever weapon had been closest to them at the time. A sword, a knife, and in Leo's case, the thickest paintbrush in his arsenal. Even Argos and Helen had appeared in the halls, ready for whatever might be asked of them. She knew Argos had been assisting the other heroes the past couple of days, but Helen's appearance had come as a surprise. Especially when Allie thought she'd glimpsed the girl sneaking out of Leo's sunroom.

No one else seemed to notice, though, as they followed Hector down one of the many hallways. The man was hard to keep up with considering his large strides, but the promise of battle made his pace even more rushed with excitement. "Just last year, we took up arms against Circe and her beastmen. That was a good time. Got to shake off some old cobwebs," answered the goliath.

"It just goes to show you we can't get complacent," Eolis said from nearby.

"Who's complacent?" Hector asked, pushing into a room Allie hadn't been in before. During her initial tour, Barcus had shrugged the space off as part of the garage, even though she'd seen the large unattached garage when they'd pulled in. Now his explanation made more sense. The room was garage-like—cement floors and unfinished walls, leaving plenty of room for the equipment that filled the large space. Not just any equipment.

Weapons.

Armor.

And… a smith anvil.

"What is this?"

"Remember I told you about a hero blessed by Hephaestus?" Barcus asked. "Hector helps make all our weapons and keeps our gear in shape for just this occasion."

"Ah." It made a strange amount of sense now that she realized it. "So he's the one that made that terrible sheath for the *Theres* Blade?"

"Terrible?" Hector turned to her, eyes wide. "My work is not terrible."

"We can discuss the merits of your craftsmanship later. Right now, we need to get a move on," Barcus urged with all the authority of a true leader. His men did as they were told, filling the space and grabbing their tools with practiced ease. There were four fully maintained sets of hoplite armor hanging on mannequins, ready to be donned. Hector's bronze breastplate was the size of a small child. Even Leo was encased in armor, the metal of which reflected the room's light with a shiny newness that called to her. Seeing the men slip on the bronze cuirass plates was a stark reminder of what they were and what they once had been.

"Are you going to wear one?" Worry tickled at the base of her throat. Would wearing that armor and facing Xanthus cause him more pain?

Barcus offered her a smile, one that was meant to reassure. "I'll be fine." He bent down and picked up his shield with ease, slipping his arm behind the inside's leather holds. When he turned it over, Allie had to suppress a gasp. The blazon on the front was a woman with wings.

"That's…"

"Hector made the shield, but Leo painted it for me." He shot a look at the young hero, who was accepting help with his armor from Hector and doing his best to look unimpressed. "I thought it was time for a change." He stared down at the shield as if he couldn't stop looking at it, and honestly, neither could Allie. The picture Leo had painted was incredible; he'd managed to make her both beautiful and ferocious.

"Would you like one as well?"

"A shield?" Allie shook her head. "I can't hold it when I fly."

"No." He turned her towards the corner of the room, where metalwork was laid out along with two additional mannequins. "Your own armor."

⚘

Barcus grimaced as he did the last clasp of his shin brace. His skin recoiled as the cool metal slipped on, but slowly he felt his muscles relax, adjusting to the familiar weight as if he had just put on a pair of old, comfortable socks. A relieved sigh escaped his lungs.

"It looks good on you." Argos stood beside him, arms crossed, as he took in the newly modified armor. "But do you really need that these days?"

"Not normally," Barcus answered. Usually, his spear and agility would be enough. But this time, things would be different. "Xanthus has a cult of heroes, trained as we were. This will be a true battle."

"I wish I could come with you…"

He looked up at the words and saw the ache on his friend's face. The desire to jump into battle, to stand beside his fellow heroes. Argos had been a part of the Order as long as Barcus. Together they and Xanthus had suffered trials and triumphs and watched new cultures be born from the bones of the old. But he'd learned long ago that Argos would not always be there to fight by his side. Now that same realization was dawning on his friend.

On Circe's island, it had been Claire fighting alongside Barcus to save Argos. His friend had been kept from battle for centuries, and now he would sit on the sidelines once again. "You have Claire…"

Argos nodded. "Yes. And my mortality. I don't regret any of it, of course. But I do wish—"

"I know."

They stared at each other. Argos dressed in jeans and a dark sweater, looking every bit like a modern man. A husband who worked to support his wife's restaurant. And Barcus dressed from head to toe in a bronze shell. Taking up the image of a man he once was. Sometimes it was easy to feel like a life of immortality meant a man could never change, but looking at Argos, Barcus knew he wouldn't be a fighter forever. After he dealt with Xanthus, he could put down the mantle and never fight again. He and Allie could have a life like his friend. One full of love and happiness instead of blood and grief.

"We will do our part," Argos promised. "Claire and I made the required calls. Within the hour, every hero in the city will be there to aid you."

"We'll need every man we can get." It would be enough to take on the small group Xanthus had with him at the gala. But if they miscalculated again, it would be dire.

"And woman, it seems. Looks like Helen will be joining you." Argos cut his head towards their collection of golden warriors. Hector and Eolis, mirror images of the fierce heroes they'd once been. Leo proudly wearing a chest plate with a lion's head emblazoned on the center. Next to them stood Allie and Ocypete, their wings out on full display as they tested them in their new armor. Barcus hadn't said as much out loud, but Hector had really outdone himself on their pieces. The front of the cuirass had ripples that made it look like golden extensions of their wings, climbing high across their shoulders and neck to protect the vulnerable arteries underneath. Their shin guards stopped just above the ankle, allowing them to fully transform their talons. Finally, an ornate Corinthian helmet with Hermes's wings on each side finished the pieces. They looked like Amazon warriors, beauty and death wrapped in golden decoration.

Helen was admiring the ensemble with clear envy. There was no armor for her. Time hadn't been on their side for such a piece, and if Barcus had the choice, she wouldn't be joining them at all. She wasn't even supposed to be here tonight, but the Fates had a way of mocking him. It would be impossible to talk the girl out of joining them now that she had gotten wind of the battle. "I should give her something for protection. A helmet or wrist guards."

"She'll be fine," Argos reassured. "I've seen what that girl can do. Besides, if you tried to keep her back—"

"She'd just follow us anyway," Barcus sighed. "Please don't tell Thalia. At least not until this is over."

"Of course."

They shook on it, sealing the promise and bidding farewell as warriors did. In silence. Even with immortality, there was no promise that any of them would come back from this unharmed. The *Theres* Blade and Xanthus's pursuit of an even deadlier weapon posed a threat to their immortal existence. The stakes were high, higher than they had been in a long time, and still the men and women around him did not hesitate to pick up arms.

Barcus felt a swell of pride as he looked at their small group. Their numbers alone wouldn't be enough, but the experience between Hector, Eolis, and himself should provide some advantage. Not to mention they had unmortals on their side. It was a small army, but one the likes of which had never been seen, and there was something to be said about that.

He came up behind Allie and let his fingers dance across the top of her soft feathers. She leaned into the touch, taking comfort from it. "Now that your wings are healed, I'm sure you could get there faster than our cars."

"I probably could," she agreed. "And believe me, I've already thought of that."

He wouldn't fault her for that. She was a free spirit, one who acted as quick as the wind. "Then you and your sister should go ahead—"

She gave him a look of disappointment. "You didn't let

me finish. I thought of it and decided against it. If Ocypete and I got there early, we wouldn't be able to take on all those heroes by ourselves. We do this together, remember?"

"Together," he promised.

Whatever came next, victory or death, he wanted to achieve it with this woman fighting by his side. He pulled her close and kissed her hard as their nearby audience pretended to adjust their armor. Time wasn't on their side, but he would take this moment to memorize the weight of her against him, the Chapstick on her lips, and the lavender shampoo that clung to her raven hair. After this battle, they would start a new life together.

All they had to do was kill the past.

XXVI

THE HEROES DIDN'T make a sound when they moved. An impressive feat given all the metal they wore. Even Allie couldn't match their stealth; she stepped carefully as they moved forward, hanging back with Helen and Leo and letting Barcus lead the way to Tartarus.

She kept her gaze set on Barcus's back, watching for any hint that his fear would overtake him again. But there was no sign of it. He moved with the same strength and reassurance as Eolis and Hector. "The staircase is narrow, and there isn't much room to hide."

The collection of heroes he'd gathered all nodded. Allie glanced at the men, with their helmets tucked against their sides, spears and swords at the ready. At least twenty of them, all there to help the unmortals trapped inside.

One by one, they crept past the unguarded doors. Xanthus was expecting them, but it was strange that there were no men posted on guard duty. She could hear music making its way up from underground, not the normal hypnotic tones that usually filled the den, but the heavy rhythm of war drums that haunted her from the gala. Allie felt her adrenaline spike, matching the call to war. Laughter and cheers echoed from behind the plush red curtain. Barcus peeled it back carefully, revealing fifty… no, seventy men.

It was significantly more than Xanthus had gathered weeks ago. She and Barcus looked at each other, the same concern reflecting across their faces. "Where did he get so many men?"

"I don't know," Barcus whispered. "There are only about a hundred of us in the Western Order. But there is some good news—he made a mistake. Look." He inclined his head to a group nearby. Allie squinted hard, taking them in as she tried to pinpoint what he meant. The heroes were dressed for combat, though their equipment was nothing as fine as what Hector had crafted. Most only wore shin braces or a chest piece, but all were armed.

Wait.

"They're all wearing armor, just as we are," Barcus whispered. "They hid amongst the Order for years without us knowing it, and now it will be just as difficult for them to pick us out of the crowd."

Barcus had a point, and suddenly the odds didn't feel so out of their favor.

Krone was nowhere in sight, but to her horror, Allie saw Oak tied to one of the pure-white columns, now stained with red streaks. He was badly beaten, the bark above his right eye torn off, but thankfully, he was alive.

"Bastards…" she hissed.

"Steady, love." Barcus reached out and grasped her wrists, anchoring them both in place. "You'll have your chance soon."

Barcus let the curtain fall and turned to the group

surrounding him. "We'll go out in waves. Eolis, Hector, and I will move first and try to find Krone. I want the rest of you to enter in small groups and spread out in the crowd. If things go bad, Allie and Ocypete will take to the air and take out as many out as possible. Helen and Leo, watch our back." No one argued against the plan, but only Allie could feel the tremble of his hands. He was putting on a brave face, but her hero was already touched by the god of fear. Blue eyes searched her face one last time—one last breath of quiet before battle. "Are you sure you want to do this?"

"Yes." She held his hands steady and squeezed. "Go find Xanthus."

Barcus leaned forward and placed a swift kiss against her lips before he threw back the curtain and stepped into the fray.

❧

As Barcus stepped into the familiar open lounge of Tartarus, not a single soul took notice.

He held his breath as they moved forward. Each step came with the risk of someone shouting out in alarm. But it never came. Instead, the enemy nodded in greeting, raised their glasses, even offered a drink. Their armor was familiar, the smile on their faces ones of companions, and the coins around their necks marked them as members of the Order. The gods had blessed these men at one time, and now here they were, defiling everything it meant to be a hero.

Eolis sucked in a breath. "Gods, they really are just like us."

"Which means they are immortal like us," Hector pointed out.

Barcus touched the *Theres* Blade hanging by his side. "That's what they think."

"Where to next?" Eolis took in the grand space with the critical eye of a strategist. Where Barcus appreciated the beauty of the structure, Eolis was taking in the nooks and crannies where a man could jump out and attack. Where the enemy had the greatest advantage.

Barcus did the same, looking for one thing in particular: Xanthus.

But the man was nowhere to be found.

"He's not here."

"He has to be," Barcus whispered. "This place is big. There is still one place we haven't looked."

He walked towards the grand columns, making sure not to look in Oak's direction for fear his sympathy would take hold. A muttered prayer fell from his lips. "Stay alive. Please stay alive." *All this will be over soon.*

The sunken theater of stone stretched out before them, and in the seats sat more men.

Hector hissed, "That's a lot of heroes."

"They're not heroes," Barcus whispered. "Not anymore."

"This is going to divide the entire Order," Eolis said.

A shadow of dread filled him as the truth sank in. Even if they killed Xanthus, it would be a long time before the aftershocks of this discovery settled. So many heroes had been indoctrinated, men who believed the same as Xanthus, that they could do whatever they pleased. How could the Order stand after this?

His thoughts were spiraling again, but he forced them down. *One problem at a time,* he reminded himself. *Focus on Xanthus and worry about the rest later.* "Come on, it looks like it is about to start."

"And when it does?"

"We'll make our move."

Eolis and Hector shared a look. It was easy to read the two's exchange as they considered the odds of fighting the crowd. It wouldn't be good. All they could do was pray the gods would be with them.

Barcus settled in halfway down the steps. Close enough that he could rush the stage if need be, but not so close that Xanthus could recognize his face. He focused on the thrum of the crowd, counting the number of men coming in and out and trying to establish the best route of escape if things went sideways. Only weeks ago, Ajax's screams had echoed off the limestone walls. Now, in a matter of minutes, new screams would replicate them.

The curtains of the stage shifted and finally parted. A roar of cheers lifted around them as Xanthus stepped out onto center stage. Unlike the men around him, the armor he wore was pure black, shaped with ragged spikes and crude molding. The outside had the look of hardened lava. There was no resemblance to the glorious armor they had once worn into battle; it was a shell made of nightmares.

At the gala, he had been in a tuxedo. Tonight, the armor showed a man who was expecting a fight. But more than that, it revealed a man who was afraid of being hurt.

Good. Barcus stared at his old friend, now his sworn enemy. No armor was perfect, and he intended to find where Xanthus was most vulnerable.

For once, it wasn't icy fear that chilled his core. No, a new feeling arose, one he hadn't felt in a long time. Rage. Pure and hot as Apollo's sun. It felt good, righteous even. If he held on to it, Barcus was sure it would be enough to help him do what needed to be done.

Xanthus smiled. His long, dark hair hung in coiled tendrils down his shoulders. "Welcome all! Isn't this a wonderful location for us tonight?"

He extended his hands, and on cue, the crowd came to life once again, cheering and howling like animals. A sharp slice of Xanthus's hand through the air cut off the cries with deadly precision. Silence hung over the room, and Xanthus basked in it. "I only recently discovered it. It was not in our records of sacred sites, yet here it is, built with stone from Medusa's lair and columns taken from Pan's temple." He inhaled deeply and grinned. "You can smell the blood and magic embedded in this place.

"This grand space belonged to monsters," he continued, shaking his head as he paced the length of the stage. "When we discovered it, news of our efforts had already reached their ears, and it was abandoned. Pity, it would have been nice to clear the world of a few more monsters, don't you agree?"

A collective "Aye!" replied in earnest. Barcus clenched his fists until slick blood collected in the palm of his hand.

"We only need two more sacrifices to achieve our goal, and tonight, I bring you those offerings." He waved a hand, and two men entered from stage left, dragging a large man in their arms. Barcus didn't immediately recognize Krone. His long mane had been shaved, showing off the dark bruises along his face. Hephaestion Chains bound him from shoulder to knee, but the stillness of the body made Barcus's throat tighten in fear. What had they done to him?

"I present the last Nemean lion!" Xanthus announced. "One of the great generals of the unmortal army. With his blood and the dryad, we will finally complete the *Athána-tos* Blade."

The name turned Barcus's stomach inside out. *Athánatos.* Immortal.

Cheers rang out. Men stood and clanked their weapons against the stone seating. One of the heroes on stage approached Xanthus, holding the blade that had slaughtered almost a thousand unmortals. Xanthus took it and stared at the reflective steel. A mad glimmer reached his eyes when he looked back at his acolytes. "But before we begin, I'd like to greet an old friend who decided to join us for this special occasion. Barcus, stand up!"

The sound of his name hit like coals in his face. A spotlight flashed on, blinding him. He reached up to shield his eyes as Xanthus's voice cut through the air. "You thought I wouldn't recognize you in that armor? I would know you anywhere."

Damn him.

Barcus shifted away from Hector and Eolis, trying to distance himself lest they be suspected. Slowly, he stood and felt the light fall away from his face so he could meet the eyes of every man surrounding him.

"You found me," Barcus said, voice carrying throughout the chamber around them.

Xanthus tilted his head up in amusement. "What are you doing here, Barcus? Didn't you learn your lesson last time?"

"I came to see what all the fuss was about," he answered with a shrug. "You've seemed to convince plenty of men to follow in your footsteps. It made me start to rethink my stance on the world."

"Oh." The unshakable confidence that always marred Xanthus's handsome features broke, but it disappeared just as quickly. "I'm sorry, but we don't accept cowards in my Order."

Laughter rolled throughout the stone stadium, but Barcus didn't buckle. His own anger was burning brighter by the minute. To his surprise, Xanthus cut the laughter off with a quick and commanding signal.

"I'm no coward," Barcus announced.

Xanthus tilted his head. "Then show us. Come, and I will let you finish what you started years ago. If you can do so without fainting, I would be happy to let you join us again."

Barcus didn't know how he did it, but he managed to descend the stone steps towards the stage. He climbed onstage with no resistance, stopping a few feet from his former friend.

Xanthus eyed the sword at his waist, the *Theres* Blade hidden by a thick leather sheath. For a second, Barcus wondered if he would stab him then and there to make an example out of him. Even without its thousandth death, the *Athánatos* Blade would be enough to kill a hero.

After what felt like an eternity, Xanthus shook his head. "Take out your blade. You'll need it."

Carefully Barcus drew his weapon, watching as Xanthus's eyes lit up at the sight of it. "Ah, what a beautiful sword. Remember all the blood it took to make it, Barcus?"

"Yes." He exhaled deeply, remembering the deaths they had been responsible for before he couldn't take it anymore. He'd walked away, but the guilt had never disappeared. "I've been wondering all this time why you left it behind in a desecrated temple when you worked so hard to make it."

"Yes, the Oracle that told me five hundred unmortal souls on a single blade would make the world's strongest weapon. But that was a lie." His followers booed on his behalf. "Don't worry, my friends. I managed to find the family of the Oracle who told us that falsehood, and I made them pay."

Their cheer was deafening. But there was something else about Xanthus's story that rang false. He remembered their visit to the Oracle. "You said the blade would help us find Argos."

A sardonic smirk curled across the Spartan's face. "Did I?"

He couldn't believe what he was hearing. For centuries, he had believed that they had killed to find Argos, to avenge him. But now it turned out Xanthus had lied to him all along.

Barcus bit his tongue against the news. If he let loose the storm of emotions inside of him, Xanthus would throw him to the wolves.

He had to get closer; he had to make Xanthus trust him. Suddenly, he heard Allie's voice in his head. *You catch more senators with wine than water.*

Xanthus's entire demeanor changed. There was confusion in his eyes, just for a moment, and Barcus knew what he had to do. He worked to make his voice as calm as possible. "If you had told me the truth from the beginning, perhaps we could have avoided the ugliness. Oh, well." He shrugged, then gave the *Theres* Blade a confident twirl. "At least I have this beautiful weapon by my side now, and I'm about to watch you create another. You were right. It is time for change, and you deserve what's coming, old friend."

Xanthus grinned as the crowd approved of Barcus's praise. His enemy stepped closer, his hand falling on Barcus's shoulder, fingers mere inches away from the scar that

Xanthus had marked him with. "Prove yourself to me now, Barcus, and I will pretend the past centuries never happened. We could go back to the way things used to be."

The new unholy weapon hovered above Krone, next to Barcus's blade, ready to drink the blood of its next victim. "Together, you and I can end this."

It was a devil's promise, one Barcus might have considered decades ago. Before he had seen the destruction Xanthus left behind and he had faced the other's hero hate head-on. He'd always wished they could find a way back to how things had been before, before Argos had disappeared, and before Xanthus had nurtured a hatred for the gods.

But this was the curse of immortality. The years went by, and without realizing it, everyone changed. For better or worse. Barcus just prayed he was changing for the better.

Looking down to Krone, the *Theres* Blade poised to strike, he steeled himself for what came next.

The lion opened one bloody and swollen eye to glare at him. His voice was a low gravel of pain. "I knew it. You are just like them. *Murderers.*"

"No, I'm not." Without warning, he swung up instead of down, carving into the arm of one of the heroes who held him hostage. It sliced through bone as easily as bread. Blood poured forth, covering the stage.

"You—" There was no time for Xanthus to utter his curse before Barcus was on him. They were so close, the *Theres* Blade needed only to land to do its damage. But Xanthus danced back, putting distance between them.

An outcry erupted from the crowd before a familiar scream pierced through it all. All heads turned to the top of the stairs, where Allie stood, a dark angel of death with her golden armor and raven's wings. She took to the air,

Ocypete following behind. As they did, their taloned feet picked up the nearest heroes and flung them against the stone wall.

Bone cracked against the stone, and everything fell into chaos.

Xanthus's men moved frantically to draw their weapons against the aerial threat while the heroes Barcus had brought drew against their neighbors, adding to the confusion of the battle.

Allie easily cut across their sea of sharp steel with barely a second glance. She made a fearful sight, like one of the furies of legend, there to deliver justice. The self-assuredness that had hung over the crowd quickly fell as the men scrambled to dodge her sharpened claws.

Xanthus's cool composure was gone. Anger drew his face tight as he snarled, "You betrayed me."

"Never. You were the one who turned his back on me, on Argos, when we needed you most." Anger crashed into him as he gestured towards the crowd around them. It was impossible to tell Xanthus's fighters from his own. Every man had the same coin, the same bronze-laced swords.

Brother fighting brother. Hero against hero. This wasn't what they were supposed to be.

"You've made a mockery of our Order."

"Open your eyes, Barcus. The Order has been in decline since the gods abandoned us," Xanthus sneered. "You insist on serving beings who no longer care about humanity when we are just as powerful! We are immortal! It is our time to take over!"

Barcus shook his head. "That is not why we became heroes."

A cruel smile twisted across his friend's face. "Maybe

not you." He turned and sprinted towards the edge of the stage, then jumped into the crowd.

Krone was weak. A mosaic of deep cuts decorated every inch of his body. There was a lot of blood. Barcus made sure to be gentle as he shucked the chains from his body and helped the lion to his feet.

"Thank you," huffed the unmortal, "for not killing me." Such simple words, but uttering them looked to have taken herculean effort.

"I would never."

Krone didn't answer him. Instead, he looked up to where Ocypete joined Allie in terrorizing the heroes.

"I need to go after Xanthus. Will you be okay?"

Somehow, a feral smile found a place on Krone's face. His teeth were bloodstained but already sharpened. "My wounds are having a hard time healing. Now that those chains aren't on me, I can finally fight back. Go, do what you need to do, but know that I make no promises about sparing your brothers."

Barcus could not fault him for the bloodlust, but they didn't need any more unnecessary killing. "I don't mind you attacking the enemy, but know my men are out there as well."

Krone's one good eye stared at him in a look that showed no sympathy, but to his surprise, the lion nodded. "I will only attack those who attack me. Now go. Don't let that bastard escape."

Barcus jumped off the stage into a flurry of steel and screams, with one goal in mind. Xanthus was not going to escape. Not this time.

❧

They took flight towards the ceiling to look down on the battle below. A few spears arched through the air, but it was all too easy to dodge them. Thanks to Barcus's heroes, the enemy seemed confused about the attack. Xanthus's men were turning on each other, calling each other traitors. Then Barcus joined in the fray, wielding one of most dangerous weapons to ever face immortals.

From above, she watched him cut down cult members with ease, dodging and thrusting like an elegant dance. With each swing of the *Theres* Blade, another hero fell and did not come up.

They were winning. They were actually winning!

"Look," Ocypete breathed, nodding towards the exit, where Helen and Leo fought back any man who tried to get past. Beside them stood Oak, cut free from his bonds and calling upon the nearby plant life to aid in their defense. The advantage of the high ground worked in their favor as they easily pushed fighters back.

Stones rumbled overhead, causing dust to fall onto her and her sister like gentle snow. Allie looked up, heart in her throat. *What now?* she thought as the building gave another shudder.

A roar cried out in answer, one that made her insides clench in fear and… hope?

She knew that roar, but Ocypete was the one to put a name to its owner. "Krone."

Allie turned to the stage, where a lion the size of a horse stood. It had been a long time since she'd seen Krone's true form. Over the years, she'd forgotten how terrifying the Nemean lions appeared. Even with his mane shaved, he was a fierce creature to behold. The stage splintered under massive paws, his dark-brown fur stained with blood from his wounds.

"He's okay," Allie sighed in relief. Seeing his bloody human form on the stage had been a cause for concern. From afar, it had been impossible to know the extent of his wounds. But a weakened Nemean lion was more than enough to help level the field between the heroes and Xanthus's cult.

Ocypete shot her a look. "I thought you hated him."

"Still do," she snorted, "but we need him, and he deserves a chance to take a bite out of these bastards." Pete was still staring at her, brows arched as if expecting more. "What?"

"It's nothing. Just didn't recognize my sister for a moment."

Allie nearly stopped flapping. "I'm still your sister."

"Yeah, but now you are the *old* Allie." Ocypete looked down at the lion, whose transformation sent men running in the opposite direction. "You managed to remember what we used to be. But not just that, you've reminded me—you've reminded Krone. I'd thought we'd lost that."

"So did I." All this time, she'd thought leaving would solve the displacement she felt. But now she was fighting alongside her sister, feeling stronger than she had in decades. She might not have managed to do that without Barcus.

Barcus, who had believed in her when no one else had done. Barcus, who had held her steady when she'd acted brash and had allowed her to fly when the time had come.

Pete gave her a playful wink. "Now let's see what I can remember from the old days." She brought her wings close and descended on a group of unsuspecting cult members. The men screamed as they ducked out of the way, but Pete was the fastest among the harpy sisters. Her clawed feet dug into the metal of one man's cuirass, piercing through to the organs underneath.

Allie got to work as well; it was easy to find the golden spark of Barcus's armor as he circled the room. She worked to pick off the men who tried to cluster around him, carving out an easier path for his search. Occasionally, their eyes met in a brief check-in before another attacker would divert their attention.

There was so much confusion. Blood coated the floors now, along with bodies. It was then that she noticed Barcus slow down. He stood in one place for far too long, head shifting from side to side in a desperate search for Xanthus. A cult member turned on him, approaching from the back, but she was there, swooping to the floor like a dark angel just in time to tackle the attacker to the ground.

"Don't lose focus!" She looked towards him to try to determine if he was alright or if the pace of battle was becoming too much. And there she saw fear.

He's gone, she thought, *just like last time.* They'd known it might happen, and she'd mentally prepared for this moment. Her mind quickly kicked into gear, assessing ways to protect him. All he needed was a few minutes and he'd be back. She just needed to reach him and—

Something hard hit her from behind. Allie fell to the floor, the impact knocking the air from her lungs. She gasped, struggling to breathe, but there was something pushing down on her back, pinning her in place. A boot, she realized. Craning her head, she caught a glimpse of her attacker's midnight armor.

Xanthus.

It was then she realized Barcus's fear hadn't been from his own demons. It had been for her.

"You've ruined everything," he seethed, pressing his boot harder into her back. She struggled to move, to fight, to scream with every ounce of strength she had. "I was hoping you would be my thousandth kill, but this will do." The light caught his sword as he raised it high into the air.

"No!" she heard Barcus shout. Out of the corner of her eye, she could see he was running towards them. But he wasn't fast enough.

"Die, monster," Xanthus growled, plunging the blade into Allie's heart.

❧

Wake up! Wake up! This is only a nightmare.

If this was truly a nightmare, it was the worst one yet. Instead of nameless faces from long ago, this was Allie. His beautiful, brave harpy, whose armor now had a jagged hole in the center. A roar erupted from him at the sight. He flew forward as if Hermes's winged boots were on his feet. A second after the sword hit the armor, not even a breath after Allie gasped in pain, he was swinging his blade.

The *Theres* Blade cut into Xanthus's arm, deep enough that it nearly severed his wrist. With a growl, Xanthus fell back, dropping his sword, while Barcus fell beside Allie.

His hands trembled as he undid the front of her breastplate, loosening it to help her breathe. Blood stained his fingers. His skin recoiled at the warmth of the liquid, but Barcus held firm. He pressed down against the wound, hoping it wasn't as bad as it looked.

Tenderly, he brushed her dark hair out of her eyes. They weren't open. Fear clutched at his gut as he called her name, once, twice…

There was no response.

No, no, this couldn't be happening.

His voice cracked on the third try. A sob on the fifth.

She was gone.

"Crying over monsters." Xanthus clutched at his unusable arm, now a mess of tissue and bone. But still, he mocked. "The Order has fallen further than I thought."

"She wasn't a monster," Barcus growled. "*You* are."

Around them the battle raged on, man against monster, brother against brother. "I wanted you to see my ascent into godhood. I would have accepted you to stand by my side. But now you've shown what a traitor you are. I'm going to put you out of your misery. A hero's blood must be as good as these creatures'." Xanthus bent to retrieve his sword, struggling to remain steady as his wounded arm continued to bleed.

Barcus clenched his fists. His sword wasn't far, but the idea of taking his hands off Allie seemed impossible. For one moment, he considered letting Xanthus cut him down. Being killed would be a mercy now. Living an eternity without Allie was too much to bear.

When he didn't move, Xanthus scowled. "Get up, you pathetic coward! Show me you can fight with honor."

"If you would strike down an unarmed man, a man you used to call brother, you have no honor."

"How would that make me any different from the gods?" Xanthus snarled. "Who trick mortals, do as they please, and leave our lives in smoldering ashes. I am what they taught me a god should be, ruthless and without feeling." Xanthus raised his sword, and Barcus braced himself for what came next.

The sword came down.

Sparks exploded as blade met blade. Helen stood in the way, using all her strength to hold back Xanthus's attack.

She grinned up at the man. "I have very strong opinions

about my gods, and unfortunately, you don't make the cut." She slashed low, breaking the contact of steel to cut deep into Xanthus's calf.

Helen moved to the side just in time to avoid another swipe. She was quick, but even with his injuries, Xanthus could best her. As they fought, it was clear how much alike the two were. An almost unlimited supply of energy fueled both in a dangerous dance. What Xanthus had once used to gain the upper hand against his enemies, Helen now used against him, keeping up a steady stream of conversation even as she ducked and rolled. Determination drove her every movement. This was what she'd been training for.

"Are you getting tired, old man? I thought gods didn't feel exhaustion."

Xanthus growled, his movements becoming more erratic. Sloppy. The wound on his arm was still hemorrhaging blood. "You're not part of the brotherhood. Who are you?"

Her grin turned feral. "Oh, I am so glad you asked that." She lunged forward, the sword swatting his away with precise speed as it sliced across the tender skin between Xanthus's shoulder and neck. He smiled, not at all concerned about the dire wound until he took in the weapon in her hands. The only weapon that could kill him.

The *Theres* Blade, her father's discarded weapon.

"Looks like you would have made a terrible god, just like you made a terrible dad."

The words struck like a blow. Xanthus's smile fell along with his body towards the floor. Helen watched the light leave his eyes and then stabbed him again.

SOMEONE WAS KNOCKING on the door. But then again, someone was always knocking on the door. The visitors showed up like clockwork, notifying Barcus of the hour and day. In the mornings, it was Hector, usually with some offering of food. The afternoons were Eolis, talking about what was going on in the world outside of the mansion. Sometimes a softer knock would come, Leo, but he rarely came in. And a few times a week, Argos made an appearance to check on him.

Barcus didn't get up to answer anymore. Each day, the bed seemed to tie his limbs down, and the effort to move grew too much.

He didn't care. What was the point, anyway? Xanthus was gone, killed in battle. Allie was gone, killed by his hand. And Barcus was alone, with only his memories.

He'd hoped at least that those would bring him comfort, but things were never so easy. Nightmares plagued his sleep, and when he woke, it was to an empty bed.

Every time, he cried. Smothering his face against the pillow and wishing for a death that would not come.

Maybe Xanthus had been right. The gods were cruel, uncaring beings to allow this kind of torture.

The knocking continued, now reaching a level below outright pounding. Barcus cracked an eye open just as the door nearly burst off the hinges.

Ah, so it was Argos's day.

His friend stood in the way, worry decorating his fine features. "So, you are alive."

"Don't tell the others," Barcus sighed, sitting up from the bed. "I'm trying to get them to accept my departure and move on."

"I do not think they are the ones you have to worry about," Argos said, coming to the side of the bed. His upper lip curled as he sniffed the air. "I am tired of these games, Barcus. Get up, get showered, and come downstairs with me. Claire sent you some food, and I intend to make sure you eat it all."

Barcus stared up at his oldest friend. He'd gone to battle to get Argos back. He'd do anything for the man. Anything.

Except get out of bed. "No."

Argos's nostrils flared as he took a deep breath. "The others told me you might say that."

Twenty minutes later, Barcus found himself seated at the kitchen island, his pride slightly damaged and his muscles whistling a soft song of pain. He wasn't dressed and he wasn't showered, but Argos had put up with it to drag him downstairs. All the time spent in bed had made him weaker than he'd thought. At least there was the delicious smell of warm crab dip and fresh homemade bread to ease the ego.

It was a compromise.

Argos stared until Barcus picked up a piece of bread, slathered on a healthy dose of dip, and popped it into his mouth. A moan followed soon after. Gods, he'd forgotten how good Claire's food was.

Across the granite countertop, Argos smiled. "Good, isn't it?"

"No." Barcus took another piece and ate.

The smile remained. Sure, it was easy for Argos to smile like that. Everything had worked out fine for him. He still had the love of his life. He could sleep at night. He could—

Stop that, Barcus told himself firmly, guilt quickly creeping up. None of that was true. Argos had spent five centuries being tortured by the sea witch. He deserved every bit of happiness in his life.

Barcus took a deep breath, forcing his thoughts in a different direction. "I'll spare you some time and cut right to the point, mmm?" Argos tilted his head in faux confusion, which he took as permission to continue. "You're going to tell me I'll get over this. That there are other women out there. That I can't spend time moping about the house and that the Order needs me, right?"

He'd heard every variation of it before and was tired of it. Tired of all the false smiles and pitying glances. Tired of the promises that someday things would get better.

Getting better wasn't what he wanted. Someday he would wake up and not remember her face, or her voice. And when that day came, Barcus wouldn't celebrate. He would mourn.

To his surprise, Argos didn't repeat any of those assurances. His friend just nodded, listening while Barcus complained, and when silence finally fell between them, he had one question. "Feel better?"

"A little." Barcus took another bite of bread, chewing as the knots in his stomach began to loosen. The food and company helped more than anything else the past month.

His friend smiled at that. "Good. Claire said talking would help."

"We never really talked before, remember? Mostly we just drank our sorrows away." And gods, a drink sounded so tempting right now. A way to forget everything, to lose himself for just a little while. But the thought of curling up in bed with that bottle instead of a harpy made his stomach turn.

Argos didn't look surprised. "I thought you might say that. I did some research and found there are other ways for us to solve this problem." He slipped something across the table. "You can talk to me or someone else. The choice is yours."

Barcus frowned at the small square and picked it up. A business card. For a Donna Zaladini, therapist. He opened his mouth, then closed it on the protest. "Who is she?"

"She is a mortal if that is what you are asking. A Mythos. Came highly recommended by Thalia. She will not say it, but I think this is her way of thanking you."

"How is Thalia? And Helen?" He hadn't heard from either since the battle. When his mind was busy reminding him of every single mistake he made, it reminded him of those two women.

"Thalia is fine. But Helen..." Argos shook his head. "No one has heard from her in a month."

A month. That was how long it had been. It felt like just yesterday a battle had divided the Order. It felt like years since he'd lost Allie.

Barcus closed his eyes against the memories. A dull

pang of worry arose at the thought of Helen. "Thalia's not worried?"

"I'm sure she is, but that woman doesn't let anyone know what she thinks until she wants to," Argos huffed. "Eolis is already putting together some men to look for her, but I do not know what good it will do. That girl will come back when the time is right. They all do eventually."

Yes, they do.

If she needed time, she deserved it. "She landed the killing blow," he told Argos. "She was the one who killed Xanthus."

His friend paused and swallowed a large bite of bread. For a second, irritation flickered across his face. "The gods should bless that girl for everything she has done for them… and us."

They should. But they hadn't. Not one of the Olympic Pantheon had stopped by to help them mourn the dead or congratulate them on another battle won.

Fuckers.

Xanthus hadn't been completely wrong. It was time to accept that the gods were well and truly done with the world.

"I do not mourn for Xanthus. Do you?" Argos shoved another piece of bread in his mouth, chewing thoughtfully.

"No." If anything, he'd come to hate the man who'd once been like blood. Xanthus had caused a civil war within their Order. He'd killed countless innocents and had taken the one woman Barcus had ever loved.

When word had reached Argos that Xanthus was dead, he'd spat on the ground. There were no toasts in Xanthus's name. No pyre to burn his remains. He would not be remembered as a hero.

Argos finished his coffee and went to pour another one. He inhaled things with the desperation of a man who'd lost years' worth of experiences. Even dressed in new clothes with his new life, this man was the closest thing Barcus had to a brother, and it was good to talk with him.

"You'll go?" Argos asked, nodding towards the card.

His fingers curved around the sharp edges of the paper. "It's worth a try."

Relief shinnied across Argos's tanned face. "Excellent."

The bread was gone, but Argos didn't seem in a hurry to rush back to Claire. He stayed, talking about anything and everything while Barcus nursed a glass of water. Though exhaustion tried to pull him under again, Barcus forced himself to stay. To enjoy these moments with his long-lost friend. He'd learned how precious such time together was and never wanted to forget it.

Old memories came up, and they laughed together. He felt lighter, as if the entire world wasn't trying to crush him with its weight. And for the first time in weeks, Barcus found the strength to face the day.

⁓

She was floating.

All sound muffled, all vision blurred. Water filled her every pore as she floated the way a child might float on their back in the open sea.

No, that was wrong.

She was floating the way a dead body floated down the river, skin and heart cold. Allie was both at the same time. She was warm, at home, yet bone cold.

How long had it been? A few minutes, maybe. A few hours. Days. Months. Her arms were weightless attachments that refused to move. The only thing propelling her forward was the gentle current of the water as it carried her… somewhere. She didn't know where.

At least she wasn't alone. Other bodies pressed against her, their gentle presence like a soothing balm when they brushed against each other, making her feel a little less alone. But still, something was missing. Surely floating wasn't all that there was in life.

Then she was poked, not by another person, but by something hard.

She frowned at the touch; at least she thought she frowned. Everything was so numb it was hard to tell if she moved or not. The thing poked her again, then it slipped under her side and lifted up.

The second her head broke the surface of the water, she inhaled. Her lungs were starving for air. The sound of her heart began to hammer in her ears, a sound that had been missing for so long. She blinked, whipping her hair out of her eyes as she tried to gain her bearings.

"Here, grab this." Something smacked the water, nearly hitting her head. Blindly, she grabbed it. Smooth wood rubbed under her palms as she was lifted out of the water and into a small boat. Blinking a few more times, she found her savior in an Einstein lookalike. His hair was cropped in wild disarray and he sported a beard that hung so low even Santa Claus would be impressed. Without pause, he stuck an aged oar back into the water and pushed the boat into motion.

Allie struggled to catch her breath. Her eyes darted around, taking in the complete darkness of the space around them, the only source of light a dull bluish glow emanating from the water that reminded her of a pool at night. She peeked over the edge of the boat. Faces stared back at her.

No, stared was the wrong word. Their eyes were closed in peaceful slumber. It didn't make the sight any less alarming. There were thousands of them, all floating alongside the boat, their bodies practically translucent.

Allie's throat tightened. "Is this…"

"The River Styx," the boatman grumbled. Charon, she reminded herself. The man had to be Charon. The boatman of the underworld, who ferried the dead to their destination.

Which meant she was dead.

"Was I…"

"In the river? Yes, I had to fish you out. Took me a while to find you. They just throw souls into the Styx and forget about them these days."

Dead. She couldn't be dead. She racked her brain, trying to recall her last memory, but nothing came. What would Ocypete do without her? Or Barcus? A horrifying thought crashed through her at the thought. "Barcus? Is he here too?"

Charon didn't even look at her. "Haven't heard of him."

That was a relief. If Barcus was okay, she could survive whatever was going to happen next. Well, survive was not really the right word here. She looked down at the water, at the hundreds of bodies floating beside them. "Why…"

"Laziness, if you ask me," huffed Charon. "There's no time for breaks down here, but all the shades complain about working too hard."

"No, why did you save me?"

He didn't look at her, but kept his eyes fixed on the misty distance. "I don't ask questions; I just do as I'm told. I imagine someone higher than me wants to speak to you."

Well, that wasn't very helpful.

A dock appeared out of the mist, anchored to a sharp

cut of rock. Torches of blue flames lined the wooden structure, illuminating three figures who stood waiting for her.

This is it, she realized with quiet finality. It had to be Hades, here to welcome her to her new home, a life of darkness and death.

The boat came to a gentle stop and Allie stood on wobbly legs and tried to walk forward. Charon caught her hand before her feet could touch dry land. "You get a trip, you give a tip. That's how this works," he rasped.

"Well, your service was lousy. I'm not tipping you. Besides, I don't have any money on me."

His dull-gray eyes shifted downward to the hand he'd captured and the ring glistening there. The ring Barcus had given her in an eternal promise. If it was with her now. It meant she had been buried with it. Allie's hand went cold at Charon's silent request. No, she couldn't. She *wouldn't* give that up. Not even in death.

Soft laughter filtered through the mist. Allie turned and found the tallest of the three figures moving towards them. As the figure stepped into the light, it was clear she wasn't an ordinary woman. Her torso stretched down until it melted into a serpent's tail with ruby red scales. Her face looked as if it were made of clay, smooth to the touch and unhindered by time or age.

A part of Allie recognized the creature, even though she hadn't laid eyes on her in centuries. "Mother?"

Echidna's face lit up in delight. "Don't worry, dear. I believe it's the motherly thing to pay for your visit." She plucked off one of her beautiful scales. Dark blood bubbled up from the tear, but the mother of monsters did not seem to mind. A quiet smile stayed on her face as she placed the payment in Charon's bony hand.

"Now, step off the boat, darling. Charon has important things to do."

The boatman grumbled his thanks and released her. "Yes, get off my boat."

Memories of her mother were few and far between. Echidna had been MIA since well before the Great Wars, and when her children were dying by the dozens, she had never appeared to help. Whatever reason brought her mother here, Allie was hesitant to hear it.

Allie had done everything possible to protect her friends and family. She'd *died* for them. And now her mother had decided to come out of hiding.

It felt like a slap to the face.

She stood her ground against the towering unmortal, arms crossed as she confronted the past. "So, this is where you've been for all these years? Are you dead? Or just hiding?"

"Neither." Echidna smiled at her. "After your father died, there was nothing much for me on the surface. I figured it was time to retire."

"Except for your children," Allie growled. "There was a war. Actually, there were a couple of wars. Our kin are nearly extinct."

Real sadness sank in Echidna's eyes. "I know. Every time one of you comes down here, my heart aches."

Allie didn't move. "Am I really dead?"

Echidna nodded, and Allie's heart broke. For herself, for Barcus, for Ocypete. As despair threatened to crush her from the inside out, one thing kept her from completely falling apart in front of these strangers. "Is… is Celia here?"

"She is," a new voice said, one Allie would know anywhere. The other figure stepped forward, and it was a testament to the darkness of the underworld that Celia's white feathers did not stand out. She was here. Perfect and unharmed and transformed into a fully feathered beauty. Allie hid a gasp behind a hand but was unable to keep a sob from escaping. Her sister's face crumpled, and they rushed towards each other.

Allie scooped her baby sister up in a hug that didn't feel tight enough. "I'm so sorry," she said, face smothered against blonde hair. "I'm sorry I couldn't save you."

"Don't," Celia said firmly. "Don't you dare blame yourself."

Allie swallowed any protests at the kind words. She focused on the solid weight of Celia in her arms, the way her sister smelled different in the darkness of the underworld, like moss and salt instead of sweet perfumes. But that didn't matter. Celia was here. Even their mother was here, and she found comfort in that.

But the pain drumming against her breastbone didn't go away. *Why?* Allie wondered, eyes clenched shut against the world around them. *Why does everything still hurt, even when I'm dead?*

"Girls," Echidna said softly. "We have matters to attend to."

Celia pulled back first, but she maintained a fierce grip on her sister's hand. "Right, time for the tour. You're going to love it here, Allie. I mean, they don't have Starbucks, or the sky for that matter. But Hades has given us our own piece of the underworld."

"Our own?" Allie repeated, looking to her mother.

"I've made a deal with Hades," Echidna stated. "He has allowed me to take refuge down here and live close to Tartarus if my children and I agree to work for him."

"Tartarus," Allie repeated, thinking of the bar she had visited so many times with Celia and Ocypete… and Barcus. There was no comparison to the real thing, the feared prison of the titans. Where evil souls went to be tortured. Where their father, Typhon, lay imprisoned.

"Yes, unmortals have come down here for centuries seeking refuge, and Hades has allowed them to work in the depths. As for those who pass on…" Her reptilian eyes fell on Celia, who was more than happy to finish.

"We have the Terassian Border. Since we're not quite mortals nor immortals like the heroes, Asphodel and Elysium are closed to us. The Border is where we can finally find peace," she sighed with a smile, talons curling against her sister's fingers. "Everyone is there. It's like a family reunion, just like old times."

Old times. Allie shivered at the words. Just a few weeks ago, that promise would have been enough for her. But now…

"What does Hades get out of it?"

"Help," her mother answered. She turned and stared at the souls floating around them, stacked on top of each other until it was unclear where one began and another ended. "Good help is so hard to come by these days. And while the other gods struggle to find their place in the world, Hades's kingdom continues to expand. It isn't easy keeping track of so many dead humans. Besides"—a smile stretched across her face, showing a row of sharp teeth—"it never hurts to have our kind on his side."

For what? Allie wanted to ask, but there were too many questions circling her mind. "So that's why you pulled me out of the Styx? To bring me to the Terassian Border?"

"Partly." Echidna pointed to the figure that still hung

back in the shadows. "Someone else wanted to meet you as well." At first glance, Allie thought he was a shade, one of the spirits who wandered the underworld, until the figure threw off his cloak.

He was short and wearing a traditional chiton that showed off powerful muscles. Brilliant blond hair hung down to his shoulders, bringing attention to the golden coin hanging around his neck. A hero.

He smiled at her, a smile that would turn any woman's knees to jelly. "It is a pleasure to finally meet you, harpy. I am Achilles."

"What?" Allie stared, blinked, and continued to stare. "*The* Achilles?"

His blue eyes lit up. Against the eerie glow of the River Styx, they were electrifying. "The one and only."

"And you wanted to meet *me*?"

"Yes, I have an offer for you."

She blinked in surprise, unsure of what to say. Her mother's face was carefully blank; even Celia had grown uncharacteristically quiet. "Why do you think I would listen to you, hero?"

His laugh was quieter than she would have imagined, not loud with confidence. It was the laugh of a man who knew one too many secrets. "Because you're the special one, aren't you? The harpy who loved a hero."

He might have thrown her back into the Styx from the impact of those words. Allie worked to hide her surprise, but it was too late. "Are you going to give me an invitation to Elysium or something? Thank me for my good deeds up on the surface?"

To her surprise, Achilles's smile widened. "Some would call what you did heroic."

"Some?" Allie waited for him to clarify. She knew how heroes liked their secrets; sometimes it was best to be blunt with them. She'd learned that from Barcus. "Who else knows about me?"

"Nearly every shade in the underworld." Celia wiggled her brows at Achilles with the last word. "The Fates were incredibly secretive about what the threads had in store for you and Barcus. It was even driving Hades crazy."

That shook her to the core. The underworld knew about her and Barcus, and one of their biggest fans was… "Hades?"

Achilles nodded. "Which is why I am here. Hades himself would like to make you an offer. You did the gods and the Order a great service by fighting Xanthus. On behalf of Hades, I am making you a hero."

Echidna made a quiet noise of disbelief but said nothing. It didn't fully hit Allie what he was saying until Achilles removed the golden coin from his neck and extended it towards her.

A storm of emotions clogged her throat, but Celia offered her the strength to find her voice. "Why? What good does it do to make me a hero when I'm already dead?"

Achilles reached into a small leather pouch and pulled out a slender golden chain. Dangling in front of her was the same coin she'd seen around Barcus's neck. "With this coin, Hades offers you his blessing. If you choose to accept it, you will be given immortality. And a second chance."

A second chance? She couldn't believe her ears. On instinct, she turned to the one person who knew her the best.

Her sister looked on the brink of tears. "Or," Celia said, "you can accept your death and stay down here. With me. The choice is yours."

It didn't feel like a choice. It felt like a cruel joke. To

finally have done something right in her life. To be recognized by the gods. But doing so meant she would have to say goodbye all over again.

Her sister squeezed her hand tightly enough that the golden ring dug into her finger. Allie looked down at the gem, remembering the promise she had made to Barcus. The dreams she'd harbored of fighting by his side, helping him, and spending eternity with him.

At one time, she'd believed she could disappear into the world and no one would notice. But that wasn't the case anymore. If she became a hero, she would be one for both mortals and unmortals.

"I love you, Cee," she told her sister, "but…"

Celia shook her head. "I know. There is so much good you can do as a hero. Ocypete needs you. Your hero needs you." She laughed, pulling Allie close for one last hug. "It seems like the world needs you now."

"Yeah," Allie breathed, her mind dreaming up a thousand different things she could do with this new status. She really could be the bridge between heroes and unmortals. She would protect them all. Convince them they were stronger together. "I think I've finally found my place in it."

"Then you should go. I'll be okay."

Echidna stood by, watching the farewell, her face stony. But in those dark, fathomless eyes, something sparkled. Pride. Allie couldn't remember ever seeing such a look on Echidna's face for any of her children.

"Are you ready?" Achilles asked.

She stepped forward and grabbed the coin from his hand. A wave of magic warmed her from the bottom up, as if giving her its own quiet assurance that this was the right decision. "I am."

D ONNA ZALADINI TURNED out to be a pleasant addition to his life. A recent graduate with her master's in psychology and another in history, they spent most of their sessions delving deep into the past.

Her family were still devoted patrons of the goddess Psyche. Had been since the fourteenth century. Their devotion bred a line of skilled psychologists who specialized in marriage counseling. Inside her office were subtle influences of her Mythos upbringing—a small figurine of Aphrodite sat on her desk while a picture of Psyche's lover, Eros, hung over the sofa. When he brought up the lack of appearance from the gods, she shrugged and explained in her remarkably calm voice, "Mortals don't need to see their gods to believe. It doesn't change much for me."

The answer did not surprise him. When he'd first considered therapy, Barcus had dreaded the idea of spilling his deepest shame to a man wearing a tweed coat and an expressionless face. Donna was the complete opposite, with her sharp orange hair and wardrobe full of stylish dresses. One might mistake her personality as loud because of her appearance, but her voice possessed a soft, cautious tone as she eased him through their sessions.

Even with her expertise, it had been hard to talk about things that had happened centuries ago. No matter what crazy story he told, Donna Zaladini didn't bat an eye. On their fourth appointment, she'd put a name to his night-mares. PTSD.

He'd heard of it. Knew it was a modern-day term for an ancient ailment. Since that day, they'd come up with ways to help him cope. But therapy wasn't like his magic potions; it took longer to see results. Sleep still didn't come any easier, and he was grieving Allie every day, but Donna's hopeful personal-ity was contagious, and every day Barcus felt a little lighter.

"What do you want to do, Barcus?" she asked out of the blue.

He blinked at her, the question throwing him off. "What?"

"A man like you needs something to occupy himself. I'm curious what that is now that you've given up a life hunting monsters."

"They don't like being called monsters," he mumbled, looking at her pristine white bookshelf.

She smiled as if she knew that perfectly well. "You're aimless."

"Yes." His chest ached at the word. "I've lost my future."

Her eyes filled with sympathy. "No one loses their future. It's always there for you. You just need to decide what it looks like."

She wasn't the first person to point that out. But the thought of picking up the pieces again was daunting.

Donna glanced at her watch and smoothed out the fabric of today's forest-green dress. That was the cue—they were out of time. Barcus stood, his limbs feeling numb after another long session. "Give it some thought, Barcus," she told him. "Try new things. Talk to old friends. They've gone through the same thing you have; they might have the answer."

"Thank you," he mumbled, walking out.

Some sessions were better than others. Today, he could feel the wheels of his mind working overtime.

Try something new. That shouldn't be hard. There wasn't a lot taking up his life these days. There was plenty of time to figure it out. A lifetime of it, to be exact. He'd officially handed off responsibility of the Western Order to Eolis, opting to take Argos's advice to focus on himself.

But it had been years since he'd put his own needs in front of those he was charged with. The only time he'd ever dared had been when he'd met Allie, when the attraction to her had been so overpowering, so compelling, he'd had no choice but to pursue it.

Sharp pain lanced through him at the thought of her. Remembering never got easier, but he would endure it to see her in his mind's eye: smiling, scowling, arguing with that fiery glint in her eye. Those memories were barbed with thorns, constantly reminding him that she was gone.

But he wouldn't give them up for the world.

Barcus went through the motions of driving home, half in his thoughts and half paying attention to the road. A cool breeze still clung to the air, unwilling to let them move on into spring. At least the snow had melted and soon life would flourish again. Maybe then things would get just a little bit easier.

The grand walls of Elysian Pointe silently greeted his return. With Eolis in the library and Hector off doing gods knew what with Leo, the usual chaos of the house was gone. The absence of the harpies and Helen hung over the house in its deafening silence. He'd never realized how large the space felt, nor how empty until now.

Barcus fought the urge to return to bed. Donna had warned him against sleeping too much. But sleeping was so much easier than talking, or exercising, or anything these days. So when the itch arose, he had to force himself to do something else.

He took in the heroic portraits surrounding him. Each one depicted a grand feat: men wrestling creatures, saving damsels, going on adventures. Maybe there was a clue in one of them as to what he could do next.

Maybe he should take up redecorating.

Barcus snorted at the thought. He turned to head towards the kitchen when something caught his eye—a blemish on the otherwise immaculate floor.

A single black feather.

Barcus stared in disbelief, all muscles frozen.

Soft footfalls echoed behind him, unfamiliar compared to the heavy steps of his comrades. Instinct took over. Just as the stranger was right behind him, he whirled, his hands grabbing whatever they could, trapping the intruder in an iron grip.

A feminine gasp reached his ear just as Barcus took in his captive.

His pounding heart crumbled into nothing at the sight of that smile.

That face.

"Just like old times, eh, hero?"

"Allie?"

⸙

She knew sneaking up on him would have consequences, but damn, she'd forgotten that Barcus could move like that. "This feels familiar…"

He didn't move. And for a second, she worried that she might have broken him beyond repair. The grip on her arms loosened, allowing one of her hands to reach for his powerful jawline. It was all she could think to do to ease that ghostly look off his face.

"You're dead," he whispered.

"I was."

"How are you here?"

"It seems the gods aren't as merciless as we thought." Her hand moved down to her neckline and his eyes followed, greedily soaking in the sight of her until they widened at the coin adorning her neck.

He sucked in a swift intake of air. "Is that what I think it is?"

There was such hesitation in the question. As if he didn't dare hope. Allie nodded. "I was given a choice. Death as an unmortal or life as an immortal. I guess the gods were pleased with our deeds after all."

Barcus shook his head, unable to meet her eyes. "No, this can't be right. I don't deserve this. I couldn't kill Xanthus. I was too weak."

Allie pulled him close, finally embracing the man she loved for the first time in what felt like an eternity. As her arms wrapped around him, she could feel the tension in his body ease out. She savored the moment, the feeling of his weight pressed against her. "It doesn't matter. We brought heroes and unmortals together. If it wasn't for us, he would have gotten exactly what he wanted."

She felt his large hands roam up and down her arms, her hair, and her neck. Each touch lingered as if waiting for her to disappear. When she didn't, he finally spoke. "I can't believe the gods would be so generous."

"I told you I'm not going anywhere. We made a promise, remember?" A promise of eternity; the ring had been her reminder of that in the depths of the underworld.

For Barcus, she had defied death.

"I'll need to make a proper tribute to Hades for allowing me to come back."

Barcus paused in his worship of her body at the mention of the Olympian, but it seemed not even that could sour his mood. "If he is the cause of this, then I will give him anything he wants. But right now, there is only one thing I'd like to worship."

Allie wrapped a leg around his torso, straddling him as their lips met again for a deep, entangled kiss.

"I love you, Barcus. I thought I might never get a chance to tell you that again." She was nearly breathless, but there had been a moment where she feared she would never get the chance to tell him those words ever again. "I hope you never grow tired of me saying that. Because I plan on doing it a lot."

His grin was perfection. It was the only answer she needed before he kissed her again. "As do I."

Epilogue

ONE YEAR LATER

I T HAD BEEN a long time since she last looked out on the city of Athens. The place was nearly unrecognizable with its new roads and newer shops. Electricity brought the buildings to life, illuminating the Acropolis in the distance.

Allie leaned out the open window, soaking in the winter chill as it penetrated her thin robe. She could feel her nipples growing hard in response. Felt her arms and legs pebble with goose bumps. Still, she couldn't take her eyes off the ancient landmark.

One year ago, it had been her dream to go off and explore the world once again. To find herself. One year ago, that dream had felt a world away.

But now…

"Close that window and get dressed. Castor will be here any minute."

She turned just as Barcus was coming out of the bathroom. His hair was a damp mess from the shower, the smell of sex and sweat washed and replaced with a spicy shower gel. A light-gray sweater and some formfitting jeans now covered his glorious body, and the always-present gold coin glistened in the dim light of their hotel room.

Ah yes, a lot could change in a year.

Not long ago, she had been held captive in a similar hotel room by this man. She had been ready to tear his throat out. Had cursed him at every opportunity. Now the sight of him made her mouth water. He and his heroes had changed her life. The proof of it hung around her neck in an identical coin while a ring decorated her finger. Both items carried with them the promise of forever.

Sometimes it was hard to believe this was her life now.

"We don't need to leave for another thirty minutes. There's plenty of time for us to relax if we want to," Allie purred, pulling at the neckline of her robe.

Interest sparked in her hero's eyes, but he shook his head. "Castor is a prompt man. He'll be here fifteen minutes before he needs to be and demand we arrive before the unmortals."

She huffed at the news. "The unmortals won't care who shows up first."

Barcus raised a brow at her. "Really?"

No, not really. The relationship between the unmortals in Greece and the heroes of the Central Order wasn't as well off as it was back home. That was why she and Barcus were here. To help them broker peace. Castor was the leader of the Central Order, a role he maintined well before Barcus joined the ranks of immortality. She'd never met the man before, but there were stories about him. Legends, really. And she wanted to make a good impression on the man.

She moved to the bed, where a selection of clothes was laid out. When she dropped the robe, she could feel Barcus's eyes devour the sight of her naked body.

"Is it a bad thing that I hope this doesn't take too long?" he asked, watching her dress.

Allie stifled a laugh. "That isn't a very heroic thing to

say, especially from a man who was once the head of the Western Order."

"*Was* is the key word in that sentence," Barcus corrected, his voice coming from behind. There was little warning before she felt the soft fabric of his sweater brush against her bare back. "That's Eolis's responsibility now."

Another change, but one for the better. After her miraculous return to the land of the living, Barcus had decided to abdicate his leadership to another hero. Xanthus was dead, and Barcus had no intention of taking on any more life-or-death quests. His body and spirit needed a break from the fighting. Instead, he had agreed to take a more diplomatic role in the Order by traveling with Allie. Together they were on their own journey to mend the relationship between unmortals and heroes.

"How does it feel to be just another hero in the Order?" Allie asked.

"I'm not just another hero," he said, the words coming close and hot next to her ear. It felt wonderful compared to the chill of the world outside. "I'm your hero, remember?"

Gods, when he talked like that, it was impossible to forget. "If you keep talking I am not going to be getting dressed anytime soon."

He laughed, and Allie spun to give him another warning, but Barcus was too fast. His hands caught her wrists and held her still against his body. Her lungs stalled as she met his gaze and saw the lust lurking in those storm-blue eyes. Any concern Barcus might have had for their visitor's arrival was gone, and Allie was just about to throw all caution to the wind—

A knock fell on the door, interrupting the moment. She had to shake her head, clearing it. "Castor's early," she whispered.

"Of course he is," Barcus sighed. "I'll go let him in. You should finish getting dressed."

"Heroes always ruin our fun."

His lips tilted into a smirk. "You're a hero now, remember?"

"Oh, yeah." She pecked him on the lips before forcing herself to step back. If she did anything more, Castor would be left waiting out in the cold.

Barcus gently closed the door behind him, leaving her to finish getting dressed. Allie darted into the bathroom to touch up her makeup. It wasn't just Castor she wanted to impress. She would be meeting with other unmortals as well. All of whom had heard the stories. In a few short months, she and Barcus had become their own kind of legend. The harpy who had become a hero. The hero who protected unmortals. The pressure was on for her to live up to those legends and do right by her coin.

Tonight, she and Barcus would bring unmortals and heroes together once again. They would establish a new Covenant and help ease Castor's men into a trusting relationship with the unmortals.

"It'll be easy," she told her reflection, fluffing her dark locks. "You've already done it once."

If she could get Krone to accept the heroes in his life, then she should be able to get any unmortal to agree.

After a few more minutes of pep talk, she stepped out into the main living space of their hotel suite. There Barcus stood talking to a tall man she could only assume to be Castor. His bald head and large build gave him an air of intimidation that would make even a football player shudder. But the outfit he wore… Allie let her eyes linger on the long leather duster and thick combat boots. Yikes, someone needed to take him aside and let him know he wasn't living in the Matrix.

Both men turned at her entrance, their conversation cut short midsentence. "Don't stop on my account," Allie said, wrapping a finger around her coin necklace. "I'm a hero, too, remember?"

Castor's eyes lingered on the coin. "I didn't believe it at first when Eolis told me, but seeing it in the flesh is…" He wisely didn't finish the thought. There were still some heroes who weren't as forward-thinking as Barcus and Eolis. But Castor had seemed willing to accept the change and ensure his men did the same when they'd talked to him earlier. It was a relief, one that made her and Barcus's job easier. But she could see there was hesitation in the older hero.

After a moment, he stepped forward and extended a hand. "It is a pleasure to finally meet the first unmortal hero."

Allie took it with a firm shake. "It is nice to meet you as well. Barcus has told me a lot about you. I'm glad we could work something out with the others."

"Yes, the others." Castor's expression soured a little at the mention of the unmortals. Allie raised a brow, urging him to share his thoughts. He cleared his throat and looked away. "I apologize. Cassandra and I have a tense relationship."

"They tried to kill each other in the past," Barcus added helpfully. "Many times."

"Haven't we all?" Allie forced a smile. She'd spoken with the leader of the local unmortals and wasn't surprised at all to hear she had a past with Castor. Cassandra was a descendant of Lamia, mother of sea monsters. She'd never been a general in any war, but wielded influence and words the same way Barcus held his spear. If she had a man like Castor on edge, she must be more dangerous than Allie had first assessed.

"Cassandra has promised to put all that aside for the good of the Covenant. It's what you both want, isn't it? Peace?"

She watched as the tension eased out of Castor's muscles. The hardness of his face softened. "I'm not doing this for peace. I'm doing it because we have to."

Allie shared a look with Barcus. They both knew of the latest dangers threatening the Order of Olympus, not just the Western Order in America, but the Central and Eastern regions as well. Xanthus's cult had created a rift amongst the heroes. Even with their leader dead, it seemed Xanthus's cult and influence lived on. They knew now that there were heroes who saw a vulnerability in a world without the gods. There were no rules anymore, no one to keep them in their place. The absence left a vacant space just waiting to be filled.

Now the Order was doing its best to clean up that mess, but it couldn't do it alone. Brokering peace between heroes and unmortals meant helping her people. Giving them protection during these changing times.

"Castor was just giving me an update on what's been happening with his men. Apparently nearly half of them have deserted the Order." Barcus crossed his arms, looking grim as the news settled over the room.

"To follow Xanthus?" Allie asked.

Castor shook his head. "It is hard to follow a dead man, but yes. My intelligence has told me that some continue to worship him as a demigod. As for the others, their decision to leave just means they've lost focus on why we do what we do. We're in a sad state these days."

"I'm sorry to hear that."

"Thank you," Castor said politely before turning back to Barcus. "There is another thing I'd like to discuss with you before we meet with the unmortals."

Barcus straightened, his jaw locking as he braced for what came next. "More bad news?"

"I don't know. There are rumors floating around the city." Castor's dark eyes glanced at Allie, and she could see the hesitation in his eyes, but Barcus put a quick end to it.

"She's one of us, Castor. If you have something to tell me, Allie must know about it as well."

"I'm sorry. I just wasn't sure how much she knows."

Allie looked between the two men, her stomach tightening into a ball of nerves. "What don't I know?"

Castor took a deep breath, as if he couldn't believe the next words coming out of his mouth. "Apparently Xanthus has a daughter."

Just as quickly as it appeared, the tension in the room dropped. Both Barcus and Allie nearly doubled over in relief. "Ah, yeah. Helen. We know about her," Barcus said. "Don't worry, she isn't a threat."

"But you've heard rumors?" Allie asked, a swell of hope filling her chest. It had been an entire year without knowing where the girl had disappeared to. The house got an occasional postcard letting them know she was alive and well, but all the heroes had been worried about the young girl. "Do you know where she is?"

"I don't know anything like that." Castor gave Barcus a look of warning. "But I'm going to need you to tell me everything you know about this girl."

"Why?" Barcus asked.

Castor's face turned to stone with his next words. "Rumor has it that the gods are interested in finding her."

Acknowledgments

This book has been a long time in the making and even longer to get right.

The idea was developed when I was stationed in Korea for a year-long deployment from 2016–2017. It was a hard year away from my family and long working days, but it was also incredibly rewarding. I was still sitting on *Holding Out for a Hero* at the time, dreaming of one day getting it published. While there, it was announced the base would be holding a special event by a nonprofit acting group called *Theater of War* Productions. They specialize in taking classical plays and presenting them to a modern audience in an effort to promote conversations about difficult topics: racial injustice, sexism, and PTSD to name a few. The cast would be performing Sophocles's *Ajax* and hosting a discussion afterward. Everyone was encouraged to attend, and I was thrilled to find the entire base theater packed! The incredible Reg E. Cathey (RIP) read the role of Ajax, and it was a performance that will haunt me the rest of my life. The theater was so quiet that you couldn't hear anything but the echoes of his screams.

Afterward, several brave men and women stood up and offered their insight into the play and their own experiences. It was then that I realized PTSD is not just a problem for the modern soldier, but a problem plaguing soldiers since Classical Greece. I, of course, started thinking about my characters who were immortal men, seeking glory and battle for hundreds and years, and wondered how that would affect them. How it would affect the world around them. And I knew I had to address it in this book. As mentioned by both Bryan Doerries (producer of Theater of War) and Dr. Jonathan Shay (author of *Achilles in Vietnam*), PTSD is a disease that impacts not just one person but their loved ones as well. Spouses, significant others, children, and friends all search for answers to help their loved ones and themselves. I did my best to research and show just one experience of PTSD and to help Barcus overcome his trauma. Below are some of the resources I dove into regarding PTSD, Greek soldiers, and the ancient world. I hope I did all wounded warriors and their loved ones justice.

I'd like to thank all the people who helped make this novel into what it is today. My beta readers, who offered insight on grammar: Riki, Karli, and Helen. My sister, who managed to get back to my emails asking for sanity checks even while she managed a five-month-old. And the women who gave me their time and insight on PTSD: Lisa Blaton, Tara Wallace, and Rebecca Matthams. As always, I need to thank the women who helped with edits, Jennifer Graybeal, Eliza Dee, and Misha Carlstedt, without whom this book would not be nearly as clean.

REFERENCES

Cartledge, Paul. *Sparta and Lakonia: A Regional History 1300–362 BC*. N.p.: Taylor & Francis, 2013.

Doerries, Bryan. *The Theater Of War*. New York, NY: Alfred A. Knopf, 2015.

Shay, Jonathan. *Achilles in Vietnam: Combat Trauma and the Undoing of Character*. New York, NY: Scribner, 1994.

Shay, Jonathan. *Odysseus in America: Combat Trauma and the Trials of Homecoming*. New York, NY: Scribner, 2002.

Sekunda, Nicholas and Hook, Adam. *Greek Hoplite 480–323 BC*. Edited Lee Johnson. Great Brighting, Osprey Publishing Ltd, 2000.

Sophocles and Aeschylus. *All That You've Seen Here Is God: New Versions of Four Greek Tragedies Sophocles' Ajax, Philoctetes, Women of Trachis; Aeschylus' Prometheus Bound*. Edited by Bryan Doerries. Knopf Doubleday Publishing Group. Kindle Edition.

Tritle, Lawrence A. *From Melos to My Lai: A Study in Violence, Culture and Social Survival*. United Kingdom: Taylor & Francis, 2000.

About the Author

Maria Shield writes adult fantasy, romance, and science fiction. She was raised in Kansas but has since lived all over the world, from Korea to Japan, finally ending up in her current location in Nebraska with her family. She is passionate about Japanese culture, ancient history, and feminist activism. When she isn't writing, Maria can often be found doing the 3 Rs: Reading, Running, and Researching. She also loves helping other writers find their communities and sharing craft tips and tricks. This often means she's participating in a critique group somewhere or starting one herself.

You can also reach out to Maria at:
Email: Mariashield.author@gmail.com
Twitter: @Mariashieldlady
Website: *Mariashield.com*

Thank you for reading. If you enjoyed this book, please consider leaving a review on Amazon or Goodreads!